T0363391

HISTORICAL

Your romantic escape to the past.

Tempted By Her Enemy Marquis
Louise Allen

The Duke's Guide
To Fake Courtship
Jade Lee

MILLS & BOON

TEMPTED BY HER ENEMY MARQUIS
© 2025 by Melanie Hilton
Philippine Copyright 2025
Australian Copyright 2025
New Zealand Copyright 2025

First Published 2025
First Australian Paperback Edition 2025
ISBN 978 1 038 93910 4

THE DUKE'S GUIDE TO FAKE COURTSHIP
© 2025 by Greyle Entertainment, LLC
Philippine Copyright 2025
Australian Copyright 2025
New Zealand Copyright 2025

First Published 2025
First Australian Paperback Edition 2025
ISBN 978 1 038 93910 4

MIX
Paper | Supporting
responsible forestry
FSC® C001695
www.fsc.org

Published by
Harlequin Mills & Boon
An imprint of Harlequin Enterprises (Australia) Pty Limited
(ABN 47 001 180 918), a subsidiary of HarperCollins
Publishers Australia Pty Limited
(ABN 36 009 913 517)
Level 19, 201 Elizabeth Street
SYDNEY NSW 2000 AUSTRALIA

Cover art used by arrangement with Harlequin Books S.A.. All rights reserved.

Printed and bound in Australia by McPherson's Printing Group

Tempted By Her Enemy Marquis

Louise Allen

MILLS & BOON

Also by Louise Allen

The Duke's Counterfeit Wife
The Earl's Mysterious Lady
His Convenient Duchess
A Rogue for the Dutiful Duchess
Becoming the Earl's Convenient Wife
How Not to Propose to a Duke

Liberated Ladies miniseries

Least Likely to Marry a Duke
The Earl's Marriage Bargain
A Marquis in Want of a Wife
The Earl's Reluctant Proposal
A Proposal to Risk Their Friendship

Discover more at
millsandboon.com.au.

Louise Allen has been immersing herself in history for as long as she can remember, finding landscapes and places evoke powerful images of the past. Venice, Burgundy and the Greek islands are favourites. Louise lives on the Norfolk coast and spends her spare time gardening, researching family history or travelling. Please visit Louise's website, www.louiseallenregency.com, her blog, www.janeaustenslondon.com, or find her on X @LouiseRegency and on Facebook.

Chapter One

Ravenham Hall, Hertfordshire—
September 5th, 1815

'But you are a woman,' the Marquis of Ravenham said.

'Yes, my lord.' The neat figure in front of him dropped the slightest of curtsies. Her face was composed, but he had the strong impression that she was amused.

'I do not want a woman—' Will stated, then broke off when he realised what he had just said.

This time he was certain of it. She was laughing at him.

One week before

'Something must be done. I cannot live in this chaos,' the new Marquis of Ravenham said flatly. 'I had no idea my late cousin's collecting had become quite this uncontrolled. This is not normal.'

He gestured around the ballroom of Ravenham Hall where, spread out before him, there were enough examples of statuary to furnish a large park, interspersed with packing cases, some with their lids off, straw spilling out.

'Virtually every space in this house is a lumber room of

paintings, boxes and objects. The only way to navigate the library is by way of paths through the stacks of volumes.' It made him feel weary just looking at it. 'Ravenham Hall looks like an Eastern bazaar crossed with a madman's attic, not a nobleman's residence.'

Arnley, his steward, coughed apologetically. 'I fear His late Lordship's enthusiasm did tend to run away with him these past few years, my lord. Mr Townsend, his secretary, found it all too much to cope with and resigned eighteen months ago. Since then, it has become worse. His Lordship appeared to value only the acquiring of objects, then neglected them when they arrived.

'I believe His Lordship did have his own methods of recording his purchases, but what they might be...' His voice trailed away unhappily. 'He was somewhat secretive, of late. No visitors were admitted beyond the drawing room, dining room and his study.'

Which would explain why his heir had no idea of the state of things. Will Lovell was a barrister, a second cousin of the Marquis who had provided a large part of his income. All their interviews had taken place in the study and it had been made clear that he was not expected to stay in the house.

The recently deceased Randolph had used Will's services in the numerous court cases he brought. Whether it was a neighbour encroaching on his land, a tenant defaulting on his lease, a dealer he suspected of not playing fair or a threat of slander, Randolph had pursued the case relentlessly.

As head of the family Will owed him respect. As the man who had paid for his education and legal training, he owed him his loyalty and, as the provider of juicy cases to get his teeth into, he owed him his attention at all times.

There was no denying that Randolph had always been eccentric. His only passions in life had been antiquities and horses and it was the latter that had killed him, along with his heir, when they had collided in the course of a curricle race.

Will had never expected to inherit. Randolph had still been young enough to wed again after a childless first marriage and his heir presumptive had been his first cousin, already married, with two daughters and ample time to produce a son. Will was only a second cousin, sharing a great-grandfather.

'I believe you will require a librarian and someone to advise on antiquities, as well as a secretary, my lord,' Arnley ventured after they had surveyed the scene in depressed silence for another minute 'I will advertise immediately.'

'Do so.'

'Mama!' Katherine Jones erupted in to the drawing room, brandishing a copy of *The Times*. 'He is advertising for a librarian *and* an antiquary.'

Her mother steadied the small velvet bolster to which an exquisite piece of Valenciennes lace was pinned and looked up. 'To whom do you refer?' She added a pin to the piece which she was repairing and set it to one side. Her skills with valuable antique lace were in high demand and a profitable supplement to their income.

'The new Marquis of Ravenham. The swine of a lawyer who ruined Papa. Look, it cannot be anyone else.'

Mrs Jones took the paper and read aloud. '"*A skilled and experienced librarian and an antiquarian scholar with a wide range of knowledge are required to assess, catalogue and advise on the arrangement or disposal of a large collection of volumes and artefacts recently inherited by a Gentleman. Applications with full details and references should be submitted to Lovell and Foskett, Lincoln's Inn.*" How do you know this is Lord Ravenham?'

'His name is William Lovell. That must be his legal practice. This is our opportunity to find what his cousin stole and to bring him to account for blackening Papa's name. I intend to apply for both positions.'

Her mother dropped the newspaper. 'But... My dear, he will never employ a female. And he will recognise the name. Besides, how can you provide references?'

'He will accept me when he realises that I am the best qualified applicant—and that he can save money by employing one person instead of two. And Lady Eversholt will give me a reference and so will some of my other clients. Miss Deben, the bluestocking, is delighted with my arrangement of her library, for one. I can choose any name that I wish and ask them to use it.'

Her mother gave a faint moan and closed her eyes. 'You are as impetuous as your father, and as stubborn. It will never succeed, although I would dearly like to see that man brought to face his just deserts.'

'Oh, so would I,' Katherine said grimly.

And I want the Borgia Ruby back, she added silently.

Precious, unique and exceedingly valuable, it had been stolen along with her father's good name and the double loss had sent him to an early grave.

'One applicant remains, my lord.' Giles Wilmott, Will's new secretary, hesitated on the threshold of his study. 'A somewhat… *unusual* candidate, applying for both posts.'

Will glanced at the last file on the desk. 'C. A. Jenson. Excellent references, I must say. Miss Deben sent an example of how her library was organised and Lady Eversholt's reply included a copy of the catalogue of her late husband's collection from his Grand Tour, with valuations and recommendations. Impressive. I have to say, the other applicants have been hopeless.'

There had been one librarian who was so vague that he made the newly retired Mr Townsend appear as sharp as a box of knives; one who wanted to impose his novel, and highly complex, system of cataloguing regardless of what Will needed; an antiquarian who clearly wanted to acquire the spoils for himself and one who was knowledgeable about statuary, but ignorant of just about everything else.

'Show him in.'

Wilmott looked as though he wanted to say something, then bowed and went out. A minute later the door opened to admit the final applicant.

Will got to his feet. 'But you are a woman!'

'Yes, my lord.' The neat figure in front of him dropped the slightest of curtsies. Her face was composed, but he had the strong impression that she was amused.

'I do not want a woman—' he stated, then broke off when he realised what he had just said.

This time he was certain of it. She was laughing at him, although not a muscle in the smooth oval of her face twitched. It was all in those hazel eyes.

'Damn it.' After a moment he got himself under control. 'I beg your pardon. Please sit down, Miss Jenson. There would appear to have been some mistake. I am advertising for a librarian and an antiquarian advisor. Not a housekeeper.'

'That is fortunate, as I have no skills as a housekeeper, my lord. As I am sure you are aware from the examples of my work I see in front of you, my talents lie elsewhere,' she said calmly. 'I have the skills and knowledge you require. It runs in the family. My father taught me. I can produce further references if you so require.'

When he remained silent, she added, 'I have some idea of your problem. The late Marquis had become notorious in the circles in which I move. I presume the place is overrun with his purchases.'

'Yes,' Will said curtly. It was useless to try to hide the facts. 'There is complete disorder.'

Miss Jenson nodded. 'As I expected. By employing me you will save on a salary. I require one hundred pounds a year, a modest suite of rooms and board and lodging for myself, my chaperon and our maid.'

'One hundred pounds? I could employ two butlers for that, Miss Jenson.'

'If you can find two butlers who can do what I am capable of, my lord, then I recommend that you employ them,' the provoking woman said politely and folded her hands in her lap.

Will had not become a successful barrister by allowing himself to be caught on the back foot for long. He leaned back in his chair and studied her across the width of the desk. Most witnesses would have begun to shift uneasily. She stared back, unabashed.

'This is a bachelor household. Surely you have a concern for your reputation?' She was clearly a lady from her speech and the quiet good taste of her sensible clothes.

'I would have my maid with me, a formidable protection against anything I might encounter, from amorous footmen to large spiders, and my chaperon, a clergyman's widow of the utmost respectability. And I assume you employ a housekeeper and maids?'

'I do. But they are servants. You would be here in a professional capacity, much like my secretary. I would expect them, and my librarian, to dine with me often, for example.'

'My chaperon, Mrs Downe, is my cousin. She perfectly used to dining at a nobleman's table. Or an archbishop's, come to that, although I imagine those are rarely invited.' When he did not reply she added, 'I assume the London town house is also awash with items.'

'If only there *was* space here for things to be awash, Miss Jenson,' he said grimly. 'However, my late cousin retired here during the last few years and the spoils of his collecting appear to be concentrated in this residence. The London house is relatively…normal. Come, I will show you around and you can see what you are offering to deal with.'

That should daunt her.

The Marquis ushered her out with perfect politeness. He was certain, Katherine could tell, that she would take one look at the task in front of her and flee in horror.

The study had been relatively tidy, with bookshelves on two walls containing volumes that seemed to be frequently used reference books and only a row of Roman busts on the mantel shelf to hint at the late Marquis's obsession. The hallway had statues and paintings, but not much more than the average home that had received the souvenirs of several Grand Tours, and the small reception room where she had waited was also relatively plain.

But once beyond those spaces, as they wove their way around the ground floor rooms, they entered a world of packing cases, of statues jostling for space, of mysterious cabinets with many drawers and paintings stacked against walls.

Somewhere was the ruby, but it did not call to her as she had felt it would. Perhaps she was being foolishly superstitious, thinking that she would sense something that had brought such grief to her family in its wake.

'What is your priority, my lord?'

'The library,' he said without hesitation. 'I want an organised collection where I can find what I want quickly.'

Of course, as a lawyer he was used to laying his hands on stacks of familiar legal tomes and the outcome of a case might depend on finding just the right one, and fast. Information and organisation would be a priority for him.

'And how do you want it ordered?'

'Logically,' he said with a look down his high-bridged nose that said he should not have to state the obvious.

'Your idea of logic may not be mine, my lord.'

'That, I imagine, is very true,' he retorted in a tone clearly intended to put her in her place.

Katherine directed a grimace at the broad shoulders in front of her. Insufferable man. But she knew that already. He was a ruthless bully, ready to crush a man simply because his lord and master directed it.

But he was a handsome bully, she had to concede. Glaring at him was no hardship on the eyes. Tall, dark and, judging by his flat stomach and narrow hips, a man who kept himself in trim and did not spend his time hunched over his law books or devouring vast dinners at the Inns of Court.

The Marquis opened a door, turning as he did so to show her in, and she looked away from the penetrating dark blue eyes. He saw too much and he would recognise dislike when it was staring at him.

'My goodness, what a very fine room.' She needed no excuse to move away from him; the library deserved admiration, or it would have done if it were not in such a state of disorder. She needed to take the upper hand, demonstrate competence now, before he made up his mind to show her the door.

'My plan would be to organise all the volumes into subjects and by author and to catalogue them by both. You can then decide which you wish to keep and which are to be disposed of. I will clean and make basic repairs as I go and make an estimate of value. I will require maids for cleaning, footmen for moving things around, ladders and trestle tables for sorting.'

She had struck a chord with him, Katherine could tell. That was what he had wanted, even if he had not put it into words, and he was a man who, professionally, had been able to turn his tactics on an instant as things changed.

'Yes,' he said. 'Very well. I will take you on a month's trial and meet your conditions.'

'Thank you, my lord. And the London house and any other properties?'

'One thing at a time. I have to be here to manage business.' For a moment she thought he looked weary, then he smiled grimly. 'It is not only the library that needs attention. When can you begin?'

'This afternoon, my lord. Mrs Downe, my maid, Jeannie, and my baggage are in a carriage outside.'

One eyebrow rose with an ease that made her want to kick him and surprise the arrogance off his face. 'You were very confident, Miss Jenson.'

'I would not travel out from London without my chaperon and maid. If you had failed to employ me, then all that would have been lost was the time spent packing my belongings. If your housekeeper can show us to our rooms and provide us with something for luncheon, I will begin work this afternoon.'

Lord Ravenham regarded her for a long moment. 'Are you confident or arrogant? Well, we shall see. Come with me, Miss Jenson.'

Katherine walked behind, not attempting to match his long-legged stride. She hid her smile when he realised he had lost her and came back down the maze of passages, his mouth set in a hard line. It might take His Lordship a while to discover that she would not dance to his piping, but she had better make certain that he found her indispensable before she irritated him too much.

There were two men waiting when they reached the hallway, one of whom she had already met.

'Miss Jenson, Mr Wilmott, my secretary, and Arnley, my steward. Arnley, Miss Jenson, her companion and her maid require accommodation. A suite with two bedchambers, a dressing room with a bed for the maid and an adjoining sitting room should answer, if you can identify such a thing in this place. They will also require luncheon, if you would be so good as to inform Cook and Mrs Goodman. My housekeeper,' he added aside to Katherine.

'Miss Jenson will begin work on the library this afternoon. I am certain she will have no difficulty in informing you both of her requirements.' With that he stalked off towards the study where he had interviewed her.

Katherine returned the secretary's quizzical look with a bland smile. 'Mr Wilmott.'

'Miss Jenson. If you could follow me, I will introduce you to Mrs Goodman.'

'Thank you. Perhaps somebody could fetch my companion and maid and our luggage from the carriage?'

'Of course.' Mr Arnley bowed and hurried off.

Mr Wilmott hesitated, then said, 'You will become used to His Lordship's manner very soon, I am certain. He is used to running a tight ship, as they say in the Navy, and the degree of disorder he has found here does not suit his temper.'

'Please do not concern yourself about me, Mr Wilmott. I am as used to creating order as Lord Ravenham is of managing it.'

And I am just as stubborn as he is, she added under her breath as the secretary showed her the way.

An hour later, a very pleasant luncheon consumed, she stood with her cousin, Elspeth Downe, and her maid, Jeannie, and surveyed the suite they had been allocated.

'I doubt it has been redecorated in ten years,' Elspeth said, eyeing the dull crimson curtains.

'It is clean, though,' Jeannie said, running her finger over the table top in the sitting room. 'And well aired.'

'I should imagine that the housekeeper was glad to find some rooms that she *could* clean,' Elspeth said tartly. 'It must be like living in a very badly organised museum. And surely those were not coffins I saw on the first landing?'

'Sarcophagi,' Katherine said, pushing the curtains aside and opening the widow. 'Ancient Egyptian.'

She would not mention the possibility that they contained mummified remains or Lord Ravenham would find himself on the receiving end of a lecture from the dean's widow on the impropriety of keeping them unburied.

Jeannie went to help the maids who were making up beds and Elspeth settled in one of the armchairs. 'Comfortable enough,' she conceded. 'And are you intent on making Lord Ravenham as *un*comfortable as possible?'

She knew that the Marquis had been responsible in some way for Katherine's father's disgrace and, after a token protest about the virtues of forgiveness, had conceded that he should be made to acknowledge the error of his ways, but Katherine and her mother had never been able to talk about what lay behind the scandal. Sooner or later, she told herself, she would have to tell Elspeth the whole story—and explain why she would be grateful for some very lax chaperonage.

'Certainly not,' Katherine said, watching as a black-clad figure on a grey horse cantered across the park in front of the window. 'I have every intention of being amiable, indispensable and of lulling Ravenham into regarding me as nothing more than an innocuous part of the household.'

Until it suits me to deliver what he is due.

Chapter Two

Katherine stood in the middle of the library and directed the
footmen who were erecting three trestle tables in as near a
straight line as they could find space for. Another had set the
rolling library steps against the first bay of shelving and was
passing books down to a man who ferried them across to a
desk where Katherine had set out notebooks, small rectan-
gles of paper, pencils, pen and ink, soft brushes and a stack of
coloured slips.

A maid came up and bobbed a curtsy.

'I need clean cloths for dusting, if you please,' Katherine said.

'Yes, Miss. I have a message from Mrs Goodman. She says
His Lordship has requested that you and Mrs Downe join him
for dinner. At eight o'clock, Miss.'

'Of course. Thank Mrs Goodman and tell Mrs Downe—after
you have found me the cloths.'

Katherine took her seat at one end of the trestle tables and
opened the case of her little travelling clock, setting it to chime
the hours. She was perfectly capable of getting so carried away
with her work that she would forget the time and she had every
intention of sitting down to dinner punctually and looking the
perfect—and perfectly innocuous—librarian.

She already had her labels ready—Religion, Philosophy,

Natural Philosophy, History and so on—and handed them to one of the men who had finished with the trestles. 'Lay these out along the front edge of the tables in the order they are now, please. Then finish emptying the first bay of shelving so that the maids can clean it.'

She reached for the nearest book, dusted it off and opened the cover. Number one of several thousand. If it were not for the thought of what she was really here to achieve, she would be enjoying herself.

At half past seven Katherine entered the drawing room with Elspeth. She was wearing a gown of dark blue silk ornamented by a frill of lace at the neck and sleeves. Her chestnut-brown hair was up and her only ornaments were cameo earrings, a cameo pendant and a bracelet of twisted gold. But the lace was antique, the cameos Roman and the gown would tell anyone who knew about such things that the simplicity was due to choice, not poverty.

Elspeth wore black with jet and silver jewellery and a small lace cap on her dark blonde hair. 'It seems we are the first down,' she remarked as they entered.

'Who are you?' A lady rose from a chair with its back to them and regarded them with narrowed eyes.

Katherine heard the sharp hiss of indrawn breath beside her, but continued into the room, revising her first impression.

Perhaps not quite a lady...

'Miss Jenson, Lord Ravenham's librarian, and my companion, Mrs Downe. Who do we have the pleasure of addressing?'

It was quite clear that if any pleasure was involved, it was entirely one-sided. 'I am Mrs de Frayne. A guest here.' She sank down into her chair again in a rustle of expensive fabric.

Katherine looked at Elspeth and raised her eyebrows. Unless she was very much mistaken, they were in the company of His Lordship's mistress. Elspeth pursed her lips, but Katherine sailed into the room and sat down on the sofa at right angles to Mrs de Frayne.

Jet-black hair, fine brown eyes, dark brows and lashes and

a figure that could best be described as lavish were set off by deep red satin and diamonds. Rather fine diamonds, if Katherine was any judge. They gleamed in her hair, at her ears, at her throat and on her bosom.

An expensive *mistress,* Katherine amended.

'But you are a woman.'

'Yes, I know. That is the second time today someone has pointed it out to me,' Katherine said.

'You are an employee.'

'We all have to earn our living in one way or another, do we not?'

Two red spots appeared on Mrs de Frayne's cheeks. She moved, a sharp twist of her body that set the folds of her gown rustling angrily and, for a moment, it seemed she would surge to her feet.

Katherine braced herself, then relaxed as the door opened and Lord Ravenham and his secretary entered.

She and Elspeth rose and curtsied. 'Good evening, my lord. Good evening, Mr Wilmott.'

'Good evening.' The Marquis took a chair opposite Mrs de Frayne, Mr Wilmott sat beside Elspeth. 'You have met Mrs de Frayne, I see.'

'Only just,' Katherine said, smiling at him. 'We have hardly begun to become acquainted.'

'I doubt you have much in common,' Lord Ravenham said.

'So do I, but that lends spice to life, do you not think? Encounters with the unfamiliar and exotic?'

The satin rustled angrily again as Mrs de Frayne turned her shoulder to Katherine and said huskily, 'My suite is draughty, my lord.'

'They probably all are, Delphine,' he said. 'There is very little choice, unless you wish to share one with an Egyptian mummy or a stack of packing cases.'

'I shall catch a chill. I should return to London,' she said petulantly. 'But I have nowhere to go. You must find me a house, William, or refurbish my suite here.' She regarded him from beneath lowered lashes. 'Or I could return and find something myself.'

'If you wish,' he said indifferently. 'Giles, make a note to have the estate carpenter see what he can do about the draughts.'

'Yes, sir.'

Well, His Lordship was certainly not besotted, Katherine thought. He has an exceedingly demanding woman on his hands and has the sense not to let her loose in London to spend his money. She must be very wearing, but presumably he found there were compensations.

Elspeth was making conversation with Giles Wilmott; Mrs de Frayne was smouldering at Lord Ravenham and he had the air of a man who very much wished himself in his London club.

'We have made a good start on the library, my lord,' she said, unable to think of a single topic of polite conversation which might engage the other woman, so turning to him instead.

'Call me Lovell,' he said abruptly. 'My family name. This incessant *my lording* makes every exchange twice as long as it need be.'

'But that is very familiar for a servant,' Mrs de Frayne drawled.

'So it would be,' Katherine agreed, 'but I am a professional. Like a doctor. Or a lawyer. Is that not so, my lord? Lovell, I should say.'

He looked at her, clearly trying to decide whether she had intended that as a jibe at his own professional standing before he had inherited. She met his gaze, thinking that the colour of his eyes was a very good match for her gown and trying not to let the frisson of awareness he provoked show on her face.

He was a very handsome man, the possessor of a fit, lithe frame and, most attractive to her, a penetrating intelligence. The fact that she thought him a ruthlessly devoid of conscience did not, for some reason, stop that little internal quiver of recognition that here was a man and that she was a woman.

'Exactly, Miss Jenson,' he said, just as the butler came in.

'Dinner is served, my lord.'

Lord Ravenham offered his arm to Mrs de Frayne and, after

a moment's dithering, Giles Wilmott recollected that he should escort the married lady rather than the unmarried one and took Elspeth in. Katherine followed behind, doing her best to appear demure. It was something of a strain.

With two men and three women the table was unbalanced. She suspected that it could be extended to seat at least twenty, but all the extra leaves had been removed and now was small enough to permit conversation. Lord Ravenham sat at the head with Elspeth on his right and Katherine on his left. Mrs de Frayne was at the foot and Mr Wilmott took the seat between her and Elspeth.

Lovell was, very correctly, making conversation with his right-hand partner. Delphine de Frayne clearly did not feel she had any obligation to make conversation with anyone and ignored the secretary. She snapped her fingers at the footman who was approaching with the wine, then sat twisting the stem of her glass between her fingers and taking frequent sips.

I refuse to believe in Delphine de Frayne as a name, Katherine thought.

Was she an actress or a singer? An actress, she suspected, given the lady's flair for the dramatic.

She smiled at Giles Wilmott. 'In the absence of anything in the middle of the table, we can converse across it, I am sure,' she said. 'Were you here with the late Marquis?'

'I was working at the chambers of Lovell and Foskett.' He cast a nervous glance in the direction of Mrs de Frayne, who ignored both him and their breach of etiquette. 'I did not find the law suited me and I had decided to apply for a position as a private secretary when His Lordship inherited.'

'It must be very interesting, helping to set all to rights after a somewhat chaotic period. I suspect the late Marquis was not overly concerned with his estates.'

'It certainly seems it was not an interest of his. Fortunately, he appears to have spent all his time here and the other estates are in the hands of capable stewards, so matters are not quite as bad as they might be.'

That was interesting and useful. It was unlikely that the ruby would be anywhere but in this house or, just possibly, at the London one, if that was the case.

Delphine de Frayne was crumbling a bread roll, ignoring her soup and already on her second glass of wine. Lovell seemed deep in conversation with Elspeth about her late husband's position as a dean at Westchester Cathedral, so Katherine risked probing some more.

'I hope that you are not expected to delve into all those packing cases, Mr Wilmott.'

'Fortunately, no. There is more than enough to be done trying to create order out of the papers. I am sure the late Marquis had a method, if only we could work out what it was,' he said with a rueful laugh. 'At the moment it eludes me.'

Katherine guessed that he was a younger son of a good family, expected to make his own way in the world, unlike the heir to whom everything would be entailed. The law would have been considered very suitable, but a post as secretary to a nobleman was also a sought-after position, perhaps leading to a political career with the influence of his former employer behind him.

They fell silent as the soup plates were removed and the entrée served. Wilmott turned to speak to Elspeth and Katherine to the Marquis.

'Have you made any progress, Miss Jenson?'

'I have made a start, but I would hardly call it progress. Your cousin does not appear to have been a great reader, which means that most of the volumes are in good condition, although very dusty. I am working through by going around the room, but if you would prefer me to identify all the books on one subject and deal with that first, I can do so.'

It was not the most logical way to proceed, but she wanted to please him with her work to the extent that he had no qualms about keeping her on.

'No, continue as you are, Miss Jenson. I want a usable library as soon as possible. In fact—'

'William, what are we doing tomorrow?'

'You may do as you please, Delphine. Wilmott, Miss Jenson and I will all be exceedingly occupied.'

'But I am bored.'

'I did warn you how dull it would be here. You can see for yourself that the house is in not fit state for entertaining. You could ride, or drive yourself. Or one of the grooms could accompany you. Go for a walk or have the coachman take you in to St Albans.' He turned to Elspeth. 'Please feel free to ride, drive or be driven, Mrs Downe. Or walk about the estate as you prefer.'

'Why, thank you, my—'

'St Albans is certain to be insufferably provincial.' Mrs de Frayne pushed her plate away, the food virtually untouched.

'That is the nature of the provinces, Delphine,' Lovell said so drily that Katherine almost choked, trying to stifle a laugh.

'I might drive into St Albans one day, if I may borrow a gig. I believe it to be an interesting city of some antiquity,' Elspeth said. 'I could take you up, Mrs de Frayne, if you would care for the outing.'

'In a *gig*? Like some farmer's wife? Certainly not.'

Katherine hastily asked a question about the neighbouring towns and villages and whether there were any local features of interest.

That occupied the three of them who were conversing until the arrival of the dessert course when it became apparent that, as well as diamonds, the Marquis's mistress greatly enjoyed sugary things. Katherine wondered if the syllabubs and bon-bons would improve her temper.

One glance told her that it was unlikely and, when the table had been cleared, she exchanged glances with Elspeth and said, 'If you will excuse us, Lovell, I think we must retire. It has been a long day.'

He and Wilmott rose and bowed slightly as they left. There was no response from Mrs de Frayne to their, 'Good night.'

'That was a most uncomfortable meal,' Elspeth remarked, low-voiced, as they climbed the stairs. 'What a frightful creature. It must be like keeping a leopard in the house and one with an evil temper, at that.'

'No doubt he finds there are compensations,' Katherine said, earning herself a reproving look. 'Perhaps Lovell enjoys danger. I wonder how long he has had her in keeping?'

'And how much longer it will last,' Elspeth said as she closed the door of their sitting room behind them.

'What do you want her for, that dowdy little sparrow?'

Will closed the door of his bedchamber behind him and sighed. He really did not need this now.

Delphine had provided several months of highly enjoyable diversion, but he had begun to feel that, despite her enthusiastic participation in bed sport, her sulks and tantrums outweighed the pleasure.

As a lawyer he had not gone to the lengths of setting her up as his mistress in her own establishment and had been on the point of bidding farewell with a generous present to sweeten the parting when the news of his cousins' deaths had reached him.

'Miss Jenson is a librarian and antiquarian, Delphine. One glance at the state of this house should tell you what I want her for.' He unpinned the sapphire from his neckcloth and began to unwind the strip of starched muslin.

Delphine was lying across the bottom of his bed, her chin cupped in her hands, her feet, bare of slippers, in the air. 'Why won't you buy me a house in town?' she said, returning to her usual complaint.

'Because I am here and will be for the foreseeable future.'

And because I do not see why I should pay for you to use my money, or my house, to amuse yourself with other lovers.

He had no illusions about Delphine.

He shrugged off his coat and draped it over the back of a chair. His valet knew better than to appear when Mrs de Frayne was upstairs.

She was sulky, provoking—and, despite that, damnably provocative, especially to a man who knew just where her talents lay.

'Surely you are not jealous of a spinster librarian with a clergyman's widow as a companion?' he asked as he emerged from the folds of the shirt he was pulling off over his head.

'She's a little pretty, I suppose,' Delphine said with a pout.

'Pretty? I hardly think so.' Will was tired and harassed, but he knew how to take his mind off that and how to stop Delphine's sulks. 'And we are both wearing far too much clothing, my dear.'

Chapter Three

Breakfast was brought to Katherine and Elspeth in their sitting room by Jeannie who had already, she reported, got her feet comfortably under the table in the servants' hall.

'They're all right,' she said, pouring tea. 'I thought they'd be all stuck up, being a marquis's household, but it seems a pretty ramshackle place, if you ask me. Mr Grigson the butler's a bit strict, but Mrs Goodman's nice enough and Cook's ready for a laugh. The other girls are all friendly and cheerful, and the lads, too.

'I'm glad to have my own bed in the dressing room, though. They say it's like a lumber room up on the top floor and they're jammed in with all kinds of odd stuff.' She straightened the toast rack. 'They're happy to have His new Lordship here, even if it does make more work for them.'

She unloaded her tray and bustled out.

Katherine passed Elspeth the toast. 'Did you sleep well?'

'Remarkably so. Now, tell me, what is your plan?'

'I must make a good start on the library,' Katherine said, buttering her slice. 'That is what Lovell most wants and it will lull him into ignoring me if I do that. Then, after a week, say, I will begin exploring the rest of the house. If I am challenged, then I will say I am looking for stray volumes and assessing the antiquities.' She hesitated. 'Elspeth, it would be helpful if your chaperonage was rather…lax. I want to be as unfettered as possible as I search for the ruby. The fact that you are here at all gives the impression of respectability and I think that is all that is necessary.'

Katherine lifted a silver dome and surveyed the platter while she waited for a response. 'They do not intend us to starve.'

'No, indeed.' Elspeth helped herself to bacon, egg and a sausage. 'I understand what you are saying and it does appear—if one leaves aside the presence of that woman in the house—that it is a safe place for a young lady to be. I believe we will be comfortable here, provided we can avoid that Mrs de Frayne, although what your mama would say if she knew you are in the same house as a woman of that kind, I shudder to think.'

'So do I,' Katherine said. 'But I do wonder just what kind of life she has had to send her down the path of becoming a kept woman. She is appallingly rude, but I shall do my best to ignore her. Annoying her hardly adds to the domestic harmony and it is in my interest to keep Lovell in a good temper.'

'So, if you are happy alone, I shall take up His Lordship's permission to take out a gig and go and explore St Albans, if you will spare Jeannie to me. Is there any shopping I can do for you?'

Katherine found her team of maids and footmen already waiting for her and looking quite happy to be involved, despite their hard work the previous afternoon, although their faces fell when she explained that she did not require the maids until the next bay was emptied and that only one footman was necessary for a while.

She picked out the one who had seemed the most interested the day before and asked his name.

'Peter, Miss.'

'Let me show you how I need to sort the books.' She led him along the trestle tables, pointing to the labels that were already there. 'As I decide which subject to place a book in, I need you it put behind the correct label and, as the sections fill up, they may need moving about to make room, but keeping together. Do you understand?'

'Yes, Miss. You don't want them getting muddled again.'

'Exactly. How accurate do you think you would be putting books into alphabetical order by their author?'

'By their surname, Miss? All the ones beginning with A together and so on? Yes, I can do that.'

He proved as good as his word and they worked steadily through several piles of books, even faster when he offered to dust them before passing them on to Katherine.

When her little clock struck half past ten she sent him off to have a cup of tea, or a glass of ale or whatever refreshment he could extract from Cook. 'And please bring me some coffee when you return,' she called as he went out.

Katherine pushed back her chair and surveyed the room. She had virtually finished the books from the first bay.

If they cleared another one, she could then see if Peter could sort some of the piles of books that sat about the room—on the floor, on the atlas stands, on the chairs—into subjects himself, dusting as he went. Then he could feed them through to her. It might speed things up, or it might cause more chaos, she wasn't sure, but she would see what was on that next set of shelves first.

The tall library steps were on wheels, with a railed platform at the top and a braking device that stopped one of the wheels moving when it was pushed down. It was stiff and she broke a fingernail freeing it, but the wheels ran easily when it was unlocked and she trod on the brake when she had the steps in position in front of the second bay of shelves.

The top shelf all appeared to be concerned with religion, which was helpful. She lifted down those she could reach and set them on the platform at her feet, then the remaining half-dozen volumes fell sideways and by stretching she could pull them towards her.

Something red fluttered at the end of the shelf and she could see a small box, tied with ribbon, at the far end. Katherine stretched and her fingertip just touched it. She could get down, of course, and move the ladder, but if she just stood on the lower rail enclosing the platform she might manage. A small box hidden—if, by great good chance, it concealed the ruby then the first part of her mission was at an end.

She climbed up, both feet on the rail, the top bar against her thighs. Her fingers closed around the ribbon, she tugged and the whole stepladder shot forward. Katherine jumped down from the rail, her feet stumbling over the heap of theological tomes, then she found herself tumbling backwards, a shower of small, hard objects hitting her as she went.

The alarming thought that the library floor was solid oak planks went through her mind in the second after she fell. Then she hit something rather softer.

It went '*ough*' as it caught her, held her and set her on her feet.

That poor footman, she thought, turning, expecting to see Peter and instead finding herself almost nose to nose with the Marquis.

'Thank you,' Katherine said. She tried to step back and stumbled on fallen books.

He reached out, caught her by her upper arms and pulled her upright again. 'I thought you were a librarian.'

'I am. I fell off the ladder—the brake does not work very well.'

'Surely familiarity with library steps and an ability not to throw volumes all over the floor are basic requirements of your profession?'

'Accidents do happen, Lovell,' Katherine snapped. 'And it is your equipment that is faulty.'

He was still holding her and that was decidedly unsettling. Not that he was gripping hard, or attempting to grope, but it was just…unsettling. And warm. And, frankly, there was nothing wrong with his equipment that she was aware of.

'You may release me now.'

He did so, very readily. Yes, she had no need to fear that her employer would be free with his hands.

'Thank you.' She tried for a more moderate tone, stepped sideways and promptly turned her foot on something small. 'Ouch.'

'What on earth?'

They both looked down at where they stood in a scatter of

colourful stones. Blood red, blue, purple, white, green—the ovals gleamed against the old oak.

As one they crouched, banged heads and tumbled into a heap.

'Oh, for goodness sake!' Katherine flailed in an effort to right herself and ended up with her hands around Lovell's neck, at which point, with horrible inevitability, the door opened.

There was a shriek of fury and Katherine threw up her arms to protect her head as something slapped down on it.

'I knew it! You are a *beast*, Ravenham. You are a liar and I am going back to London this moment and you can keep your plain little miss. Librarian? *Pah.*'

Delphine de Frayne swept out, dropping the copy of *La Belle Assemblée* that she had been belabouring them with as she went.

'I am quite all right, but you had better go and explain,' Katherine said, uncurling herself. How it had happened she had no idea, but somehow, she had become thoroughly entangled with Lovell and her skirts were up to her knees.

'I don't think so.' Lovell got to his feet and extended a hand to haul her to hers. He showed not the slightest interest in the expanse of calf and ankle that was exposed.

No doubt, she thought, her very ordinary legs in their cotton stockings bore little resemblance to a courtesan's silk-clad limbs.

When Peter appeared a moment later, a tray with a cup of coffee on it in one hand, Lovell took it from him.

'Tell the stables to have a carriage ready to convey Mrs de Frayne to London, send her woman to her to pack and inform Mr Wilmott that I would be obliged if he would provide the necessary expenses for her journey, to be given to her with my compliments. And the blue Morocco case from the safe.'

'What?' he demanded as the footman hurried out and he turned to put down the tray.

'You are very ruthless in disposing of your—er, I mean I am sure she would understand if it was explained.'

'I do not appreciate being called a liar, I do not tolerate anyone abusing my staff and I did not invite her here in the first place. She *was* my *er*,' he added with a sardonic smile for her evasion. 'She is no longer.'

Unable to find any satisfactory reply to that, other than, *Of course you are a liar. You are a lawyer, I have heard you in court,* Katherine drank her coffee in one quick gulp.

'And what the devil are these?' He crouched down again and began to gather up the confetti of fallen stones. 'Intaglios.'

'Oh, lovely.' Katherine joined him on hands and knees with the box, carefully checking each engraved oval for chips before she put it back. 'They are a mixture, I think. Some are Roman and some later. Renaissance, perhaps. I need to see them with a magnifying glass in good light. I don't think any are damaged.'

'Where were they?' He looked up when she pointed to the shelf. 'Are they of any value?'

'To collectors, yes. The Renaissance ones more so, because they are often very fine work and, of course, they are semi-precious and precious stones. They could be set in jewellery or displayed under glass. Where would you like me to put small valuable items that I come across?'

'Give them to Wilmott.' Lovell stood up. 'He can use the strongroom.' He looked at her, his face expressionless, although Katherine had the strong impression that he was angry. 'I apologise for Mrs de Frayne's personal remarks and for her insinuations about your character.'

'I do not regard it,' Katherine said as she tied the ribbon on the box.

It was disconcerting to find that this man whom she despised recognised that an employee had feelings, let alone that it mattered if they were hurt. Although, of course, she thought as he walked away without another word, he, too, had once been employed.

'Please pick up the fallen books, Peter,' she said when the footman returned. 'Where is the strongroom?'

'In the basement, Miss, next to the silver safe and the butler's room.' He straightened up with an armful of books. 'I don't think there's any damage to these.'

'Oh, good,' Katherine said absently.

Why hadn't she thought of a strongroom? The late Marquis had fought through the courts to retain his hold on the ruby and it was logical that he would protect it.

She would have to let Mr Wilmott become used to her coming and going until he left her alone in the room and she could search. She could hardly ignore Lovell's direct order to begin on the library in order to pretend to catalogue the small valuables. If he could dismiss his mistress so abruptly, he was not going to forgive a mere employee for disregarding his orders.

Best to become indispensable first, she concluded, whisking a soft brush over a commentary on the early Church Fathers, then she might expect more flexibility from him.

He had certainly been flexible when he had caught her, she mused, her mind wandering. And when they had ended up in that undignified tangle on the floor. Strong and flexible—

Katherine pulled herself together with a muttered curse. The Marquis was an unscrupulous bully and the fact that he was good to look at—*and to feel,* a treacherous little inner voice murmured—did not make him any less the enemy.

He had looked imposing in court, too, his face stern and unyielding under his lawyer's wig, the black gown swirling around him as he paced in front of judge and jury. The occasional flashes of humour were as nothing in mitigation, either.

Elspeth returned from St Albans, full of interesting facts about the abbey—'Sadly tumbledown, I fear'—the quality of the shops—'Very good. Rather too good, in fact. I allowed myself to be tempted into buying some lace, some soap and a pair of gloves'—and the attractiveness of the countryside.

'Not that I expect you will have much time spare to drive about,' she said, clearing some books off a chair and dusting it with her handkerchief before sitting down and surveying the library. '*What* a mess.'

'It is at the *getting worse before it can get any better* stage,' Katherine said.

In fact, she was rather pleased with progress. Peter was proving a helpful assistant and she had hopes of having everything in a preliminary order by the end of the week. Then she could write up the catalogue in the evenings and, hopefully, start searching through the small boxes.

Perhaps she could persuade Lovell that it would be a good

idea to locate and deal with anything portable and of value before worrying about statues and sarcophagi.

'But you missed all the excitement,' she reported. 'Mrs de Frayne has taken herself off to London in a huff, with Lovell's parting gift in her baggage.'

'Excellent. The woman created a tension and unpleasantness wherever she was. What caused the rift, do you know?'

'I did,' Katherine said ruefully, checking that the door was closed and Peter still off searching for more black ink. 'I fell from the ladder, was caught by Lovell, we ended up on the floor somewhat entangled and me with my skirts up to my knees, and in walked Delphine. She put the worst possible interpretation on the scene, belaboured us with a copy of a fashionable journal—painfully—and stormed off.'

'My goodness.' Elspeth was wide-eyed. 'How embarrassing for you. The Marquis did not—that is, I hope he...'

'He behaved like a perfect gentleman. I was of about as much interest to him as the sack of potatoes I fear I resembled. Our instincts about there being no need for me to be closely chaperoned were quite correct, it seems.'

The more she thought about it, the more insulting it was. *Of course* she hadn't wanted him to take advantage of the situation, that would have been appalling, but she had to admit it would have been gratifying to see a gleam of interest, or to gain the impression that he was tempted by her loveliness and manfully restraining himself.

'Excellent,' Elspeth said briskly. 'I can see I need have no qualms about leaving you.'

'None whatsoever.' The door opened to admit the footman carrying a bottle of ink. 'I must get on. Do you think you can find out whether we are expected to dine with the Marquis tonight, Elspeth?'

'Mrs Goodman and Grigson believe we are expected to dine every evening, unless told otherwise,' Elspeth said several hours later when they were in their sitting room drinking tea. 'Jeannie!'

'Yes, ma'am?' The maid emerged from the dressing room where she was putting away Elspeth's purchases.

'It seems we will be dining formally every evening, Jeannie. Have we enough gowns, do you think?'

'Only two each.' She frowned in thought. 'But we can add and take away lace collars and trims and there is the net over-skirt to Miss Katherine's blue gown. That could go with your amber-coloured one, ma'am. With different shawls we could make it seem more varied.'

'I did see a dressmaker's shop with some elegant but simple gowns on display in the window when I was in St Albans,' Elspeth said. 'I went in and enquired—one never knows when one might need a reliable seamstress—and I have their card. The terms seemed reasonable.'

'I'll order something,' Katherine decided. 'In the meantime your ideas are excellent, thank you, Jeannie.'

When the door closed behind the maid Katherine said, 'I do not know why I am so concerned. It will just be the two gentlemen every evening and I am certain neither of them is fretting over boring us with the same waistcoat night after night. Besides, I doubt whether Lovell would notice if we were in full dress or bathing costumes.'

'I doubt he is quite that unobservant,' Elspeth said and they both gave way to a fit of the giggles.

Chapter Four

The two women were in high spirits Will noticed as he joined them in the drawing room. He could almost believe they were laughing at *him*, but that was probably because his own mood was so foul he was prepared to think he was bring mocked.

The departure of Delphine had been accompanied, so Giles informed him, by a great deal of flouncing and her absence, along with her moods and dramatics, was a relief in many ways.

On the other hand, she had been spectacular in bed and he was going to miss that. In fact, he already was, which did nothing for his temper, already provoked by having to spend all day wrestling with paperwork.

The sight of Miss Jenson, cheeks pink, eyes sparkling with suppressed laughter, brought back the memory of her body hitting his and the feel of warm, yielding femininity under his hands.

She is not a beauty, he told himself now. *Not even pretty. An ordinary oval face, ordinary hazel eyes, ordinary brown hair, not quite chestnut. And she is a respectable young woman which means I should not even be thinking about her in that way.*

Giles, who was talking to Mrs Downe, pushed away from the mantel shelf where he was leaning as Will entered and the ladies made as though to rise, then sank back as he gestured for them to stay sitting.

They were ladies, he thought irritably, even though one was an employee. Ladies had not stood for him when he was plain William Lovell and he saw no reason for them to do so for the Marquis of Ravenham.

'You have no ill effects from your fall, Miss Jenson?' He stood on the other end of the empty hearth from Giles, one foot on the fender. 'The locking mechanism on the library steps has been repaired, I understand.'

'I am quite unharmed, thank you.' The laughter was still in her eyes and he thought he understood why when she added, 'I had quite a soft landing.'

Was she implying that he was flabby? Will pulled in his already perfectly flat stomach and managed not to glower. Confound it, he knew full well he was in good trim. Lawyers risked becoming stooped and weak from hours spent at their desks, but he had always taken care to ride daily, to spar at one of the capital's boxing salons and to keep up his fencing practice. This bright-eyed female was making him self-conscious and that was a novel and unsettling feeling.

He did what he always did when he sensed a threat, he went on the attack. 'It would be as well if you kept off ladders in future, Miss Jenson. That is what footmen are for.'

'Librarians climb ladders of necessity,' she said composedly. 'However, I will check the brake on any others I ascend in future.'

And that was supposed to be an acceptable answer to a direct order?

'Dinner is served, my lord.'

Will bit back the words he had been about to utter. 'Thank you, Grigson. Mrs Downe?' He offered his arm and she rose to take it.

'Thank you, my lord.'

'Lovell,' he reminded her, aware of Miss Jenson's voice behind him, speaking to Giles. Why was it that he sensed hostility under her calm words to himself and yet there was none there when she spoke to his secretary? Imagination, obviously. She had no reason to resent him: he had, after all, agreed to everything she had requested.

Perhaps she found dealing with a marquis intimidating and was unable to truly relax around him. Will smiled wryly to himself, still not quite able to comprehend his sudden rise in status.

He seated Mrs Downe on his right and gestured to Giles to take the foot of the table which had now been reduced to a smaller rectangle. That put Miss Jenson on his left, to be conversed with during the second remove.

He should have known better than to rely on her to observe the formalities.

'Have you found any papers relating to the collections, Lovell?' she asked as soon as they were seated. 'Some provenance and an indication of the price paid for each item would be very useful.'

'We have discovered little and what there is has been put to one side unexamined,' he said. 'There is too much else to deal with. The estate here has been badly neglected, Mawson at Home Farm tells me he despaired of being given any clear direction, the tenants' cottages are in poor repair—no doubt you can imagine the problems.'

'At least you have the experience in handling large numbers of facts, of sifting through documents and creating order from them,' she said as a footman placed a bowl of soup in front of her.

'Close attention to documents is not a problem. In many ways my career in the law relied upon it, but now I have to learn an entirely new language, that of estate management,' Will admitted.

'If I come across anything relating to the subject I will inform Mr Wilmott. I saw map cabinets behind some of the piles of books. If there are any estate plans in there, shall I have them brought down to you?'

She was thinking like one of his clerks, he realised. Anticipating his needs, planning to satisfy them. As he thought it, she smiled suddenly at Giles who had passed her the bread rolls and Will caught his breath.

He was, he knew, a man of strong appetites, but he had never failed to keep them under control as a gentleman should. Mistresses had come and gone over the years, usually with far less drama than Delphine had provided. They expected, and received at his hands, respect, maintenance and, at the end of a relationship, a civilised parting gift. He had experienced a number of perfectly satisfactory liaisons in the nine years since he had first been able, at the age of twenty, to afford such a luxury.

Wives and families involved a considerable investment for an ambitious lawyer—a respectable town house, more servants, a carriage, large bills from modistes and milliners.

It would be time to take a wife when he was thirty, Will had decided. He had a year to that deadline and in the meantime had felt no need to flirt with respectable young ladies beyond what was expected in polite society.

It was a shock to discover that the thought of Miss Jenson satisfying his needs, combined with that smile, should be so arousing. Will rearranged the napkin on his lap with some force and told himself that men who lusted after those in their employ were no gentlemen.

Besides, now that Miss Jenson had ceased smiling and was regarding him with the air of someone about to ask a difficult question, the heat of desire ebbed away.

'Yes?'

She blinked a little, deliberately as a reproof for his abruptness, he was certain. 'I expect to have made the library usable, although not completed, by the end of the week,' she said coolly. 'I could then divide my time between completing it in every detail and, for example, directing the clearance of any other room you wish to have in use. Or I could scour the house for small, portable items of value, such as those intaglios, and ensure they are safely locked away.'

'You distrust the staff here?'

'I have no reason to, although I do not think it right to leave temptation in front of them. You have no idea what you have, or where it is. And this is a large, rambling house. Anyone could get in and pillage it to their heart's content, I imagine.'

The fact that she was perfectly correct, and it was not fair on the staff to put them in such a position, did nothing to soften his mood.

'Very well,' Will said shortly. 'From tomorrow spend half the day on the library and the rest searching for anything portable and valuable. Giles, I assume there is space in the strongroom?'

'Sir?' Wilmott had been deep in conversation with Mrs Downe.

Interrupting the lady was bad mannered and he forced himself to apologise. 'I beg your pardon, ma'am.'

She sent him a sunny smile of forgiveness. 'Not at all, Lovell.'

Now he felt a boor as well as a libertine. He must have been mad to employ a female, let alone saddle himself with two respectable ladies living in his house.

Before they had arrived he had merely felt harassed by a deluge of demands that required knowledge and skills he did not yet possess and resentful of his cousins for being such confounded fools and getting themselves killed. No doubt the rest of the world considered the inheritance of a title, lands and wealth as an astonishing windfall, Will could only feel aggrieved.

Common sense told him that eventually he would have all this under control and could begin to enjoy his privileged position, but just now he felt that he was having to work harder than he ever had in his entire life.

With an effort that felt almost physical he enquired, 'And did you have an interesting visit to St Albans, Mrs Downe?'

Although it was very satisfying to observe that the Marquis did not appear to be enjoying his elevation to the peerage and it was tempting to tease him a little more, Katherine decided that an early night might be strategically sensible. She had no wish to irritate him to the extent of sending her packing.

'Lovell is not a happy man,' Elspeth observed as she poured tea in the privacy of their sitting room. 'One would think that the departure of that woman might have improved his temper.'

'Not if he is missing the, er, benefits she provided.' Katherine dropped a slice of lemon into her cup and resisted adding a small lump of sugar.

'True, although she is hardly out of the door—surely he cannot be missing her already.' Elspeth gave a little shake of her head. 'What an improper conversation for an unmarried lady to be having. Stop speculating about his private life, Katherine, and explain more about this ruby you are hunting and why you hate him so much. I know he was perfectly dreadful to your poor father in court, but I never quite understood what it was all about.'

'There is this jewel made in the sixteenth century—a large cabochon ruby in a wonderful gold mount and with three baroque pearls—those twisted freshwater kind—hanging below. There is a portrait of Lucrezia Borgia wearing it, which is why it is known as the Borgia Ruby.'

'She was the natural daughter of one of the popes, wasn't she?'

'Yes, Alexander VI, and she has a reputation as a poisoner, which I'm not sure I believe. I have always suspected it was a question of putting blame on any attractive young woman.

'Anyway, this wonderful thing disappeared for a while, then there were reports of it being in Venice, the possession of a great courtesan and mistress of the Doge in the early seventeen hundreds. It vanished from sight again and then the Venetian Republic was overthrown by Napoleon in 1797.'

Katherine refilled her teacup and drank while she got the rest of the story in order. 'Then Papa heard a rumour that it had been looted by a French army officer, lost in a game of cards and had ended up in the possession of a dealer in Lyon. That was in the April of 1814, just before Napoleon abdicated. The war was over, everyone thought, and it was possible to travel in France, so he went and found the dealer.'

'How on earth could he afford such a valuable item?' Elspeth asked. 'I know your father did some buying and selling, but mainly he was employed for his scholarly knowledge, was he not?'

Katherine nodded. 'He scraped together everything he had and, when he found the man, discovered that he was in fear of his life. He had made many Royalist enemies who were out for his blood now the monarchy was being restored. He agreed to a very reasonable price if Papa could get him safely out of France, which he did.'

'So, your father was back in London with the jewel. How did the late Lord Ravenham become involved?'

'Papa needed to recoup his investment and Ravenham was the collector most likely to buy it. The Marquis was interested, but said he wanted his own jewellers to assess it. Papa was reluctant to leave it with him, so Ravenham paid him two hundred pounds as a surety and Papa signed the receipt.'

'Oh, I can guess what happened then. Ravenham maintained it was an outright sale and kept it.'

'Exactly. It is worth perhaps ten times that, perhaps more, if handled with the right publicity, although Papa had no hope of achieving that figure. He asked for six hundred and when Ravenham refused to either pay the difference or return the ruby, he took him to court.'

Elspeth put down her cup with a rattle. 'Of course he did, it was theft.'

'He might have had a chance,' Katherine said, 'but William Lovell, then Ravenham's lawyer, defended his cousin, made out that Papa had obtained it in France through dubious means and that it was probably not the real Borgia Ruby in any case. Papa was branded a liar and a fraudster and, even worse, someone who traded with a supporter of Napoleon.

'The two hundred was what he had paid the Frenchman, so he did not lose that, only the costs of his travel and getting the man out of France safely, but the money hardly mattered. Nobody would employ him again. There were even rumours, after Lovell's very strong hints in court, that Papa had been a spy during the war and had been in league with the man then. The disgrace killed him.'

'Do you believe that William Lovell knew that his cousin had, in effect, stolen the jewel?'

'I have no idea. But lawyers don't care, do they? It is their job to defend their client regardless, even on a murder charge. It must have been he who discovered that the man from whom Papa bought it was a Bonapartist and that he had smuggled him out of France. I imagine that employment for a marquis must be very well paid,' she said bitterly.

'It is terrible,' Elspeth said hotly. 'No wonder you are so determined to retrieve it. Lovell and his cousin ruined your poor father's name, took his livelihood, sent him to an early grave and now your mother must trade in lace and you seek employment.'

'It is fortunate that both of us enjoy what we do and are able to support ourselves by it. Not that it would make any difference to Lovell if we hated it and were poverty-stricken. But at least the one thing he could not do was ruin us financially.'

'But what can you do about it?' Elspeth said. 'The man's a marquis and possession is nine-tenths of the law, even without a court finding in his favour. You certainly can't steal it back— that would be a hanging offence, taking a gem of that value.'

'I know.' Katherine reached for the teapot again. 'I am attempting to get him used to me as a vaguely irritating, but useful, presence. He already seems able to accept me as more than a servant. Soon, I hope to have the free run of the house and be able to pry into files and documents. Somewhere there might be the original correspondence between the late Marquis and Papa and the genuine receipt. When I have those, I can prove my ownership, bring him to court or use the evidence to make a public scandal of the way Papa was treated.'

'I wonder that you manage to be so pleasant to the man. I am not certain that I will be able to, not now I know the whole story.'

'Please try, Elspeth. As for me, I would smile and be pleasant to the Devil himself, if necessary.'

'You know what they say about taking a long spoon if you wish to sup with *that* gentleman,' Elspeth warned.

'I will take care, but I *will* have Papa's good name restored, I *will* expose Lovell for the lies that he told, I *will* claim the ruby—and William Lovell can go to the Devil himself.'

Chapter Five

There was one problem with Katherine's plan, she acknowledged to herself, and that was the fact that she found the Marquis of Ravenham attractive. Not his personality, of course, that was beyond forgiveness, but his looks.

She was resigned to spinsterhood unless, improbably, she found a reclusive antiquarian to fall in love with. Anyone else would shun an alliance with the daughter of the disgraced Arnold Jones. And she knew who to blame for that.

Although it was possible that she might encounter such a person, it did seem unlikely that he would be her soulmate and would love her in return and she was not given to hopeless daydreams, although it was not always so easy not to yearn, just a little, whatever common sense told her.

But she was twenty-six years old, a healthy female, and whatever her brain was telling her, the rest of her body was informing her that it was in the presence of an attractive specimen of the opposite sex. It asked, quite insistently, what she was going to do about this because, it kept reminding her, it had very much enjoyed landing in his arms and being entangled with him on the library floor. It even made suggestions by means of dreams about how it would like matters to proceed.

The answer, that she would do nothing, was not helping Katherine's sleep and, for the second night in a row, she found herself at three in the morning wondering why Giles Wilmott wasn't filling her dreams instead of his employer. He was a nice man: intelligent, kind and perfectly pleasant to look at, being tall, slim and possessed of a pair of kind brown eyes and a head of thick blond hair, yet he did not arouse the slightest flicker of an improper thought in her mind.

It had never occurred to her that it would be possible to find someone she hated attractive and it was not a pleasant realisation. Clearly, she had very poor taste and it was fortunate that William Lovell appeared quite impervious to whatever charms she possessed.

That was not surprising, Katherine had to admit. Her looks, she considered, were perfectly pleasant. Brown hair tending towards chestnut, an oval face, hazel eyes and nothing objectionable about her nose, chin or figure. There were thousands of women as ordinary as she was and none of them, unless they had a vast dowry or near-royal bloodlines, would be of any interest to a marquis.

At which point she pummelled her pillows, pulled up the covers, reminded herself that the said nobleman was the enemy and attempted to sleep by counting as many authors of commentaries on the Bible as she could recall.

Katherine was in no mood at seven the next morning to exchange bantering conversation with Lovell over the breakfast table, which was fortunate, as he barely acknowledged her presence beyond half rising, before burying himself again in a pile of correspondence.

On the other hand, she needed to be certain he was still in agreement with the programme she had outlined the previous evening.

'I will be working in the library this morning, Lovell,' she said, reaching for the toast.

'Indeed?' He did not look up, allowing her to observe that he had a full head of hair with no sign of thinning on top.

'I will see what estate maps I can find.'

'Good.' He tossed the letter on to a pile on his left hand and reached for another.

'And this afternoon I will begin searching for small valuable items to put into the strongroom, as agreed.'

'Yes.' That letter went to the right and he opened another.

Giles Wilmott came in, greeted her and apologised to Lovell for being late.

'As long as you are in the study at half past, the time you eat your breakfast is of no concern to me, Wilmott.'

Katherine caught the secretary's eye and pulled a wry face. He grinned back. Yes, a very pleasant gentleman and when she looked at him her heart remained as steady as a metronome.

She decided she would take a day or two bringing him items for the strongroom. Then, when that had become routine, she would innocently enquire where the paperwork relating to them might be and offer to search for it herself—in a spirit of pure helpfulness, of course. If the late Marquis had kept records about such *objets de virtu,* then the papers relating to the ruby might be with them.

Lovell looked up, his gaze locking with hers. Katherine controlled the instinct to look away and he broke the contact first, returning to his scrutiny of the correspondence in front of him. If it were possible to shrug with the eyes, she thought, he had just done so.

That indifference was excellent, of course. He clearly regarded her as of much interest as his footman, which meant he detected nothing amiss, no threat to himself.

And of no interest as a woman, a small, resentful voice murmured in her thoughts.

'Is there anyone in charge of the woodlands?' Will asked, looking up from the account books spread on his desk. 'I haven't seen anything relating to timber sales and we are surrounded by beech woods. I can recall suing a Mr Atherton to the east over forestry boundaries several years ago.'

'I have seen nothing in the wages books for a forester or a wood reeve, as I believe they are called in some parts, sir.' Wilmott gestured towards the stack of ledgers on a side table. 'If the late Marquis was concerned enough about his boundaries, you would expect him to take equal care of the actual property.'

Will shook his head. 'It was all about ownership. He had to *have,* but once he possessed something, he lost interest. Ask the outside staff later, will you, Giles? If you are correct and nobody is employed, then we will advertise. Timber is a valuable asset. Have you seen any maps that show the extent of the woods? There must be something somewhere or I'd not have been able to prepare that case.'

'Nothing here, sir. The only estate plans we have found so far are the grounds around the house. Perhaps Miss Jenson has unearthed something in the library—she did say she would look.'

Will pushed back his chair. 'I will go and see and make sure while I'm there that the confounded woman isn't lying on the floor with a broken neck after clambering up the map stand.'

He ignored the muffled snort of laughter behind him and strode off down the corridor, his progress impeded the further he went by statues and packing cases.

The library, when he reached it, was a scene of well-ordered chaos. The piles of books he recalled were still there, but neatly stacked. Trestle tables held even more volumes, bristling with paper tags, and George, one of the footmen, dodged back and forth between the desk, where Miss Jenson sat, and the trestles.

Two maids were dusting empty shelves and Peter, instead of working with his colleague, was seated and appeared to be sorting more slips of paper.

Will cleared his throat and, like a game of Statues, everyone froze. Except of course, Miss Jenson, who finished the line she was writing, put down her pen with care and then looked up.

'Lord Ravenham.' She rose to her feet. 'Good morning. We have beaten a path to the map cabinets, but I have not investigated their contents yet. Peter, could you remove anything that looks like an estate map to that empty trestle for His Lordship?'

Will approached the desk as the man threaded his way to the back of the room. 'You have acquired yourself a secretary, I see.'

'An assistant, certainly.' Miss Jenson lowered her voice as she sat again. 'He is an intelligent young man and ought to be aspiring to something more. A clerkship in a legal firm, for example.'

'He can rise where he is, if he has the ability.' Was the confounded woman equating his own legal training with what a footman could achieve?

'He is the fourth footman, I believe. This is not the army where one can expect those above you to be killed off on a regular basis. Unless, of course, there are more hazards in this house, like those library steps.'

His retort was cut short by Peter coming back. 'I have laid them out on the table, my lord. Do you wish me to carry out a preliminary sorting?'

What on earth had she been teaching the lad? 'Thank you, no. I will look for myself.' He made himself smile at the footman. It would not do to take out his temper on an innocent party when the cause of his irritation was sitting right next to him.

And the very fact that she was irritating him was an annoyance in itself. He had wanted access to the plans and Miss Jenson had given him that, speedily and efficiently. Will gave her a brisk nod of acknowledgment and went to look at what Peter had laid out.

As he sat down and began to unroll the first, someone put something down on the table. He looked up and saw her, hands full of small bulging objects. She set some more beside him.

'Weights. They will hold down the rolled-up maps without damaging them.'

She turned and went back to her place before he could thank her. Will stared at the innocuous pale brown lumps, each about the size of a child's fist, then picked one up. It was heavy, made of a close-woven cotton, tightly stitched in dark red and with KJ embroidered on the side.

Thoughtfully he unrolled the first map, weighting its corners. Miss Jenson was obliging, efficient, polite and good-humoured. She even engaged in light banter on occasions. So why did he sense something else behind that pleasant smile? Dislike? Or something even darker?

That was ridiculous, unless of course she was of a radical disposition, inclined to hate those possessing power, privilege and wealth on principle. He re-rolled the map which showed the park and reached for another, giving a mental shrug while he was about it. Even if Miss Jenson did hate him, it was of no matter, provided she did her work and did not attempt to poison his tea.

In his career as a lawyer he had often been hated by those he opposed and, on a few occasions when he had failed to achieve what a client wanted, had received blustering threats. He ignored them all—they were part of the cut and thrust of the legal process. If a lawyer allowed himself to be intimidated by them, then he would never last long in the courts.

But Miss Jenson was a puzzle. He had done nothing to thwart her, so either she had a general dislike of aristocrats, she objected to something about his person or, more likely, he was imagining things.

The map in front of him dragged his attention back to where it should be. The whole estate lay before him, the blocks of woodland shown in green. Yes, he definitely did need a wood reeve to manage this significant resource. The estate was going to cost a great deal to set right, but there was every indication that, properly managed, it could pay for itself.

Will rolled the map up, tucked it under his arm and began to walk out.

'One moment if you please, Lovell.'

He stopped by Miss Jenson's desk and raised an eyebrow as she held out a hand for the map.

She took it with a nod of acknowledgement, unrolled it enough to see the title and date in one corner, made a note on a slip and handed it back.

'Am I not allowed to take my own property without permission?' he enquired acidly.

'Of course, my lord. But that has not been catalogued. Now I know what it is and where it has gone.'

She looked back at him with a hint of challenge in her eyes.

Go on, that look seemed to say. *Argue and we'll see who wins.*

'Excellent, Miss Jenson. A most sensible idea,' Will said with a condescending smile calculated to make any right-thinking woman wish to slap him. 'Carry on.'

'Oh, I will, my lord,' she said, perfectly composed.

Now, who won that round, I wonder? he thought as he closed the library door with a gentle *snick* of the catch.

After luncheon with Elspeth, who had spent her morning exploring the overgrown and neglected gardens in front of the house, Katherine left Peter cleaning a pile of books with feathers and squirrel-hair brushes and set out on her own journey of discovery.

First she asked Giles to unlock the strongroom for her and surveyed the shelves with him. Other than a few dead spiders it contained only a pair of rather ugly silver candelabra, which they moved to the butler's silver safe.

'Any ordinary person would store their collections in an orderly manner and would keep small portable items securely in the strongroom, or in locked display cases,' she observed to Giles as she placed the box of intaglios on a shelf.

'Attributing logic to the thought processes of the late Marquis is clearly time wasted,' he replied.

The previous Lord Ravenham was clearly a magpie, she thought, surveying the first cupboard she opened in one of the cluttered and unused reception rooms. It yielded several fossils, some pleasant miniatures, seven books on various subjects which she set aside to take to the library, a pair of old riding boots and a whip.

An acquisitive magpie with, apparently, the attention span of a five-year-old child, she amended.

But if the man had not been logical, then she must be. There was sure to be a plan of the house with the others in the library. She would make a copy and then search room by room in an orderly manner, making sure no possible hiding place was neglected.

Katherine scooped up the armful of books and opened the door. Which way to go? She could retrace her steps back to the hall and from there she knew the way to the library. But was that the quickest route? Another corridor led off to her left and her sense of direction told her it must lead towards the rear left-hand side of the house where the library lay.

She set off, dodging between packing cases and encountering nobody. Clearly, this was not an area that received much attention from the staff, judging by some spectacular cobwebs draping the cornices.

As she thought it, she did encounter someone going about their work. A large tabby cat padded around the corner, tail up. She greeted it, but it gave her the disdainful look that only cats and dowager duchesses can produce and stalked past.

'Go and catch a mouse,' she called after it and received a twitch of the tail in response.

Katherine turned a corner, then another, beginning to lose confidence that she was heading in the right direction. Then she found a staircase leading upwards. It had finely carved balusters and an impressive newel post and was clearly not a service stair, although it hugged the wall and was only wide enough for two people to climb side by side. Perhaps it was a relic from one of the earlier stages of the house.

But what seized Katherine's attention was the group of statues that were crowded into the space beside the first flight and under where the second turned at a half-landing. There seemed to be seven or eight and, although the figures at the front were clearly Roman, there was one at the back that made her catch her breath. Greek, surely? And not a Roman copy.

She put down the books, climbed up a few steps and leant over the handrail to see better. It certainly looked beautiful and behind it was not a stone wall, but a panelled one with doors in it. A cupboard, hidden. Where better to keep something precious? At least, if you were an eccentric who appeared to have forgotten he possessed a strongroom.

The sensible course would be to summon some footmen and have the statues moved out into the corridor. But that would reveal the cupboard and she wanted to look inside it before anyone else did.

Katherine stood in front of the group and decided it would be possible to wriggle her way through to the back, despite them standing in such an untidy muddle, some almost half turned, some facing forward, some back.

Cautiously she began to slide between them, sucking in her breath as she passed a spear point, curving her back to negotiate the bulge of a shield, then sliding past the lifted arm of a nymph ineffectually hiding her modesty with a stole.

Then she was in the small space at the back and could open the cupboard doors. The space inside came only as high as her waist, was perhaps an arm's length deep and its shelf held a mass of heavy, folded fabric. A tapestry, she realised, running her hand over to feel the texture.

'Drat.' Katherine closed the doors, turned to wriggle back to the corridor and found herself trapped like a lobster in a pot.

All the parts of the statues that she had squeezed past were turned towards her: arms, a spear, a trident and a scroll. There was no smooth polished marble surface to slide across, only jabbing projections. She crouched down, thinking to get out on hands and knees, but plinths and sandaled feet, even a leaping dolphin, barred that way.

Could she climb and reached the staircase, haul herself up and over the handrail? Several attempts proved that, no, she could not.

Katherine took a deep breath down to the bottom of her lungs. 'Help!'

Half an hour later, to judge by the distant, faint, chimes of a clock, she had a sore throat and the nasty feeling that she was well and truly stuck. Old tales of young women lost in ancient mansions, trapped in cupboards or chests only to be found as skeletons in fine gowns many years later, came into her mind to haunt her.

'Nonsense,' Katherine said sharply to her own overactive imagination. She would just have to try to push a statue over and she could see just the one, a very inferior Roman figure with the head of a jowly man set on the body of an athletic youth, the kind of thing churned out in their hundreds for men who wanted to show they had a wise old head on a healthy body. If it fell, it was unlikely to hit anything else and should create a space to crawl through.

She didn't like damaging any antiquity, but she was certainly not going to perish for the sake of that one.

Katherine reached through the tangle of limbs, put the one hand that would reach on the torso and pushed.

It did not as much as sway.

Chapter Six

'Help!'

Will stopped in his tracks and listened. Nothing—clearly his imagination. Then the call came again. But from where? The ground floor where he was, he decided. It did not sound as though it was echoing down a stairwell, but there was a maze of corridors at the rear of the building, inefficiently linking the various phases of construction, and he had already noticed how sound was distorted in this house.

'Keep shouting,' he yelled and it came again. A woman, by the sound of it. A maid fallen down some back stairs?

'Here!'

It was closer now. He turned a corner and saw in front of him a huddle of full-sized statues, one of which appeared to be calling out.

'Where are you?' he shouted.

'Here, behind the statues.'

Not a maid. It was the infuriating Miss Jenson. Not that he could see more than the top of her head and glimpses of her sensible dark blue morning dress.

'What on earth are you doing?'

'I got in—I can't get out.' At least she did not sound hysterical, although why she thought she was trapped, he was unclear. He was certain he could see a way through.

Will took hold of the nearest statue, a partly draped female nude, and rocked her on her base in an attempt to widen the entrance.

'Careful!' Miss Jenson called. 'That's one of the good ones. If you get some footmen, they can shift them without risk of damage.'

It hardly seemed necessary. She had clearly panicked and, if he was with her to help her out, there would be no problem.

Will took off his coat, breathed in and began to thread his way between the obstacle course of bare buttocks, awkwardly placed elbows, painful spears and jabbing hands.

'No, *no*,' Miss Jenson said. 'Of all the... Oh, why will men *never* listen?'

He had to force his way through the final pair of statues and saw her grab for one as it rocked.

'Do be careful! This is valuable. Genuine Greek.' Miss Jenson looked at him over her shoulder. 'And now we are both stuck,' she announced in a tone of resignation.

'Nonsense. Just follow me out.'

Will turned, not an easy thing in what was now a very small space with an irritated librarian fending him off every time he went too close to her prize statue, like a chaperon with a well-bred virginal debutante to protect.

'All we need to do—' He broke off, faced with a bristling array of limbs and weaponry.

'I told you. We are in a fish trap.'

Will swore under his breath. 'I'll push one over.'

'There is only one that is relatively valueless and that won't take anything with it and I can't even manage to make it rock.' She pointed.

Will stretched out one arm and made contact. 'Why is this one disposable?'

'The bodies—rather unsubtle athletic types—were churned out in their thousands and then portrait heads were put on top. You can see the join.'

'Why? The man is in his sixties, at least.' The head was of

a man who was bald and jowly. It looked ludicrous perched on the youthful body.

'"*Mens sana in corpore sano*",' she quoted. 'A healthy mind in a healthy body. Age and wisdom coupled with a fine physique was the ideal for the Romans. Anyway, you have at least three other examples of that about the house.' She patted the shoulder of the youth she was next to. 'While I might consider going hungry for *this* one, I wouldn't miss dinner for *that*.'

'Right.' Will flattened his hand against the statue and pushed. It stayed perfectly still. He shifted position, managed, at the cost of a marble elbow in the stomach, to get his other hand in place and tried again. Nothing.

Well, that was humiliating enough, without a critical female audience.

'Unfortunately, I cannot get close enough to exert sufficient pressure.'

'No,' she said with a sympathy that grated. 'There's never a broom handle when one needs one.'

Will rotated cautiously again. 'What's in that cupboard?'

'Folded tapestries. Useless at the moment, but worth getting out eventually, I suspect. Shall we shout again?'

It was the logical thing to do, but Will disliked the thought of having to be rescued by a party of footmen in his own house. He looked up. 'If I lifted you, could you get to the outside treads of the stairs, do you think?'

'And then walk down to the ground facing inwards and holding on to the handrail?' Miss Jenson tipped back her head and studied the nearest accessible tread, about three feet above the top of Will's head. 'Yes,' she said with a brisk nod.

Will crouched, made a stirrup with his clasped hands and she put one foot in it, holding his shoulders as he rose slowly to his feet. She was a perfectly healthy, well-built young woman and it hurt his fingers. He gritted his teeth.

'I'm the wrong way around,' she said. 'I can't get hold of anything.'

Except my hair and ears, he thought with a wince as she clutched at him for balance.

'I'll put you down.'

That was even harder than lifting her and she slid down his body, landed with a bump and pitched forward on to his chest.

Will, his arms suddenly full of well-nourished young lady, registered warmth, curves and the fleeting pressure of long legs. He took a deep breath. 'I am sorry. Are you hurt, Miss Jenson?'

She laughed, the maddening female, and stepped back. 'Not at all and do call me Katherine, it is ridiculous to be so formal when we are in such a fix. Shall we try it the other way around?'

'If you wish… Katherine.' He bent, she stepped back into his clasped hands and he lifted. This was a little easier because, he guessed, she was steadying herself on the wall. The curve of her hips and bottom passed his face as he resolutely thought of crop yields and cold custard, then he was blinded by the folds of her skirts.

'I can almost reach the step. Can you push me a bit more so I can stand on your shoulders?'

Will set his teeth and pushed and then his face was buried deep in smothering wool, her feet were planted one on each shoulder and the weight on his arms was suddenly relieved. He made a grab for the back of her calves as she swayed, then they were still.

'Oh, for a nice safe library ladder,' the voice over his head said. And then, so quietly he hardly heard it through the muffling cloth, 'And a pair of trousers.'

'What now?' Will asked, turning his head to free his mouth.

'If you can take hold of my ankles and push me up, I can pull until I can swing one foot on to a step.' She sounded breathless.

Ankles? Gentlemen were not even supposed to acknowledge that young ladies had such a thing. On the other hand, this was not the time for such scruples.

Will got a grip on each, trying not to think about the fine bones under the thin knitted cotton. 'Ready?'

'Yes.'

He pushed, shoulders aching, arm muscles protesting, and then she shook her right foot free and the weight miraculously reduced.

'Just keep pushing,' Katherine panted. 'I'm almost…there.' Then, 'Yes! Let go.'

The folds of skirts flapped away and Will looked up, caught a scandalous glimpse of garter, stepped back as far as he could and saw that she had pulled herself up, her body draped over the handrail, her toes on the outside of a step.

'Take care coming down,' he called up. 'Catch your breath first.'

He should have known she would take no notice. Katherine simply rolled over the handrail and landed with a bump on the stairs. 'Ouch.'

After a moment he heard her get up, then she hung over the rail, looking down at him. 'Wait there.' She disappeared and he heard her footsteps vanishing down the corridor.

Wait here? What the devil does she think I'm going to do instead? Levitate?

Will studied the Greek statue Katherine had liked so much in an effort to appear as unruffled as possible before his staff arrived to view him, trapped like a lobster.

Ten, perhaps fifteen minutes had passed. Had she got lost? Then he heard a strange scraping sound that got louder until something began bumping up the stairs.

'Mind your head.' Katherine appeared, pushing a ladder over the handrail.

It was one of the gardeners' fruit-picking ladders, wider at the base than the top, and, when it landed, he saw it was about seven foot tall. Not high enough to reach to the top, but tall enough for him to climb on to the outside of the steps and roll over the rail as Katherine had done.

He landed in an undignified sprawl on the uncarpeted wood, which inflicted several painful bruises, and she plumped down beside him.

'Phew.' She fanned herself with her hand and grinned. 'I am sorry it wasn't a longer one, but I couldn't manage the biggest I found. I thought you'd prefer it to a rescue party.'

'How did you manage even that?' He needed to get some feeling back into his arms before he tried pulling it up.

'Dragged it. They had left it against one of the trees at the side of the house and I noticed it yesterday.'

Will got up and began to haul the ladder up, an undignified process as he had to lean over the handrail to reach it. Katherine came to help once he had hoisted it high enough and they dropped it on the stairs with a thud and let it slide to the ground.

'Now what shall we do with it?' she asked, walking down and picking up a pile of books.

'I'll carry it around the corner and tell the next footman I see to return it to the garden,' Will said, dusting off his hands. 'How it got there will remain a mystery for ever.'

'Life in an aristocratic household holds excitements that none of us lesser mortals could dream of,' Katherine remarked as she waited while he propped the ladder up.

Will shot her a look, uncertain whether that was sarcasm or not. That cool, rather judgemental look was back in her eyes, replacing the laughter she had allowed to show as they had sprawled side by side on the stairs.

He gave a mental shrug. It was no concern of his whether an employee liked him or not, provided they did what he paid them for.

'I wonder if it would make life easier if we identified all the large statues that you would like to dispose of,' she remarked as they made their way back to the hallway. 'We could send those off to auction and make some space. I'd suggest we send the poorest specimens to various local auctions where less well-off buyers might take them for their gardens. I cannot imagine Mr Christie's customers would give you much for the one we tried to push over just now. There are auction houses in St Albans and Hertford and Aylesbury, I'm sure.'

'Spread them around a little? Yes, that seems a good idea. When will you do that?'

'We could start this afternoon.'

'We?' They had reached the hall and he stopped. 'Why do you need me?'

Katherine pursed her lips, but not before he caught a glimpse of a wicked smile. Clearly, she didn't *need* him at all.

'Because it must be your decision on what is sold. It would put me in a very difficult position if I made such decisions without your direct approval.'

When he shrugged and nodded, she asked, 'Do you have any of that pink legal tape?'

'Rolls of the stuff.' Lawyers never travelled without it for tying up documents—the original 'red tape'.

'Then I suggest we walk around and tie some on each of the statues we identify for sale. I was going to see if there is a plan of the house in the library I could copy and use to make certain I checked every room. We can mark that up with the statues for sale as well.'

It appeared that his librarian was going to organise his working day as well as the house and its collections. On the other hand, he was profoundly weary of endless ledgers—his skill was with words, not numbers—and exploring the place was appealing, even if it was in Katherine's rather uncomfortable company.

'Very well. I will collect the tape and meet you in the library.'

'Bring scissors!' she called after him.

Uncomfortable and *managing.*

The library was empty when Katherine returned to it and she sat in her chair and fanned herself with a pamphlet on pig breeding while she recovered from that encounter.

For a moment, as they had collapsed on the stairs, she had almost thought that Lovell had a sense of humour. He certainly was not a man who stood on his dignity, although perhaps he had not had much option under the circumstances.

And, if she was spending a moment being fair to him, he had not attempted to grope her legs. Possibly he recognised that any attempt to do so would have resulted in a sharp kick on the nose, but even so, many men would not have resisted sliding their hands up her calves, or making a veiled but suggestive remark about the view.

But there was no time to sit there marvelling at the fact that the wretched man had one or two redeeming features. Only an inhuman monster or a pantomime villain would have none and she had never thought him that, only ruthless, uncaring and without conscience.

There was a plan of all the floors of the house among the

rolls of maps and she spread it out and made a rapid copy of the basic outline of rooms on the ground floor. That would be more than enough to begin with.

Lovell reappeared as she was finishing and she waved the sketch plan. 'Shall we begin in the hall and work around clock-wise?'

He shrugged, clearly not caring how they proceeded, so she led the way to the entrance. 'I think they are all of reasonable quality here. Are there any you don't like?'

'I am supposed to *like* them now?'

'Well, you do have to live with the ones you keep. Surely you wish for your surroundings to be aesthetically pleasing?'

Lovell turned from studying a simpering nymph and shrugged. 'All I require of my surroundings is that they are adequately comfortable, efficient and well organised.'

'No wonder—' She bit off the words *you have no soul.* 'It is no wonder, if you have been working so hard as a lawyer,' she amended. 'Now you can create a pleasing ambiance, somewhere to take pride in, somewhere to relax.'

Lovell snorted, but he turned back to the nymph. 'This can go. I cannot abide smirking females.'

'It is actually quite a good piece, so it can go to Mr Christie.' She dug in the capacious pocket she had sewn in to the seams of all her working dresses and produced a spool of blue tape. 'This is for making book markers. I will use that for the better items. Anything else? No? This room then.'

By six o'clock they had surveyed about half of the statues on the ground floor, identified five to go to the London salerooms and twenty for the provincial ones.

After the first half an hour or so of apparent boredom Lovell had begun to show an interest and to ask questions. Then, by the third room, to express quite decided opinions, often at odds with Katherine.

'That is a much-copied piece, positively clichéd,' she said of a crouching female nude he was studying as the clocks struck six. 'It is well carved, I'll admit.'

'It is charming. Why should I care if there are other versions around? There is only one here. At least, as far as we have found,' he amended, coming close to where she was bending over the figure. 'I like it.'

'In a minute you are going to say, *I don't know anything about art, but I know what I like,*' she said.

'And what is so wrong with that? You are an elitist, Katherine.'

'And you are an aristocrat, Lovell,' she retorted. 'One cannot be any more elitist than that, short of being a member of the royal family.'

'I was not talking about blood lines, but opinions.' He ran one hand over the smooth shoulder of the figure. 'She should have a pool to gaze into, perhaps the one on the South Terrace.'

'It is good marble and would be perfectly safe out there. That is the first time I have heard you express an opinion about how this house should look,' Katherine said.

Lovell straightened up, almost nose to nose with her. 'You really do think me a philistine, don't you?'

'No, I think you are—' she bit off the words just in time '—my employer, who has little time for such considerations.'

They were so close that she had to tip back her head to look into his face.

And I think you are a much better-looking man than I had allowed myself to consider.

Those penetrating blue eyes held intriguing darker flecks, his hair was thick and invited touch and the way he was regarding her held intelligence and humour, both of which were attractive traits in anyone.

This close she was aware of the faint drift of a very discreet cologne, a little peppery; the good smell of freshly ironed linen; the elusive scent of warm, clean male.

Something changed in that deep blue gaze. There was a question there now, one her body had no difficulty interpreting and very much wanted to answer in the affirmative.

Chapter Seven

Katherine ignored the impulse to move closer to Lovell. He was asking her to say *yes* and she had no intention of doing any such thing, much as everything female in her was clamouring to be kissed by that severe mouth with just the hint of a curve in one corner.

William Lovell might be a very attractive man, if one ignored the character of a pit-fighting dog crossed with a snake, but she had no intention of ruining herself and her mission for the sake of a kiss. Or whatever else he had in mind, which, given that his mistress had departed in a temper, doubtless involved his bed.

He had not spoken, so neither did she. Stepping back was all that was required, coupled with a look that even the densest man, which he was most certainly not, could read as a negative.

'I think we have done all we can for today,' Katherine said composedly, ignoring the distracting fluttering sensation in the pit of her stomach. 'As far as I have seen so far there are no large statues upstairs, so a few hours when you can spare the time will deal with the rest. Then the footmen to move and pack them and I will write to the various auction houses and get them on their way. And out from underfoot,' she added as she stubbed her toe on the nymph's base.

'Very well. Tomorrow after luncheon. As you say, let us be done with it.'

Lovell turned on his heel and walked away, leaving her with her hands full of pink and blue tape, a pair of scissors and uncertain just what he meant would be *done with.* A flirtation that had not even begun? At least she need not add a tendency to snatch kisses to his list of sins, which was a relief.

Katherine made her way back to the library to leave the equipment. No forced attentions…yet. It would be as well to be on her guard. This was a virile man who had only recently lost an energetic bed partner and was stuck in the depths of the countryside. A man who was ruthless about getting what he wanted.

But I felt safe with him, that treacherous feminine voice in her head whispered. *I wish he had kissed me. I wish I was a lady...*

What on earth was she doing daydreaming about the man who was the cause of her now being completely ineligible for a respectable marriage?

'Idiot,' Katherine snapped as she opened the library door, making Peter start and drop the book he was dusting.

'Miss Jenson?'

'Not you,' she assured him, picking up one of the books he had been working on. 'You have done a very good job with these, Peter.'

'Thank you, Miss Jenson. I had best go now or Mr Grigson will be chasing me to get ready for dinner service.'

'Yes, of course. Thank you, Peter.'

Katherine sat down and began to tidy her desk without having to think about it. What had she achieved that day? Good progress on the library and the identification of some statues to help reduce the clutter. Both exactly what the Marquis believed he had employed her for.

Two cupboards checked with absolutely no sign of jewellery or related records, let alone the Borgia Ruby itself, and nothing else to take to the strongroom to establish a pattern of using it to lull future suspicions.

And to cap it all she had become far closer, in every sense of the word, to William Lovell, a man she should be keeping at pitchfork-length from her both physically and emotionally.

She had even discovered a few good points to his character and she did not want to do that. She needed a one-dimensional villain, a shadow-play cut-out figure to despise and defeat. Now she had a human being and one she had a suspicion was going to dominate her dreams. And those would not be nightmares.

'Sorry, Papa,' she murmured. 'I will do better from now on.'

Will took his place at the head of the dining table in no very good mood, not that he allowed it to show. Arnley, his steward, had pointed out to him that it was desirable for the spiritual well-being of his staff if he employed a chaplain.

This, he was told, was especially necessary as one of his ancestors had cleared not only the historic village as part of his landscaping schemes, but had appropriated the parish church as a private chapel, currently unused in the absence of a domestic chaplain. This meant that the staff must walk over a mile to the church in the new village of orderly and picturesque cottages.

When Will had enquired exactly how one went about hiring a chaplain—the local staff registry office, perhaps?—Arnley winced slightly and suggested writing to the bishop.

The steward then enquired whether Miss Jenson would be fulfilling the role of archivist, the previous incumbent having been found cold and still among the dusty boxes and files in the muniments room eighteen months previously.

Will had snapped that he would think about both, then made himself apologise to Arnley for his short temper.

Will supposed that the librarian he would appoint when Katherine Jenson had finished her work and departed could take on the joint role. The library would not need much attention then and the man—it would be a man, *definitely* a man—could concentrate on the archives.

Which led him to think about Katherine—*Miss Jenson*—something he really did not want to do.

She was sitting on his right now, talking across the table to Giles. She was neat as a pin in a simple evening gown and showing not the slightest awareness that a few hours earlier he had been manhandling her over some banisters and trying not to admire her ankles. Or, more recently, that he had very much wanted to kiss her.

And she had known what he had wanted. There had been perfect comprehension in that cool gaze, although he was quite certain she was as respectable and virtuous a young lady as she appeared to be and should have had no idea about such things.

Don't be an idiot and a prig, Will told himself. *Young ladies aren't foolish and unobservant, even if they are brought up to behave as though they haven't a thought in their little feather brains. They know perfectly well why they are told not to be alone with men and if married ladies can feel passion, why can't a single woman, however respectable?*

But it was hard to shake off the accepted belief that ladies felt only pure emotions and accept that Katherine Jenson might desire to kiss him, but at the same time, not like him very much. Or, at all. There were many things to be read in those expressive hazel eyes, but fondness was not one of them when they were looking at him.

It was not until he caught the eye of Mrs Downe and saw her steady, judgemental look that it occurred to him to wonder just why the two women regarded him with such disfavour. A career as a barrister was one that ensured many people disliked him and, in some cases, positively hated him. You could not defeat someone in court in a civil case, or see them found guilty of a crime, and expect them to love you in return.

But these two sparked no recognition at all. Perhaps they simply found something about him not to their liking, which was reasonable enough. He did not set out to be liked and was not at all certain he could charm someone if he tried.

A small devil of mischief prompted him to wonder whether he should attempt just that, make an effort to charm Miss Jenson out of her froideur. He would have to be careful. He did not want to raise expectations in her breast or toy with her affections—that was the work of a rake and a scoundrel. No, just see whether he could coax a smile at best, a reduction in the dislike at worst.

Best to begin with the chaperon. Will smiled at Mrs Downe,

enquired whether she was finding her stay at Ravenham Hall comfortable and how she was filling her time.

'Most comfortable, thank you. I find that walking, sketching and reading pass the hours unexceptionally. The countryside is delightful hereabouts and I shall presume on your kindness in letting me drive out in the gig again very soon.'

It was all said pleasantly, with a smile. But barristers have to learn to be actors in order to win over juries and present their cases with confidence, however much they might be out of sympathy with their client or bored with a routine case.

Mrs Downe was acting a part, that of complaisant companion, he was certain of it, but that might simply be because she was here out of duty and would have much preferred to be in London.

As for Katherine, she remained a mystery. She was clearly exactly what she said she was—a perfectly competent librarian. She was hard-working and she had the knack of training at least one of his footmen.

She also appeared to be very knowledgeable about Classical sculpture—she had not been acting there, he was certain. There had been a focus, an intelligence, that was far from the glib utterances of someone playing a part.

And yet, something was awry. A mystery, Miss Jenson. But then, Will enjoyed mysteries.

Katherine looked up from her timbale of salmon to find that Lovell was smiling. At her, or about her? she wondered. If one did not know that he was a ruthless, manipulative hunter without a conscience or scruples, one would think him a handsome, likeable man. A desirable one, too. Unfortunately, that impression showed no signs of diminishing.

She turned her head and asked Giles a question about the history of the house, hoping to find the reason for the staircase where the statues had been stored. He admitted he did not know any details and the conversation became three-sided, drawing in Elspeth who said she was certain that the central block was Tudor in origin.

'1493,' Lovell said, making them all jump. 'So just into the reign of Henry VII. Extended under Charles I, one wing demolished as a result of a siege during the Civil War, extensively remodelled under Anne and the version you see now dates from the reign of George III.'

'You take an interest in architecture?' Katherine asked, surprised.

'Not at all. I found the only book in my bedchamber was a history of the house written by the late archivist. He probably died of boredom with his own company, if the prose is anything to judge by. I couldn't sleep the other night, so I read that.'

Why couldn't you sleep? Katherine wondered.

If that was habitual, then she must take care if she wanted to do any exploring by night.

The men had excused themselves from the after-dinner tea tray, so Elspeth had it carried up to their sitting room.

'What on earth were you doing all afternoon with statues and the Marquis?' she asked, dropping a slice of lemon into her cup. 'I thought you were devoting the time to searching for the...object.'

'I was. I just became, er, distracted. And getting rid of some of those statues will make it easier to move about the house.'

'But to spend so much time in Lovell's company,' Elspeth persisted. 'Surely that is the last thing you wanted to do?'

'It was. Is. But I am getting to know him better and knowing one's enemy is always a good thing, don't you think? And I am lulling him.'

'That man does not need *lulling*,' Elspeth said grimly. 'He needs shutting in the cellar while we search this place from top to bottom. He is suspicious of something, I'm certain. Why, he even tried charm on me at dinner.'

He tried out-and-out seduction on me, with those blue eyes and that wicked mouth.

She had thought at the time that it was as simple as a man feeling carnal desire, but now she wondered. Was he suspicious of them? Of her? What lengths might Will Lovell go to if he was distrustful of her?

'I would not like to attempt to subdue him and lock him in

the cellar,' Katherine said with an attempt at humour. 'He is hardly the stooped and weedy lawyer one expects. But it will not come to that. I will carry on searching and doing my level best to lull any suspicions he might have.

'But what can he be dubious about? My references were impeccable and genuine, he can see I know what I am about and he has never encountered me before. In court I was always veiled. I do not take after Papa in looks, so, even if he recalls him— which I doubt—I would not stir any memories. I am quite safe.'

My secret might be, my mind might be, but my foolish emotions, they are not at all safe.

The next morning Katherine attacked the library with determination, keeping Peter and another footman and two maids busy cleaning, clearing and dusting.

The collection was beginning to take on form now, with very little religion, but a substantial amount on art and antiquities, languages, the Classical writers, history, travels and memoirs. There was not much law, but then, why would the late Marquis need books on the subject when he had a tame lawyer on call?

The work absorbed her, as it always did, and Peter made her jump when he came and said, 'Luncheon is served, Miss Jenson.'

'Thank you. Can you be spared to carry on with cleaning the books this afternoon?'

'Until four, Miss.'

She thanked him and went in search of Elspeth, whom she found in the small dining room with Giles Wilmott.

'Is Lord Ravenham not joining us?' she asked him when she had helped herself to a slice of cold chicken pie and some salad from the sideboard.

'He has ridden into St Albans,' the secretary said. 'I have no idea how long he might be away. Did you need to speak to him, Miss Jenson?'

'No, just idle curiosity,' she said with a smile.

Inside she was delighted. Lovell's disturbing presence was out of the house which meant she could rummage to her heart's content all afternoon.

* * *

With her sketch plan of the ground floor, she began in the room where she had left off, opening every cupboard and drawer, removing a few books and stacking them to be taken to the library and placing anything easily portable of any value on a table.

It was important to be as open as possible, to make a point of displaying everything. She was in a position of trust and had no intention of betraying that, other than with the one exception. And it was all too easy to raise suspicions, handling small valuables when one was all alone.

The haul in that small room was not encouraging. There were no records about purchases or lists of items and the only jewellery was a bracelet made up of Roman cameos, a set of Whitby jet mourning jewellery and a pearl necklace. They looked more like family pieces that had been there for years, rather than recent acquisitions.

Katherine numbered the room on the plan, made a list of what she had found in her notebook and carried the jewellery in search of Mr Arnley, the steward, to have them locked away in the strongroom.

When she went back to collect her notebook she paused just inside the door and studied the panelled walls. Was it possible there might be a concealed cupboard? It was worth checking, although the panelling was fairly plain, with none of the carved ornamentation one read about in Gothic novels, where a careless twist of a boss would send the heroine tumbling into a skeleton-hung passageway or the lair of the arch villain.

She began by walking around, tapping each section of panels from floor level to as high as she could reach. At every point there was the dull sound of solid wall behind the grey-painted wood.

One wall, then the second, passing the fireplace and on to the third. Her shoulder was getting stiff from constant raising, stretching, then lowering. Katherine sighed and leaned against the next section, flexing her arm.

'What the devil are you doing, Miss Jenson?'

Lovell's voice made her start and she came upright, twisting to see him standing in the doorway.

'Searching for hidden compartments, of course,' she said. There was no other remotely believable explanation she could think of.

'Really?' He raised one dark brow incredulously.

'Yes, really.' She half turned away, tripped over her own foot and hit the wall, putting out one hand to steady herself. It slid down the panelling and something gave way under the pressure.

Katherine jumped back and found Lovell by her side. 'There. You see?'

'I do see.' He smelt of fresh air and leather and, not unpleasantly, of horse, and sounded exceedingly dry. 'And I see that you, Miss Jenson, are the most accident-prone female I have ever encountered. You fall off ladders, you find yourself trapped behind statues and now you throw yourself through walls.'

'I have not thrown myself through,' she pointed out. 'I am this side of the wall, with you.'

'Yes.' He did not sound as though that was necessarily a desirable outcome. 'I suppose we had better see what you have found.'

They reached the black space together, shoulder to shoulder, and bumped heads when they both stooped to look inside.

'My wall, Miss Jenson. My secret cupboard.'

Chapter Eight

Katherine stepped back and did her best to control her impatience. Lovell appeared to be doing something inside the panelling, then an entire section swung inwards, like a door.

'How wonderful, I've always wanted to find a secret passage.'

'It is probably a priest hole,' he said, his shoulders still blocking her view. 'We must be within the original Tudor building.'

'I'll fetch a lantern.'

'Whatever for?' Lovell turned back, dusting his hands together.

'To explore, of course.' Katherine stopped halfway to the door. 'Surely you want to see what's in there, where it goes, what it contains?'

'It is absolutely no place for a lady to be scrambling about in. Ask Wilmott to join me and bring two lanterns.'

'Yes, my lord, whatever you say, my lord,' Katherine muttered to herself as she ran along the corridor towards the study. 'And just you try to keep me out of there.'

Giles looked up when she burst into the study. 'Is something wrong?'

'I have found a secret room and Lord Ravenham wants you to come and explore it with him and bring lanterns,' she panted.

'A secret room?' Giles suddenly looked about fourteen.

'There are lanterns in the hall,' he added, jumping to his feet and striding off, Katherine on his heels. He snatched up two and lit them both from the fire that was kept burning all day long in the draughty entrance. 'Where?'

'The little room at the end of that passageway.' Katherine pointed, waited until he was out of sight, then lit another lantern and followed. When she reached the doorway, she stopped outside and listened.

'I should go first, my lord.'

'Very noble, Wilmott, but I doubt there is anything more perilous down there than some spiders and a rat or two.'

Their voices faded and Katherine looked in to see the light of their lanterns dwindling away. This was certainly more than a simple chamber if there was a passage. She tiptoed across the room and stepped in through the panelling, telling herself that spiders and rats were more scared of her than she was of them and that there were two large men between her and the skeletons or whatever else this secret way held.

The walls were brick and narrow, twisting sharply in a series of dogleg turns, making it difficult to keep a sense of direction. The top was low, brushing her hair unless she ducked her head—the men must be bent over uncomfortably.

Then the voices in front of her were suddenly closer and she could see the light from their lanterns clearly. They must have stopped, so she did, too.

'Very well,' she heard Giles say and before she realised it, he was around the corner and right in front of her.

'Shh,' she whispered.

He grinned. 'We've found a door,' he murmured back. 'I'm going to locate it outside.'

It was a wriggle to pass each other but, being the gentleman that he was, Giles turned to face the wall, and so did she and they squeezed past without too much embarrassment, at least on Katherine's part.

She could lurk where she was or she could go and look at this door. Katherine decided that she might as well risk Lovell's wrath and brazen it out. Lantern high, she went around the corner.

'That was fast, Wilmott.' Then Lovell turned and saw her. 'What do you think you are doing, Miss Jenson?' Obviously tired of stooping, he had crouched down on his heels and was leaning back against the wall. He made no effort to rise.

Your valet is going to have something to say about the state of your coat, she thought, deciding she would not mention the large cobweb draped across one shoulder.

'I found this, so I think it only fair that I explore it, too.' Katherine held up her light and saw the passage ended in a door, so dark that she could not make out what it was made of until she reached out and tapped it. Solid oak, by the feel of it.

'Is it locked?'

The lamplight shining from beneath made Lovell's face look devilish, a mask of dark shadows and flickering flame. If she had seen it without knowing he was there, she would have screamed the place down, Katherine admitted to herself.

'Yes, Miss Jenson. That is why I am sitting here in such comfort.'

She took a deep breath and ignored the sarcasm. 'This cannot be a priest hole.'

Lovell looked around, then up to the brickwork curving over their heads. 'I agree. It was built as part of the house, not carved out afterwards, and that means it is too early for there to be any need to be hiding priests of any denomination, Protestant or Catholic.'

'Mr Wilmott is taking a long time.'

'Have you seen the state of the garden on this side of the house? He will probably need the gardeners armed with bill-hooks and saws to get through the tangle.'

'At least he knows roughly where it is,' Katherine pointed out. 'He needs to locate the window of the room, then go around the corner. The walls must be very thick.'

'When this was built it was in the early years of the first Tudor king. The Battle of Bosworth was still fresh in the memory, I imagine. This would have been a defensive manor house—it certainly had a moat once, long since filled in—and I think this must have been a sally port, an escape route for the defenders to get out at the back if they were attacked.'

'The late Marquis would have found this fascinating.'

Lovell grunted. 'I doubt it, at least in his last years. He coveted objects, not history.'

She had been wondering how to lead round to discussing his cousin, now he had handed her the opportunity.

'Was he always so…obsessive? I had assumed he was a connoisseur, that his collections would be beautifully curated and well displayed.'

Silence. Clearly, she had presumed too far. Then Lovell sighed. 'He was, when I first knew him. There are three other houses—the town house, a hunting lodge in the Shires and a very pleasant estate near Bath. They are all well furnished and appropriately decorated.

'But he began to change about eight years ago. He stopped visiting the other houses, he started buying wildly—horses and objects—and he retreated here. I hadn't realised quite how bad it had become, because I never got beyond the most public rooms and the study.'

It seemed the near darkness had made him feel able to confide, so Katherine ventured, 'He had many horses?'

'Almost forty. I have sent all but a few to Tattersall's for sale. Not that he rode or drove all those, of course—he collected fine bloodstock to gloat over, it seems. That is what killed him. His heir, the only first cousin he had, apparently twitted him about a pair of match bays he had bought at great expense.

'Randolph flew into a passion and challenged James to a race. He hadn't driven for months, perhaps years. The bays were so fresh the grooms tried to stop him, but he flew into a rage with them, laying about them with a whip, they told me. He lost control, careered into James's rig and they were both killed.'

'Forgive me, but was he, perhaps, no longer in his right mind?'

'A polite way of putting it, yes. He had become like an old dragon, hoarding objects and animals like fabled gold, creating a great pile of it that he guarded jealously.'

'He was not always like that?'

'No, not when I first knew him. Randolph had been indulged since birth, the longed-for son after his parents' years of childless marriage. He was self-centred to the extreme and with no consideration for others, but he was rational.

'He believed I had the mindset for the law and decided I was likely to be of use to him if I had the proper training. He paid for my education, made certain I had the right contacts at the Inns of Court, saw me trained to be a lawyer.'

'You didn't resent it?'

'I am the elder son of a younger son of a younger son. My destiny was to manage a small estate, hardly more than a farm. Randolph gave me an education, access to the wider world, a career that interested me, enough money to ensure my younger brother has all he needs to make our family estate prosper. I could put up with his demands, his...eccentricities—I owed him my loyalty.'

Katherine waited, but that seemed to be all he was prepared to say. It was more than she had hoped for and enough to reassure her that the Borgia Ruby must be in the house somewhere. And it gave her an insight into why Lovell had fought so fiercely for his cousin and employer, even though he clearly hadn't felt any affection for the man. It still didn't excuse—

Thud.

She jumped as Lovell rose to his feet in one smooth movement and pounded on the door with his clenched fist.

'No way of unlocking it from this side.' Giles's voice penetrated faintly. 'I'll come back.'

Lovell stooped to pick up his lantern. 'After you, Miss Jenson. I suppose it is too much to hope that you will not now go and fight your way through the undergrowth to view the door from the other side?'

Katherine stepped out into the room, blew out the candle in her lamp and shook out her skirts. 'My lord, it is your house. If you tell me that you do not wish me to satisfy my antiquarian curiosity then, of course, I will obey you.'

'You amaze me.' Lovell emerged, too, rolling his shoulders as he straightened up. 'I would have thought that nothing would stand in the way of your curiosity, Miss Jenson. Of course you may go and look, but do not expect to bring suit against me if you sprain an ankle or fall into some unfilled section of moat. And what, might I ask, is amusing you now?'

'You have cobwebs in your hair.'

With a muttered curse he went to look in the over-mantel mirror.

'I do have a comb.' Katherine dug in her pocket and came up with the small one that she always carried to repair the effects of dusty shelves on her appearance. 'No, let me,' she added as he reached for it. 'They are all over, especially at the back.'

To his own surprise Will stood still and let the managing female comb his hair. It was that, he reasoned, or risk going out with cobwebs on the back of his head.

It had nothing to do with the fact that she put one hand on his shoulder to steady herself as she reached up, her breath tickling over the nape of his neck. And, ridiculously, it amused him to be ordered about by the woman, a novelty, given that he was used to barking orders and having them obeyed.

Or perhaps he was just lacking in female company and ought to give more thought to wooing a wife. There was the succession to think about now, the title, the entails.

'I'm sorry. Was that a knot?'

'What?' He stared at Miss Jenson as she stood, comb in hand.

'You frowned so fiercely that I thought I must have pulled a tangle.'

'No. I was considering something that fills me with a singular lack of enthusiasm. Come then, if you really want to plough though bogs and brambles.'

'I will just go and change my shoes. I can make my own way.'

She vanished through the door in a flurry of skirts before he could call after her that she, too, had her back hair covered in cobwebs.

She found him and Giles and two gardeners standing in front of the tangle of briars that had once been a rose garden. Miss Jenson was dressed in a drab coat and a pair of half-boots that could only be described as *stout*. She had more concern for practicality than appearances, he noted, then saw with a smile that she had combed her hair and all her cobwebs had vanished.

'That was a singularly foolish place to choose for a rose garden,' she observed, pulling her left foot out of the mud with a squelch.

'That it be, Miss,' Tompkins, the head gardener, said, nodding sagely. 'The old moat be under there and it's fed by springs. You can drain it all you like, fill it in like they did, but you can't make it dry. They don't mind a heavy soil, they favour a clay, do roses, but waterlogged is another matter. In fact...'

He rambled on as Will tried to remember how many gardeners he had. Just the two, he rather feared, because he had to get this house looking respectable if he was going to bring a bride to it. A garden, not a wilderness, was essential, any lady would expect it.

'Miss Jenson!'

'Yes?' She was already well into the narrow pathway Wilmott and the two men had managed to cut through to the wall.

'What do you think you are doing?'

'Looking at the door, of course.' She didn't add, *You idiot*, but he could almost hear the words hanging in mid-air.

Will refrained from rolling his eyes: one did not criticise one member of staff in front of others. 'Come along, Wilmott. You wait here, Tompkins and—'

'Smith, my lord.'

He fought his way along the narrow path, cursing the mud sucking at his boots, until he was at the door where Miss Jenson was bending down to peer at the lock.

'We need a key,' she announced. 'Or can you pick locks, my lord?'

'Why should we want to open it? This is more secure left as it is.'

'I suppose so.' She sounded disappointed as she looked around. 'It is very well disguised, isn't it? Set back in the angle of that buttress. I think it would be quite hard to see when the moat was full.'

'If they kept a small boat in the tunnel, then anyone wanting to escape the house could open the door, launch the boat and row across,' Wilmott said, arriving behind Will.

'All very interesting,' Will lied. 'I'll have this undergrowth cleared and drains dug,' he added, looking at his secretary's feet which appeared to be sinking into the mire. 'It must increase the damp in the—'

With a strange sucking rumble the ground opened up around Wilmott and he vanished into the hole with a shout of alarm.

Will grabbed for him, was too late and found himself tipping forward, only to be hauled back by a pair of determined hands on his coat tails.

'Wilmott!'

'Here, sir.' He sounded unhurt, at least, although he was not in sight. 'The springs that fed the moat must have been working away and undermined the fill. There's quite a cavern down here.'

'Stay still. Don't risk moving about. We'll get ropes and a ladder down to you.'

'Right you are, sir. Very interesting, this. I can see the stone walls of the foundations.'

'Never mind the damn architecture! Tompkins, Smith—ladders, planks ropes, more men, on the double.'

He looked across the hole. A good eight feet, too far to jump with no run-up. They were stuck on this side, although at least they had firm stonework to stand on. 'You still all right, Wilmott?'

'Yes, sir.' His secretary sounded less confident now. 'I think this could have gone at any time, all the way along. Bits keep dropping off, I can hear them hitting the water.'

Will listened to faint splashes. Worrying. If more fell, Giles could be buried. Or if water gushed through, he might be swept away. He made his voice as indifferent as possible. 'Well, stand under the opening, then.'

There was a faint laugh from below and he settled his shoulders back against the door. Miss Jenson sat on the step at his feet.

'What was I saying about you being accident-prone?' he asked.

'I am not down that hole and I wasn't anywhere near him when he fell,' she protested.

'You create an aura of chaos.'

'I do not! I create order out of chaos, or haven't you seen your library recently?'

'True.' It was he who seemed to be plunged into chaos by her, in ways he couldn't quite pin down. 'What is your given name?'

'Katherine. I did tell you, I am certain.'

'Probably.' And probably he had been too busy grappling with the fact that he'd been demented enough to employ a female librarian and antiquarian to recall it.

'Well, Katherine, what do you make of this situation?'

'That if we had a key, we could get off this ledge.'

A snort of laughter escaped hm. 'Do you always say what you mean?'

'No, very frequently I have to bite my tongue,' the infuriating female said from the level of his knees.

There was another loud splash from the hole.

'Mr Wilmott? Giles, are you still safe?'

She sounded very concerned about him, Will thought, then mentally kicked himself. Of course she was concerned, anyone would be. He wasn't becoming jealous of his own secretary, was he?

'Sinking a bit,' the voice from the hole confessed, sounding rather more anxious.

'Hold on, we'll soon have you out. I had best lie flat and reach down to him,' he added to Katherine and began to shrug out of his coat.

Katherine stood up. 'Then I will hold on to your ankles and then Giles can catch hold of your hands. It had better be you, your arms are longer,' she pointed out, unanswerably. 'But hurry up.'

And, curse her, she was right. Not about who would have to do the lying down—there was no way he would allow a woman to do that—but that something must be done now.

Goodness knew where the gardeners had got to. Will crouched down, testing the ground in front of the step, then spread out his coat and stretched himself full-length on top.

As he began to work closer to the hole, hands caught hold of his ankles. He levered himself over the edge and let his arms hang down at full stretch.

'Thank you,' Wilmott said fervently from below and he felt hands fasten around his wrists. 'I'm up to mid-calf, but I think I've stopped sinking now you are taking my weight.'

'Excellent,' Will said, wondering just how heavy the man was. His secretary was not fat, but he was tall and it all seemed to be bone made of lead. 'I was just thinking how difficult this was going to be to explain to the coroner. Accidental drowning in a non-existent moat, perhaps.'

That made Giles laugh, which was not helpful. Will felt himself move a little and dug his toes in. The grip on his ankles tightened.

'I can't get a good hold through the leather,' Katherine complained. 'And you are sliding.'

'I had noticed that.'

'Dig your toes in some more while I try something else.'

The hands on his ankles vanished and the next thing he knew a weight descended on his backside.

'There. I'm sitting on you now. That should do it.'

Will realised suddenly that he was grateful for the burning ache in his shoulders, a powerful distraction from the fact that Katherine Jenson's admirably neat posterior was pressed to his rump.

Chapter Nine

'Did you say something? Are you all right, Lovell?'

'Umph.'

Fair enough, she thought. She was sitting very firmly on his backside. *His very admirable backside...*

A lump of earth fell off the edge of the hole and Giles gave a startled yelp.

Where were those gardeners?

They appeared even as she thought it, accompanied by two grooms, carrying three ladders and two planks between them. They laid the ladders across the hole on either side of Lovell, then laid planks on top of the rungs, before the smallest groom edged out with the third ladder.

There was a splash and a squelch as it was dropped into the hole and then Giles's head appeared.

The groom seized him by the collar and helped him out to sprawl on the far side. 'Best crawl away, sir,' the man advised and the secretary, black with mud, found the energy to drag himself clear.

He rolled over and sat up. 'Go and help His Lordship!'

'Gerroff me.'

It was a growl and Katherine shifted back to Lovell's thighs, then his knees and finally to the doorstep, grabbing his ankles again as he scrabbled backwards, sending clods of earth into the hole.

'Stay there.' He gestured at the two men who were beginning to edge out across the planks. 'Move the ladders together.'

The skinny groom wriggled across and pulled up the ladder in the hole and was dragged back by his feet, then the others shifted the makeshift bridge until the ladders touched.

Lovell stood up, his face and body thick with mud. 'Well, Katherine? We can wait for a locksmith or brave the gaping cavern.'

It was beginning to look exceedingly cavernous now and the way across seemed rickety, to put it mildly, but she was not going to sit shivering on the doorstep for however long it took to find a locksmith and get that door to yield.

'The cavern, of course.' She took a step forward towards the plank and was swept off her feet, up into his arms, and Lovell was running, striding across the gap, planks clattering, and on to firm ground.

He skidded to a halt, chest heaving.

Around them the men were talking excitedly, there was the sound of the ladders and planks being hauled back. Katherine was aware of it vaguely, a background buzz to the sound of Lovell's breathing, the sensation of being held, the strangely not unpleasant smell of hot man and mud.

'You can put me down now,' she said.

He did not reply, simply walked off, around the side of the house, up the steps to the main door which, as it was ajar, he opened by the simple expedient of kicking it and into the hall.

This time she could hear the babble of voices clearly and one cutting right through them.

'My lord, is Miss Jenson injured?'

Katherine lifted her head from where it was resting very comfortably against Lovell's sodden shirt front. 'I am perfectly all right, thank you, Elspeth.' She tried wriggling. 'You can *put me down* now, my lord.'

'What, and make this floor even muddier? Grigson, a great deal of hot water is going to be required for Miss Jenson, myself and Mr Wilmott, who will be along shortly.'

And then the wretched man marched past the gaping servants and carried her up the stairs, into her bedchamber, through into the dressing room and deposited her, in a state somewhere between hysteria, fury and excitement, in the empty bath.

He stepped back and assessed the object she was sitting in. 'Am I mistaken, or is this a sarcophagus?'

'Yes. Roman,' Katherine said faintly. 'It isn't very practical because the marble doesn't hold the heat.' She rallied slightly, but found standing up was beyond her. 'What do you think you were doing, carrying me?'

'I thought that bridge wouldn't stand up to two of us going across, so speed and one pair of feet seemed sensible.' He stretched and began to roll his shoulders.

'I can understand that, but then to carry me inside—you must have strained your arms holding Giles for so long like that.'

He shrugged. Or perhaps it was simply another exercise. She averted her gaze from the disconcerting sight of muscles moving under the wet fabric.

'I am hardly a featherweight.'

'I had already discovered that, remember? You stood on me to get away from those statues and then you so obligingly anchored me down.'

You are supposed to disagree with me!

'In fact, I am clearly feeding my staff too well. Wilmott is deceptively hefty.'

Katherine took a grip on her temper and ignored the other sensations that were disturbing her internally. 'He is a very well-built gentleman. Well, thank you very much. I can manage now.'

Lovell looked down with what she had become to think of as his lawyer look: unreadable but penetrating.

Katherine thought he was about to speak, then Jeannie came in, Elspeth on her heels.

'Miss Katherine!'

'Lord Ravenham, you are in a *lady's dressing room.*'

He turned to Elspeth with a smile. 'So I am. Fortunately the lady is fully clothed. I will see you at dinner, Mrs Downe, Miss Jenson.'

'What on *earth* is going on?' Elspeth demanded as the outer door closed behind him.

'We have a moat again,' Katherine said, beginning to struggle with the water-swollen fastenings of her gown. Not that it was fit to be called a gown any longer. 'Jeannie, you might as well cut this off me. I think it is beyond saving.'

She began trying to explain everything to Elspeth. 'I found a secret passageway and we explored it and it came to a door. So we all went around to locate it from the outside. Giles Wilmott fell in to the remains of the old moat and Lord Ravenham and I were trapped against the house wall. He had to hold on to Giles's hands to stop him sinking any deeper in the mud and I had to hold on to him to stop him falling in after Giles.'

'A moat?' Elspeth ran to the window and looked out. 'I don't see it.'

'It was filled in ages ago, apparently. Springs have been scouring it out over the years, I assume. I do hope Lovell thinks to check the plans to find out the extent of it before half the house falls down.'

It was incredible. She sounded quite calm and rational and inside she was in chaos.

'There's hot water coming,' Jeannie said. 'Lots of it. Thank goodness we can drain this thing, because we are going to need to fill it at least twice.'

Whoever had conceived the idea of making a marble sarcophagus into a bath had at least considered the practicalities. It was raised on blocks and there was a drain hole in the bottom with a pipe that vanished into the wall.

Katherine stood passively while they stripped off her clothes and, with the plug out, poured water over her until the worst of the mud had gone. Then she replaced the plug, sat down and wallowed in clean hot water while Jeannie took away her clothes, holding them at arm's length.

'I shall go and have a look at this moat for myself,' Elspeth declared. 'At a safe distance.'

Alone at last, Katherine tried to get her emotions in some kind of order. The day so far had revealed Lord Ravenham to be arrogant, authoritarian and quite without consideration. No new insights there.

But he had rescued Giles without hesitation and had kept his temper, despite having his arms half pulled from their sockets, finding himself face down in mud, being sat on by his librarian—female—and ruining a very good pair of boots. That all had to go on the plus side of his account, however reluctant she was to see it growing.

Where to put the fact that she had found herself alarmingly aroused by him, she had no idea. All that male physicality, the way he had lifted her, the sensation of being in his arms... None of that should go to his account in either column—positive or negative. It was all down to her inexplicable reaction to the man.

The next morning Will spread out the three house plans that he had found in the library, holding the corners down with the little weights Katherine had shown him.

Infuriating woman, but efficient, even if that efficiency involved sitting on his rump to stop him falling into the moat that he hadn't known he owned. Add immodest to infuriating and quick-thinking to efficient.

He growled under his breath as stretching to unroll the paper made his abused arm and shoulder muscles complain. A hot bath and a night's sleep had helped, but even so, they ached.

His stomach growled in company and he would go and have his breakfast soon, but he had wanted to look at these plans before the library was full of maids, footmen and a certain librarian. If nothing else, he needed to be certain the house wasn't going to collapse into the other three arms of the hidden moat.

'Oh, good, you have found plans that show the moat,' a voice said behind him, making him let go of one corner.

'I will call you Kat,' Will said, reaching out to flatten the roll again without looking around. 'You creep around like one.'

'Ladies walk quietly and with decorum,' she said piously, ignoring his shortening of her name. 'What date are they?'

'These are dated seventeen-five and show the house before and after the major works at that time. Here is the moat.' He pointed to the plan on the next table. 'That is the present house, drawn up in eighteen hundred.'

Kat moved to stand beside him, bringing a faint, distracting, hint of jasmine scent with her, and studied the oldest plan. 'The moat enclosed a large area and the new house was built well within it.'

Will pointed to the top of the left-hand arm. 'The springs feeding it come in there and were managed by a sluice gate here. 'He indicated markings at the bottom of that arm. 'The other three sections were filled by that one source. The water overflowed into a stream that led down to the lake.'

He moved to the plan showing the Queen Anne house. 'As far as I can make out, they channelled the spring water through some kind of pipes down to the sluice and out. I think these symbols show that they blocked up each arm of the moat and then filled the whole thing in, assuming that the water would be safely channelled away through the new drains.'

Kat moved to stand between the two tables, looking from one to the other. 'The present house is definitely safely inside the hidden moat, except perhaps the orangery over here.' She tapped the small extension on the far side from the door to the secret passage.

'I agree. It does not appear that we are about to plunge into the abyss,' Will agreed. 'The pipes they used to contain the spring water must have burst or rotted and the fill has been gradually washed away into the lake which is probably silted up with it, if we could only hack our way through to inspect it.

'The mass of tangled roots must have been all that was holding up the earth. No wonder Wilmott went through it. I'll have to get new pipes laid.'

'Why not have the moat excavated on that side, repair the sluice, make certain the blocking to the other arms of the moat is sound and then have a water feature? It wouldn't make much more work than digging down and laying pipes,' Kat pointed out. 'You could build a little jetty where the sally port is and the ladies of the house would be able to drift about in boats on hot summer days. Charming.'

'Which ladies?' he enquired, lifting the weights and letting the plans roll up with a snap, resisting the urge to say that he had employed her to organise his library, not landscape his grounds and certainly not drift about in boats.

'You will be marrying soon, I imagine,' Kat said, collecting the maps up and tying the tape around each. 'Title, entails, heirs.'

He had been mentally filing that thought under 'To Be Attended To Later' in his list of things to be done and had no intention of contemplating it now.

'Improving the grounds to appeal to a wife will have to take second place to clearing the inside of this house. No lady is going to want to be faced with this as her country seat.'

'There are always the town house and the others you mentioned.' Kat bent to slide the plans back on their shelf. 'But I suppose, if one marries a marquis, one wants the principal seat to be in order for entertaining and flaunting and so forth.'

'Flaunting?' Will raised one eyebrow in the manner which always used to reduce an unsatisfactory witness to stammering incoherence.

'If one has become a marchioness then I imagine one would want to flaunt the fact. Discreetly and in the best possible taste, of course,' she added in a tone that hinted at suppressed amusement.

Will considered the suggestion that someone would consider marrying him a matter to be flaunted, then reminded himself that he was no longer simply a lawyer. The cachet of being a marquis would trump every fault from doddering old age, through poor personal hygiene to an obsession with pig breeding in the eyes of ambitious parents and his personal attributes would have nothing to do with it.

'Have you eaten breakfast yet?' he asked to change the subject. 'Or, like me, did you first want to be certain the house was not going to collapse around our ears?'

'Exactly that,' Kat agreed, joining him as he walked towards the door.

'And how to you expect to fill your day, now that you are reassured on that point?'

'In the library this morning, then completing our survey of

the statues, if you can spare the time. Thank you,' she said as he opened the door for her. 'I have written to the various auction houses and expect a reply very soon.'

'I will certainly join you, provided you can assure me my life is safe on this occasion, Kat.'

'Your life?' She looked up at him and he seemed to see both amusement and alarm in her expression. A strange combination.

'To date you have flattened me by falling from the library steps, you have trapped me behind statues and compelled me to climb staircases from the outside, you have lured me through secret tunnels and you have almost precipitated me into the abyss.' He followed her in to the empty breakfast room.

'The library steps incident was the result of a fault in the equipment of this establishment,' Kat retorted as she sat down. 'I warned you not to come into that group of statues. *You* insisted on going into the passageway and I prevented you from falling into that hole. Would you care for coffee?'

'Thank you, Kat. You have an answer for everything.'

'I hope so, at least, for those things which fall within my sphere of knowledge.' She passed him the coffee cup. 'I do not recall giving you permission to shorten my given name, Lovell.'

'It suits you,' Will said, earning himself a look from narrowed eyes. 'Can I fetch you anything from the sideboard?'

'I doubt I should be flattered,' she said tartly. 'A little bacon, thank you.'

She sat there neat as a pin, dressed plainly in her simple cotton working gown, her soft brown hair firmly trapped in a snood of knotted black ribbon, and answered him back as composedly as another man would have done. She countered his accusations, she flattened his teasing, she remained perfectly polite—and positively exuded femininity all the while.

Will, forking bacon on to one plate for her and eggs, sausage and bacon on to another for himself, confessed he was baffled by her.

Kat was pleasant and yet he could not shake off the nagging suspicion that she disliked him.

It was not the caution and mistrust that any single lady might feel being alone with a man, he was sure of that. She had shown not the slightest concern about being in that tunnel with him, or in any of the rooms. When that inexplicable urge to kiss her had come over him she had understood perfectly well and had shown no uneasiness in wordlessly rebuffing him.

And it was not as though he necessarily expected to be liked. He was demanding, authoritative and determined, he knew that, and people could take him as they found him. So why was this young woman making him even think about the matter?

It was because she *was* a cat, he told himself, buttering toast. They were quite capable of unsettling anyone, just by sitting around and staring.

He should avoid her as much as possible...yet he found her company stimulating in much the same way as he enjoyed the clash with a good opponent in court. It made his brain work harder, his blood flow faster. Very strange.

Chapter Ten

Katherine ate luncheon alone with Elspeth. Lovell and Giles had apparently taken theirs in the study.

'They've got all kinds of ledgers out, Miss Jenson,' Arnold, one of the footmen, explained as he brought in a jug of lemonade. 'Something about crop yields, I think. His Lordship sounded a bit…testy-like and Mr Wilmott looked fit to tear his hair out, if you'll pardon the expression.'

'Lovell is going to have to employ a new estate manager by the sound of it,' Elspeth observed when they were alone again.

'I expect he wants to understand the problems before he hands them over to someone else,' Katherine said. 'I know I would. If things are in a mess, he will not want to start a new man off like that.'

'How is your own work progressing?' Elspeth asked.

'Very well in the library. Peter the footman is proving an excellent assistant. I really must encourage Lovell to find him better employment—he is wasted as it is.

'I hope to identify more statues that we can send for sale this afternoon, which will be a start on setting the house to rights, but it sounds as though Lovell may not be able to join me for a while yet. How do you intend to spend the afternoon?'

'Catching up with my correspondence, which has been sadly

neglected while I have been spending so much time out of doors sketching.'

'Well, do not be tempted around to the west side of the house or you'll risk plunging through, like poor Giles did.'

'How is the *other matter* progressing?' Elspeth said, keeping her voice low.

'Hardly at all, but now I think I am lulling Lovell into not noticing where I go or what I do, so soon I will be able to explore where I want.'

Elspeth looked up from her bread and butter with a frown. 'I think you need to be very careful with the Marquis. He is formidable, for all that he is being very pleasant to us.'

'I can be formidable, too,' Katherine said darkly. 'And I am not a woman to be intimidated.'

Katherine was able to finish inspecting all the large statues by herself within an hour and went back to her room feeling decidedly weak at the knees with excitement. Where was Lovell? Surely crop yields couldn't take much longer?

She made her way downstairs after washing her hands, tidying her hair and removing the large apron she wore when she was working. Possibly she looked cool, calm and collected, but inside she was bubbling with excitement.

As she passed the study door it opened and Lovell strode out, Giles behind him. The secretary rolled his eyes at her, looking like a man very much in need of a tankard of strong ale.

'Ah, Kat. Have you been waiting on me?'

'I do have the remainder of the statues for you to consider and I think—' She broke off at the sound of someone knocking at the front door.

Arnold, the footman, trotted past and they heard his voice. 'I will ascertain whether His Lordship is at home.'

'Now what?' Lovell muttered as Arnold reappeared, bearing calling cards on a silver salver.

'That was Lady Bradley's footman, my lord. Her Ladyship and her three daughters are in their carriage outside, enquiring whether you are receiving.'

'No.'

'Excuse me, Lovell, but you are going to have to start receiving neighbours very soon,' Katherine said. Her news could wait, she told herself. Its subject had for several thousand years, after all.

'The drawing room is in a perfectly acceptable state and you do look as though you would be better for a cup of tea.'

'Where is Mrs Downe?'

'In our sitting room, I believe.'

'In that case you and she will join me, if you please. And you, too, Wilmott—I can see you trying to slide off. If you think I am going to be trapped alone drinking tea and making banal conversation with four ladies, you are much mistaken. Some dilution is needed.'

It would be amusing to witness Lovell having to be civil to a matron and her three daughters, all no doubt exceedingly interested in the arrival of a titled, young and single gentleman of high rank.

'I will go and fetch Mrs Downe,' Katherine offered, managing, somehow, to keep a straight face. Revenge came in many forms, it seemed.

'Very well. Arnold, invite the ladies in to the drawing room and order tea.'

'I will just go and make sure I'm respectable,' Giles said with a meaningful cough.

'What? Hell, I suppose I had better do so, too.' Lovell stalked off and Giles and Katherine exchanged grins before both hurrying for the stairs.

Katherine and Elspeth entered the drawing room first and both curtsied to the group of fashionably dressed ladies waiting there.

'Good afternoon, Lady Bradley,' Elspeth said, looking every inch the senior clergyman's wife that she had been. 'This is Miss Jenson, His Lordship's librarian, and I am Mrs Downe, her companion. We are sorry to have kept you waiting. Lord Ravenham will be down shortly and refreshments are on their way.'

Lady Bradley, a handsome matron of, Katherine estimated, forty-three or four, bowed in return, managing not to look too surprised at Katherine's role. 'Good afternoon. These are my daughters Claire, Millicent and Penelope Bradley.'

The three young ladies curtsied, at which point Lovell and Giles came in, the introductions were performed all over again and everyone sat down. The young ladies, seated in a demure row on the sofa, kept their eyes modestly lowered while their mother, Lovell and Elspeth went through the ritual of small talk.

'My late cousin was not someone much given to socialising, I believe,' Lovell said after the weather, the pleasantness of the drive from Westhaye Manor and Lord Bradley's intention to call very shortly had all been disposed of.

'We certainly found that to be the case,' Lady Bradley said. 'I understand the late Marquis was much involved in scholarship and was somewhat of a recluse. I do not recall him ever holding any social events of any kind at the Hall. Even the village Midsummer festivities were no longer held here, as they have been for many years. A sad disappointment to the neighbourhood.'

The hint that Lovell should remedy this lack immediately hung unspoken in the air.

'My cousin was a great collector, which means that most of the rooms here—including the ballroom—bear a close resemblance to a warehouse,' Lovell said. 'I regret to say that it will be some time before I am able to offer any hospitality beyond morning calls.'

Katherine noticed with amusement that he avoided any mention of the fête, let alone a commitment to hold it next year.

'There is no ballroom?' Miss Bradley asked plaintively with what, Katherine guessed, was intended to be a melting look at Lovell. 'Oh. We were *so* much hoping you would be holding a ball, my lord.'

'Not for some time. I am sorry to disappoint you.'

Oh, no, you are not, Katherine thought, amused. *You are delighted to have such a good excuse not to entertain.*

'Wilmott and I are much involved in restoring the estate and Miss Jenson, although an indefatigable worker, is still imposing order on the library.'

'A lady librarian,' Miss Bradley remarked. 'How very unusual.' She seemed undecided over whether to be shocked or intrigued by this phenomenon.

Giles, who had been silent after the greetings, suddenly said, 'Miss Jenson is also a learned antiquary.'

'Good heavens,' Lady Bradley said faintly. 'Whatever do your parents have to say about that?'

'My father, who educated me, is dead. My mother completely approves.'

'My dear late husband, who was Dean of Westchester Cathedral, always said that we ladies should use what talents we have been blessed with,' Elspeth remarked with the air of one quoting sacred writ.

Katherine bit the inside of her cheek to stop herself laughing. Dean Downe had been a clergyman who firmly believed in exercising his own talents for good living and would have been completely incapable of believing a female had any intellect at all.

She suspected that Elspeth was twisting a remark of his about housekeeping or sewing. Managing the Reverend Algernon Downe had required considerable skill and tact and it must have helped that he had clearly never realised just how intelligent his wife was.

The other ladies looked suitably impressed. They clearly thought it strange, but faced with a clergyman's widow as chaperon, Katherine's accent and simple, but good, clothes, even the most suspicious mind could hardly put a scandalous interpretation on her presence in the household.

'I do hope you will be able to call, Mrs Downe,' Lady Bradley said graciously, accepting a second cup of tea and launching into a description of all the good works and charitable causes in the area that she was certain a clergyman's widow would wish to be involved with.

Whether it was deliberate or not, this forced Lovell and Giles to converse with the young ladies and all three proved that they had learned their lessons in innocuous chit-chat and modest flirtation perfectly.

If it were not for Will and his late cousin, I would have been a young lady like that, flirting in an unexceptional manner with eligible gentlemen, looking forward to marriage. A family...

Lovell's face was a mask of polite interest, but Katherine knew him well enough now to tell that he was seething with impatience. There were several of what she understood card players called 'tells': he fiddled with his cuff, tapped one finger on his knee and his smile became harder and more fixed.

Should she rescue him? She supposed it was only charitable and Giles was looking positively cross-eyed with the banalities he was forced to utter whenever Lovell fell silent.

'Would you care for another cup of tea, Lady Bradley?' she enquired sweetly. 'I can ring for more hot water.'

'Goodness, is that the time? How it does fly in congenial company.' She rose to her feet. 'Come, girls. Delighted to have met you, Lord Ravenham, Mrs Downe. And Miss, er... Mr...'

Lovell showed them out himself. It was not so much a courteous gesture, Katherine thought, as a fervent desire to make sure they really were off the premises.

He came back and collapsed into his chair. 'Why on earth did people think it is a good idea to raise young ladies to pretend to be lacking in any intelligence at all? Goodness knows what those three are like behind the curls and simpering. One would assume they had feathers for brains.'

'I believe many gentlemen feel threatened by female intelligence and so it is thought best not to challenge them with any evidence of it,' Katherine said.

'Something went wrong with your upbringing in that case,' Lovell remarked.

Did she detect a shadow of a smile? Katherine pretended to ignore the comment. 'You will have to brace yourself for more of the same as soon as Lady Bradley has boasted all around the district that she was the first to call.'

'In which case I expect all of you to rally around in support, regardless of what you are doing at the time.' He got to his feet. 'Which reminds me, I promised to inspect statues with you, Kat.'

Katherine saw Elspeth's eyebrows rise at the shortened name, but she said nothing.

'Yes, it should not take long. I have been around them already and noted some.' She followed him out and along the corridor to the next group, suppressing her excitement over her find. Let him judge for himself when he saw it.

'This and this are poor Roman work,' she said as they reached the first two. 'This, I am sure, is a modern copy and—'

'Thank you, Kat.' Lovell put one hand on the shoulder of a Roman matron who looked stiffly out at the world from under a tightly curled mound of hair.

'What for? This is what you employ me for.' He was very close, but not precisely looming.

'For rescuing me just now. That was not agreed when I took you on.'

'I was rescuing all of us,' she said. 'Besides, I thought you were about to explode like a keg of gunpowder.'

'Did you? I was certainly seething with impatience, but I had not thought I was so easy to read.'

'I have begun to know you, my lord. I am sure that acting in court taught you a lot about control, but some things betray you.' She tapped her finger on the statue's other shoulder in imitation of his gesture.

'Acting in court? It is not a stage.'

'But surely it is? You cannot truly be feeling indignation on your client's behalf about every petty matter, nor feel outrage about every alleged fault, let alone hide your feelings about every defendant who is dragged before you under a mask of disapproval and disbelief about each one of them. Or can you?'

'My feelings in a case are neither here nor there. It is a lawyer's role to present his client's side of the matter in the strongest possible form.'

'Even when you do not believe in it? What if you are certain your client was a murderer? Or a thief?'

'I rarely take—*took*—criminal cases.' There was a flush of colour up over his cheekbones now.

Irritation or embarrassment?

'No, I suppose your late cousin's endless civil litigation kept you well employed.'

And I am going the right way to getting myself dismissed, she realised with a shock.

Something had released this hostility and she had an uneasy feeling that it was Lovell's closeness, the warmth that had been in his voice when he had thanked her.

'I apologise,' she said hastily. 'I knew someone who was badly...bullied in a court case. Very unfairly. I still feel annoyed about it on their behalf.'

'Passionate, I would have said.' Lovell's hand slid across the back of the statue and caught hers. 'Now who is showing their agitation?'

His grasp was warm and compelling, but not so fierce that she could not have slipped her own fingers free. Skin to skin she could feel his pulse, strong and perfectly steady whereas hers was all over the place.

I want...want you to kiss me.

For a hideous moment she thought she had said it out loud, then realised he would hardly be standing there, unmoving, if she had. Either he would have turned on his heel in disgust or...

'What do you feel about this statue?' she asked, moving her hand down the arm as though testing the quality of the surface. His fingers slid away and Katherine found she could breathe again.

'She looks as though a puppy has done something regrettable on the best Axminster carpet,' Lovell said. 'Or whatever the Roman equivalent was. I can happily part with her.'

He sounded perfectly calm and not at all like a man in the grip of an urge to do something unseemly with his librarian, so it was clearly her own imagination.

And as for her reaction, that surge of desire, that was inexplicable. She hated the man. She wanted to show him up for the liar, cheat and the bully that he was, she wanted him to apologise, grovel. Not kiss her.

'What about these?' Her voice sounded too high-pitched, but Lovell did not seem to notice.

Soon he would see the thing that had taken her breath away and she hoped, very much, that he would feel as she did about it, although why that should be important, she could not have said.

'Those can go,' he said, frowning at a group of very dull senatorial types. 'But this...'

He moved slowly towards the pale figure of the youth, carved in yellow marble. The figure stood tall and straight, the folds of his robe falling in precise folds to his sandaled feet. His gaze was fixed somewhere over their heads, one hand was lifted as though holding something and Katherine felt the same awe she had experienced when she first saw it.

'It is Greek and early, I am certain,' she said, not trying to hide her excitement now. 'It is something very special and I think you should ask an expert to assess it, perhaps one of the scholars at the British Museum. If I am right, then it is precious.'

'It is incredible.' He sounded almost awe-struck. 'Stylised and yet so real it seems to breathe. Who was he?'

'A charioteer, I think. He was holding the reins, perhaps at the start of the race.'

'Wonderful.' Lovell prowled around the figure. 'Powerful. Where are we going to put it?'

We?

'You want to keep it?'

'Of course. I'd happily throw out everything else I have found in this house to keep this.'

Will watched Kat as she backed away from the statue, head cocked to one side, considering. He had the clear impression that his enthusiasm had made her very happy, as though she was responsible for conjuring up the charioteer.

But no, he realised as she stopped and frowned in thought. *She is simply happy that someone understands and shares her enthusiasm.*

'I know,' she said suddenly. 'The perfect place. Come on!' She caught his wrist and ran and Will let himself be towed along, fascinated to see what Kat had thought of, disarmed by the way that she had so far forgotten herself in her excitement as to take hold of him.

She skidded to a halt in the hallway and gestured at the far wall opposite the front door. 'That niche. We paint it a darker colour—blue, perhaps? The statue would look superb standing there. The guardian spirit of the house.'

'You are a romantic, Kat,' Will said, making no effort to free his wrist. He rather thought she was unaware she was gripping it.

'Of course.' She looked amused by his surprise. 'You would have to have a heart of stone to study the objects and the stories from the past and not find romance in them.'

She tugged again, impatient to inspect the niche, and he followed her. A few minutes ago he had wanted to kiss her. Now he knew that he would like to sweep her up in his arms and carry her to his bed while this glow of excitement was on her.

Will made himself study the alcove. It was semi-circular in plan, cut back into the wall and with a domed top. It was clearly meant for a full-sized statue and the charioteer would stand there comfortably, safe from knocks.

'A dark blue, definitely. What do you think?' she demanded.

'Evoking the seas of his homeland?' Will suggested.

She was making him as romantic as she was. Perfectly ridiculous. He was the least romantic person he could think of. Lawyers had no business languishing over rugged landscapes or tales of chivalry or storm-tossed oceans.

'Oh, yes.'

She spun around and instinctively he gathered her in to him by the hand she held and suddenly there she was, warm and happy and bubbling with enthusiasm, almost pressed to his chest, laughing up at him.

'I want to kiss you,' he said harshly, knowing he was warning himself as much as her.

Chapter Eleven

The laughter drained away from Kat's face, leaving not the rejection Will expected, but a warmth and a curiosity.

'Yes,' she said and went up on tiptoe to touch her lips to his.

The kiss was sweet, fleeting, almost innocent. She dropped his hand and stepped back immediately, leaving him on fire with desire, wildly out of all proportion to the cause.

'Goodness,' Kat said. There was colour in her cheeks and her eyes were wide, but she seemed considerably more composed than he felt. 'Goodness,' she repeated. 'Well, there's a warning about getting overexcited about romantic things! And it isn't even as though he's a statue of Eros.'

'I must beg your pardon,' Will said, holding her gaze. *Please do not look down...* 'That was unconscionable. Be assured such a thing will never happen again.'

He turned sharply on his heel before she had the opportunity to notice just how aroused that had made him and strode off to the study. By the mercy of whichever guardian spirit looked after marquises who had temporarily taken leave of their senses, there were no servants in sight.

As he thought it, Arnley came around the corner. Will halted and the steward stopped, too, awaiting his pleasure.

'The hall is to be redecorated immediately. Have someone discuss colours with Miss Jenson.'

'Miss Jenson, my lord?'

'Yes. I intend placing a statue in the niche there and she knows what will best set it off.'

'I understand, my lord. I will see to that at once.' He bowed and hurried off, leaving Will to reach the study with a sense of relief. Sanctuary.

'Sir?' Wilmott put down his pen and stood up.

Will waved him back to his seat and sat down himself. At least the shock of almost running into Arnley had subdued the evidence of his arousal.

His secretary gestured to a pile of papers in front of him. 'I was just summarising the decisions you reached this morning, sir, and making a list of actions, but is there is anything else you prefer me to be doing?'

'No. Carry on. I have some things to think about.'

Like what the devil had possessed him to find Kat Jenson so damnably tempting. She could not be further from the kind of woman who normally took his fancy. In fact, if one were to consider what was the exact opposite of Delphine de Frayne, Kat was the image you would come up with.

Pleasant enough to look at but, compared to the face of a wicked angel, masses of jet-black hair, flashing eyes and a lavish figure, there was no competition from regular features, smooth brown hair, calm hazel eyes and a neat figure.

A passionate temperament would surely trump calm good sense, and a virgin with a fine mind could, surely, never hope to compete with the sensual skills that Delphine possessed.

But Kat was not competing, was she? That kiss was the product of high spirits and curiosity. She was no wanton. A quick pressure of her lips and she had gone.

Now, he assumed, she would analyse the experience, probably catalogue it under 'What on earth is all the fuss about?' and pretend it had never happened when they next met.

Will shifted uncomfortably on his chair. Was that what he should do, too? Ignore it?

A respectable young lady would expect a declaration after

a kiss from a gentleman, however fleeting. Was a librarian a respectable young lady? Kat was certainly respectable, young and a lady, even if of apparently modest standing.

He supposed her parents were country squires or something similar. Go back a generation or so and you would probably find connections to titles and great names, just as you could with his bloodline.

But… He could still swear that she did not like him, that she disapproved of him in some way. He had caught her sometimes watching him with a cool appraisal that sent a shiver down his spine. Was that the calculation of a husband-hunter? Was that what she was after—a title?

If so, she was going about it in a very strange way.

'Sir?'

'What?'

Wilmott was looking at him strangely. 'You sighed, sir. Heavily.'

'Heavy thoughts.'

'If it is any help, I have drafted an advertisement for a wood reeve.' His secretary passed a sheet of paper across the desk. 'I can send that off today, if it acceptable.'

'Yes, excellent. When you have done that, please consult with Miss Jenson about moving as many of the large items of statuary and the crates into the ballroom as possible. Then Mrs Goodman can set to work on having everywhere else thoroughly cleaned. If she requires more maids, or to employ women from the village for the rough work, then tell her she has *carte blanche* to hire however many she thinks necessary.'

'Yes, sir.' Wilmott looked somewhat startled, as well he might, Will conceded. They had been working through estate matters thoroughly, at a steady pace and not considering the house at all, now that Kat was employed.

'I want the place in a tolerable state by early summer next year,' he said, with the distinct feeling that he had just jumped off the edge of a cliff. 'I intend staying in London for the coming Season and finding myself a wife.'

'The London house is in a reasonable condition, sir?' Giles asked.

'Yes. It will simply require a thorough early spring clean,' Will said vaguely. He had committed himself now, he had said it out loud. He was in search of a wife and he intended doing so by means of the Marriage Mart that was the Season's focus.

'I have no reason to be secretive about this. Warn the staff that there will be a need to prepare the London house during February.'

Wilmott was already making notes. Given the way that news spread about a large household, his plans would be common knowledge by dinner time and Kat would be warned that she should harbour no expectations. Not, of course, that she had any, but it was best to be on the safe side.

Strangely this did not make him feel any more settled, but that was probably the prospect of the bear pit that was the Season, something he had only touched the very fringes of before. But he knew enough to be aware that he would be prey, that he might as well have a target painted on his back labelled *Very Eligible Nobleman.* Ambitious mamas would be circling like sharks that had smelt the blood in the water.

'Right. What is next?' He sat up straight, pulled his chair up to the desk and pushed all thought of marriage, women and hazel-eyed librarians to the back of his mind.

That had been... Extraordinary. Extraordinary that Lovell had wanted to kiss her. Extraordinary that she had let him, or, rather, that she had kissed him. And completely extraordinary that such a fleeting brush of the lips should make her feel so very peculiar.

Katherine sat down on one of the hard shield-back hall chairs to get her breath back. Something inside her seemed to fizz with excitement, she felt decidedly warm and, incredibly, she could still taste him on her lips.

It was probably also extraordinary that Lovell had immediately apologised and left her. One heard so many stories about predatory employers taking advantage of defenceless females. Governesses and maidservants seemed particularly vulnerable to such attentions.

But Lovell *hadn't* taken advantage. Yet more confirmation

that this man was not the ogre she had thought him to be, he was something much more complex.

And as for her own behaviour... Well, she would not think about that now. Probably it was the result of high spirits after finding that wonderful statue. She would feel quite calm in a minute.

'Ah, Miss Jenson. I was hoping to find you.' It was Mr Arnley, the steward.

Katherine stood up, fixed what she could only hope was a vaguely intelligent expression on her face and smiled. 'Yes, Mr Arnley. How may I help?'

He launched into an explanation about painting the hall and Katherine nodded and promised to see the painter the next day. 'And are you the correct person to ask about crating statues that Lord Ravenham intends to send to various auction houses, Mr Arnley?'

He was, so now she could add discussions with the estate carpenter to her list of things to do tomorrow. At least paint and sawdust should keep her mind off other, completely inappropriate, things.

She parted from the steward, went to check on the library and glanced at the clock. Incredibly she still had two hours in hand before she needed to change for dinner. Time to begin checking the room next to the one with the door to the secret passage, perhaps.

She left the door wide open, set her notebook and pencil on the small table it contained and looked around, wondering what purpose it had served. A small parlour for the ladies, perhaps. There would have been a good view of the grounds in the days when they were properly cultivated.

As it was, it housed four tea chests, what looked like a canvas-wrapped painting, a large chest of drawers, several upright chairs and a fire screen on a pole. She would start with the chest of drawers.

Katherine lifted the clock, to the table, making a note in her book.

French ormolu clock. Mid-eighteenth century. Out of fashion and not a well-known maker.

Then she began lifting out the drawers, one at a time, and stacked them on the floor, allowing her to shift the carcase away from the wall. Nothing hidden behind it, nothing under it.

Now she could tackle the drawers, one by one. Katherine replaced the clock on the top of the chest and carried the lowest drawer to the table.

She was halfway through the third drawer when she felt the warning tingle that she was being observed and glanced up.

Lovell was in the doorway, leaning against one jamb, arms folded, watching her.

She put down the box she was examining and stood up, but he waved her back to her chair.

'You left the door wide open, there must be a draught.'

That was certainly a more prosaic opening than *And just why did you kiss me?* she supposed.

'Yes, but I am going through rooms that contain all kinds of objects, many of them small and valuable. That could lay me open to the suspicion that some might find their way into a pocket, so the more open I am, the better I feel about it.'

She saw Lovell glance at her notebook where she listed everything she had found, drawer by drawer.

'I select my staff with care and I choose to trust them,' he said.

Katherine opened the box she had been looking in, lifted out a ring and handed it to him. 'A nice, if small, diamond. So easily hidden. Very tempting.'

'My assessment of your character, Kat, is that not only are you too honest to pocket as much as a seed pearl, but that you what makes you honest is not fear of being caught committing a capital crime, but your own self-esteem and sense of what is right.' He handed back the ring with barely a glance at it.

She could only stare at him, surprised. It was true, when she did find the Borgia Ruby—and she would—then she would not simply take it. That would be wrong—some money had been paid for it, even though in the course of a fraud, and Lovell had some stake in it until she had returned that.

He had not known what his cousin had done, she was certain of that now. If he could assess her character, then she thought she was beginning to understand his. But she could not forgive him for the way he had fought that case. Never.

'Thank you,' she managed to say. 'Even so, the sooner the small portable items of value are in the strongroom, the better. This is a large house and, if we had an intruder, we might not realise it.'

We? This is not your house, she reminded herself sharply.

'So, you are moving these.' He poked one long finger into the tray of snuffboxes, two necklaces, a few rings and a miniature in a jewelled frame, stirring them about. 'What else?'

'Books go back to the library. Furniture, paintings and clocks stay where they are. I am no expert on any of those, so it is a matter of your choice when we, I mean, *you*, come to arrange the rooms.'

Why was she beginning to feel so possessive about this house? To cover up her slip she chattered on. 'I know people who can give you reliable estimates on anything you do not care for. Reliable, that is, if they realise you are not about to sell to them directly and instead employ them on a fee.'

Lovell smiled, the twist of his lips cynical.

Such nice firm lips...

'Are you telling me that not all experts can be trusted?'

'If they are also dealing then, naturally, they will be looking to make the best profit for themselves. But they would expect you to compare estimates. I would not recommend anyone to you who I would not be prepared to trust personally. Not all dealers are criminals, no matter what the late Marquis thought.'

His gaze sharpened and she swallowed hard. Had she given herself away, revealed resentment?

'It is a small world, word gets around,' she explained. 'Your cousin had a reputation for prosecuting anyone he thought had done him down.'

'He was a vindictive man.' Lovell shrugged. 'Carry on, then, Kat. I have ordered that all the packing cases and all the remaining statuary are to be moved into the ballroom. That should make things easier.'

There was a tap on the door frame and they both looked around to find Giles Wilmott holding a letter. He had an expression on his face of mingled amusement and alarm.

'My lord, the bishop is sending you a chaplain. He should arrive tomorrow. The Reverend Quintus Gresham.'

'Good G——, that is, how the blazes did he know I wanted one?' Lovell frowned. 'I am not even certain I *do* want one.'

'In that case, I beg your pardon, sir. I fear I have exceeded my authority, but I assumed after your conversation with Mr Arnley on the subject...'

'Very well. I suppose he was right. It is a long walk for the staff to get to church and next year the household will have expanded.'

Will it? Yes, of course, Katherine realised. Once the house was habitable again, Lovell would want to entertain. His new wife certainly would and that meant more servants, from scullery maids to ladies' maids to grooms.

The pang of something perilously like jealousy surprised her. Of course, she was growing to know the house and its contents, but she had not expected to feel such a sense of ownership. The library, of course, was becoming exactly as she had hoped and it would be painful if someone changed that—not that she would be here to see it—and she most definitely felt possessive about the charioteer statue.

'Kat?'

'I am so sorry, I was wool-gathering.'

'Will you and Mrs Downe be available to greet our new chaplain tomorrow?'

'I will, certainly, and I am sure, even if Elspeth has any plans, she would be happy to change them. But will you not be interviewing him first?'

Lovell grimaced. 'If the bishop has sent him, then I suppose he will be suitable for the position. I have no idea how to interview a chaplain. I shall offer him a month's trial—he may take a dislike to us, after all.'

Us. He meant the household and himself in particular. But the word had given Katherine another uncomfortable little jolt.

She was becoming very attached to this place and she would be sorry to leave, she realised. It was almost as though her mission to find the ruby, and to expose the lies about her father, was something apart from the day-to-day life she lived at Ravenham Hall. And that was a very unsettling thought.

Chapter Twelve

'The Reverend Gresham, my lord,' Grigson announced.

They were all gathered in the drawing room drinking coffee. Elspeth had taken it on herself to order it every day and then to extract Lovell and Giles from the study and Katherine from the library for, as she put it, 'a conversable twenty minutes to refresh us from our labours'.

Her own labours were the result of volunteering to survey all the hangings, curtains and upholstery in the house with Mrs Goodman and to decide what needed cleaning—all of it—what required repair—much of it—and what was beyond help.

As they all put down their coffee cups and prepared to greet the new arrival Katherine wondered enviously how Elspeth managed to stay so pin-neat and free from dust. At least she herself had washed her hands, tidied her hair and taken off her apron before taking coffee, so she was not in too much of a mess to greet a clergyman.

They all stood as he came in and Lovell went forward to shake his hand. Beside her Katherine heard Elspeth's sharp intake of breath and closed her own mouth with a snap.

Oh. My. Goodness.

The bishop must have sent them the most beautiful clergyman at his disposal. Blond hair, blue eyes, straight nose, strong chin topped a slim six foot of youthful manhood.

Katherine blinked, fastened a smile of welcome on her face and waited to be introduced.

'Mrs Downe, Miss Jenson, Wilmott, this is Mr Quintus Gresham. Gresham, Mrs Downe's husband was the late Dean Downe of Westchester cathedral. She is companion to Miss Jenson here, our librarian. Giles Wilmott, my secretary.'

Everyone shook hands, Elspeth rang for more refreshments and they sat.

Mr Gresham was about twenty-six or seven, Katherine thought. His manner was modest and his accent well bred. Presumably, with the name of Quintus, he was the fifth son of a gentry family with elder brothers taking the roles of the heir, the spare and the Army and Naval officers.

She often wondered how the careers of younger sons were decided. Did they have any choice in the matter? Perhaps they all sat down together and decided who would look best in scarlet and rode well, who didn't get seasick and who had an aptitude for study. Or, more likely, it depended on what influence their father had, and with whom, at the point they were of an age to leave home.

Was having the looks that would excite someone creating a stained-glass window of angels actually an advantage for a young clergyman? Probably not.

After twenty minutes of polite conversation about the bishop's health, his journey and his interest in a county he had never visited before, Mr Gresham finished his coffee and Giles offered to take him to his suite and help him settle in.

When the door closed behind them Elspeth fanned herself with her hand. 'My dear, what an extraordinarily good-looking young man!'

'Incredibly so,' Katherine agreed. 'I was thinking he could model as an angel for a stained-glass artist.'

Lovell cleared his throat pointedly.

'Well, he is handsome,' she said. 'Poor man.'

'Poor man? Even I can tell that he is likely to excite the interest of every female for miles around, including you ladies. I saw your faces when he walked in.' Despite his joking tone, Katherine suspected Lovell was not that amused by their reaction.

'Exactly my point. Just think how difficult that must be for a parish priest. He would be hunted by every hopeful spinster and would have to take particular pains never to arouse gossip or speculation. On the other hand, many matrons would be very glad to secure him as a husband for their daughter. That may well be why the bishop has sent him here, to a household.'

'And how am I expected to protect him from over-amorous housemaids?'

'It is not the same situation at all,' Katherine snapped, suddenly discovering she was finding this no more amusing than Lovell was. 'In a well-regulated household the female staff are safe from unwanted male attention and the same should be true in reverse. The balance of power is quite different between a domestic chaplain and one of the staff and a parish clergyman who might find himself compromised in any number of ways.'

'And this is a well-regulated household, is it?'

'You have an excellent housekeeper, butler and steward, my lord. It would be better if there was a lady of the house, of course.' She put a slight emphasis on *lady* and saw his eyes narrow.

Yes, my lord, I am suggesting that having your mistress in the house was not fair on the staff.

'That will have to wait until after the Season, when I intended to remedy that lack,' Lovell said. He spoke so politely that it was clear he was nettled.

'Then, providing Mr Gresham is of upright character, which one sincerely hopes he is, given the bishop's recommendation, there should be nothing to worry about,' she retorted, just as politely. 'Now I must get back to work.'

It was always satisfying to get the last word, so why was she feeling so unsettled? Safe in the library again, Katherine tied her apron strings, sat down at her desk and stared unseeing at a pile of harmless local histories that Peter had dusted and placed ready for her attention.

The honest answer was that it had been a shock to hear Lovell announcing his intention to seek a bride. It should have been no surprise—of course he was and they had spoken of it only the other day. So why...

Because I want him.

The words popped in to her mind with a suddenness that startled her.

Well, of course you do, she argued back. *You are female, possessed of good eyesight and he is an attractive specimen of the opposite sex. You kissed him, didn't you?*

It isn't that, came the insidious little whisper. *You are jealous that he wants to marry another woman.*

No! Stop it. Remember who he is, what he did. Remember why you are here. Remember why you are no longer able to marry any gentleman of good standing, let alone a marquis.

A marquis? What is the matter with me?

She felt herself go hot and then cold.

'Is something wrong, Miss Jenson? Those books are the ones you wanted me to work on, aren't they?'

Peter, brush in one hand, was regarding her with some anxiety.

'Oh. Yes. Absolutely correct, thank you, Peter. I was just thinking of something rather…rather unpleasant. I had no intention of glaring at you.'

He returned her smile. 'Shall I do the rest of the shelf?'

'Yes, please.'

And I will apply myself to my work and to avenging Papa.

And what was all that about? Will wondered, staring at Kat's retreating back.

Her shoulders were back, her head up and she was positively radiating irritation.

Was it because he had teased her and Mrs Downe about admiring Gresham's looks? Whatever it was, the conversation had moved rapidly to what felt remarkably like a lecture on the management of his household. Had that been a covert reproof for having Delphine in the house? He rather thought it had been.

Kat was creating an excellent library for him out of chaos and her work with the statues had not only revealed some fine pieces and the magnificent charioteer, but had already begun the work on clearing the house. But she was a disturbing presence to have around, not least because he found her mysteriously alluring. She was not the type of woman who normally attracted him, not at all. But she was the first female he had found himself living with in a domestic setting since he had left home. He was coming to know her as a person—at least, as far as she allowed him.

Perhaps the attraction was because of the slight edge of hostility that he sensed from her. Was that simply a challenge to his masculinity adding a perverse erotic frisson? And why, bizarrely, had he felt disappointed when she had virtually ordered him to marry for the sake of the household?

Surely, he wasn't such a coxcomb that he expected her to want to take that position herself? That he hoped she wanted him for more than a fleeting, experimental, kiss?

He was a marquis, Will reminded himself, still finding the concept faintly incredible. Marquises married the daughters of aristocrats, not librarians, and Kat knew that perfectly well.

And he had more immediate worries—like what, exactly, was he supposed to do with a chaplain?

Kat solved that problem for him at luncheon by asking Gresham straight out what a domestic chaplain in a great house did.

He had regarded her solemnly. 'I have to confess I asked my lord bishop precisely that question when he spoke to me about this position. I understand that I will be ministering to the spiritual needs of the household and holding a service, or services, as Lord Ravenham requires, on Sundays. I can also hold morning and evening prayers for the household, if that is you wish, my lord.' He directed a slight bow in Will's direction.

'If baptisms, weddings, the churching of women and funerals are required, naturally I will perform those,' he added. 'Then there is the welfare of the tenants, to whatever extent you require me to be involved, my lord.'

'Call me Lovell, or sir,' Will said. 'I do not know to what extent the tenants will wish to attend the chapel here as opposed to the village church and I assume that you will need to form some kind of working relationship with the Vicar there, Mr James.

'As for services, Matins on Sunday will suffice, I think.'

Across the table from him Mrs Downe cleared her throat. 'And daily morning prayers, do you not think, Lovell? Until the ballroom is cleared, and while the staff is relatively small, the drawing room, perhaps, will be large enough.'

'And grace before meals, of course,' Kat added with a sweet smile that was clearly intended to tease him.

'As you say, ladies.' Will smiled back. 'However, I suspect that you may find work needs to be done on the chapel before it is fit for services, Gresham. It was the parish church—fortunately a very small one—and in recent years the late Marquis did not use it, except, perhaps for storage.'

'You have not seen inside, my…sir?' Gresham looked a little daunted as it began to dawn on him that his employer was probably not a deeply devout man.

'I have not. But I am sure Miss Jenson will enjoy exploring it with you. She is a notable antiquarian and excellent in organisation.'

He had said it to tease, expecting that Kat would demur, make an excuse that she was too busy. Surely she didn't want to spend time poking about a dirty church with a clergyman?

She smiled at him. 'You are too kind, Lovell. I would be delighted to explore the chapel with you, Mr Gresham.' The chaplain received a far warmer smile.

Apparently Kat would welcome being given leave to spend hours with the handsome chaplain. He hardly thought that spiders and leaking roofs were the attraction.

'Shall we go and look now, Mr Gresham?' Katherine suggested as they rose from the table. 'If there is work to be done, then the sooner it is begun, the better. I expect it will be locked. Do you have a key, Lovell?'

'I have no idea. I suggest you ask Arnley. My steward,' he explained to the chaplain.

Mr Arnley had produced a heavy iron key on request and Katherine led Mr Gresham across the gravel carriage sweep, down the overgrown path through the shrubbery and up to the wall of the little graveyard.

'This could do with the attentions of the gardeners,' she said. 'But you can say that about the entire gardens and I should warn you about walking around close to the wing of the house where they are clearing the undergrowth—the ground is unstable there.

'The late Marquis was, to put it politely, eccentric. To be more accurate, he was an obsessed collector who was losing his grasp on reality and who neglected everything else except the objects of his desire.'

'I see,' he said, clearly not doing so in the slightest. 'Allow me.' He took the key from her and, by dint of using both hands, managed to turn it in the lock. 'Oil is required, I think.'

The door opened with a screech of rusty hinges that would have not been out of place in a Gothic novel and Gresham stood aside to allow Katherine to enter first.

It was a dubious privilege, she thought, lifting her skirts clear of dust and the evidence of both bats and pigeons.

'At least it has not been used as a storehouse,' she observed. 'I can see nothing that a thorough cleaning will not remedy. It is rather charming.'

'I agree,' Gresham said, earning her approval. 'Modest and simple. The glass all appears to be intact and I can see no trace of leaks in the roof.'

'Oh, look.' Katherine stopped by a table tomb topped with the effigies of a knight in armour, his lady at his side. 'How lovely. They are holding hands and look at his lion and her lapdog at their feet. I can't see an inscription, but it looks fourteenth century to me. I wonder who they are.'

'Perhaps Lord Ravenham's archivist can tell you.' Gresham prodded a kneeler with the toe of his shoe. 'Mice, I fear.'

'There is no archivist yet, although I rather suspect that I will be given the task as soon as the library is in order.'

The chaplain was clearly consumed with curiosity about her employment and, contrarily, Katherine felt no compulsion to explain herself. He was simply going to have to accept that a lady might have respectable employment outside the schoolroom.

'Is there any church plate, do you know?' Gresham opened a door. 'This looks like the vestry, but I can see no lockable cupboard to store it.'

'It is probably in the house, although, when you come to look around, you will see that it might be a while before we find it.'

'I have my travelling communion set,' he said, shaking out a ragged surplice with a grimace of distaste. 'That will suffice for the moment.'

'Shall we go back and find Mrs Goodman, the housekeeper, and see what she can do about finding some women from the village to clean inside? You cannot hold services as it is now.'

They walked back through the shrubbery. 'Where were you before you came here?' Katherine asked. 'A parish?'

'No, I was only ordained a month ago. I was expecting to be sent somewhere as a curate, so this was a surprise,' he admitted.

'Do you mind?' she asked bluntly. 'Would you have preferred a parish?'

'I am happy to serve wherever I may be of use,' he said, sounding, to Katherine's ears, rather stilted.

'May I be impertinent and ask whether a great house, and estate, of this size is something you are accustomed to?' Katherine risked a quick sideways glance and saw he was biting his lip.

'No. Our family is gentry, I suppose. My father has a small estate in Wiltshire. But the bishop is his cousin, so I owe this preferment to him.'

'This is an unusual household,' she said. 'You may already know that the Marquis has only recently inherited from a second cousin who was, as I said, eccentric. Things are at sixes and sevens and you will find us very informal. Lord Ravenham is unmarried, so there will be much to do connected with the welfare of the tenants, I am certain, even if the household is rather small at present.'

'Thank you. That is reassuring,' he said with the first unforced smile Katherine had seen. 'I am anxious to be able to contribute, but I am aware that I am not experienced.'

'I am glad to be of help,' she said, smiling back as they entered the hall.

It had not taken Kat and his new chaplain long to become friends, Will thought, emerging from the study in time to see them coming in through the front door, smiling at each other.

'Oh, Lovell.' Kat turned the smile on him. Was it his imagination that it was several degrees cooler?

'We were just on our way to see Mrs Goodman about getting the chapel cleaned. It will take quite a few women, and men with ladders as well, but the building seems sound. You don't happen to know where the communion silver and the altar candlesticks are, do you?'

'I suspect the candlesticks may be the large brass pair in my bedchamber. I'll ask Petrie to bring them down. My valet,' he added to Gresham, who was looking somewhat subdued. The effect of being organised by Kat, no doubt.

'I hadn't realised you had one,' she said brightly. 'Although, of course, you must do. He is somewhat reclusive, is he not?'

'He is used to a lawyer's chambers and wigs and gowns and had been looking forward to my spending a great deal on fashionable clothes and residing in considerable splendour. This does not come up to his expectations. He tends to lurk and has embarked on a campaign to eradicate the clothes moth as an outlet for his ill humour.'

Gresham was looking blank and Kat patted his arm. 'I told you,' she said, 'this is an unusual household. Shall we find Mrs Goodman?'

She glanced back as they passed Will and he could have sworn that one eyelid dropped in a wink, then they had gone and he could hear her voice fading as they reached the baize-covered door to the servants' stair.

'Sir?' Wilmott said from inside the study. 'I have found those rent books for the missing years that we needed.'

'Excellent.' He turned back to his desk. 'It appears that my new chaplain is seized with nerves at the strangeness of us and my librarian has decided to mother him.'

Wilmott, head bent over a dusty ledger, snorted. 'If she is feeling motherly, then at least she's not going to fall in love with him, then.'

'Don't be ridiculous,' Will snapped.

Chapter Thirteen

To Katherine's relief morning prayers went well the next day. The staff seemed to appreciate it, Lovell clearly approved of the brevity of the service and Mr Gresham did not make the mistake of prosing on, but introduced himself and then led the household in the Lord's Prayer and read a blessing.

At breakfast he asked whether Lovell had any particular tasks for him. 'I had thought of speaking to the indoors staff individually this morning, if that is acceptable. Just a quick word so I can learn names and encourage them to come to me if they think I can help. This afternoon, I wondered if I should begin visiting the tenants, but I do not know how many there are and how long it might take me to call on them all.

'I did not presume to bring a horse,' he added with the air of a man willing to tramp for miles if that was what it took.

'Take any mount from the stables that you think will suit, except for the big grey,' Lovell said.

'Or I could drive you in the gig,' Katherine offered. 'You will need a map, a notebook and your travelling communion set in case anyone is sick or infirm.'

Lovell's brows drew together and she added, 'I have been inside for days and I declare I am feeling quite frowsty. I would appreciate the fresh air and change of scene, if I may have a half-day off.'

'I have a list of the tenant families,' Giles said. 'I can plot them on a sketch map for you if that would help.'

'Then that appears to be your day organised, Gresham,' Lovell said.

Katherine wondered just what was putting him so out of temper—behind the smile there was coldness in the blue eyes.

Well, if she was in disgrace for taking a few hours after luncheon to help the chaplain and to, hopefully, bring some comfort to the tenants, then so be it.

'The tracks seem to be in very poor condition, dear,' Elspeth warned. 'The main carriage drive is not so bad, but I confess I did not have the resolution to try any of those through the park when I have driven out.'

'I am sure neither of us has any intention of proceeding at anything but a walk, believe me,' Katherine said with a laugh. 'After luncheon then, Mr Gresham?'

It was a relief to escape from Lovell's brooding presence. Katherine glanced back as she reached the door and found that he was watching her, his expression cool. She shivered. Was he suspicious of her? Surely he could not have discovered her true identity?

'This should be the correct way,' Gresham said, Giles's sketch map unfolded on his knee. He sounded doubtful as they began to follow the track, Katherine guiding the pony around ruts and hollows.

'Elspeth was not exaggerating about these tracks,' Katherine said. 'I am not at all surprised by how neglected this is,' she said. 'You recall I told you how eccentric the late Marquis was. He neglected everything, it seems.'

'I took the liberty of exploring the house a little, in between speaking to the staff,' Gresham said. 'It will take a great deal of effort to restore it to the state one would expect of a nobleman's dwelling.'

'I know,' Katherine said, with some feeling. 'But the people matter more than the mansion and I suspect that in the absence of a caring lord, let alone a lady of the house, their interests will have been sadly neglected.'

'I will do my best, Miss Jenson,' Gresham said stoutly.

She glanced across and saw he was looking determined, the travelling communion set held firmly on his knee, the map balanced on top of it. This was his first experience of ministering to a flock, of course. He must be nervous.

'My goodness, look at these potholes! If anyone is in need of labouring employment, then mending these tracks will be a good start.'

'I will make a note of it,' he said, wriggling on the seat in an effort to get his notebook out of his pocket one-handed while steadying the box and map with the other.

Katherine leant to one side to give him more room while she guided the pony on to the grass to get around yet another deep rut.

They were just back on the track again when a deer erupted from the bushes almost under the pony's nose. It threw up its head in panic and began to back rapidly.

Katherine was momentarily blinded by the map flapping up in her face, then the gig lurched abruptly, a sharp object jabbed her in the ribs and she felt herself falling. She hit the ground with a thump that almost knocked the wind out of her, had a moment to be grateful for the thick grass, and then something hit her head from above and the world became black.

Will walked along the terrace at the back of the house, picking his way over uneven slabs and tufts of grass and weeds.

More gardeners needed.

More of everything needed and, in his case, more patience and less suspicion, he acknowledged ruefully.

As a lawyer he was trained to be suspicious, to be constantly looking out for lies and evasions, to expect hidden motives and to think the worst of people.

Now this household, the estate and the tenants were in his care and his responsibility was to trust and nurture them. If he couldn't begin by trusting his chaplain, let alone his hard-working and intelligent librarian, there wasn't much hope for him.

The statue of the crouching nymph that he had ordered to be brought outside and set by the little pool at the end of the terrace was in place and he went to look at it.

Not close enough to the edge, he decided, bending to push it nearer so she could look down into the murky green water. He could see his reflection behind her, dark and blurred as he grunted with effort and finally managed to get the statue into a better position.

Will straightened up, stretched to ease his back and suddenly laughed at himself for his sour mood. It was ridiculous to be brooding because the handsome Mr Gresham appeared to have made friends with Kat. Surely friends were all they were.

It was excellent that someone was making an inexperienced young man feel at home, excellent that Kat had someone else to talk to instead of him, prowling irritably about the place.

All that was wrong with him was insufficient exercise and an excess of accounts. He would take his hunter Ajax out for a gallop, get some fresh air and see if he could find a few tenants. It would not be right for his chaplain to know them better than he did. Besides, Kat might need some help—he had no idea how well either of them could drive.

Half an hour later Will turned the big grey stallion off the carriage drive and down the first turning he came to, keeping the impatient horse to a steady trot. This was no track for speed. He added road mending to his mental list of things to be done and noticed the fresh marks of carriage wheels crushing the grass to the side of the worst potholes. Kat and Gresham must have come this way, too.

The track curved, then rose and, as Ajax crested the slight rise, Will could see several hundred yards of track in front of him. Halfway along was the gig, stationary, and a man was standing by it. There was no sign of Kat.

She could have stopped and descended for any number of reasons—the pony had gone lame, she had seen an interesting flower, the track was too damaged to continue. Even as those explanations flashed through his mind, he knew something was wrong. Careless of ruts or holes, Will sent the horse down the track at a gallop.

By the time he reached the gig and flung himself out of the saddle Gresham was on his knees next to Kat's sprawled body. Beside her head silver vessels glinted incongruously in the grass. There was no blood, he saw with relief.

'What the hell happened?' He pushed Gresham aside and knelt, wrenching off one glove to search for a pulse at Kat's throat. Beneath his fingers he felt it beating strongly under her jaw. Alive, then.

'A deer frightened the pony, it backed into the hole and the gig lurched. Miss Jenson lost her balance and I lost my grip on the wooden case holding the communion vessels. She landed on the soft grass, but the case struck her head.' The chaplain sounded anxious, but he was reporting rationally.

Will judged the distance between the gig's seat and the ground, felt the turf. The distance was not great, the uncut grass was soft enough and without stones. It seemed unlikely that Kat would have suffered more than bruises from the fall. It was the blow to the head they must worry about.

'Can you drive?'

'Yes, my... Lovell.'

'Then turn the gig. I'll lift her.'

A gig had no space for anyone but the driver and passenger and there was nowhere to lay Kat flat. Gresham led the pony around on the grass, rather than try to turn on the track, which showed sense, Will thought through his anxiety, then he climbed up and tied the reins around the whip in its holder.

'If you pass her up, sir, I can hold her while you climb in.'

Lifting a completely limp young woman was not the easiest thing, even for a fit man. A twinge reminded Will that he had been heaving lumps of marble about recently, but he rose steadily to his feet and got Kat on to Gresham's knees.

Will tied Ajax to the gig then, at an agitated word from the chaplain, picked up the chalice and paten, stowed them in the box and jammed them between the young man's feet.

Kat stirred slightly when he took her back in his arms, but

was silent again as he arranged her safely, her head on his shoulder, his arms tight around her.

It was extraordinary the wave of protectiveness that swept over him. Presumably, he rationalised while bracing himself to hold her steady and trying not to shout at Gresham to whip up the pony, this was the effect of being the Marquis and responsible for a large number of people in his employ.

'Kat?' he murmured as she stirred. 'Keep still, you have had a bang on the head, but we are almost home now.'

Home? He had never thought of Ravenham Hall like that before, only as a huge liability that he had inherited. Now he realised that it *was* home and that Kat was part of it, presumably because she had been there almost as long as he had.

'Take us around to the stable yard, there's level access into the house from there,' he ordered Gresham, pleased at how steady the young cleric was.

It took only a moment after they entered the yard for the grooms to realise that something was wrong and four of them clustered around as Gresham climbed down and went to the pony's head.

'Fetch a hurdle and something clean to put over it,' Will ordered and two of them ran off, returning minutes later with one covered in grain sacks.

They laid it on the ground, then came and stood two on each side of Will so he could hand his burden down to them. They were strong, fit, young men and they managed easily, placing Kat gently on the sacks.

As Will jumped down Gresham led the pony to the wall, tied it up and then ran for the house.

Mrs Goodman and Mrs Downe were waiting for them as they negotiated the kitchen door.

'My room, I think, my lord,' the housekeeper said. 'Then we don't have to manage the stairs until Miss Jenson is feeling a little better. I have sent Arnold for the surgeon, Mr Henderson. He's good on a horse is young Arnold, he'll be as quick as may be.'

'Just lay her on top of the bed, my lord,' Mrs Downe said,

preceding them into the housekeeper's parlour and through to the bedchamber.

Will lifted Kat from the hurdle and carried her to the narrow bed with its patchwork quilt.

'Now, what happened, exactly?' she asked as he stepped to one side.

'She fell from the gig over rough ground. I do not think that was serious or caused any damage—she landed on soft grass. But the travelling communion set fell out after her and struck her on the head.'

'Tsk. Not wearing a bonnet, I suppose,' Mrs Downe said as Will smoothed back the tumbled hair over Kat's forehead.

'Her bonnet came off and blew away as she fell,' Gresham said from the doorway.

'There's a lump at the back, but no bleeding,' Will said, his fingers exploring gently. 'It seems as though the box hit her with a side, not an edge or a corner.

'Thank Heavens for that,' Gresham said.

Will thought, but managed not to say, that Heaven should not have been allowing anyone to be struck with such a container.

He slipped his hand out from under Kat's head and she opened her eyes, clear hazel staring bemusedly back into his.

'Ouch,' she said faintly. 'Where am I and what happened?'

Will bent closer and was relieved to see that her pupils both seemed to be normal. The danger with head injuries was the damage inside the skull, he knew that. But at least she was rational. Bleeding from the ears and nose—that was another danger sign, he recalled and peered closely at all three.

'And what on earth are you doing?' Kate demanded querulously. 'My head aches.'

'You fell out of the gig and were hit on the head by the box containing the communion set.'

'Goodness,' she said faintly. 'How bizarre.'

'You are now on Mrs Goodman's bed and I am just checking there is no bleeding.'

'My lord, if you were to perhaps move…'

Will straightened up abruptly. 'Yes, of course, Mrs Downe.

We will send the surgeon down as soon as he arrives and if there is anything you need, you only have to ask.'

She would be perfectly all right, he told himself as he left the room, pushing Gresham in front of him. 'Out. She does not need either of us, I am glad to say, in your case.'

The back of the younger man's neck and his ears turned red. 'You refer to the last rites, my lord? Yes, we must indeed be thankful that it was not more serious. But I blame myself.'

'Really?' Will caught up with him as they emerged into the hallway. 'And why is that?'

'I should have been driving. Or perhaps I could have caught her.'

'If Miss Jenson wanted to drive, it would take a stronger man than you to stop her, Gresham.' The chaplain still looked wretched so Will added, 'If you had caught at her you might well have pulled her under the wheel. As it was, she fell on the grass clear of that danger.'

What was the matter with him? He was becoming soft, trying to soothe an anxious young man and worrying himself over a slightly dented librarian.

Over a young woman who was his responsibility. A hardworking, intelligent, spirited young woman who was somehow—and probably without the slightest intention of doing so—reconciling him to this monstrous house and the weight of duties that went with it.

Grigson hurried past him to answer the knocking on the front door and a tall, ugly man stalked in, shedding coat and hat into the butler's arms as he came.

'Henderson,' he said tersely. 'Where is my patient?'

'Ravenham,' Will snapped back, secretly amused by the surgeon's no-nonsense approach. 'She is downstairs, conscious, making sense, but complaining of a headache, which is unsurprising as she was hit on the head.'

'By what?' Henderson demanded.

'The box of a portable communion set.'

Silence. Then the surgeon glanced at Gresham in his sombre black with the white clerical bands at his neck and remarked, 'I would suggest you employ a chaplain with a less militant approach to the spread of the faith, my lord. I have always found that simple persuasion is the best method of conveying information.'

'It was an accident. This way.' Suppressing a smile, Will turned towards the back stairs. 'Down there. You'll find Mrs Goodman, my housekeeper, in charge.'

He dismissed Gresham to do whatever chaplains did—write a sermon, perhaps?—and went to scan the post that Giles, who had ridden into St Albans, had left on his desk in the study.

He had left the door open and, less than twenty minutes later, emerged at the sound of footsteps striding down the hall.

Henderson stopped when he saw him. 'Nothing broken, no signs of concussion. I have given her something for the headache and told her to rest. An intelligent young woman, she'll know if she needs to see me again. Good day to you.'

'And good day to you,' Will replied as the surgeon let himself out, banging the front door closed behind him.

Not a man with a soothing bedside manner, but he had more confidence in the surgeon than all the smooth-talking doctors he had encountered. They, of course, despised surgeons as mere technicians because they worked with their hands, despite the fact that, with their practical approach, they saved more lives than the medics.

The house would certainly be calmer with Kat confined to her bed, he thought, going back to the letter from Truefit, the chief clerk at his legal chambers. Will was a sleeping partner now, leaving his two barrister colleagues to run the firm, and Truefit wanted to know what to do with the paperwork relating to the Ravenham estate and his late cousin's cases. Did His Lordship wish it to be stored at the chambers or sent to him, and if so, to where?

'Send everything relating to the Ravenham estate and to my late cousin's affairs here to the Hall,' Will wrote. Then as an afterthought added, 'Is there an opening for an intelligent young man? I have an under-footman who shows promise.'

He answered a few minor points the clerk had raised and was sealing the letter when he heard the door to the service stairs open. It would be Mrs Goodman coming to report on Kat, no doubt, he thought, going out to meet her.

Instead of the housekeeper, the figure doggedly making its way towards the foot of the main stairs was Kat. She was sporting a rakish bandage around her head, her hair was in a long plait and she was wearing a brown wool robe that barely skimmed her ankle bones. Her feet were bare.

'What in Hades do you think you are doing?' he demanded.

'Don't shout,' she said, glaring at him. 'My head hurts. I am going to bed.'

'You *were* in bed and told to stay there. And of course your head hurts. If you will go throwing yourself out of moving vehicles, you should expect it to.'

'*My* bed. The rest of your observations are inaccurate and unfair,' Kat said with dignity. This was somewhat undermined by her appearance and the fact that she was steadying herself on the wall, then on the console table as she shuffled past it.

'How the devil did you persuade Mrs Goodman to let you out?' Will demanded, advancing on her.

She was pale, there were scratches on her check from the dried grasses she had landed on and, from her expression, every step jarred her aching head.

Something inside Will shifted, painfully.

'I didn't tell her. She left me to sleep. I can't take her bed, poor woman—she was intending to sleep on the sofa in her sitting room.'

He could stand there, argue with her, tell her that the housekeeper could have the pick of any empty bedchamber in the house. Instead, he took two strides, picked her up and carried her to the stairs. He was coming to know the feel of her in his arms. To like it.

Kat gave a gasp of alarm, then held on tight, and whatever it was inside him twisted again.

Chapter Fourteen

Infuriating man. Domineering creature.

Katherine wanted to protest, to kick, to demand he put her down, yet, somehow, she did none of those things, but tightened her arms around Lovell's neck, let her aching head rest on his shoulder and closed her eyes.

It was because she was feeling so sore and shaken from the fall, of course. It was nothing to do with the fact that being carried up a sweeping staircase again by a large, strong man who smelt of leather and citrus and male skin was breathtaking and she did not want it to stop.

Lovell shouldered open a door, walked across a room, through another door and Katherine found herself being deposited firmly on the side of her bed.

'Get in and stay there,' he snapped, jolting her into reality again.

Standing in front of her was not the dashing hero of a Minerva Press novel who had just come to the rescue of the heroine, but an irritable, overbearing lawyer-turned-marquis who was every bit as disagreeable as she had always thought him.

The thought crept into her mind that climbing the backstairs had almost exhausted her and that she would probably have had to manage the main staircase on hands and knees if he hadn't found her, but Katherine was in no mood to be reasonable about this.

This man was the enemy, the man who had destroyed her father and, foolishly, she had let herself become friendly with him, attracted to him. Somehow she had managed to separate William Lovell, King's Counsel, from Will Lovell, the Marquis of Ravenham, and that was a betrayal of her parents. And it was all her own fault.

'Go away,' she said.

'Get into bed.' He rested his balled fists on each hip and looked at her through narrowed eyes.

'I will. Now *go away.*'

She closed her eyes.

Go away because I want to have a good weep, you horrible man. My head hurts, I have been an idiot and I still haven't found either the ruby or the evidence of your lies. I have let myself enjoy being here, my work here. You.

Lovell shifted, turning away. There was the soft tread of retreating footsteps on carpet. The sound stopped.

'Kat, are you crying?'

'No!' She opened her eyes and, through a blur, saw him in the doorway staring at her.

'Yes, you are.' He sounded exasperated, angry even. Now he would go away because men could not cope with tears.

'You infuriating female.' He strode back, sat down beside her, thrust a large handkerchief into her hand and gathered her efficiently against his shoulder. 'Use that. Don't make my shoulder wet.'

'I'm not infuriating, you are,' she managed to say through a layer of linen, her cheek pressed against superfine coating.

Lovell snorted. 'I'm an idiot.'

'Yes,' she muttered.

Hate you.

But despite his words, his tone, he was holding her gently and rubbing her back with his free hand, his palm making warm circles though Mrs Goodman's sensible dressing gown.

She must be strong. She must rest and then get back to work. She *would* find the ruby and the evidence that would clear her father. And she would not allow herself to fall in... To *like* William Lovell.

Katherine wriggled free, blew her nose loudly and inelegantly and said, 'Thank you. I will go to bed now. Perhaps you would be good enough to let Mrs Goodman and Mrs Downe know where I am.'

Lovell released her with unflattering speed and walked away. 'I will.' She thought she heard him mutter, 'I should lock the door. She needs a keeper.' Then, even more to himself, 'Bloody fool.'

Katherine spent the next day in bed, her headache diminishing as the bruises from the fall flowered into purple glory.

Elspeth lectured her on imprudence in between dosing her with bitter willow-bark tea and dabbing the bruises with arnica. She reported that Ravenham was out of temper, Mr Gresham appeared to have pulled himself together and had gone out visiting tenants all by himself and Mrs Goodman had hired five women and two men from the village and set them to cleaning the chapel.

'It is beginning to look rather fine now that the men have gone up ladders to clean the windows and have dusted the ceiling and beams. They even found some charming medieval floor tiles in what must have been the Lady Chapel. I have begun making altar cloths from linen and some brocade curtains. The kneelers are in a deplorable state. Mice, no doubt. Perhaps the kitchen cat...'

Katherine let it all wash over her as she lay there, turning over and over in her mind what she would do when she found the evidence that Lovell had fabricated the charges of dealing with the French enemy against her father.

The first thing would be to send it somewhere safe where he couldn't find it. But then... Her father had not been charged with any crime, so appealing to the Lord Chancellor to have a conviction overturned was irrelevant. It had been a civil case and it was Papa's reputation that had been destroyed.

There were newspapers that were radical in sympathy and might well take up the case provided they were confident they had proof—standing up to a marquis was not for a faint-hearted editor who feared charges of libel. Several editors had ended up in the stocks for that.

Or she could confront Lovell. Threaten him with exposure and demand that he make a public retraction of his 'evidence' against her father. That might be the better course—then she had the newspapers to fall back on if he refused.

It would mean standing up to him, of course, and she quailed inwardly at the thought. But, she told herself, she would draw on her anger and that would give her strength.

And, in the meantime, she must constantly remind herself just who she was dealing with and not allow herself to drift into a kind of friendship with her employer. Or allow herself to look at him as an attractive man, one she wanted in the most basic of ways.

For the next week Will felt as though he was living in the midst of a hurricane, which was decidedly strange, as the household was beginning to run like clockwork around him.

Men arrived to remove the crated statues destined for the salerooms, gardeners cleared and repaired the terraces to the extent that many of the less valuable statues could be moved outside, rooms opened up.

His chaplain, his secretary and his steward seemed intent on bombarding him with decisions to be made until he snapped and ordered them to talk to each other.

Gresham could liaise with Arnley and Mrs Goodman over what the tenants needed in terms of repairs and assistance, he declared. Wilmott could talk to everyone and draft advertisements for whatever positions were still to be filled. Mrs Downe—who he really must speak to about recompensing her for her efforts—and Mrs Goodman could supervise the cleaning and reordering of the various rooms and deal with the textiles.

And somewhere in the centre of this whirlwind was Kat and it felt as though she was the axis on which everything spun, leaving him like some cog that somehow did not mesh with the machinery. Yet he still gave the orders, the staff still deferred to him and he hardly saw Kat except at meals and morning prayers.

Was she avoiding him? She professed that she was quite re-covered, had no headache and needed to work.

Finally, he took himself off to ride alone through the park-land, letting Ajax have his head, trusting the horse's intelligence and sure-footed stride to keep them out of trouble.

When he set off he told himself he would look for the second lake that showed on the estate plans, somewhere off towards the low hill crowned by a building with a hole in its roof. Then he promptly forgot about it in thoughts of Kat. When Ajax skid-ded to a halt with a snort, his front hooves sunk into a muddy bog, Will almost went over his head.

He had found the lake or, more accurately, its ghost, a small pond in the middle of a reed bed. Will surveyed it with a sigh. More expense to get this clear.

Turning Ajax, who was mincing disdainfully through the mud like a society lady suddenly finding herself in a puddle, he looked back the way he had come and saw where a stream must run from this bog towards the house. It would join up with the lake that the moat drained into and would make a handsome feature through this valley.

Add landscape gardener to the list.

But the work would create a great deal of employment for the local men and that was important. He must remember to think like a landowner, someone with responsibilities to the community, and not like a lawyer with one hand tight on the purse strings.

Will guided Ajax around the edge of the reed bed, making for the folly. At least, he assumed it was intended as a *faux* ruined temple and wasn't simply a copy of one that had been allowed to tumble into disrepair by neglect.

The latter, he discovered as he reached it and swung down from the saddle, leaving Ajax to crop the grass that grew long and lush around it.

It was a little circular building with an arcade of Classical columns surrounding a central drum-shaped room, clearly cop-ied from etchings of Roman temples. The double doors creaked open when he pushed at them and pigeons flapped up in a panic as he found himself standing in the rubble where part of the domed roof had fallen in.

It was a mess now, but it would be a delightful spot with a view down the valley over the lake if both it and the watercourse were restored. And, he realised, it was another location where the statues, of which he still seemed to have an unnecessary number, could be placed.

Which brought him back to thinking about Kat. Will sat on the low platform that supported the ring of columns and stared out towards the chimneys of the Hall that could just be seen above the trees.

He had kissed her once. A mistake that had haunted him ever since, with guilt for taking advantage of someone in his household and a nagging desire to do it again. And again. And more.

Perhaps she had sensed that when he had carried her upstairs and that was why she was avoiding him now. He did not think he had let his feelings show, but Kat, even through a headache, was probably sensitive to atmosphere. She might be a virgin, but she was not naive.

She had accused him of having to be an actor as a lawyer. Perhaps that was true. Whether it was or not, he had to act now as though he was completely indifferent to her as a woman. In a few months she would be out of his life, because he could not imagine that his new marchioness, whoever she might be, would be accepting of a female librarian with the same status in the household as his secretary or chaplain.

The mental image of this unknown lady was vague in his mind, her face hazy, although for some reason she had brown hair. She would be organised, efficient, raised to manage the demands of an aristocratic household and the social life that went with her rank.

Will realised that up to that point he had been thinking about this theoretical wife in much the same way he would have done about a court case that was still some way in the future. He had been making preliminary lists of actions to carry out, research to be done.

This unknown young woman who would take his name,

bear his children, was a cipher, an object to be obtained, and he suddenly felt ashamed of that. And then irritated with himself.

What was he supposed to do? As plain William Lovell, barrister, he had been free to choose a wife, follow his inclinations and fancy, although she would be intelligent, from much the same background as he was himself, able to entertain and to support a man rising in his career.

Now he was constrained by rank and duty. He could curse his cousins for their recklessness, leaving him shackled to the title and all that went with it.

He got to his feet, grinning ruefully at his own thoughts. There would be few other men who would be so ungrateful as to resent a high title, estate, wealth—if there was any of it left in the coffers by the time he had beaten his inheritance into shape.

Having to restrict his choice of bride to a small circle of eligible ladies was a small price to pay for all that, surely?

From her sitting room window Kat watched the rider on the grey horse cantering back towards the house. She had come upstairs to wash her hands and tidy her hair before luncheon and had been feeling decidedly pleased with herself.

The library was now in a state where all that was needed was for Lovell to decide what he wanted to keep and what was to be disposed of. There was space for anything else that was found scattered around the house and her draft catalogue was complete. Now she was free to search all day, every day, until she found the ruby and the documents that related to it.

Now, the sight of Lovell upset her equilibrium, as it did every time she encountered him. It was as though she was a piece of paper that had been torn neatly down the middle. On each side was a picture of Katherine Jones, alias Jenson, but one of those Katherines wanted to expose William Lovell for what he had done to her family. The other Katherine simply wanted him.

She had been avoiding him because of this, she was well aware. That must stop, because she did not want him to suspect that anything was wrong, that she was anything but what she should be—a hard-working expert set on ordering the chaotic collections he had inherited.

Katherine willed the corners of her mouth to turn up in a faint smile and opened the sitting room door.

The small dining room was empty when she reached it, but Elspeth joined her after a few minutes, followed by Mr Gresham and Giles Wilmott. They were deep in a discussion of the restoration of the chapel when Lovell came in, seeming to bring with him a breath of fresh air and the scent of the outdoors, despite the fact that he had changed from breeches and riding boots to pantaloons and Hessians and had donned a different coat.

When he had helped himself from the sideboard and taken his seat, Katherine said brightly,' I saw you riding back just now. What a very fine horse that is.'

He seemed slightly taken aback at her smile, but answered readily enough. 'Ajax? Yes, a fortunate purchase. A grateful client was selling him and gave me first refusal.'

'Were you exploring the estate or visiting tenants?' she asked.

'I had not intended to do more than take a ride at random, but I have discovered an upper lake and what might be a rather charming building—an eyecatcher. Or it will be charming, when it has been repaired. There are holes in the roof and it needs cleaning.'

'A sham castle, perhaps?' Elspeth asked. 'Or a hermit's cave?'

'No, this is a little circular temple with a view down the valley towards the lower lake. It would make an excellent summer house for picnics when I begin to entertain. I thought it might be a suitable location for some of the superabundance of statuary.'

'What a good idea and, as it is not a hermitage, you are saved the expense of employing a hermit to live in it,' Katherine said with a perfectly straight face.

'Do people really go to those lengths?' he asked, knife poised over some cold salmon. 'I had assumed it was a joke.'

'Oh, no, there are at least three that I know of. Pa— Er... someone I was acquainted with in the antiquities trade was employed to find suitable pieces of ruined churches—small windows and so forth—for one and, when he arrived to supervise their setting, he found there was already a hermit in residence and he knew of two others.'

Goodness, she had almost blurted out *Papa* just then. And

then it would be no great feat to discover which landowners had real hermits in their employ and the names of the advisors on the design of their dwellings.

But there is no reason for Lovell to do that. Not unless he is suspicious of me, Katherine reassured herself.

'Thinking about follies and restoring silted-up lakes—I assume it is silted? Yes, of course, it would be—must be a great change for you, Lovell. You will miss the cut and thrust of the courtroom, I imagine' she said, anxious to steer him away from her slip of the tongue.

'Yes,' he agreed, apparently not offended by the personal question. 'I enjoyed the research before the case came to court and the interest of the adversarial contest. One has to think on one's feet, literally, and there is little of that here.'

'You clients will be sad to lose you,' Elspeth said, unwittingly helping Katherine, who was wondering how to probe further.

'My partners continue the practice,' Lovell said. 'I shall retain an interest, but no longer be actively involved. Which reminds me, I must find a secure room to house the files of cases relating to the estate. I have just instructed the clerk to send them here.'

Katherine suppressed her smile of delight and covered her smile by taking a mouthful of lemonade. That would save her having to search for any documents that the late Marquis kept here, or, at least, made finding them less urgent, because, surely, what she would need to confront Lovell with his libel of her father would be with the legal documents. The old Marquis would have kept the real receipt, she reminded herself ,and she still needed to find that.

'I believe you have a proper muniments room,' she said. 'There will be many old documents, files of papers and so forth, that are no longer in use. It will all be stored together and would be the perfect place for your legal records.'

'I believe it has been locked up ever since the previous archivist died there,' Giles said.

They all stared at him and he hastened to add, 'He isn't in there! He was buried, of course.'

'Do show me later, if you would,' Katherine said. 'It would be best to check that it is as fireproof as possible. It needs to be secure, but accessible, with all the essential records kept together, so that if there is a fire, they can be removed quickly to safety.'

'It is in the basement,' Giles said. 'Just before the strong-room.'

'That is excellent. If I find anything that I think should be in there I can take it directly.'

He blinked at her eagerness and Katherine realised she might have let her delight in what everyone else would think a very dull and mundane subject show.

'Please pass the butter,' she said hastily.

Chapter Fifteen

After luncheon Katherine inspected the room Giles had described and agreed it was ideal, although much in need of tidying and dusting. But there was a table and some spare shelves and two keys.

Giles gave her one. 'You might as well keep this as you will be the person putting most items in there, I imagine,' he remarked, putting the other back on his key ring along with the one for the strongroom.

Katherine had made a point of not asking for one for that because she wanted to establish a clear pattern of seeking out valuables and then bringing them to be secured. Building up a trust that, she was very well aware, she intended to betray.

But it is justified, she told herself as she marked off yet another downstairs room on her plan of the house and carried a small trove of valuables along to Giles.

'Some silver, but not the chapel silver, I'm afraid,' she said. 'And these are some rather nice Italian micro-mosaics. I've found a folder of family genealogies. That can go in the muniments room.'

'What progress are you making?' The deep voice from right behind her had Katherine spinning around. She lost her balance and had to be caught by Lovell.

'Goodness, you made me jump!'

His hands were still resting on her arms just above the elbows where he had steadied her, not holding, merely making her feel as though they were resting against bare skin.

'Progress? Let me show you my plan.' That gave her an excuse to move away slightly and unfold it on the desk. 'You see? I have ticked off each room I have searched and made a note of what items of furniture remain and what I think the original purpose of the room was.'

'Excellent progress,' Lovell said. 'But you haven't found what you are searching for yet, have you?'

Whatever was the matter with Kat? She was staring at him as though he had grown another head.

'What? I—'

Damnation, I have alarmed her again by grabbing hold of her.

She out up a hand as though to brush back a lose strand of hair and Will was momentarily distracted by the way the light brought out hidden golden highlights.

He moved back a couple of steps. 'The chapel silver,' he explained. 'There ought to be a chalice and a paten and a jug at the very least, surely? You mentioned it the other day. And the candlesticks, of course. I must bring down the ones from my bedchamber and you can see if they are suitable.'

'Oh, of course. I am sorry, I was confused because I am attempting to find everything portable of value. The candlesticks would be brass, I believe, if they date back to before your cousin's time so, if the ones from your chamber are large, then they may well be from the church.'

Kat seemed to be talking almost at random and he wondered if she was still suffering the after-effects of the blow to her head.

'You should get outside,' he said abruptly. 'Out in the fresh air.' He saw her cast a glance out of the window and added, 'Not now, it is becoming overcast. But tomorrow, if the weather is fine. Do you ride as well as drive?'

'Why, yes, although it has been some time.'

'Then we will ride out tomorrow and I will show you the little eyecatcher temple. There is a very steady mare in the stables. It looks as though it would be a positive armchair ride, so you need have no anxieties about another fall.'

'Ah, I see what it is,' Kate remarked in a rallying tone, seeming to recover from her moment of imbalance. 'Not so much a holiday for me but work to be done assessing your folly.'

Will winced inwardly. It was not a building that was his folly, he was well aware. It was becoming too attached to his librarian for propriety. Or wisdom.

'But of course,' he said, echoing her tone. 'I will be a positive tyrant until we get more of those confounded statues out of the house.'

'Very well, provided you really can find me a ride that is prepared to tolerate a sack of potatoes on its back.'

'Having had you sitting on me when poor Wilmott was being swallowed by the moat, I am sure the cob will be able to cope.'

Now I have made her blush. I used to have a sure touch with women. What has changed?

'After breakfast then, Kat?'

'Very well. After breakfast tomorrow.' She glanced at the old-fashioned German clock on the wall. 'Now I have just time to finish the next room this afternoon. It is more of a closet than anything and shouldn't take me long.'

She smiled at them both and left the room, once more neat, composed and industrious.

Will realised he was still staring at the closed door when Wilmott cleared his throat.

'Sir?'

'Yes? Sorry, I was brooding on the pair of brass candlesticks in my bedchamber.' His secretary was looking blank. 'From the chapel.'

'Oh, yes, sir. I believe Miss Jenson is quite correct and most churches had brass. It isn't something one notices, but I seem to recall...'

Will stopped listening, thinking instead of what he would take with them to the folly. A sketchbook, perhaps, so he could draft out some thought about landscaping the lakes from the viewpoint of the temple. A rug to sit on, some refreshments. It would not do to have Kat getting overtired.

'I'll just go down to the stables,' he said, cutting across whatever Wilmott was saying. Something about drains? 'I want to make certain that mare is as reliable as it looks.'

Her riding habit was at least three years' out of date and possibly had moth holes, Katherine thought as she made her way to her next room. But that hardly mattered. This would be a ride over rough parkland on an old cob, not Rotten Row at the fashionable hour, and the last thing she wanted to do was look dashing or attractive.

The door, when she reached it, opened on to a windowless space and it was hard to see what its original function might have been. Now it was a store cupboard for items that looked more suited to below stairs.

Katherine began to carry out brooms, buckets, long poles with feathers on the end which must be cobweb dusters, a box of clean rags that someone had thriftily hoarded for cleaning and which seemed to have been home to several generations of mice, and several useful small stepladders. Of course, staff not wanting to carry cleaning equipment up and down stairs might well have found this hidey-hole, confident that the old Marquis wouldn't care.

She could have done with those stepladders when she and Lovell were trapped behind the statues, she thought, carrying the last one out.

That just left a very dusty Buhl cabinet. A rub with one of the rags showed fine inlaid woods and brass and it certainly did not deserve to be hidden away there.

The curved double doors at the front opened with a reluctant creak to reveal six shelves stuffed with small boxes.

Jewellery boxes. Katherine's heart seemed to jolt inside her. Had she found the dragon's hoard of gems?

It was hard to resist simply sweeping everything off the shelves and opening each one, scrabbling through until she found the ruby, but caution stopped her. Everything must seem open and above board—she must hide the thing in plain sight.

What she needed was to carry all the boxes through to a table in one of the rooms she had already searched, lay them all out and list them. Then everything could be taken to the strong-room and she would make a great deal of the discovery—of everything except the Borgia Ruby which would never reach the strongroom.

If it was there…

The disappointing thing was that there appeared to be no paperwork with the boxes. Somehow, she was going to have to get into the files that Lovell's clerk was sending from London. But that could wait. She needed a large tray, or a box—

A cry of pain and the crash of falling objects made her leap to her feet and run to the door to find George the footman entangled in the buckets and brooms she had taken out.

'Are you hurt?' She helped him to his feet. 'I am so sorry, I should have realised that anyone coming around the corner would fall over these things.'

'I'm quite all right, Miss. I wasn't looking where I was going.' He dusted down his livery and peered at what surrounded him. 'Where did these come from?'

'Out of this little room. When you are recovered, George, please will you see they are taken below stairs and added to the cleaning equipment there?'

'Of course, Miss.'

'What the blazes?' It was Lovell, Giles at his heels. 'I heard what sounded like someone dropping several suits of armour from a great height.'

George scooped up an armful of brooms and hurried off, leaving Katherine to face the men over a fallen stepladder and half a dozen rather dented buckets.

'I have discovered a large number of jewellery boxes,' she announced. 'And I would welcome some assistance in carrying them to a room with a table.'

'Buckets,' Lovell said, picking two up and handing them to her. 'You fill them, we will carry them.'

Breathe. In plain sight, she told herself, taking them and turning back to the cabinet. *Show no interest, make this seem ordinary.*

'Thank you. The second room along to the right has a table that would be suitable.' Katherine made herself start filling the pails without studying the boxes and handed out the first two as the dressing gong rang.

'If we can clear them before we go to change for dinner, then I can lock the door,' she said brightly, taking the next bucket from Giles. The timing was perfect, both men in too much of a hurry to be tempted to open the boxes or take much interest in them.

'This is rather a nice cabinet,' she added as a further distraction. 'Buhl, of high quality. Shall I have it moved to the drawing room? It would look rather well in there once it has been polished.'

Lovell, taking the final bucket from her, nodded as he passed it to Giles. 'Certainly.' He regarded her quizzically. 'I have to tell you, Kat, that you have a smudge on the end of your nose and your skirts look as though you have been using them as dusters.'

When she gave her nose a swipe with one hand and shook out her skirts with the other, he added, 'Run and change for dinner. We will lock these away for you.'

There was no way to protest that she wanted to do it without appearing suspicious. 'Thank you,' she said with a smile and turned away, then added over her shoulder, 'Just leave them as they are—the buckets were quite dry and the boxes will come to no harm.'

Dinner was purgatory. Katherine itched to go and examine the jewellery boxes, search through them for the Borgia Ruby—there had been at least a dozen cases that would have fitted it—but instead found herself making polite conversation about the desirability of whitewashing the interior of the chapel and whether Mr Gresham should use his travelling communion set in the chapel in the hope that the original pieces would be found in the house or whether a new set should be ordered.

'You could write to the Goldsmiths' Company in London to ask for a recommendation,' Katherine suggested to Lovell. 'They must have members who specialise in church silver. Or

I can make enquiries among my contacts and see if there is an old set on the market, if you prefer.'

'Neither,' he said decisively. 'I know exactly what would happen—the moment I have committed to considerable expense, the originals will turn up in this madman's attic of a house.'

'Very true, my lord. I agree that all efforts should be made to find the original vessels and my small set is quite adequate for now,' Gresham said earnestly. 'I am happy to say that, thanks to the efforts of Mrs Goodman and her workers in cleaning and the repair work that has been carried out, I can hold our first service this coming Sunday. I must also thank Mrs Downe for creating a most handsome altar cloth. I believe the chapel will present a very decent appearance.'

Katherine tried to reply appropriately and join in with the conversation as it turned to the chaplain's visits to the tenants and the good news that he had found no cases of severe want.

'What a relief,' she said vaguely, her mind on the ruby. She could not go and search through the jewellery boxes that evening. She had never worked after dinner before now and doing so now would only draw attention to her. She could ask for the room key and then search late at night, she supposed, but that would be impossible to explain if anyone found her. Lovell had said he was a light sleeper, she reminded herself.

It would have to be in the morning, a rapid search and then when she had located it, she could go to the library and be observed placidly cataloguing books.

'I went to the stables to look over that mare I had mentioned as a nice quiet ride for you, Kat,' Will said as the soup plates were removed and the fish course brought in.

She stared at him blankly and it seemed for a moment that she was a hundred miles away and wondering who on earth he was.

'For our expedition to the temple folly after breakfast,' he said patiently and saw her gaze sharpen and focus.

'Oh, yes, of course. Forgive me, I was—'

'Miles away?' he suggested.

'No, not at all. I was quite definitely *here,* but I was making mental lists of things to be done tomorrow and had quite forgotten the temple,' she said, smiling.

Something in the very brightness of Kat's tone did not ring true and Will glanced at her sharply. For a second as their eyes met, hers widened, then the shutters seemed to come down and Kat was once again the perfect young lady with a demure smile and, apparently, not a thought in her head beyond small talk.

Will found himself strangely affected and it took him a moment to work out why. Desire was there, of course, that flash of unwilling attraction that he felt whenever he was close to her. And the answering spark that made him think that it was mutual, however careful she was not to show it.

But the strange sense he had that Kat disliked him, despite that attraction—that had gone and what he had seen in her eyes just then had been impatience, quickly veiled.

Not impatience to be in his arms, that was for sure, he thought. He watched her shift her position as though to make herself more comfortable on the rather hard dining chair and in the process moving so that she was angled away from him. Their eyes would not meet now if they both glanced up at the same time. Was that deliberate?

The others at the table were engrossed in a vehement discussion about some aspect of parish relief, from what he could make out. That was what happened when one put a clergyman, a clergyman's widow and a man responsible for keeping an eye on his employer's expenditure together, he supposed.

'But you must agree, Giles, that it is the responsibility of landowners to support the needy in the communities on their estates,' Mrs Downe was saying.

'Yes, but all those in prosperous situations in each parish should also have an obligation—'

Abruptly Will turned away again. Nobody was going to go hungry in any parish or estate where he had a responsibility and that was enough for him.

He looked at Kat's profile. She was carefully probing her fish for bones, her profile giving nothing away.

On impulse he said, 'Why do you dislike me, Kat?'

She dropped her knife on to the plate with a clatter and made a business of picking it up again.

'Dislike you? What an extraordinary question, Lovell!' She put down her knife and fork as though giving up on the fish. 'What have I ever said to give you that impression?'

'Nothing,' he admitted.

It isn't what you say.

'Well then. My goodness, but this fish is difficult. Tasty, but as bony as a kipper. I declare it has defeated me.'

Will tried it and found himself unable to speak through a mouthful of bones. Once he had dealt with them it occurred to him that not only had Kat not answered his question, she had not refuted the statement either.

Miss Jenson's thought processes were proving as obscure as the waters in what remained of his lakes was muddy.

Chapter Sixteen

It was a long night and, when Katherine could snatch at sleep, the dreams crowded in on her.

Why do you dislike me, Kat? Lovell asked himself, looking at her out of a strange fog, the Borgia Ruby pinned to his coat over where his heart would be, the stone seeming to pulse like blood. Then, as she reached for the stone, he had faded back into the mist and there was just his voice echoing faintly. *Why... why...why...*

Katherine came down heavy-eyed to breakfast early the next morning in her old riding habit and ate a hasty meal with Elspeth for the look of it, almost quivering with impatience. She would forget the dreams, forget Lovell. Only one thing mattered.

'I will just run along to see Giles for a moment,' she said. 'If Lovell comes, tell him I assume it is at nine o'clock that he wants to ride out and I will meet him at the front of the house then. There are one or two things I want to check up on first.'

She found Giles standing in the study sorting through the post which had just arrived.

'Good morning. Could you let me have the key to the room we locked those jewellery boxes away in last night? Only, I woke in the night with a positive conviction that, although the buckets were dry, there might have been rough surfaces which would damage the boxes, and that would be such a pity.'

She smiled at him, positively radiating fussy female anxiety, and Giles dug the key out of his pocket.

'Yes, of course. Keep it.' He handed it to her, his attention already back on the opened letter in his other hand. 'What the devil is this about, do you think? It appears to have been written by a drunken spider during a thunderstorm.'

'Try it the other way up,' Katherine suggested, already half-way to the door, pursued by Giles's snort of exasperation.

Her hand shook as she turned the key in the room where the men had stored the jewellery cases, half afraid it had all been a dream and she hadn't found them after all. But there they were, a prosaic row of four domestic buckets, incongruously brim-full of small cases and boxes. There was fine Morocco leather in a rainbow of colours, shagreen, plain polished wood, metal...

Katherine tipped the nearest bucket out on the table, rapidly pushing the contents around to sort them. Small ring boxes here; the thin, flat ones that would hold necklaces there; larger ones for parures of jewels... Nothing was the right size for the Borgia Ruby.

If she could only recall the box when Papa had brought it home... But she had been too excited to look at the jewel itself and she had hardly registered the case it came in.

Another heap, then another. One bucket left. She emptied that, pushing aside the precious contents with a haste that she would never normally have shown.

And suddenly, there it was. A scuffed, dark blue leather case, large enough to fill the palm of her hand, domed to a height of about two and a half inches and secured with an elaborate, and clearly very old, catch.

She scrabbled at it, broke a fingernail and made herself stop. The box was an historic artefact, too, original, part of the provenance of the jewel, and she was in danger of damaging it.

Katherine took a deep breath, put the box down carefully and waited for her hands to become steady. She reached for it again.

'There you are, Kat.'

It was impossible that her heart could have leapt up and

lodged in her throat, but something seemed to have done so. With an effort that made her dizzy, Katherine reached out and lifted two other boxes of much the same domed shape and placed them next to the ruby's box. Then she turned.

'I could not resist gloating over such a hoard,' she said with a light laugh—a triumph considering that she seemed to have no air in her lungs. 'And I had a foolish fear—you know the way worries strike you at three in the morning?—that the buckets might be rough inside and would have damaged the cases. But all is well. Is it time for our ride?'

Lovell barely glanced at the table. He certainly did not seem greedy for gemstones.

Winning, control, that is what matters to him, Katherine reminded herself. *Not so very different from his cousin, only with Lovell all is rational, sane and orderly.*

'Yes, the horses are ready, if you are.'

'Oh, I expect I can drag myself away,' Katherine said, following him out and locking the door behind her. When Lovell strode off in front of her, she slid the key down inside her habit shirt, snug under the edge of her stays. She had the ruby now, that was all that mattered. That and finding the documents relating to it.

There was something different about Kat that morning, Will thought, as they trotted away from the house and turned on to the track that led to the folly.

There was an excitement about her that he could sense fizzing under her usual calm demeanour. It was not anything she said—she had not spoken since thanking him for boosting her into the saddle—nor even something in her expression. Her face showed nothing except mild pleasure at being out in the open air.

He was becoming sensitive to her mood, he realised, and the thought made him uneasy. He was already finding her too attractive for comfort, or propriety, and he did not want to consider what this awareness indicated about his feelings for Kat.

For Miss Jenson. For my librarian. For my employee.

'Is your mount to your liking?' he asked abruptly, more for something to break the silence than for any concern that she was having difficulties. The mare was moving easily and he could see Kat's confidence in her relaxed hand on the reins and her gaze, sweeping over the view and not tensely focused on the path ahead.

'She is delightful and a very easy ride. Is she one of your cousin's horses that you retained when you inherited?'

'Yes, I thought she would be suitable for my—for any lady visitors.'

He almost said, *my wife,* because that had been in the back of his mind when he had made the selection of which animals to keep. He could have achieved a good price for her, but the mare's breeding and manners made her an ideal mount for a lady of status. A marchioness.

Or for the contrary female at his side. She might be out of practice, as she had said, but Kat had a natural grace in the saddle and a firm but gentle hand on the reins.

'Look, there is the folly ahead now.' He pointed to where it was just visible and Kat brought the mare in close alongside Ajax who sidled a little, showing off to the mare, Will supposed.

'Steady,' he said to the horse. 'She's not interested in you, you fool.'

He might do well to apply his own words to himself, he thought, as Kat gave a little snort of amusement. The mare ignored Ajax with as much uninterest as her rider habitually showed the stallion's master.

'Will you breed from her?' she asked. 'These two would make a fine pair.'

'I had not given it any thought,' he said shortly, shifting slightly in the saddle and trying to think of some remark that would get them off the subject of mating.

'Did you say there is a lake here?' Kat asked, to his relief. She shaded her eyes, peering ahead at the long grass and scrubby bushes that lay between them and the temple on its little hill.

'It was a lake, but it is about as impressive as a village duck-pond at the moment. I almost rode straight into the marsh surrounding it. In fact... Yes, here is where I had to turn.'

Kat followed him as Ajax, still with the air of a cat who had been dropped in a muddy puddle, picked his way through the boggy ground to the foot of the hill.

'It is going to be an incredible amount of work to clear this,' she observed when she could ride alongside him again. 'But I imagine the employment will be very much welcomed in the village and all around and the effect of two lakes between here and the hall will be magnificent.'

'It would put your little boating pond in the old moat in the shade,' he said, straight-faced but intending to tease.

'That will be *romantic*,' Kat retorted.

'*I* am *not* romantic.'

Again, that slight, barely ladylike, snort of amusement which he was finding perversely endearing.

'I know,' she said. 'You are a lawyer to the bone.'

'And lawyers are never romantic?' Will demanded. What was the matter with him? Were they flirting?

'Oh, I suppose there are some,' she said airily. 'Noble, idealistic types who set out to defend the innocent and right wrongs. I imagine you would have to be a romantic to try to do that, given the way that our legal system works.'

'Here is the folly,' Will snapped quite unnecessarily as they had arrived in front of it.

'Now this is delightful.' Kat kicked her foot out of the stirrup and slid to the ground without waiting for him to dismount and help her. She had tossed the reins over a bush and was running up the steps on to the circular platform ringing the temple before he had reached the ground.

He was not going to chase after her, damn it. Will took the mare's reins and led both horses into the shady spot he had found before, loosened their girths and tied them so they could crop the lush grass.

When he returned there was no sign of Kat, but the doors stood open. He found her inside gazing around.

'The roof is the priority,' she said without turning as his boots crunched over the broken plaster on the floor. 'Once that is fixed all it will need is cleaning and a coat of limewash.'

'White?'

'No, more a stone colour, as it was originally.'

Yes, ma'am. Your orders have been noted, ma'am.

'What is this door?'

'I have no idea.' To be honest he hadn't noticed it before.

Kat had already opened it and disappeared inside. 'Oh, how ingenious,' she called. 'There's a little scullery on one side and a privy on the other. This place was clearly designed as a summer house for picnics. Come and see.'

Will pretended he hadn't heard and went out again. His interest in inspecting sculleries, let alone privies, was limited and he had no intention of finding himself in a confined space with Kat.

She found him again after a few minutes, still bouncing with enthusiasm. 'This is perfect. We can have statues all around this plinth looking out between the pillars. That should take care of virtually everything left in the house and will finish this to perfection.'

'I had thought a mown area in front.' He gestured down to the gentle slope that ran from the steps for perhaps ten feet before it became steeper and plunged down towards the bog. *Lake*, he reminded himself.

'And some seats to go around up here against the wall.' Kat gestured vaguely behind herself. 'They will need to be curved, but quite simple in style, I think. Nothing beyond the abilities of the estate carpenters. The interior needs some furniture too. Day beds, perhaps, and a dining table and chairs.'

Will's imagination leapt at the thought of day beds, of making love in this secluded place with the doors thrown open to the sunlight. Or by moonlight. There might be nightingales…

'I shall assess the best position for the mown area,' he announced and, before his brain supplied pictures to go with the imaginings, jumped down to ground level and strode off to where he had left the horses.

He came back with the saddlebags he had ordered to be packed with food and drink and the large blanket that had been rolled up and strapped behind.

When she saw what he was doing Kat ran down the steps and helped him spread it out. She sat down in the middle, jumped up and moved it a foot to the right. 'That's perfect now. Perhaps a little terrace could be cut here. Just look at the view.'

Will sat, too, carefully keeping to the far end of the blanket. He pulled one of the saddlebags towards him and took out the sketch pad and pencil it contained, sitting with one knee up as a makeshift easel.

He was going to need someone with expertise in moving earth and directing rivers, he thought, drawing as best he could the lie of the land and then cross-hatching where he imagined the restored lake would go.

What would happen to all the mud dredged from the marshy areas and how long before the scars of the work healed? What would this bride he was planning to bring home next year make of a landscape that looked as though a major battle had been fought over it?

But then, the daughter of an aristocratic house would understand about the need to improve the estate, create a fine park and grounds. Many of the famous grand landscaped parks still had not matured into the form their designers had projected decades ago. Aristocrats built and planted for their heirs, he reminded himself.

Which brought him back to the reason for marrying—practical considerations. It was hardly as though he was planning on making a love match and needed a romantic hideaway to bring his bride to.

As he thought it Kat said, 'Why did you ask me that last night?'

'What?' He dropped his pencil and scrabbled for it in a tangle of blanket fringe and dry grass.

'You asked me why I disliked you. What have I ever said that made you think such a thing?'

'You never have—unless it was to show your mistrust of lawyers generally. No, it is the way you look at me sometimes,' he admitted, carefully not glancing at her as he spoke. 'Obviously it was my imagination,' he lied, convinced it was no such thing.

'I can be judgemental,' Kat admitted. 'Perhaps it shows in my expression. You have many admirable qualities, Lovell.'

'I do?' Surprised, he turned to look at her and saw amusement and, under that, a steady, unsettling, watchfulness.

'You have intelligence, a willingness to work hard, occasional humour. You treat your staff well, you take your responsibilities seriously.'

'I thank you for such a glowing report,' he said, torn between being flattered and nettled. 'And what is there in the balance in my disfavour?'

'You are a lawyer,' she said simply, her gaze steady on the long view down the valley. 'And like all lawyers, you persecuted those less strong, simply at the whim of your employer.'

'We are back to my regrettable lack of romance, I assume.'

'You cannot help it, I expect,' she said in a kindly tone. 'It must be like having red hair, or blue eyes.'

As he opened his mouth to retort she flopped back on the blanket, staring upwards.

'Look how lovely the sky is this morning. What kind of clouds are those?'

'I have no idea.' To his surprise Will found he was lying down, too, the sketch pad at his side, the pages ruffling in the light, warm breeze. 'You will have to ask a librarian, if you can find one, and they will look it up. Surely there is a book on the subject.'

She gave a little gasp of laughter and suddenly he found his irritation ebb away. It *was* a beautiful morning, the sky was blue with those strange little white clouds, looking as though cherubs were blowing puffs from celestial pipes. This place belonged to him and, just now, he was lying on a blanket in the open air with bird song all around and an attractive—if confusing—woman next to him.

Something touched his hand and Will realised that he had reached out, and so had Kat, at the same moment. Their fingers brushed, curled together, clung.

He turned his head slowly and found that she was looking at him, those hazel eyes a deep and rather lovely green that seemed to catch both sunshine and shadows and trap them there in fathomless depths.

'Those are not the eyes of a woman who dislikes me,' he said.

'No,' she agreed after a moment, her voice a little strained. 'But they may be the eyes of one who is having very dangerous thoughts.'

Already his body was heavy with need, tight with the effort to control it. Will rolled on to his side, facing her. 'Irresistible thoughts?'

'I hope not,' Kat said seriously but, as she spoke, she curled over towards him, her free hand reaching to touch his cheek. 'But we could find out?' she added, frowning, as though confused by her own words.

Will caught her in his arms, rolled so that he was above her, his weight on his elbows, his body cradled between her thighs, his legs tangled in the folds of her habit.

A foolish garment for seduction, he thought, then told himself that he was not in the business of seducing virgins and, surely, Kat was one—and what the devil was he doing now in that case?

Satisfying my curiosity, a wicked little voice in his head said, nudging aside his conscience.

And satisfying hers as well, it seemed. Kat's mouth opened, warm and generous under his, and she wrapped her arms around his shoulders, her fingers exploring the nape of his neck in a way that had him exerting every ounce of self-control in an effort not to rip at the fastenings of her jacket.

Will thrust with his tongue and, after a tiny start of surprise, she answered him, hers tangling and challenging in return, bold and brave and, he realised as he sank into the glorious warm femininity of her—innocent.

Yes, she knew what this was about, but it was new to her and he should stop now.

Now, he reminded himself, perhaps a minute later as his hand found her right breast and she sighed into his mouth. *Now, while you still can.*

Will rolled away and lay panting, half on, half off the blanket.

'That,' he said when he recovered his breath, 'was a very bad idea.'

Chapter Seventeen

Don't stop. Please don't stop.

Katherine sat up and her head spun. She drew up her knees and rested her forehead on them, arms clamped around, as though she could disappear into a tight bundle, somehow safely containing all her tumbling emotions.

I am in love with him.

'That was a very bad idea,' Lovell said, his voice harsh.

Katherine lifted her head, but found she could not look at him. 'Certainly, it was,' she managed to say after a moment.

Was falling in love ever a good idea? This, most definitely, was a disaster.

'I apologise,' he added. It sounded as though he meant it, as though he was regretting those few frantic minutes very much.

'There is no need. It was…mutual.'

There was a kestrel hovering over the marsh below, focused on something far beneath it. Something small and quivering and fearful, no doubt.

Like my heart.

'You are an innocent. I do not seduce innocents.'

That shook her out of her frozen state and she turned to stare at him 'I am not an innocent. I knew perfectly well what we were doing.'

'In theory, no doubt.' He was lying at the far edge of the blanket now, eyes closed, mouth hard. 'You are a virgin.' It was almost an accusation.

'Yes.'

'And in my employment. My responsibility.'

The kestrel stooped like a bullet and vanished into the tall grasses. Something had probably just died.

Katherine kept her lips tight closed. Anything she said might betray her and she had already betrayed herself, and her father, by falling in love with this man.

Lovell was still speaking and she made herself listen. 'My honour demands that I protect you, not ravish you.'

At which point, mercifully, Katherine lost her temper, although with whom, she could not have said.

'That is, of course, excellent. As long as *your* honour is satisfied, nothing else matters,' she snapped.

He sat up abruptly and they glared at each other.

She swallowed hard, fighting back all the words that were clamouring to be said. Instead she remarked politely, 'Your neckcloth is under your right ear.'

'You have two buttons undone,' he countered, equally helpfully.

Who smiled first, Katherine was never certain. Perhaps it was simultaneous. And then they were laughing.

'We are two healthy adults who, apparently, find each other attractive,' she said when she had recovered herself a little. 'It was not wise to test our willpower like that. Thank you for ending it.'

Lovell ran one hand over his face as though to scrub away his feelings of guilt. 'You are generous. I deserve a slapped face at the very least.'

I love you. No amount of slapping is going to make that right, ever again.

After a moment, Katherine shrugged. 'As I said, we are adults.'

She shuddered to think of the consequences if they had made love. What if Lovell had decided he was honour-bound to offer to marry her? Or he thought that as she was so loose in her morals she should become his mistress? Katherine had no idea which was a worse prospect—to find herself in a marriage brought about solely because of 'duty' or for the man she loved to so misunderstand her as to offer a *carte blanche*.

But now she was in love with her enemy, the man who had ruined her father, the man she had vowed to revenge herself on.

What was the right thing to do? She knew now that he could be trusted not to take advantage of a woman foolish enough to offer herself to him. Should she tell him about the ruby, have faith that he would accept her father's innocence, his cousin's lies and the part he himself had played in her father's disgrace? Or was she asking too much, blinded by her own feelings for the man?

She must be cautious, she decided. These feelings were too new, too untried. Unreliable. She must secure the ruby, find the papers, be able to prove without doubt to Lovell that she was telling the truth.

'I have a simple picnic in these saddlebags.'

'Perhaps not,' she said, regretful. 'We should go back now, Lovell.'

'Call me Will.'

Katherine got to her feet, careful of the trailing skirts of her habit. 'That would lead to suspicions that our relationship is something it is not.'

He seemed taken aback, as though he had not considered them as part of the household, but as some separate entity. 'You are right. That was thoughtless. You have blurred my mind, but that is my fault, not yours.'

'Perhaps you should recall your mistress,' she suggested, taking one end of the blanket to help him fold and roll it.

'Delphine?' Lovell stopped, the fabric half gathered in his hands, and stared at her. 'You know, I had completely forgotten her.'

'Now that is a difficult feat, I should imagine,' Katherine said drily, collecting up his sketchbook and pencil.

Will grimaced. 'She was exceedingly hard work.'

Will. I wish I could use his name. I like its simplicity.

'But it had its compensations?' she asked, aware how shocking the question was.

'It did,' he admitted. 'But I find I have lost my appetite for over-rich fare. It was like dining at the Regent's dinner table for every meal. But I should not be making such thoroughly improper observations to a lady.'

'Amusing, if improper,' Katherine said, stuffing the sketchbook into the saddlebag and handing it to him.

The horses seemed glad to see them, bored, perhaps by being left so long. The big stallion snorted, stamped one hoof and then butted Lovell with his nose.

'Ajax is impatient,' he observed, tightening the girth, then moving to Katherine's mare to do the same. 'He fancies your mount, but she is not receptive.'

That is not his rider's problem, Katherine thought. *Lovell—Will—finds himself with a female who is all too receptive and he has to exercise self-restraint for both of them.*

She put her booted foot in his cupped hands and was tossed up into the saddle.

'Are you eating properly, Kat?' he demanded as she gathered up the reins and found the stirrup.

'Yes, of course. Why?'

I have not yet reached the stage of pining away for love of you. That may yet come.

'You seem lighter than when I lifted you out of our prison of statues,' Lovell said as he swung up into the saddle.

Katherine averted her eyes from the long, muscled legs. 'There is all the difference between briefly tossing me up to a saddle and having to hold me up for minutes at a time while I trample all over your head and shoulders.'

He gave a snort of amusement. 'Of all the things that I imagined myself doing when I inherited this title, tossing librarians over banisters was not one of them.'

As they rode down the hill in silence Katherine added another good quality to her mental assessment of Lovell's character. Surely virtually any aristocrat in the land who had found himself trapped in such a way would have lost his temper and shouted for help, not scrambled to freedom in a thoroughly undignified and practical manner and then been able to joke about it days later.

The scales she was using to weigh his character were tilting more and more in his favour. Only the lead weight of his treatment of her father kept the balance on the opposite side.

Her father, and who else had he ruined on behalf of his cousin, the man with the power, the man with the money? The man Lovell himself admitted was not a sane and reasonable person and yet whose orders he had followed, whose interests he had defended.

As soon as they had squelched through the marshy borders of the lake she touched her heel to the mare's side and let her run.

Behind her she heard Lovell curse. Ajax, seeing the object of his desire racing ahead, must have wanted to chase and she suspected that Lovell was in no mood to give him his head. If the master could not satisfy his desires, then he was not going to allow his mount to do so.

Although there the comparison ended. The bay mare was in no mood for the stallion's attentions and, Katherine suspected, any attempts on his part would be met with teeth and hooves. But Lovell had received no assistance from her to control the situation.

She let the mare gallop as far as the carriage drive, then trotted around to the stables where grooms came running to help her down.

'His Lordship is right behind me,' she said over her shoulder as she gathered up her long skirts and strode towards the side door into the house. The ruby was calling to her now, the desire to finally hold it in her hands almost overriding her confusion of feelings about Lovell.

Jeannie was in the dressing room when she reached her room and tutted as she helped Katherine out of the habit. 'Did you fall off, Miss Katherine? There's dry grass all over the back of this.'

'No, I sat down to admire the view from a hilltop and the grass is untended and rough. Just my plain working dress, please, Jeannie.'

She washed her hands, bundled her hair into a net and made herself walk downstairs calmly.

As she passed the study door, she could hear three male voices and slowed for a moment. It was Giles Wilmott and Mr Arnley the steward reporting progress to Will.

Lovell, you idiot, she chided herself.

'...on the moat. The underbrush is being dragged away and burned, the material they are digging out will be spread on the fields on the upper ground. It is very thin chalk there and that rich silt will benefit the crops considerably...'

Katherine hurried past, the door key tight in her hand, dodging around the dust cloths and trestles that the decorators had set up as they began painting the hallway. She paused for a moment to touch the statue of the charioteer, shrouded in dust cloths.

You know about luck—wish me luck.

At last.

The boxes were just as she had left them and she reached instinctively to close the door. But, no, that would not do. She had always made a point of working in an open room and must do so now. With her back to the opening, she sat and pulled the box towards her.

The antique clasp was complex and stiff and cost her another broken nail before she could release it. The lid with its faded impressed gold ornament opened stiffly and she held her breath.

The interior lined in faded velvet was empty.

Ridiculously, Katherine shook it, as though the jewel might be somehow hiding, but not so much as a gold link fell out. It was definitely the correct box, its interior carefully moulded to hold each element of the ornate piece in place.

With great care she placed it back on the table, then burst into tears. The storm lasted only a moment, then she wiped her eyes, blew her nose and forced herself to think.

The late Marquis would not have sold the ruby without its box—he would know as well as she did the importance of keeping the two things together—so the jewel was still somewhere in the house, perhaps with the papers that related to its acquisition. *To its theft.*

Panicking and flapping about searching everywhere would

do no good. It was known she had discovered the collection of jewellery boxes, so she must sort through them, list the contents and take them to the strongroom. Anything else would be highly suspicious.

Katherine returned to the task after luncheon and, having checked all the boxes that might just have held the Borgia Ruby, had the idea of asking the chaplain to help her as she listed the contents.

'I have noted twenty rings, five sets of necklaces and earrings and two pairs of bracelets so far,' Mr Gresham said after an hour. 'What on earth did a bachelor want with these? Surely, they are not all family pieces?'

'They are a magpie's hoard,' she said. 'He collected for the sake of collecting, of owning. It seems he did not even wish to display what he had acquired—merely to know that he had all this was enough until he had the urge to buy something else.'

'Poor soul,' the chaplain said compassionately. 'An empty life, indeed.'

'Indeed,' Katherine echoed. However, though her feelings about Lovell were shifting and becoming more nuanced, she could not find one ounce of sympathy or forgiveness for his late cousin. And Will Lovell had aided him in all his bullying, spiteful prosecutions.

The two of them carried the first stack of boxes to the strongroom, set out on trays instead of bundled into the buckets, and Giles opened the heavy door for them.

'Did you find anything of interest?' he asked as they were arranging the final items on the shelves along with Katherine's inventory.

'They all need assessing by a good jeweller—Rundle, Bridge and Rundle, the royal jewellers, for example,' she said. 'I suspect some pieces are very good. If Lovell wants to pay for clearing and landscaping his lakes, then he need look no further than what we have just brought in.'

'A string of pearls for a string of lakes?' It was Lovell, materialising silently behind her.

Katherine fumbled with the last box that she was straightening on the shelf before she turned to him.

'Some of these were empty,' she said, gesturing to the ones she had put at the end. 'Have you any idea what your cousin might have done with the contents? I am rather concerned to think of valuable pieces unprotected by their cases.'

'Well, he didn't lavish them on opera dancers or courtesans,' Lovell said.

Giles cleared his throat. 'Er, he was not interested?'

Katherine knew what he was implying. She'd had an uncle who, her mother had explained, was not 'the marrying kind'.

'No idea,' Lovell said wryly. 'But I suspect that most women aren't prepared to sit around being items in a collection to be gloated over and ignored as human beings. Especially those who were lovely enough to attract his collector's eye. They would have far better prospects with gentlemen of equal wealth who would give them a much better time.'

Mr Gresham cleared his throat and shifted, clearly uncomfortable at the turn the conversation was taking.

Katherine caught Lovell's gaze and saw he was thinking exactly what she was—thank goodness the young cleric had not encountered Delphine de Frayne. She bit her lip to stop the laughter that was bubbling up at the mental image that evoked and Lovell turned away, coughing.

'Come and see the hall, Kat,' he said and strode away without waiting for an answer.

She ran after him and found him around the corner, leaning against the wall and laughing.

'Whatever would Delphine have made of him, do you think?' he managed to choke out after a moment.

'Breakfast,' Katherine said crisply. 'And probably dinner, too. She would have made a dead set at him, just because she could, or because she wanted to make you jealous,' Katherine speculated. 'He is very good looking, after all.'

'He is that attractive?'

'Goodness, yes. An archangel just waiting for a wicked woman to push him over the edge into darkness. I expect that is why the bishop sent him to us—he would be stalked unmercifully in a parish, poor thing.'

I said, sent him to us, *not* to you, she thought, wondering if Lovell had noticed her slip, but, if he had, he made no comment.

'And he is a very nice man. I like him very much,' she added.

'Just as long as he doesn't send us any more handsome clerics in need of sanctuary. One is more than enough,' Will said with no humour in his voice.

'Now, come and see what you think of the new paint,' he demanded and the coldness had gone as though it had never been. 'They have just cleared the ladders away.'

He caught her hand and pulled her towards the front of the house and Katherine made no effort to free herself. His hand was strong and warm, with rider's callouses rough against her softer skin. She could feel his pulse against hers and a wave of longing swept over her. It was all she could do to let her hand lie passive in his and not to twine her fingers into his.

'Close your eyes,' Lovell said as they neared the archway into the hall.

Blind, she allowed herself to be led to where she guessed the front door was, then he turned, so their back was to it.

'Now you can look, Kat.'

Katherine blinked. It was so much lighter, the dingy old walls painted a light creamy buff, although she hardly noticed that because facing them from his niche, pale and timeless against the blue of the Aegean Sea, stood the charioteer.

'Oh. Oh, *Will.*'

'Thank you for finding him, Kat. I could so easily have called in some dealer who would have taken all of those statues and never told me what a wonder I had.'

'He would have taken your nymph as well,' she said, teasing a little, because she was embarrassed by the emotion she was feeling.

'You are unkind to mock my nymph. She looks very well by her little pool on the terrace.'

'I imagine she has great appeal to gentlemen.' The crouching figure possessed a very pert backside and an expression which showed she was well aware of the fact.

'She is very lovely, but she is only stone and has no heart. I prefer flesh-and-blood beauty, Kat.'

And that puts me in my place, she thought, catching a glimpse of herself in the mirror that hung facing the foot of the stairs. *A very ordinary young woman. Perfectly acceptable looks, perfectly common or garden colouring and features. Well past the age of being eligible for anything much except genteel employment. Very firmly on the shelf. Just because a handsome aristocrat who is missing his mistress decides to kiss you, almost makes love to you, that is nothing to be proud of. There is no foundation to build castles in the air upon.*

'A penny for them.'

'What?' She almost jumped. Lovell was still holding her hand.

'A penny for your thoughts.'

'Nothing. I mean, all I was thinking was that this light buff colour would be perfect for the interior of the temple folly. And you are holding my hand.' She gave it a little tug.

'So I am,' he said, continuing to do so. 'I had no desire to put you to the blush, Kat.'

'You have not,' she protested.

'Then why are you that charming shade of pink?' He lifted their joined hands, kissed the tips of her fingers where they emerged from his hold and then released her.

'Because you are flirting with me,' she said hotly, turned on her heel and fled.

Faintly, from behind her, she heard Lovell's, 'Damnation', but she did not stop until she reached the safety of the library.

Inside all was blessed calm: a housemaid polishing the atlas stands, Peter the footman sitting in front of a pile of dusty almanacs, soft brush in hand, and one of the estate carpenter's assistants measuring a broken cupboard door.

This was her world: books, ideas held between their covers, emotions described, but safely contained—and no perilously attractive marquises in sight.

Chapter Eighteen

'Damnation.' Of all the idiotic things to do, to kiss Kat's hand like that when only hours earlier things had almost gone so disastrously wrong between them that he might have ended the day discussing the arrangements for a wedding with his chaplain.

She wouldn't expect it and he had not the slightest suspicion now that Katherine Jenson was out to entrap him. Oh, no, she had no need to—he was proving quite careless enough without any assistance from her.

'My lord? Is the new paintwork not to your liking?'

Will turned to find Arnley regarding him anxiously. 'I think it is excellent work,' he said. 'I was merely remembering something. Nothing to do with redecoration at all.'

'Are there any other rooms I can have the men work on, my lord?'

Will almost said that he had made no decision, then thought of the library. It would please Kat to have that decorated, surely? Suddenly it felt important to hold out some kind of olive branch.

'Yes. Ask Miss Jenson what she wishes to be done in the library.'

'Certainly, my lord.'

Will watched his steward bustle off towards the library,

thinking vaguely that the man walked like a partridge, head forward, backside sticking out. The comparison made him smile.

'Good news, sir?' It was Wilmott, the inevitable papers clutched in one hand.

'Just a foolish thought about game birds. What have you there to plague me with?'

'A response from the landscape gardener that I approached—the one that Lord Larchfield recommended. If you recall, I wrote to His Lordship on your behalf, having read his article in the *Gentleman's Magazine* about the work he had done at his Shropshire estate.'

'And what does he say?'

'That he will be arriving as soon as possible with his assistant and will draw up proposals and costings for you.'

'The man's eager,' Will said, suspicious.

'He writes that the prospect of improving the estate of so notable a personage would be an honour. He professes himself greatly stimulated by the grounds that, from what I described, offer such scope for radical transformation.'

'Hmm. The problem is, I have no idea what work of this kind should cost. He could lead me by the nose.'

'Ah.' Wilmott was looking decidedly smug. 'I have taken the precaution of making enquiries about works carried out at a number of estates by a variety of landscapers and have a very fair idea of what is entailed.'

When Will raised an eyebrow he added, 'We secretaries do our best to help each other out—where it can be done without compromising the private affairs of our employers, naturally.'

'Excellent work, Wilmott. Now, write to the three most prestigious London jewellers and tell them each to send someone to assess the jewellery Miss Jenson has located. I want it valued and I want to know what they will offer for it.'

'You intend to sell it all, sir?'

'No, but there is a great deal I will not wish to keep. I can see no point in hoarding antiquated pieces no future marchioness will wish to wear. Although I suppose somewhere in all this chaos there are papers relating to which items are entailed, so nothing can be sold until those have been identified.'

It was about time he started thinking about this theoretical marchioness who would be wearing the family gems, instead of worrying about his librarian and his decidedly inconvenient attraction to her.

Redecorating the library should please Kat. Will caught himself up. His future *wife* would probably not care if he had the library painted purple and green. What she—his *wife*—would want would be a delightful bedchamber, a boudoir and the public rooms done out in the very latest fashion.

Which probably meant being formal and uncomfortable, not a place where a man could fall into a sagging, but comfortable, armchair after a ride without having to change out of breeches and boots. That was what he had now, a pleasantly informal retreat where his household gathered around in the evening before dinner with embroidery, books and the chess board.

Mrs Downe and Mrs Goodman between them had transformed the drawing room, the smaller parlours and the dining room into calming places to be, even though the furniture was old fashioned, the fabrics faded and the scheme of decoration left much to be desired.

Comfortable and homely. He would just have to make the most of that while he had it. Which made him think of his own bedchamber. It was decidedly gloomy, cluttered and cramped.

It was not the master suite, of course. He had taken one look at his cousin's rooms and shuddered, shutting the door firmly on them. Now, having seen what could be done, he wondered whether they had possibilities.

The windows faced south-west with what would be a fine prospect across the park and the new lower lake when that was completed and the rooms were probably spacious, once nine-tenths of the contents were removed, with a bedchamber, a dressing room and a small sitting room.

Tempting, if he could only remove all traces of Cousin Randolph. And, of course, the adjoining suite would have to be prepared for his bride.

Will mentally shied away from that thought. Presumably there were fashionable London decorators one could employ to give one's rooms the very latest touch. Let Wilmott find one of those and give him his head; he would probably enjoy it more than searching for drainage experts or tabulating crop yields.

Meanwhile, perhaps he should let Kat loose in the master suite. She would enjoy exploring the contents and perhaps retrieving some hidden gems in the process. In fact, now he came to think about it, that was the most likely place for the late Marquis to have secreted the jewels missing from their boxes, if they were special items he wanted to gloat over.

Which reminded him that there had been no sign of the pride of his cousin's collection, the Borgia Ruby. Randolph had shaken off the claims of that double-dealing agent, the one whose relations with Bonapartists proved his undoing, in order to secure the title to it. Or, rather, he had set Will on the case.

Kat had no need to warn him about the motives of dealers—that one had the brass neck to maintain that he had merely received a deposit from Randolph when, clearly, the document that his cousin had shown Will had stated it was a sale, even though it was possibly at a bargain price.

But then, the man had been, if not a traitor, someone with very dubious connections and he had probably realised too late that he had been too eager and had sold at a low price. After that he had stopped at nothing, including perjury, to claim a higher return.

Strange that there had been no sign of that jewel yet, but if it was in the house, he could rely upon Kat to ferret it out. She might not be a jewellery expert, but she would find that a particularly interesting piece, he was certain.

He would tell her about the suite over luncheon, by which time she would, perhaps, have recovered from his clumsiness in the hallway. It had broken the magic of the charioteer and he was angry with himself about that. This might please her.

It did not occur to him until he was halfway down the stairs that it was not usual for marquises to worry about the happiness or otherwise of their librarians.

Will—*no*, Lovell. *Stop thinking about him like that!*—came in to the small dining room as Katherine was discussing tapestries with Elspeth.

Her companion seemed to have developed a passion for textiles that matched Katherine's mother's for lace. Having unearthed the hangings from under the stairs where Katherine and Lovell had been trapped, she was lamenting her lack of knowledge.

'I have been studying that book on tapestries you found for me in the library, dear, but it is such a vast subject, I feel most inadequate. The other fabrics are much easier—I can tell what material they have been made of and guess at ages from the designs and so forth, but tapestry is another matter.'

'I know they were exceedingly expensive when they were made, at least, the Tudor ones I have read about,' Katherine said. She broke off as Lovell took his place at the table.

'Is this something else that we need to summon an expert from London to deal with?' he asked.

'I fear so. Or even one from the Low Countries if these are Flemish,' Elspeth said, passing him the bread rolls. 'But for the moment I want to have them aired and hung up somewhere dry and clean so that the creases can begin to drop and we can see if there is any damage from the moth.'

'Might I suggest the chapel?' Mr Gresham said suddenly, from his place at the far end of the table where he had been quietly working his way through a large plate of cheese and cold meats. 'It is clean and dry now and has long expanses of windowless wall.'

Katherine helped herself to butter and left Elspeth to enthusiastically engage with the chaplain on the subject of how the tapestries could be hung and whether they were of religious subjects and therefore suitable as a permanent feature in the chapel.

There was no sign of Giles Wilmott, which left her rather uncomfortably aware of Lovell carving himself slices of cold roast chicken with the air of a man who has not seen meat for a week. There was nothing wrong with his appetite after this morning's events, which was more than she could say about hers.

She broke her roll into small pieces and began to butter them slowly.

'I have been thinking where the missing jewellery might

be,' he said casually as he poured himself ale from the jug by his place.

Katherine dropped her butter knife and thanked the footman who picked it up for her while she forced her expression into one of polite interest and reminded herself that several of the boxes had been empty, not just the one that contained the Borgia Ruby.

'Really? There is a safe or locked chest that you have recollected, perhaps?'

'No, none that I know of. But it occurred to me that if there were items my cousin wished to keep by him, his suite of rooms would be the most likely.'

'Surely you would have noticed them by now?'

'I am not using the Marquis's suite,' Lovell said, adding pickled red cabbage to his plate before attacking the chicken.

'No?' Katherine reached for the water jug, gave a mental shrug and poured herself ale instead. She suspected she was going to need it.

'When you see it, you will understand. If you are not busy in the library, I was hoping you could deal with that suite next, as the ground floor is now in good order.'

When she hesitated, he added, 'I will be out all afternoon. I must start making calls on my neighbours or they will consider me as eccentric and unsociable as Randolph.'

'Certainly, I will have a look. I need to speak to Mr Arnley about paint colours in the library, but that should take little time, as only a small area of wall is exposed and the ceiling is very plain.'

'Thank you. You might also look at the Marchioness's suite next door as well, although I doubt my cousin ever set foot in there. It seems to be full of all the things he wanted moved to make way for his own acquisitions.'

'That could be very interesting.' Katherine looked up and met his gaze, smiled politely, then found herself unable to break the connection.

There was something in Lovell's eyes that held her, something she could not read. Not desire, she knew that look now.

No, this was rueful, perhaps a little puzzled, as though he was looking at something he did not quite understand.

Perhaps it was simply that he was the archetypal male baffled by women and not understanding why she was not making a great fuss and to-do about what had happened between them that morning.

Or perhaps, she thought with a sudden stab of alarm, perhaps he could read something in her expression that betrayed her feelings for him. He had sensed her distrust at first, however careful she had been to hide it. Now could he see the opposite?

How ghastly if he realised she loved him. Was that better or worse than him thinking she wanted to marry him?

Stop thinking about marriage. Stop yearning for what you cannot have.

Katherine took a too-hasty gulp of ale, coughed, apologised, flapped her napkin and, by the time she had recovered, Lovell was assuring Mr Gresham and Elspeth that they could do whatever they wished with the chapel walls and the tapestries.

She indulged herself by studying his profile while he was distracted. Will Lovell was a good-looking man, she admitted to herself. He was not pattern-book-handsome like Quintus Gresham, but he had a more masculine type of beauty that relied on strong bone structure and underlying character and vigour. He would still be a striking figure when he was an old man, looking distinguished in a magnificent family portrait.

Along with his well-bred marchioness and their brood of fine children.

'What is wrong, Kat?'

'I—I was thinking that I haven't seen a family portrait gallery, which I'd have expected, given that this is the main seat,' she improvised hastily.

'The Long Gallery runs along the west side of the house. I had a quick look at it and was plunged into gloom by the sight of so many portrayals of the family nose. Or the chin.'

'Which do you have?'

'Neither, I am happy to say. My father inherited the nose, so I suppose it might appear in my offspring—hopefully the boys, not the girls. Randolph had both the chin and the nose. Go and look for yourself some time.'

'I will do,' she promised, intrigued and also depressed at the thought of Will's potential family.

Lovell, Lovell, Lovell, she chanted silently.

She dared not let herself think of him so familiarly in case she said the name aloud and somehow betrayed herself.

Lovell rode off after luncheon in elegant tailcoat, immaculate breeches and highly polished boots to make his calls. Giles remarked that Petrie, the valet, was smug because at last his talents had been utilised.

'He lives in hope that His Lordship will throw a dinner party and his genius with neckcloth and curling tongs will finally be appreciated.'

'Curling tongs?' Katherine stopped at the foot of the stairs, one hand one the newel post and stared at him. 'Lovell?'

'A valet may dream. I am off to discuss with Mrs Goodman where we can accommodate a landscaping expert and his assistant. They arrive tomorrow, along with the expert in water management and drains who will supervise the moat repairs. I only hope His Lordship appreciates the disruption we are heading for.'

'Do landscape and drainage experts eat *en famille?*'

'I imagine so, given how much they charge. I understand they rate themselves as highly as society portraitists. The assistants, I believe, are accommodated below stairs.'

'It should please Cook, at any rate. I understand she considers her talents as wasted as Petrie does and is pining for Lovell to throw dinner parties.'

They exchanged grins as Giles took himself off to the study and Katherine climbed the stairs in search of the master suite.

She found it after a few false starts. It looked like something from one of Horace Walpole's Gothic tales, hung with gloomy fabrics at the windows and around the bed. It made her shiver with its musty atmosphere and it gave her the uneasy feeling that she was in a nest of something dark and brooding.

Katherine pulled the bell cord by the bed, half expecting no response, but both Arnold and George were at the door within minutes.

'Strewth, thought it were a ghost, Miss Jenson,' George said. 'Nobody's rung from here since His late Lordship died.'

'Well, the current Marquis has decided that this is the next room to be cleared. Please can you fetch ladders and remove all these curtains so I can see what I am doing. You had best give them to Mrs Goodman and Mrs Downe, although whether they will thank me for them remains to be seen,' she added when Arnold shook out one curtain and started sneezing.

While they were away looking for ladders, she opened the windows wide and could appreciate why this was the main suite. The view was already fine and, when the lakes were cleared, would be delightful.

She turned as thumping and some muffled cursing heralded the return of the footmen with the ladders and stood aside as the curtains fell in clouds of dust.

'His Lordship never liked anyone coming in here, you see, Miss,' George explained apologetically. 'I don't know when it last got cleaned properly.'

Once all the fabric was removed she set them to taking down the pictures which she suspected might be quite good seventeenth-century Dutch and Flemish works.

'Where shall we put them?' Peter asked, eyeing a somewhat fleshy nude inadequately clad in a few inches of gauze.

'In the Long Gallery, please. Stack them carefully so the canvas isn't damaged.'

Left alone, and with some light to work by, Katherine began to explore properly. Where, if she was a collector and a hoarder, would she put the small articles she wanted to gloat over?

The bedside tables yielded nothing but some literature which made her raise her eyebrows and set to one side, a sticky jar of something labelled *A Sovereign Remedy for Congestion of the Lungs* and several auction catalogues. Tipping them up and removing all the drawers revealed no secrets.

She eyed the bed, a very fine half-tester which had, thank goodness, been stripped of its covering down to the mattress. No sign of slits in the side, nothing underneath as far as she could slide in a groping hand on either side. The pillows, when shaken, produced feathers but nothing else.

Would an elderly man want to be hopping in and out of bed to examine his treasures? The panelled headboard produced nothing, but the ornate tops of the posts at the foot, each just sticking up a foot above the height of the mattress, looked promising. She twisted and turned the one on the right. Nothing. The one on the left yielded immediately and lifted away, to reveal a hole down into the hollowed-out post and the top of a narrow drawstring bag.

Katherine pulled it out and upended it on the mattress. Necklaces slithered out, snakes of diamonds, emeralds and sapphires. A handsome Renaissance medallion fell on to them and then, flashing blood red in the afternoon sunlight as it flooded in through the window, the Borgia Ruby.

Chapter Nineteen

It lay in her palm, beautiful and strangely sinister, this jewel that had belonged to the lovely fair-haired daughter of a pope, a woman who had been labelled a poisoner and was probably no more than the pawn of the powerful, dangerous men around her.

Blood-red in its elaborate Renaissance setting, the twisted baroque pearls hanging from it like frozen tear drops, it seemed to pulse as the light hit it.

A living thing and, like so many great jewels, a thing of danger and desire.

There was a sound behind her and, without conscious thought, Katherine slipped the ruby into her pocket, then turned to see Lovell standing in the doorway.

I have done it now. I am a thief.

Or she would be in Will Lovell's eyes, never mind that his cousin had kept the pendant when all he had paid was a surety deposit.

'You have found them, Kat? The missing jewels?'

'Most of them, I believe,' she said, wondering at how calm she sounded. 'I didn't count the empty boxes. These are certainly finer than the pieces that were still in their cases—look at this pendant with its fabulous enamel work.' The ruby seemed to be growing heavier as she spoke. Heavier and hot, as though it was burning through her pocket with guilt.

It isn't theft. It is ours—mine and Mama's—and this man helped steal it and ruined Papa.

Somehow that no longer seemed enough.

It's because I love him, she thought miserably. *Now I have no idea where my loyalties lie, although I know where they ought to be.*

'Is something wrong?' Lovell came in and picked up the pendant she had indicated, but his attention was on her face.

'Oh, it is this room—so gloomy, it is enough to cast anyone into a depression. Taking the hangings down helped and let in some light and I had the paintings moved to the Long Gallery in case that revealed any secret cupboards in the walls. Some of the paintings are very good, I suspect.'

'And did it reveal any cupboards?' He looked around the room and she noticed that the wind had brought out the colour in his face and his hair was tousled from where he had carelessly removed his hat.

'I haven't looked. These were in the bed post. Did you have a pleasant afternoon?'

'The ride was stimulating, the calls, not so enjoyable.' He pushed his hand through his hair, disordering it even more, and she clenched her hands against the need to smooth it.

'I am not enjoying being the local lion and the target of so many hopeful mamas,' he added, walking away to scrutinise the nearest wall.

'An unmarried marquis under the age of ninety and in possession of both his wits and his teeth?' Katherine said over her shoulder as she went to scan the surface of the opposite wall. 'You might as well have a target painted on your back.'

The surface was plaster, not panelling and, other than the marks where the paintings had hung, there was nothing to be seen. She began to open drawers, finding folders of etchings and watercolours, some documents in handwriting that she thought might be Tudor and trays of coins.

'These are Egyptian.' Lovell had opened the cabinets on the other side of the room to reveal an army of small figurines, pieces of what looked like wall plaster painted with vivid birds and stylised plants and alabaster statues. 'More treasures.' He sighed. 'And what to do about this suite...'

'I haven't looked at the other rooms, but this could be lovely. Take everything out, paint it in pale blues and greens to reflect the park outside, have curtains and bed hangings just a little darker. Choose paintings that you like and just a few pieces of furniture. Buy a new mattress—this one looks as though it is an ancient Egyptian piece.'

He laughed at her attempt at humour and opened a door. 'Very well, you have convinced me. This is the dressing room. I'll tell Petrie to organise and decorate that as he wishes. And here's the sitting room. Hmm. I think we had better remove the mummy cases.'

Katherine came to look. 'Goodness. Six of them.' Aloof, ancient, unreadable faces stared back at her. The only furniture was an armchair facing the cases, as though the late Marquis had sat and conversed with them.

'Do you think they answered back?' Lovell said with a visible shudder, clearly thinking the same thing. 'They are beautiful workmanship and they are definitely leaving this house!'

Katherine tried the remaining door and found herself in another bedchamber. She wriggled past crowded furniture and flung open the curtains.

'Oh, how pretty.' It was a charming room in the style of the previous century, all white and soft blue and hung with light, flowery, embroidered fabrics at the windows and around the bed. All kinds of furniture of the same period had been jammed in, so it was like a lumber room, but the essential light-hearted elegance still shone through the clutter and the dust.

She heard Lovell come in and turned, facing him across the width of the bed. 'See?' She ran a hand over the bed covering. 'It is all hand-embroidered. Exquisite.'

'Exquisite,' he echoed and she looked up to find him watching her with an intense look in those dark eyes. There was desire there, she knew him well enough now to see that, but there was something else—liking, perhaps, or affection?

The ruby in her pocket suddenly felt like a lead weight. Will

Lovell trusted her, liked her—and she was betraying that trust, lying to him day after day. If she had known him for what he truly was, from the beginning, then she would have told him the truth, told him what had happened with her father and his cousin, trusted his integrity and judgement to asses her story fairly.

But it was too late now.

Kat stood by the elegant bed, vivid and interested, wanting to share her pleasure at this charming room with him. She looked so right there, naturally graceful, bubbling with an intelligence that he had never expected to find combined with such femininity.

So right.

What was the matter with him, gritting his teeth and forcing himself to plan for a Season negotiating the shoals of the London Marriage Mart in search of a suitable bride. He had her here.

The thought hit him like a blow and he sat down abruptly on the nearest chair.

True, he would be expected to marry an aristocrat, but, damn it, dukes married actresses, so why couldn't a marquis marry a perfectly respectable young lady who might be a commoner, but whose upbringing had clearly been perfectly respectable?

Kat would be a perfect choice for him. There was mutual desire; she was already taking an enthusiastic interest in transforming the house and estate; she was healthy, intelligent and would make a wonderful mother, he was certain of that.

Their eyes met across the width of the bed and he saw her change, the enthusiasm ebbing away as she turned a little pale, an expression that he was shocked to read as shame crossing her face.

For a second Will was confused, then he realised what Kat must be thinking. He had almost seduced her there on the grass that morning, he had made her uncomfortable by kissing her hand, and now he was staring at her across a bed with goodness knew what visible in his expression.

Kat was a virgin, a respectable young woman, and she had let herself be carried away for a reckless moment. Now she was ashamed, embarrassed and wary of him. It was his fault, his responsibility and, somehow, he had to make it right.

What could he say? *I'm looking at you with a view to marriage?*

She would imagine that his conscience had driven him to it after that passionate incident. Or perhaps that he was attempting to complete his seduction with false promises and would cast her off once he had succeeded.

Somehow he had to retrieve the situation. He stood and walked across to the window, pretended to be looking at the view when all he could see was that look of shame and hurt in her eyes.

'I am sure Mrs Downe and Mrs Goodman can restore this suite. It is, as you, say, charming. Perhaps you could have a word with them about it and instruct Arnley as you see fit about any works that are required. I am sure, with your combined taste, it will make a fitting set of rooms for a marchioness.'

'Certainly, as you wish,' Kat said, her voice colourless.

'And I will tell Wilmott to write to the trustees of the British Museum about those mummy cases,' he added. 'You have no need to trouble yourself about those.'

'Very well. I will continue the inventory for both suites and also move any books I find to the library and any more small valuable items to the strongroom.'

When he looked around Kat was already half out of the door and into the master bedchamber. There was not a great deal to be read from either the set of her shoulders or her businesslike tone.

'In that case I will leave you to it,' he said, opening the door on to the corridor. One thing was certain, he wasn't following Kat into any more bedchambers in the near future. 'Until dinner time.'

There was a vague mumble from the other room. He closed the door behind himself and leaned back against the panels. Now what to do?

Court her, of course. Court her in the most respectful, proper manner. Do not be alone with her, do not follow her into bedchambers, kiss her hand—touch her. Somehow convince her that your intentions are pure—

No, they are not, his conscience reminded him sharply. *You want her. You want her naked on that flower-strewn coverlet, her limbs relaxed into pleasure, her face soft with the after-math of your lovemaking, her skin pale against that green silk.*

Very well, he must hide his intentions, Will resolved. This would be the most proper wooing in the history of courtship and Kat would never have to meet his gaze with that look in her eyes again.

Katherine wondered if she was going to be sick. She felt strangely hot and her stomach churned. She made herself go back into the Marquis's bedchamber and sat down on one of the heavy carved chairs until the wave of nausea passed.

What should she do? She fingered the outline of the ruby through the folds of her skirts. She could hide it somewhere and then 'discover' it—preferably with a witness. Or she could keep it until she had found the incriminating papers, the docu-ments that proved it had been obtained by a deception and the court case that had ruined her father had been a fraud from start to finish. Or she could find it again, let Lovell have it and still seek the papers.

Whatever she did, other than pursuing this to the bitter end, would mean she was betraying her father and bringing more grief to her mother who was relying on her to clear his name. And anything other than walking away leaving Will Lovell with the gem was to betray the trust of the man she loved.

There really was no choice, she decided after half an hour of wrestling with her thoughts. She was nothing to Will other than a useful servant who had provoked some desire in him. There was nothing between them *to* betray, other than the duty of an employee to her employer, and she was not stealing, she reminded herself, simply retrieving what was hers.

He would be angry, annoyed that his actions on behalf of his cousin and client had been shown to be less than honourable, but that was all, surely?

She knew him too well to believe that he would harm her vindictively and what else could he do to her, after all?

Nothing, except break my heart, she thought with a shiver.

But she couldn't sit there all day. She got up and went to her room, wrapped the ruby in a large handkerchief and tucked it into the middle of a skein of knitting wool. She had brought her basket of knitting with no very firm intention of actually doing any, although ladies were expected to occupy themselves with some hand work in the evening, so Mama had added it to her bags. Now it served as the ideal hiding place—out in plain sight on the dresser.

'I wonder if you ladies would care to drive out with me tomorrow,' Lovell said when the soup plates had been cleared at dinner time. 'My coachman informs me that he has had the landau he found in the carriage house cleaned. It is rather an elderly vehicle, but he assures me it is perfectly roadworthy.'

'That would be delightful,' Elspeth said. 'Are you making calls, or perhaps visiting some of the tenants?'

'No, I propose merely an excursion for pleasure. Tompkins the gardener has a reputation as a weather prophet, apparently, and he forecasts a fine day. Wilmott, Gresham—why do you both not come, too, on horseback?'

Both men agreed and began to discuss possible destinations, but it seemed that Lovell had already made a decision.

'I propose driving westwards. There are fine beechwoods and some splendid views across the Vale of Aylesbury, I understand,' he said. 'We can take a picnic luncheon.'

Why is he doing this?

Katherine smiled and nodded and did her best to seem enthusiastic about the plan, but the thought of the ruby, hidden in her room, of the pressing need to find the papers that would prove the deception, nagged at her. She could not afford to waste time now, not when she had the incriminating gem in her possession.

It was an effort to look interested and to contribute to the discussion that Giles began about the study of rocks. 'There is so much to learn,' he enthused. 'I have been greatly interested in the writings of James Hutton, the Scottish geologist, on the formation of the earth. The fine view we will see tomorrow is due to the great ridge of chalk on whose slopes we are now. Mr Hutton proposes…'

'You were very quiet about tomorrow's expedition,' Elspeth said when they finally retired to their own sitting room.

'Was I?' Katherine asked vaguely. 'I do hope you were not offended by Giles's enthusiasm for Mr Hutton and his belief that the earth is hundreds of thousands of years old,' she added in the hope of turning the subject.

'Archbishop Ussher calculated it to have been created in the year 4004 before Christ,' Elspeth said. 'It has always seemed to me to be something impossible to calculate, especially as he was insistent that it occurred on the twenty-second day of October in that year. Not that I ever mentioned my doubts to Mr Downe, of course. He would have been most shocked.'

Katherine listened with half her attention to an amusing tale of the Bishop of Bath and Wells and his views on the likely fate of those blasphemous scientists. What on earth had possessed Lovell to propose an excursion? Sober lawyers faced with mountains of work and onerous new responsibilities did not take their entire retinue out for picnics.

Perhaps he was trying to throw her together with the two young men. Yes, that could explain it. Lovell was alarmed at the attraction for him that she had betrayed and was attempting to distract her by placing her in a relaxed, social situation with Giles and Quintus.

'Well, I am for my bed,' Elspeth announced. 'But first I will warn Jeannie that we will require light day dresses, our prettiest bonnets and sunshades. This September weather is still pleasantly warm and we must look our best as Lovell has devised such a pleasant treat for us.'

Yes, Katherine decided. She would make a real effort to look her best and she would gratify Lovell by flirting in the most unexceptional way with both young men, while treating him with solemn respect.

If he was beginning to suspect that her feelings for him went deeper than desire, that she had thoughts of entrapping him into marriage, then she must act decisively to quell those suspicions. And somehow she had to keep the love she felt hidden somewhere deep inside.

Chapter Twenty

'Ladies, how delightful you both look.' Lovell stood at the foot of the staircase as Katherine and Elspeth, who had breakfasted in their rooms, descended, followed by Jeannie.

The maid was laden with parasols, shawls in case of breezes, fans in case of overheating and a basket containing all manner of items that she considered essential for ladies venturing out into the uncivilised world of the English countryside.

The party had become more elaborate, it seemed. Jeannie would join them, to see to their comfort, and she and the footmen had already been despatched with hampers, rugs and cushions to establish the picnic site, guided by one of the grooms, a local man who could recommend the perfect spot.

There was even, Jeannie had reported when she brought their breakfast, a little tent containing a close stool and a washstand for the ladies' comfort and convenience.

'Why, thank you, my lord.' Elspeth preened a little as she reached the foot of the stairs. It was not unjustified, Katherine thought. Her friend was attired in a pale green gown with darker ribbons and a ruffled hem and was wearing a pale straw poke bonnet with matching ribbons.

Katherine was wearing a new gown in jonquil yellow with white trim and a Villager straw hat with a wide satin ribbon of golden brown, both ordered from the shops Elspeth had discovered in St Albans. If she said so herself, she thought she looked rather fine.

She bobbed a curtsy as she passed Lovell and kept on, out of the front door to where the landau was drawn up and Gresham and Wilmott waited, already mounted.

'My goodness, how fine we will feel in such a carriage and with such handsome outriders to escort us,' she exclaimed, attempting to sound like her youngest cousin, Elizabeth, who was a shocking, and very successful, flirt. Mama disapproved of her and, it was true, she had many admirers, but never a declaration that she felt inclined to accept, but her charming little tricks certainly appeared to make an impression on the gentlemen.

Both riders seemed about to dismount to assist her into the carriage, but Lovell ran down the steps and they settled back into their saddles as Elspeth exclaimed at the fine appearance of the landau.

It might have been an elderly carriage, but it had been polished to a high shine and two matched dapple greys were in the shafts.

'Are those more of your late cousin's horses?' Katherine asked as Lovell turned from helping Elspeth into the open carriage and offered her his hand.

'Yes. I kept them intending to buy a coach and then discovered I possessed this. Randolph's travelling coach is not fit for service,' he added, climbing in after her and taking the backward-facing seat. 'I must purchase a chaise and, I suppose, a town carriage.'

'Oh, yes, the Marchioness will certainly require those,' she said chattily. 'Although I imagine this landau is really a town vehicle, is it not? I suppose much depends on whether the hoods are still weatherproof.'

'Quite.'

She was not certain how to interpret that. It did appear that mention of his future bride was not a particularly welcome topic, but was that because he feared she was angling for the role, or because he was not looking forward to the effort of the

Season or simply because he had no intention of discussing his private affairs?

Ignoring the nasty little pang under her left ribs, Katherine fixed a bright smile on her lips and waved to Giles Wilmott whose bay gelding was keeping pace alongside the carriage while Quintus Gresham had ridden ahead on a neat black hack.

Giles tipped his hat in response.

'What a very fine sight we must present. A fine carriage and horses, handsome young men as outriders,' she said. 'Just what the villagers expect from their new Marquis, I am sure.'

As she spoke, they began to rattle over the cobbles of the village street and Katherine looked around with interest. 'Several people have doffed their hats or curtsied.'

Looking profoundly uncomfortable, Lovell raised his hand in acknowledgment of the courtesies. Katherine kept her gaze firmly on the back of the coachman, not wanting to give the impression that she might be pretending that this was her carriage.

If it was... If I were the Marchioness, married to the man sitting opposite me...

For a moment she indulged the fantasy, mentally moving Lovell to sit beside her and furnishing the other seat with a row of children. Two boys and a girl? Two of each? They would have blue eyes and dark brown hair and, given their parents, would probably be thoroughly stubborn and a complete handful.

'The church appears to have a Norman tower,' Elspeth remarked, jerking Katherine out of her dangerous daydream.

'It does?' Lovell asked unwisely, earning himself a lecture on rounded arches and pointed Gothic arches and various infallible methods of dating churches.

Katherine, meanwhile, discovered that she could converse quite comfortably with Quintus Gresham who had fallen back to ride alongside the carriage.

'How have you found the Vicar here?' she asked. 'Is he a congenial colleague?'

'Oh, most welcoming, despite the fact that reopening the chapel has reduced his congregation. But he is a fount of information on local affairs.'

'I am so glad,' she said warmly, watching as he cantered ahead again as the road narrowed.

'About what are you glad, Katherine?'

Startled by the use of her full name, she turned and looked at Lovell. 'Why, that Quintus has found the local Vicar congenial. He is such a nice young man, it would be sad if he found himself isolated from the support of a more experienced cleric. I wonder if the Vicar has daughters.'

'You are inclined to matchmaking?' There was a sharpness in his voice as he put the question and something in his expression that made her think it was not a casual remark.

'One always wishes to see one's friends happy, although, of course, I am not so foolish as to imagine that matrimony is the answer for everybody's contentment.'

'You do not see yourself as a clerical wife?' Lovell said lightly.

'Why, what an idea!' She managed to looked confused, wished she could blush to order, but settled on fanning herself with her gloved hand. 'I am sure Elspeth would tell you that I would be a most unsuitable match for a man of the cloth, although perhaps a wife with scholarly interests....' She let her voice trail off as she looked at the riders ahead of them.

'Or perhaps your talents would best fit you for being the helpmate of a politician.' He still sounded as though he was intending to tease.

Puzzled, and vaguely suspicious, Katherine shook her head. 'I have no idea, nor do I have any strong political allegiances myself. But, as I am unlikely to encounter any politicians, the situation is unlikely to arise.'

There was just the slightest flicker of a glance to one side where Giles was now riding.

'You believe Giles has ambitions towards a government career, or taking a seat in the Commons? Goodness.' She did her best to sound thoughtful, but let a little smile curve her lips, as though she was tempted. Best not to be too obvious, perhaps. 'Who is matchmaking now?' she challenged lightly.

Lovell had the grace to colour slightly. 'I was merely jesting, although, naturally, if it is a question of the happiness of members of my staff, I would exert myself to assist.'

So, he thinks it would be a good idea to marry me off to his secretary or his chaplain, does he? Either it has not occurred to him that I would be constantly in his company if I did or he is intent on keeping me close at hand in order to... To what?

Katherine felt her smile harden. 'I have my work and I am Mama's companion,' she said, trying to sound just a little wistful.

The only man she wanted to marry was out of her reach and, apparently, amusing himself by teasing her with talk of matchmaking. It hurt, a little, but, naturally, she must be glad that Lovell no longer wanted to kiss so much as the tips of her fingers.

If she had been a more unprincipled and ruthless character, Katherine realised, she could have made an outcry about being ruined by him and demanded either marriage or a substantial sum in compensation.

No wonder Lovell had suddenly become so distant, had stopped called her Kat. This talk of marriage must mean that he had realised just how close to the wind he had been sailing in making love to her.

What is sauce for the goose is sauce for the gander, my lord.

She could be just as formal.

'What a charming drive, my lord. I had not realised how picturesque the villages were around here with their flint walls and little churches.'

As though sensing something wrong in the atmosphere, Elspeth began to talk, commenting brightly on the cottagers' gardens and the charming picture a young goose girl with her charges made on a village green.

Katherine sat back and silently watched the passing scene, responding politely to any remarks directed at her, or when Lovell offered to open her parasol in case the sun was too bright or fell to his knees to retrieve a dropped handkerchief.

They eventually reached thick beech woods, the tall, smooth greyish-green trunks rising to the thick canopy overhead. A ride had been driven through, edged by grass verges, and the carriage slowed to negotiate the uneven surface.

Fallow deer bounded away as they approached, dappled hindquarters and white tail scuts vivid against the undergrowth as the two riders cantered off in front of the carriage.

Then suddenly they were out of the woods on to short, rabbit-cropped grassland with a wide view over the Vale perhaps four hundred feet below the steep scarp they were on.

'The wagon has arrived, just ahead,' Katherine said, leaning out to look. 'It is certainly a marvellous place.'

'From what I heard, I thought it might please you,' Lovell said, then added, 'You ladies, that is.'

Was that an afterthought? Katherine descended from the carriage with Lovell's assistance and watched him thoughtfully as he handed Elspeth out. Was this a treat for both of them, or even the four, including the two men, or had he devised this for her alone and the others were some form of concealment?

But to what end? If Lovell was set on seduction, then taking his victim's chaperon and his own chaplain along was a very strange way to go about it.

She gave a mental shrug and decided to simply enjoy the outing. The sun was shining, the day was warm and the breeze that stirred the trees was soft enough to be refreshing, not cold.

Rugs had been spread out in the shade of some tall hawthorn bushes, cushions piled in abundance, the ladies' retiring tent was set up at a discreet distance and Cook herself had come along to supervise the food.

Or possibly, as Elspeth suggested in a whisper, to have herself a holiday because the footmen were certainly doing all the work while she supervised from her seat in the wagon.

Lovell established Elspeth and Katherine among the cushions, checked that they had the most pleasing view, opened parasols and went to fetch them lemonade.

'My dear,' Elspeth whispered, 'I do declare the man is courting you!'

'What? Nonsense,' she retorted sharply. 'He is paying you just as much attention and, besides, what man intent on courtship brings along the lady's chaperon and half his household?'

'A man who wishes to establish the complete honesty of his intentions,' Elspeth said. 'He impresses the chaperon with his restraint and observances of all the niceties and he impresses the lady with attentions that he hopes will be pleasing to her, while ensuring she feels quite safe from any, shall we say, *warm* behaviour.'

'And what I see is a man who wants a change of scene,' Katherine said. 'Lovell has been cooped up with all those ledgers and all the chaos that his cousin left him. If he ventures out socially, he is stalked by hopeful young ladies and their parents. He hears about this wonderful view and so what is more natural than to declare a holiday?'

She broke off as Lovell approached, a glass in each hand. 'Why, thank you.' She remembered her resolution to be formal. 'My lord.'

He quirked an eyebrow. 'Not at all, Miss Jenson. I had thought to have luncheon served in about an hour, if that would suit you, ladies?'

'Delightful,' she murmured. 'I wonder what Giles is about?'

Giles was lifting something from the rear of the wagon and called Quintus over to help him. They spent a few moments apparently unravelling something, then walked towards Elspeth and Katherine carrying something large and multi-coloured between them.

'Look what I found in a cupboard in the office,' Giles said as he reached them. 'A kite and it is a beauty. It looks a good age—it must have been a childhood plaything of the late Marquis. I had to make a few repairs, but I believe it is sound now.'

They all stared at the thing, its slightly faded harlequin colours patched here and there with brighter coloured paper.

Quintus was carefully straightening its long tail of paper bows. 'We should try it now,' he said, suddenly sounding about twelve years old.

Both men took off their hats and coats, Giles held the roll of string and Quintus walked away towards the edge of the scarp, holding the kite above his head as the string unravelled.

'The wind is catching it now,' he called. 'Shall I let it go?'

'Yes!'

The kite soared, hesitated, then climbed again, Giles letting out the string and leaning back against the pull. It rose higher and higher and he began to run along the break of slope, making it swoop and soar, Quintus running with him, both of them laughing like boys.

Giles handed him the roll of string and they ran back, the kite climbing higher.

'Goodness, how fit and happy they look. Do you not want to try it, Lovell?' Katherine asked.

He was standing, hands fisted on hips, watching the two experimenting, arguing noisily about the best way to gain height.

'Childish nonsense.' His eyes were fixed on the kite.

'Innocent fun,' she countered. 'Or perhaps you do not have the skill.'

As she suspected, at that Lovell took off his hat, stripped off his coat and strode down to the kite flyers. They surrendered the string at once, but their groan as the fragile kite plunged earthwards was audible to the two women.

Then Lovell found the knack and it climbed again, sending a buzzard that was soaring on the updraught swooping away in alarm.

'My mother used to say that all men are boys at heart,' Elspeth said.

'And mine says that if you want work done, one boy is worth half a man, but two boys are only worth half a boy. What three are worth, I cannot imagine, but we cannot expect much sense out of these lads until they have exhausted themselves.'

They settled back against their cushions to watch, sipping their lemonade. The three men were all under thirty, all tall and fit and full of energy and they made a sight that would gladden the heart of any young lady, Katherine thought.

Quintus Gresham was the best looking and, perhaps, Giles Wilmott, the more athletic, but there was no mistaking who had the most power, the finest figure.

The now-familiar tightening in her chest caught her again, a mixture of love, desire and depression. Will Lovell was all she would ever want and she could never have him.

'Are you all right, Katherine? That was a very heavy sigh,' Elspeth said. 'Is your head paining you again?'

No, my heart.

'I am quite well, thank you. I was just allowing thoughts of what remains to be done to oppress me. I should make the effort to forget work and enjoy this holiday.'

Giles had control of the kite now, making it swoop and loop. Then the wind must have changed in some way and it dropped, hitting the ground heavily. When Quintus ran to pick it up it drooped in his hands.

'One of the struts is broken,' he called and trudged back up the slope, a picture of despondency.

'Never mind,' Elspeth said when he drew level with them. 'I am sure you will be able to repair it when you get back to the Hall. And it will soon be time for luncheon, I imagine.'

All three men, looking slightly embarrassed at their demonstration of boyish enthusiasm, came and retrieved their coats and hats.

'Please do not feel you have to put those on again on our behalf, gentlemen,' Katherine said. 'We have no objection to your shirtsleeves or bare heads and it is very warm now. And, surely, the footmen can be excused their livery coats, too.'

That was greeted with smiles of relief all around.

The staff was laying out the picnic on a trestle table covered, incongruously in such a wild and natural setting, with a pristine white cloth. The gentlemen went to view it, then came back to report to Katherine and Elspeth for them to make their choices. Clearly, it was expected that neither should rise from their cushioned seats to serve themselves, Katherine thought with an inward smile.

'Cold chicken, a roll and some of the salad for me,' she requested, while Elspeth asked for the salmon.

That was duly brought, along with more glasses of cool lemonade, and the men settled themselves on a second rug in front of the ladies. As this was slightly downhill, Katherine had the sensation of being some Eastern potentate with her retainers at her feet. It was an amusing fancy, but it did not stop her wondering what, exactly, Lovell was about.

He was watching her closely, although subtly, and she was very aware of him. When she put down her empty glass he was on his feet at once, taking it to be refilled, rather than waiting for a footman to attend to it and when a wasp took rather too close an interest in the sweet liquid he produced a clean napkin to lay over it.

Could Elspeth possibly be correct and Lovell was wooing her? But to what end? A man did not court a mistress in such a manner, she was certain of that, but the only alternative was marriage and he was a marquis, for goodness sake!

It was simply her friend's romantic soul and her own yearning for him to love her as she loved him that was making them both see something more than gentlemanly politeness in his attentions.

He had allowed himself to become too familiar with a member of his staff and now he was backing away, taking refuge in formal politeness, that must be the answer, she told herself.

Then he looked up suddenly, caught her gaze as she studied him and suddenly time stood still. The sound of Giles and Quintus bickering amiably over what village down in the Vale was the nearest faded away, her surroundings seemed to blur, and all that was left was Will Lovell's face, those intense blue eyes locked with hers, full of desire and something more. Something deeper and far more complicated.

Katherine knew she was returning that look without reserve, without trying to hide any emotion from him. Could he read her love in her eyes or was he as confused as she was at what he was seeing?

Chapter Twenty-One

'Oh, Katherine, do look at that enchanting little blue butterfly!'

Elspeth's touch on her arm jolted Katherine out of her trance and she pretended to follow her friend's pointing finger, although everything was still a blur.

'So pretty,' she agreed. 'I have never seen one like that before,' she added brightly when it finally came into focus.

'Those are butterflies of the chalk downlands,' Quintus said, twisting to look. 'We have them in plenty where my family lives, in Sussex.'

Elspeth immediately started asking him about his family and whether they knew her acquaintance, the Fanshaws, who also lived in Sussex.

Katherine let it all wash over her, pretending to follow the dancing flight of the little butterflies.

Had she just imagined that look? Will—she abandoned the attempt to think of him by his family name—was engrossed in a discussion with Giles about land drains, surely not a subject that a man with romance, of any variety, on his mind would think of.

Perhaps she wasn't well. Perhaps that blow to the head when she fell from the gig was causing her to have delusions, see things that were not there. But she had no headache, her vision seemed perfect.

'I think I will just rest my eyes for a little while,' Elspeth announced. She removed her bonnet, made herself more comfortable against the piled-up cushions and appeared to drop off to sleep immediately.

The two men stopped discussing drains and, with a muttered word to Will, Giles stretched out on his back, a cushion behind his head and tipped his hat, a woven straw, over his face. Quintus had strolled off. He appeared, from the way he kept crouching down and examining the turf, to be looking at wild flowers.

The footmen had cleared away the picnic and had retired to the shade of the wagon where they were playing cards and smoking while Jeannie looked over their shoulders at their hands and, from the occasional burst of laughter, was teasing them with suggestions on strategy.

When she looked around again Will was on his feet, one hand extended. 'A stroll to admire the view?' he said, his voice low. 'I believe we have a perfectly alert chaplain as chaperon, even if Mrs Downe is resting.'

Katherine stood up without taking his hand, no easy thing to achieve gracefully on slightly sloping ground amid a scatter of cushions and a sleeping companion.

'I feel no need for a chaperon with you, W—er, Lovell,' she said once she was a few steps away. 'And a walk would be welcome.'

She had almost called him by his first name, he realised as he offered his arm, but all Will said was, 'Take care, this turf is somewhat slippery in places.'

Kat tucked her hand into the crook of his elbow and they began to walk, close to the break of slope.

'What fun for children to slide down this,' she observed, looking down the precipitous grassy scarp. 'Although rather dangerous, perhaps.'

They walked a little further in silence. The winds rising up that had sent the kite high into the sky was still blowing, sending Kat's skirts across his legs and making her clutch at her wide sun hat with her free hand.

What to talk about? How did one go about this courtship business? He knew how to flirt, but that was out of the question at this stage. Will cleared his throat. 'An amazing view, is it not? One was hardly aware of being at any height when we drove here and yet there is this virtual cliff. It must be almost five hundred feet at this point.'

Kat was still silent, then she said abruptly, 'I do not understand.'

'We are on chalk, which I believe, if I understand the writings of James Hutton on the science of geology correctly, is a rock that has been much bent and lifted by the movements of the earth over time. The same thing may be observed on the South Downs, in fact—'

'That is not what I mean,' she said, almost impatiently. 'I do not understand what this…this *formality*, is about. You used to call me Kat, now I am Miss Jenson, or you carefully avoid calling me anything. Before, you never cared about chaperons, now you make a point of it. And this outing—you have seemed committed to your labours with Giles and anxious that I continue my work in the house, yet you suddenly declare a holiday. You probe as if testing my attraction to Giles and Quintus.

'I am, my lord, confused.'

Damnation. He had been so concerned about moving slowly, being scrupulously careful, that it had not occurred to him that such behaviour would, in itself, appear strange. Now what? Laugh it off, pretend Kat was imagining things—or be honest?

Honesty, of course. This was Kat, too intelligent to have the wool pulled over her eyes, too important to lie to.

'I was attempting to begin a courtship, Kat. Apparently, I was not going about it the right way,' he confessed ruefully, wishing he could see her expression, but the wide brim of her hat hid her face completely.

Her reaction was unmistakeable. She jerked her hand free of his arm and took two abrupt steps away from him, up the slope.

'I will *not* become your mistress.'

Now he could see her face and there was more than indignation or shock there. She looked hurt.

'I am not asking you to,' he retorted, anger at himself making his voice harsh.

'Then what do you want?' Kat demanded.

Will shot a glance towards the picnic party, but Wilmott and Mrs Downe still appeared to be dozing and all that could be seen of Gresham was his distant figure vanishing into a clump of bushes, apparently still in pursuit of butterflies.

'I want you to marry me,' he said flatly, trying to keep his voice down and succeeding, he realised, in merely sounding exasperated.

Kat took two rapid backwards steps, stumbled and sat down on the grass with a thump.

'Is this your idea of a joke?' she demanded, tugging at the ribbons of her hat that had slipped. She jerked it free and tossed it aside.

'No. It is my idea of how to make an inept proposal,' he snapped back. 'Are you hurt?'

'Merely my dignity.'

Surely those were not tears he could see gathering in her eyes? Kat turned her head and stared out across the Vale, lips tight.

Will sat down, a cautious arm's length away. 'I may not be going about this the right way,' he admitted, 'but my intentions are serious and sincere.'

'You, *my lord*, are a marquis. I am a librarian from a gentry family. You require a wife who has been bred and raised to marry a man of high rank. An ability to set your library in order and an unfortunate physical attraction leading to an ill-judged episode in the long grass does not make me an eligible candidate.'

Will took a deep breath, let it out slowly and started to pick his way through the quagmire it seemed he had created.

'You are a lady. You are educated and intelligent. You have the skills and the interest to manage a large household and to be concerned for tenants and dependents. And, as you say, there is a certain attraction between us. I had thought to go to London to take my seat in the House of Lords and to participate in the Season, but—'

'But you have no desire for the tiresome business of attending Almack's and fending off matchmaking matrons and sorting through the ranks of young ladies on display in the Marriage Mart.'

'Well, yes,' he admitted. 'But—'

'How much less effort is required if you are already married. No simpering misses, trained to show not an ounce of the intelligence most of them undoubtedly possess. No need to be constantly alert for attempts to compromise you in the conservatory, no tiresome parties or overheated balls.'

'If I might be allowed to finish a sentence?' he enquired and received an icy nod.

'I do not deny that I was not looking forward to the Season. However, if I had not felt both liking and attraction to you, I would not have made this declaration.'

'You consider liking and attraction to be sufficient, do you?' Kat snatched up her hat, jammed it on her head and was on her feet before he could regain his and offer his hand.

'Yes, certainly.' Will stood, trying to read her face. Surely any young lady would be delighted to receive a proposal from a marquis? Or, at least, from one they were prepared to let kiss them, one with who they had co-existed with on an amiable basis for almost a month.

Although just how amiable *had* it been in reality? There had always been that edge, that uneasy feeling that Kat harboured some antagonism towards him.

'What do you consider sufficient?' he asked.

'Love,' she said flatly. 'Love and trust, as well as liking and attraction.'

Love? Aristocrats did not make love matches. Aristocrats made strategic marriages: blood lines, political influence, wealth, lands—those were the considerations. Everything else might, or might not, follow.

But then, he was not making a proposal with any of those things in mind. He was proposing because he wanted Kat. And Kat wanted something from him he was not sure he could give.

Trust, yes. He trusted her already to have the run of his house and control of its valuables. He trusted her to say what she thought.

But love? What was that? His parents had enjoyed a happy, amiable and long marriage without, as far as he could tell, ever professing love for each other. None of his married friends ever rhapsodised about feelings of romance when they were court-ing—the young ladies were attractive, healthy, had the makings of excellent hostesses and had useful connections in the legal world. The lawyer's equivalent, he supposed, of what aristo-crats looked for.

Love, he was given to understand, involved a burning desire to pen poetry to the beloved's eyebrows and a sensation of hope-less surrender to the emotion, including lack of sleep, inatten-tion to anything else and an inability to find fault in the lady.

Will was sleeping perfectly well, was not aware of any ab-sentmindedness and was as indifferent to poetry as he had always been. In addition, he was all too aware of Kat's faults—including, but not exclusively, stubbornness, a complete refusal to regard masculine pronouncements as infallible and a pair of perfectly ordinary eyebrows.

'I do trust you and I hope you feel you can trust me,' he said.

Her mouth set in the firm line he had come to know all too well.

'Perhaps if you were to allow me to court you, other…emo-tions might develop,' he suggested, wondering as he did so why he didn't simply wash his hands of the whole idea. Kat had re-fused him and London during the Season would be full of young ladies only too happy to accept a proposal from a marquis.

He opened his mouth to inform her that he would take *no* for her answer and would trouble her no more and found the words did not come. He didn't want those other, faceless, young la-dies. He wanted Kat.

And, miracles of miracles, she seemed to be wavering. 'I… Yes, of course I trust you,' she said. 'But you do not *know* me.'

And that, Will realised, was true. There was something in-side her that was hidden. Kat had secrets, even if they were only secret feelings.

'I would like the opportunity to do so. Can we not be Kat and Will? Can we not work together as we have been? I will stop trying to court you in proper form, I will forget about chaperons and formality. Give it a month, Kat—we may surprise ourselves.'

It was fascinating to try to read the emotions that she was trying so hard to suppress. Was he fooling himself that she wanted to say *yes*, but that something was holding her back? And that something was in her, not in him?

'Yes,' she said after what seemed like a year. 'Yes, let us take a month, Will. Then we may know what we truly feel.'

He held out his hand to her and she took it, her own soft and warm within his fingers, and they walked slowly back towards the others with nothing more said.

Katherine told herself that she had bought time. Time to assemble her evidence, time to think of a way to confront Will with it and somehow salvage whatever it was between them.

She owed it to her parents to clear her father's name, she told herself as the landau bumped its way slowly back through the woodlands. She owed it to herself, too. And she also deserved, surely, a chance at love? Whatever it was that had prompted Will to make that proposal, there was more to it than a man's lazy disinclination to face a London Season, she could tell that.

Men, her married friends had told her, were not sensitive to feelings, even their own. Often it took the emotional equivalent of a blow to the head to make them realise that what they were feeling was love.

She closed her eyes for a moment, imagining Will in love with her, what that would be like, what it would mean.

'Are you all right, Kat?' he asked.

'Just a little tired,' she said with a smile. 'All that fresh air. And unlike some people, I did not take a nap after luncheon.'

'I was merely resting my eyes,' Elspeth said with dignity. 'I was quite awake the entire time.'

'Of course.' Katherine did not point out that when she and Will had returned it was to find Elspeth's soft snores making a strange duet with Giles's more robust contribution.

* * *

Her friend made no comment in the days that followed when Katherine called Will by his first name, nor did she mention her theory that he was courting or wonder why he suddenly seemed indifferent to chaperonage again.

Because Elspeth is matchmaking, Katherine thought as she threw herself into her work.

She finessed the library arrangement and spent every other spare daytime hour searching the upstairs rooms.

She found more small valuable objects, far too much furniture and clocks, even for a house of that size, and finally reached the Long Gallery and the family portraits a week after that disturbing picnic.

'I think the last room I have to look through is the Long Gallery,' she reported at luncheon. 'There is very little furniture, but there is any amount of panelling that might conceal cupboards.'

Will had spent every day shut in the study with Giles, wrestling with a crisis that had just blown up over leases which had been inaccurately dealt with in his cousin's time. In the evenings he and Katherine had been going through the library catalogue, discussing whether there were any items he wished to sell and identifying gaps where he might wish to strengthen the collection.

It had been a very amicable collaboration, although she had had a tussle to prevent him disposing of every book of sermons, arguing that many of his future guests would wish to read such books on Sundays. But, amiable as it was, it had not done much to advance their easy friendship further towards anything else and Katherine wondered if Will was regretting his stated intention of returning to the question of marriage after a month.

Now he put down his glass and remarked, 'I will come and search through it with you. We have finally beaten those confounded leases into submission and Giles deserves an afternoon off. It is time I confronted my illustrious ancestors.'

Will clearly felt like a boy let out of school and approached the serried ranks of his forebears in a frivolous spirit.

'What an array of stiff-necked bores,' he remarked.

'Oh, not all of them,' Katherine protested. 'Look, this little Tudor sketch is charming—it might be by Holbein. And there are some very good portraits among those that seem to date from late in the last century. Now, this gentleman looks like you, don't you think?'

'My great-grandfather,' Will said, coming to stand beside her. 'And the two small boys must be my grandfather and his older brother, Randolph's grandfather.' He took a step back. 'You think I look like him?'

'You are better looking,' Katherine said. 'He is too perfect and he knows it. Or perhaps the artist smoothed away all imperfections and gave him a suitably haughty look.'

'And I am not haughty?'

'You are not,' she said, smiling at him over her shoulder as she stopped back. 'You can look very forbidding when displeased, but—Oh!' Her foot caught in her hem and she staggered back.

'Kat.' Will caught her, turned her in his arms. 'What have I said before? Accident prone. Thank goodness there are no library steps, or steep scarp slopes in here.'

She laughed up at him and suddenly they were both still, arms around each other, eyes locked together.

'Kat?' he said again and this time it was a question.

It was not a proposal of marriage again, she knew that, but suddenly she did not care.

'Yes, Will. Oh, yes.'

Chapter Twenty-Two

There was a wide window seat, almost a day bed, made to look like a Roman couch, presumably so that a reader could lounge elegantly while perusing a volume, but there was little elegant about the way that they fell on to it, tangled together, mouths locked in a kiss that was almost desperate.

Katherine found herself on her back, Will's weight over her and him looking down at her, so close their noses were almost touching, so near she could have counted the darker flecks in his eyes.

'Are you sure, Kat?'

Sure that I love you? Sure that I want you? Sure that I know this is madness, that there will be heartbreak—but I do not care?

'Yes,' she said. 'Certain.'

There was no hope for them, she knew that now. She would not, could not, betray her father and so Will would understand that she had been his enemy from the very first and that nothing would deter her from her vengeance.

It was not romantic, this coming together. The doors were unlocked, their need urgent. Neither made any attempt to undress the other and that, for Katherine, was a bitter loss. She wanted to feel Will's skin under her hands, learn the texture, the warmth of it, discover muscles and lines and those secret, sensitive spots that even a tough man must possess.

Then the heat of his mouth on hers blurred her thoughts and the caress of his hands over her breasts, even through layers of fine cloth and underwear, sent her own fingers exploring from the nape of his neck to the taut curve of his buttocks.

Her skirts were rucked up, he was reaching between them for the fastenings of his falls and they were both clumsy because they did not know each other's bodies yet.

Then Katherine felt the texture of Will's breeches against her bare thighs, felt the muscles bunch and slide against her softer flesh, and parted her legs to cradle him where he fitted so well.

She felt his fingers caressing her there where she was already so very ready for him, felt the pressure, curled her body up to meet it, rode on a wave of desire and new, surging, feelings and then they were joined and Will was abruptly still.

It had hurt, a little, she realised with what part of her rational mind was still functioning, but that had gone now and she needed him more, needed something she could not define.

'Will, *yes.*'

And then they were moving together, as though they had always known the rhythm, understood how to be together.

I love you, she thought as the pressure and the need built and then suddenly broke apart, unravelled, throwing her into a whirlpool of feelings and emotions as she clung to him blindly.

Then he moved abruptly and she cried out at the loss of him as there was heat and wetness on her skin and the weight of his body, sprawled boneless, on top of her and then darkness.

'Kat?'

She was curled up against him, holding on tightly, quite still and quiet. Will was not certain whether that was a good sign or not, but they couldn't stay here, like this.

'Kat.' He pressed her shoulder gently, then took one hand in his. Under his fingers her pulse beat steadily.

'Mmm?' When her eyes opened he was caught in the look that seemed miles deep, centuries old. And then she smiled.

'Lie still,' he said, just touching her lips with his.

How did he feel? Will wondered as he carefully disentangled himself, did his best to restore his clothing to some sort of order.

His legs felt as though he had run ten miles, his brain didn't seem capable of focusing on anything but what had just happened and his body felt so good he could hardly believe it belonged to him.

He handed her the clean handkerchief that he found in one pocket, then tactfully turned away when she sat up.

She would marry him now, he knew that. It wasn't why he had taken her in his arms—that had been quite unplanned, utterly spontaneous—but it would result in her agreement, he was certain.

Kat had been a virgin and he knew her well enough to be certain that she would never be free with that virginity.

Behind him he heard her get to her feet. Lord, they hadn't even taken off their shoes…

'This does not mean I will marry you, Will,' she said, her voice just a little unsteady.

'What?' He spun around to confront her as she stood there, skirts smoothed down, pinning a few locks of hair back into place. 'You have to marry me now.'

'I do not think so.' She looked quite composed, if flushed, but he sensed she was holding on to that composure by her fingernails. 'You did not intend that in order to force me, did you? You would not have taken precautions against my conceiving if you had. We have just lain together because we both wanted to, very much. But that is all it was, all it can be.'

'Why?' He felt as though she had slapped him.

I love you.

'I… I cannot.' And she turned on her heel and ran from him, down the length of the Long Gallery, through the door. It banged closed behind her.

What could he do? He couldn't force her, although if his precautions failed and she was with child, he would have a damn good attempt at it.

Will paced slowly after her down the length of the gallery, conscious of the gaze of dozens of painted eyes on his back. Judging, pitying or sneering?

It was not until he was halfway down the stairs that it occurred to him that he had stated that Kat must marry him because he had taken her virginity. He had said nothing about his feelings for her, although he had demonstrated physical desire clearly enough.

Her pride, at the very least, must be hurt. Could he be honest with her? Dare he? That was rather closer to the truth. To admit that new-found love was to risk rejection, pity. Scorn, even.

But then, what was love if it did not hazard itself for the beloved? He had to tell Kat. Lay out his heart to be trampled on, if that was what it took. Trust her with the truth. But not yet, not while they were both reeling from what had just happened.

'Miss Jenson, excuse me.'

Katherine stopped dead in her headlong flight, composed her face into what she could only pray was normality and turned.

'Yes? Oh, it is you, Petrie.'

Will's valet stood outside what she realised was the old Marquis's bedchamber door. He was as serious and immaculate as usual.

'His Lordship asked me to put the dressing room in order, but I have found a cupboard full of papers and I believe that you are sorting those. I do not wish to overstep.'

She took a deep breath and smiled. He did not recoil, so she supposed it had looked all right. 'I can certainly look at them for you. Probably they can all be taken down to Mr Wilmott.'

'May I assist you?' he asked. 'Otherwise I have done all I can in there until it is cleaned and repainted.'

'No, thank you. I am sure you have a lot to be getting on with. I can always ring for a footman if there is more than I can manage.'

'Thank you, Miss Jenson. I am much obliged.' He made a prissy little bow and walked off.

She supposed she could go and look at this cupboard now. It was as good a place to hide as any and it would have to be cleared sooner or later.

Petrie certainly appeared to be efficient. The room was neat, all the drawers empty and the cupboards and presses with their doors slightly ajar. To air, she supposed.

In one corner was a small cupboard, about eighteen inches deep and waist high. When she opened it she saw a far tidier arrangement than any other of the old Marquis's. It was empty except for the top shelf on which manila card folders were stacked neatly and when she pulled one out she saw it had a label written in a pinched hand: *Mummy cases.*

The next read *Manuscripts.*

Excited, she pulled them all out, scanning the labels. And there it was, on top of the second pile. *The Borgia Ruby.*

Her hands shook so much as she opened the folder that the papers it contained spilled across the floor and she dropped to her knees. Letters in her father's hand. Copies of the Marquis's replies. The draft of a letter to his lawyer. To Will.

And there, at last it was—the top half of the receipt, the part that showed clearly that the payment the Marquis had made to her father was a deposit, a surety, only. It had been cut neatly, but when she held it up to the light, there was the betraying watermark, sliced across: the two pieces would fit.

Katherine bundled it all back, slid the folder into the middle of the pile and carried the whole stack to the door, leaving the cupboard empty. There was nowhere better to hide something than in a mass of similar objects.

She carried it downstairs, through to the muniments room, and slid it on to a shelf next to some similar files.

Now she had virtually everything she needed to confront Will. All that was missing was the evidence that he had concocted the accusations against her father.

Her hand was on the door when she heard voices outside.

'Sir, the boxes have arrived from your legal clerk. They are in the study now, but shall I have them brought down to the muniments room?' That was Giles.

'Yes, do that. There is important material in there, so it is the best place for it.' Will.

Was it her imagination or did he sound strained, unlike his usual self when he was talking to his secretary?

It would be a wonder if he did not sound different after what had just happened.

'I'll have that done now, sir. They are taking up a considerable amount of room where they are.'

Will replied with a comment she did not catch and their voices faded away until she felt safe enough to look out. The passageway was clear and she left, closing the door behind her and turning the key.

Elspeth was very full of news at dinner, so excited that nobody appeared to notice that Katherine and Will were unusually silent.

She had discovered some wonderful embroidery, Elspeth explained, and she thought it might be Elizabethan, perhaps an altar frontal.

That, of course, greatly interested Quintus Gresham. It also provoked comment from the two new arrivals who had, apparently reached the house late in the afternoon—the drainage expert, a Mr Perkins, and the landscape designer, Cosmo Peronne.

Katherine did not believe that name in the slightest, but she was too grateful for the presence of two strangers to provide distraction from herself and to compel Will's attention.

Once Elspeth had talked herself to a standstill Will and Giles engaged the two men in an esoteric discussion on water management, discussing the moat, the stream and the silted-up lakes.

It all sounded exceedingly technical, with discussion about angles of slope, water pressure, sluice gates and depths, and Elspeth, Quintus and Katherine made no attempt to follow what they were talking about.

With the other two now exchanging comments on the latest Court news—something that never interested Katherine at the best of times—she was left to brood on what had just happened.

Her body was still tingling with the after-effects of their lovemaking and she still felt off balance. What had she been thinking of? Besides the obvious desire and love, of course... What had it been that had broken her determination to hold herself aloof until Will's month of courtship had expired?

It was almost as though something within her was determined to push this to a crisis, end it once and for all. Although quite how losing her virginity would achieve that was a mystery.

Then the discovery of those documents, the half of the receipt that proved beyond doubt the late Marquis's crime—it was almost as though she had somehow known that this was the end game, that everything was rushing towards the dénouement and she had snatched at the last chance to lie with Will, to somehow show him her love before she turned on him.

She did not linger and wait for the tea tray when she and Elspeth left the men to their port. 'If you do not mind, I will retire,' she said. 'I am tired and I really cannot face more discussion on drains and how to dispose of tons of mud, which they are sure to still be talking about when they come through,' she apologised.

Elspeth smiled and waved her off. 'Sleep well, dear.'

It would have to be tonight, Katherine thought as she sat at her dressing table while Jeannie brushed out her hair and put away her few items of jewellery.

The ruby was in her evening reticule, making the embroidered bag bulge more than usual, but she did not dare leave it anywhere. 'Leave that, Jeannie,' she said, putting her hand over it when the maid reached out. 'I want to look closely at the inside seams, I think one has split.'

Then she was alone with her thoughts. *Plan*, she told herself fiercely. Anything was better than feeling.

The sooner she searched the box of legal papers relating to the old Marquis, the better. She knew where they were and they might be moved later to somewhere she could not access so easily. And the sooner she had all the ends tied up, the sooner she could act.

The sooner I can leave here. Leave Will.

So, tonight. What to wear? She was in her nightgown with her robe over it and both were simple, practical garments. If she was seen, then wearing those meant she could pretend to sleeplessness and the need to go down to the library to find a book, and the slippers would be soundless on the stone floors.

She had the key to the room, but would the boxes be locked? She guessed that legal boxes would be, not because they contained valuable items, but as a simple act of preserving the privacy of the individuals they related to.

Fortunately her father had taught her to pick ordinary locks because so often the keys to items he had bought had been lost. Katherine sorted through her hairpins and selected three, each of a different thickness, and slid them into her hair. If the locks were more complex then she would be faced with the choice of trying to find the keys or breaking into the boxes and she did not want to have to do either.

She slipped the ruby into the pocket of her robe, somehow wanting to keep it, and everything relating to it, together and sat down to wait. The household kept country hours: by one o'clock all would be quiet. She would allow another half-hour to be on the safe side.

Will paced up and down in his bedchamber. He was still wearing his evening breeches and shirt, with a heavy silk banyan over the top. He wanted to appear at Kat's door decently clad because this was going to be tricky enough without appearing as though he wanted to come to her bed.

Which he did. But not tonight.

He hoped that Mrs Downe was a good sleeper—he thought she was from remarks he had overheard at breakfast time—because he was going to have to negotiate the ladies' shared sitting room before he could tap on Kat's door.

He could leave this until the next day, of course, yet he knew he would never sleep and he rather thought that Kat would not either.

He would tell her he loved her, sink every ounce of his pride if that was what it took, beg her to marry him, not because he had compromised her, but because he was certain now that they belonged together.

The clock stuck the half-hour and he glanced at it in the candlelight. Another half-hour. Two o'clock.

There were three of the big black tin boxes that lawyers used for their clients' papers to keep them safe from vermin and damp. Each had *Ravenham* painted in white on the lid, but it was possible to tell which was the newest because the paint was freshest.

She lifted it down, set it on the table and looked at the lock. Yes, just a simple mechanism designed to keep out the curious and secure the lid in place. A few minutes' work with two of the hairpins and it clicked open, the sound echoing in the small room.

Katherine took a deep breath and told herself to keep calm. The house had been silent and still as she had come downstairs, only the snores of whichever footman was on duty in the deeply hooded porter's chair in the hall disturbing the peace.

She delved into the box, lifting out thickly filled folders that were clearly to do with the Marquis's death and the inheritance of the title.

Below them was another labelled *Borgia Ruby*. Heart thudding, she opened it on the table and began to sort through it until she found what she was looking for, a letter from Will to his cousin.

> *Agents report that the man Jones purchased the gem from was a supporter of Bonaparte who had to flee France to evade the retribution of local loyalists. He has achieved this thanks to Jones's efforts and money.*
>
> *One can only deduce from this act, which must have put Jones to considerable expense and involved some risk, that they were already confederates.*
>
> *I can use this to demonstrate what a blackguard the man is and to undermine whatever sympathy the court might have for an apparent 'underdog' in conflict with a peer of the realm.*

She spread the letter out, set the doctored receipt beside it, laid the ruby itself on top as a glittering paperweight. She had it all now.

A draught disturbed the papers, lifting one corner.

'What the devil do you think you are doing?'

Will stood in the doorway, staring at her. Then he looked at the table where the ruby glowed balefully in the candlelight.

Katherine reached out instinctively to cover the gem.

'And what are you doing with that?'

Chapter Twenty-Three

She looked the picture of guilt, Katherine realised. Beside her the legal box stood open, her picklocks beside it. Papers she had no right to look at were spread out in front of her and she was clutching a valuable jewel.

'That is the Borgia Ruby. Kat—'

'It is mine.' She found herself on her feet, confronting him, the ruby clenched in her fist. 'Your cousin stole it—see, here is the half of the receipt he cut off to make it look as though he had bought it, when instead of paying a security while he had it appraised.

'And here—' she jabbed one finger at the letter he had written '—here you are suggesting how a good man, an honest, loyal, *patriotic* man, might be cast as a traitor, a sympathiser with the enemy, in order to make his word in court worthless.'

Will had not moved. 'Who are you?'

'Katherine Jones, his daughter. And this ruby belongs to me and to my mother. She is a widow. Did you know that? The story you told in court broke my father, ruined him, killed him.'

'I trusted you. I—'

'Papa trusted the court for justice. I worked hard for you. I have done everything you employed me for.' She made her voice cold. 'And do not think I have robbed you. Not one item that does not belong to me has been taken. Only this, which is mine.'

'You could have told me.' He looked bleak and somehow... empty.

'Yes? Told you what, Mr "We Can Use This" Lawyer? That you cousin was a liar and a cheat? That Papa helped that pathetic little man escape because that was part of the price of the ruby? The war was over—what harm could he do? You had not one scrap of evidence that my father conspired with Bonapartists before that, because there was none to be found.'

'It was my duty to present my client's case in the best light,' Will said.

'It was your duty to tell the truth!'

'So you came here hating me. But then... Are you such a good actress, Kat?'

'Yes, I came here hating you.' Something forced the truth from her. 'And then I started to like you, to desire you. It still did not make anything right, even when I—' She almost said it. *Loved you.*

'I wanted to marry you,' he said. 'What did you want?'

'For you to clear Papa's reputation. To tell the world that he was not a traitor, not a confidence trickster. To have the ruby's ownership clear so Mama can sell it.'

'Give me that receipt. Both pieces.' He held out his hand, those long fingers that had held her, caressed her.

She should not trust him with it. All he had to do was snatch it away, set the candle flame to it and her proof was gone. She could read in his eyes that he knew what she was thinking, saw the bitter twist of his mouth.

'Here. Hold the pieces up to the light and you will see that the watermark matches.'

He took them, read them, then held them together between finger and thumb of one hand while he reached for the candle.

Katherine held her breath. All it would take is one touch of the flame...

But he held it behind the paper and looked closely at the point where the two parts joined. There was a long silence, then, 'Keep it.' Will dropped the two parts next to the ruby. 'Keep the receipt. Keep the damn jewel. Be gone from this house at daybreak—a carriage will be ready for you.' He raked her with a look that left her feeling scorched and turned to the door. His hand was on it, then he looked back.

'I was searching for you because... No.' He shook his head. 'I had not thought myself quite the fool I clearly am.' Then he was gone.

Katherine found she was sitting again, although she had no recollection of it. In front of her, on the litter of papers, lay the ruby, glowing like a malevolent eye.

There were always tales about the great historical gems, stories of spells and magic, of love affairs and murders. Katherine had dismissed them as amusing romantic nonsense.

Now, for the first time, she believed them. This stone was cursed and it had ruined their lives. It had killed Papa, plunged Mama into deepest grief and now it had ruined whatever was between her and Will.

Why was he looking for me? Does he feel something, something more than desire? If he did, he doesn't now. Not any more. Not now he knows I lied to him, deceived him, did not trust him even when we had become so close.

Katherine stood up, steady suddenly with a kind of frozen calm. She returned the legal papers to their box, used her hairpins with a steady hand to snick the lock closed, returned it to the shelf. Then she folded the receipt and Will's letter into the ruby's box and placed the jewel on top, touching it only with her fingertips, and closed the lid.

She would take it home and sell it as soon as she could find a buyer. With the receipt intact at least it would be clear that Mama had title to the thing, even if dealers knocked the price down as a condition of handling something from the daughter of a ruined man.

Then she locked the door behind her and climbed the stairs to her room to pack. They would be ready at first light: she had no desire to face Will Lovell ever again.

'I still cannot believe he gave it up,' her mother said two days later when Katherine was at last able to tell her what had taken place. Not all of it. There were no mentions of kisses, of her lost virginity, of marriage proposals and her broken heart.

'Nor can I,' Katherine agreed wearily. 'I think he just wanted to be rid of me—and of it.'

'Will we be able to sell it now?' Her mother was eyeing the box with the same wariness she might have shown a small un-exploded mortar.

'I think so. I will start to make enquiries.' Just as soon as she had shaken off this clinging lethargy, the feeling that she would never smile again, never find anything amusing or pleas-ant or worthwhile.

'...it must have been so unpleasant for both of you,' Mama was saying and Katherine forced herself to pay attention. 'Poor Elspeth was most distressed by having to leave in such a clan-destine manner. I do wish she had stayed on with us for a while.'

'So do I. She was a great support and I feel I haven't thanked her enough,' Katherine admitted. 'Neither of us was in a fit state for long conversations on the journey home.'

'The morning papers, ma'am.' Jeannie came in with the three they normally took and laid them on the table, then went straight out again instead of stopping to relay any gossip she had gleaned from the newspaper sellers that morning.

'Jeannie is not happy either,' Katherine observed. 'I rather suspect a dalliance with one of the grooms. I only hope it was not serious because—'

'Katherine! Oh, Katherine, look!' Her mother thrust the copy of the *Morning Post* at her. 'See? There. Read it out loud.'

There was a full column in the legal section headed *Jones v the Marquis of Ravenham.*

'"...as the lawyer acting on behalf of the late Marquis of Ravenham I can disclose that the evidence presented on be-half of the Marquis was incomplete and lacking an essential element which proves, beyond doubt, that the jewel known as the Borgia Ruby was the lawful possession of Mr Arnold Jones and remains that of his heirs. Further, it is indisputable that the suggestion raised during the case that Mr Jones was in any way in league with Bonapartists, or was in any manner disloyal to* *his country, is entirely false and based on erroneous evidence. William Lovell, Third Marquis of Ravenham."'*

Breathless, Katherine turned the pages of the other two papers. 'It is here, too—*The Times* and the *Chronicle*.'

She realised her mother was drying her eyes. 'Mama?'

'You did this. You brought that dishonourable man to realise what he had done. My darling Arnold's name is cleared.'

No. It was Will's sense of honour that led him to do this. He had no need to.

To find that she could think like that after all that had happened surprised her, confused her. Katherine realised that she should be delighted, happy beyond words that she had achieved what she had set out to do—to have her father's good name restored and, less important, to secure the return of the ruby.

But I am not. I feel hollow, as though my chest has been an echoing void.

'Mama, I am going out for a walk. I need to clear my head.'

'Of course, dear.' Her mother was still dabbing at her eyes. 'I will write to Elspeth—if she has not seen the newspapers she will be so glad to hear our news.'

Will spread the previous day's *Times* out before him. His communication had been printed exactly as he had written it, he saw, checking carefully. Beside lay a furious letter from his partners in the law firm, demanding to know whether they should expect a suit for damages from the family of Arnold Jones.

He picked up his pen and wrote across the bottom of the letter.

No. They are honourable people. R.

He folded it and tossed it across the desk to Giles who was radiating tact to a painful extent. 'Readdress that to the Chambers, please.'

He had been furious with Kat. Hurt and furious. She had lied to him, betrayed his trust and yet...

He looked down at the newspaper again, at what he had written. What else could she have done? If she had arrived on his doorstep claiming that his cousin, a peer of the realm, had deliberately falsified a document in order to steal a valuable jewel, what would he have done?

Thrown her out, of course.

And that matter of her father and the Frenchman. That had been badly done. He had thought his cousin's case was fully justified and that he was dealing with a rogue and a thief. What was more likely than that Jones was disloyal into the bargain?

I should have checked. I should have dug more and Kat owed me absolutely nothing but her hatred.

Yet she had worked hard to do what he had employed her for. That was honest and she had been that. There had been endless opportunities for her to have robbed him blind, but she had not.

What hurt, he realised now, was that as she had come to know him, as they had grown so close, she still had not been able to trust him with the truth of her mission, because that was what it had been, as much as any intelligence officer infiltrating behind enemy lines.

But I am not the enemy, Kat. I love you.

There was a scratch at the door and Giles got up to answer it.

Behind him Will heard murmuring, a muffled exclamation and then his secretary went out. A tenant at the door, perhaps.

If I go to her now, tell her that I understand her deception, that I honour her devotion to her father, that I love her—what then?

He could not hope she would forgive him, let alone return his regard in any way, but he knew he could not live with himself if he did not at least hazard it. Hazard his heart, hazard his future.

The door opened and closed again. 'Giles, I am going to London. This afternoon. Bring me anything that must be dealt with immediately.'

'There is only an ex-employee to deal with, my lord,' said the person behind him as he became aware of a faint scent of jasmine, of a tingling down his spine. 'I fear she must be dealt with now, as she has something to say.'

He came to his feet as he turned. It was not an hallucination brought on by sleepless nights. It was Kat.

* * *

It was not encouraging. Will's face was blank of emotion, his body tense. Katherine swallowed and launched into her carefully prepared speech.

'I have come to thank you, my lord, for the notice in the newspapers. My mother and I are deeply relieved that Papa's good name has been restored. After the way in which we parted, I realise that you could well have done nothing.'

'I thought it was the only honourable thing to do when I realised that your father was innocent and that, therefore, his supposed connection to the French needed further exploration,' Wil said, very formally, very much the Marquis of Ravenham.

'And I am sorry that I deceived you when I sought employment here,' Katherine added.

'You performed everything I hired you for to an excellent standard. I can hardly fault you on that. In fact, I realise I owe you your wages.'

They were both so stilted, formal. So very correct—an armour to get the through this.

'Don't! Don't make this about money,' she burst out. 'Not after…'

Silence, then Will said, 'I am curious. How had you intended to play this out once you had the ruby and the evidence?'

'I would have come to you, told you what I had discovered, demanded that you did what you have just done.' She gestured towards the open newspaper.

'And if I had simply taken it all back from you, dared you to do your worst, countered your accusations with the story that you were a discarded and spiteful mistress?'

'You would never have done such a thing. You are a man of honour.'

'You think that now, perhaps.' In his turn he indicated the paper. 'But were you so certain then?'

'No,' she admitted. 'But I would have risked it. Lo—' Katherine froze.

Will closed his eyes and she saw him draw a deep, shuddering breath. 'One of us has to say it,' he said, almost to himself. 'One of us has to risk it all.

'Kat, I had decided to drive to London this afternoon and, when I was there, I was going to call on you.'

'Why?' she whispered, her heart beating too hard.

'To tell you that I understood. To tell you that I was sorry. To tell you that I love you. I don't even know if you heard me before. I can't imagine that you would have believed me.'

She sat down, hard. Thankfully, there was a chair just behind her.

'You love me? I thought perhaps you would feel you had to make a declaration after we had lain together.'

'It is why I was looking for you that night. To tell you that I love you and want to marry you. Not because we made love, not because I had in any way compromised you or that I thought I owed you something. Because I do not think I can ever be happy again without you and I suspected that perhaps you felt the same, despite your denials.'

'I realised that I was falling in love with you after that morning at the temple,' she confessed.

Is this a dream? Is Will really telling me he loves me, just as he does over and over in my dreams?

'It was…dreadful. I felt I was betraying Papa *and* you. It was a struggle to know where my loyalties lay. I didn't dare trust you,' she concluded miserably.

'You were right to choose as you did,' Will said. 'I couldn't understand you, how what I sensed from you was so changeable. Now I see what you were struggling with.'

Then, at last, he smiled and there was so much love, so much tenderness in his face that Katherine gasped.

He held out his hand and came towards her and she stood, took it in her own, felt the emotion that flowed between them and was suddenly, and completely, happy.

Will stooped, scooped her up in his arms and somehow opened the door.

'Will? *Will!*'

He strode across the hall towards the stairs, passing his butler, his chaplain, the landscape designer and the drainage engineer.

'Grigson, the lady's suite is to be made ready. Perkins, I want that moat pond finished and a rowing boat on it by the end of the week. Gresham—see about a special licence, will you? The name of the bride is Katherine Jones.'

'Katherine Amanda Jones,' she said, breathless, over his shoulder as she was swept up the stairs.

'Rowing boat?' she added as Will reached the landing.

'This house is going to have everything you want. You said you wanted to make a boating pond out of the moat and you will have it.'

'Will, the house already has all I want—you.'

'My lord?'

'Petrie, out.'

As the door closed behind the valet Will lowered her to her feet beside the bed. 'I love you. I want very much to show you how much. May I? This time without our shoes, on a proper bed and with no disapproving ancestors looking on.'

'I cannot think of anything I would like better,' she admitted, pushing his coat back from his shoulders.

They undressed each other, urgently and then, when it was the last few garments, slowly, carefully.

Katherine had expected to be shy when she stood in front of him naked, but she was too much in wonder at the sight of him to be self-conscious.

Will lifted her on to the bed, followed her and lay beside her, caressing her, kissing her, and she let him for a few moments, then began boldly to stroke and kiss him in turn, revelling in the way his body reacted to her touch, gasping in pleasure at the magic his hands were weaving.

When he came over her and she cradled him against her body, where he fitted so well, she felt no fear. They had joined before and this time would be even better.

'Love me, Will,' she whispered as he entered her.

'Always. Fly with me, my lady.'

'For ever,' she promised and let him take her soaring up into the fireworks and the velvet darkness and, finally, to rest.

A long time afterwards she turned her head on the pillow. 'What did you just say, my love?'

'"*Who can find a virtuous woman? For her price is far above rubies. The heart of her husband doth safely trust in her,"'* Will said. 'It's in the Bible. I looked it up when I realised that I didn't care about rubies, or my title or anything else. I just wanted you, needed you. That I could trust you with my heart.'

'Always and for ever,' she promised and kissed him.

* * * * *

The Duke's Guide To Fake Courtship

Jade Lee

MILLS & BOON

Jade Lee has been scripting love stories since she first picked up a set of paper dolls. Ball gowns and rakish lords were her first loves, which naturally led her to the world of regency romance. A *USA TODAY* and Amazon bestseller, she has a gift for creating lively worlds, witty dialogue and hot, sexy humor. She's earned an MFA in screenwriting from the University of Southern California, published seventy novels and won several industry awards including PRISM Best of the Best, RT Reviewers' Choice and *Fresh Fiction*'s Steamiest Read. Check out her devilishly clever historical romances at www.jadeleeauthor.com.

And lest you think *Bridgerton* is her only fav fandom, she's got a few other fancies. She adores shifters and writes about them as Kathy Lyons—visit www.kathylyons.com. But her biggest love is for her grandkids. They inspired her foray into picture books as Kat Chen—visit www.kat-chen.com.

The Duke's Guide to Fake Courtship is
Jade Lee's debut title for Harlequin Historical.

Look out for more books from
Jade Lee, coming soon.

Author Note

Who doesn't love a fake courtship? It's one of my favorite tropes, and I got to really indulge with this book because it's not only one fake courtship! Just how many people are pretending to be in love? Hard to tell, honestly, because our characters aren't exactly sure what they want or how they feel. Isn't that the way love works? One moment we're being polite, exploring possibilities with a handsome earl, and then the next, everything changes. A duke shows up, meddling parents destroy our peace and we're trying to be honest about our feelings—but what exactly are they? There's love, intrigue and some very good spice in this tale. I hope you enjoy it as much as I did!

For Soraya, my amazing editor.
This book would never have happened
or been as awesome without you.

Chapter One

Declan was a temperate man.

He did not consider that a virtue. It was an act of self-pres-ervation against a father and uncle, a drunkard and a wastrel respectively. Not to mention nine previous generations of vi-cious arseholes who all carried the Byrning name. Once upon a time, that had been an asset. The Byrnings had helped tame England and had received titles and coin in reward. But now Declan lived in a civilised time where intemperate rages were frowned upon.

His mother had declared—when he was three years old—that he would be a temperate man or she would destroy him. He had done his best to comply. What boy didn't want to please his mother? And so no one knew the fury that seethed beneath his exterior.

Unfortunately, it was very close to the surface now. His mother was banging on his chamber door the morning after his birthday celebration and he was imagining violently ripping the door off its hinges and throwing it out of the window. Unfortu-nately, he knew even that show of temper would not deter her.

'Good God! Shut her up!' he growled into his pillow.

'Brisley is handling it, Your Grace,' said his valet, his words thankfully very muted.

'He won't last for long,' he retorted, because his mother was nothing if not determined.

So he forced himself upright and grabbed the restorative offered by his valet. Declan doubted that it would help, but it could hardly hurt. He choked it down, then forced himself into the wingback chair next to the shuttered window. A minute later, he opened the newspaper, as if he didn't wish himself at the bottom of the Thames.

Only then did he bid the man open his bedroom door.

'Good morning, Mother. Have you come to wish me a belated happy birthday?'

'I fail to see why one should celebrate the mere fact—'

'Of living another year,' he finished for her.

She said something to that effect every year. Fortunately, his father had been more jovial in that and every way, so there'd been happy birthdays throughout his thirty-one years. The former Duke had also been more violent and hateful, so the memories were a mixed bag. In any event, this had been the first birthday celebrated without his father, and that had made it a commemorative one.

'Don't interrupt me,' his mother snapped.

'Don't burst into my bedchamber or pound on my door.' He'd almost said his father's door, but of course it was his now. 'You don't live here, Mother.'

And she hadn't for several years. At present, she resided with her sister-in-law in a neat townhouse far removed from the London ducal residence.

'But I am still responsible for seeing to the seemly disposition of the family.'

Yes, she had taken on that mantle, hadn't she? She and his aunt had set themselves up as the moral authority over the entire extended family. And, given that they both held inordinate influence over polite society, she did have some power in that regard. But if she planned to chide him for celebrating his birthday, then she was—

'Cedric is in trouble,' she pronounced. 'You must stop him.' She pulled out a pocket watch from her reticule. 'You have until teatime.'

He frowned—a painful act—as he set the paper aside. This unseemly display was about his cousin?

'Where is he?' Last he'd heard, the man had travelled to China with the East India Company.

'You'll find him at the docks, on a boat called *The Integrity*. As if naming a thing is enough to give—'

'When did he arrive in London?'

And why hadn't the man contacted him? Declan certainly would have invited his cousin to his birthday celebration. The two had been at school together, and though not quite the same age—Declan was older by three years—were close enough to be friends.

'How should I know? He sent a note this morning, informing his mother of the details. He intends to bring some chit to tea today.' She shuddered. 'I shan't be there, of course. It would be inappropriate for me to overshadow my sister's tea just because she lives upon my indulgence. And besides, we have agreed that you will stop this nonsense immediately.'

Of course they had agreed. Never mind that Declan might have a different opinion. But, rather than address any of the many objectionable things she'd said, he decided to focus on the most important.

'Cedric is engaged?'

'Not officially, of course. That's what you have to stop!'

Good Lord, the woman's voice was a near shriek—and she was a woman who never raised her voice. He waited for her to continue while simultaneously hoping that she would expire upon the spot.

She did not do either. In the end, he had to prompt her.

'Why should I stop it?'

'Because the girl is miserably unsuitable. His mother and I have discussed this often. We have decided on the ladies who will serve the Earldom. This chit does not.'

Yes, he knew that the two women had developed lists of eligible girls for their sons. It was their favourite discussion and they never thought to involve their sons in any of their decisions.

'Who is this woman?'

'She's the illegitimate child of Lord Wenshire, and Cedric is

bringing her to tea.' She made a face as if the man was bringing spoiled fish.

'Shouldn't you meet the woman before—?'

'Unsuitable!' she snapped.

He winced. 'Yes, I heard that.'

'Fix it.'

He waited a moment, staring at his mother's rigid face. He
wondered for a long, self-indulgent moment what she would do
if he refused. There were several hundred ways she could make
his life unpleasant, but at the end of the day it would merely be
uncomfortable. He was now the Duke, she the Dowager Duchess. Officially, he held all the power. He could refuse her at
his whim.

But that was the response of a child, not an adult, and certainly not one of a duke. His cousin's choice of wife was significant, not simply because Cedric was a future earl. Cedric stood
shoulder to shoulder with Declan as leaders of their respective
branches of the family. A wife would influence the family for
better or worse in very significant ways.

Declan owed it to everyone to meet the girl.

'Very well,' he said as he set aside the paper unread. 'I will
go.'

His mother nodded with a self-satisfied smile. 'I knew you
would rise to the occasion. I hope you see now how intemper-
ance one night makes the next morning nearly unbearable.'

He gritted his teeth. Damn the woman for being right. Several caustic words burned on his tongue, but he swallowed them
down. She was still his mother, not to mention a duchess, and
therefore deserved some respect. Also, cutting into her for her
overbearing, supercilious, condescending attitude would be like
scolding a dog for having fur. It was simply who the woman
was, and he had ceased tilting at windmills some time in his
early adolescence.

He did arch his brows at her, in an attempt at ducal arrogance. 'I cannot dress with you here,' he said. 'And therefore I
cannot depart for this boat.'

She sniffed, as if his words had an actual smell. 'First you
will deal with your cousin, and then I should like you to attend

Almack's this Thursday. There are several girls I have selected who will make excellent duchesses—after my instruction, of course. Select one this week and you can be well on your way to filling a nursery this time next year.'

He didn't bother interrupting her. The woman rarely stopped speaking even when interrupted. So he waited in stiff silence until she was silent. Then he gave her a single, hard word.

'No.'

'What—?'

'No.'

She rolled her eyes, then abruptly decided on a gentler approach. She settled herself in the chair opposite his and spoke calmly.

'Declan, think. If you are to avoid the legacy of your name, you need a wife who is calm, who doesn't invite rages, who is unimpeachable in character and lineage. There are precious few of those around. Indeed, I have inspected every one within a decade of your age.'

He shuddered to think of how that process had gone.

'Mother,' he said dryly, 'you will not be selecting my bride.'

'Well, of course not!' she snapped, her softer tone gone. 'I have just narrowed the field—'

'I will select my own bride. Soon. You will not dictate that. Do not even try.'

She tsked deep in her throat. And then her brows went up and she took on *that tone*. The one she'd used all through his childhood. The one that told him exactly what she was about to say now.

'You are too mercurial to make this decision. It is the Byrning legacy, you know. High temper, irrational actions. It will destroy you as it destroyed your father.'

It was true. It was the dark spectre that hung over his family. Not just his family tree, but his own flesh and blood.

His father's unbridled rage at a servant had caused his sister's death. His little sister had stepped into the fray to protect her nanny, only to receive a blow herself by accident. It had killed her. His father had become a drunkard that day, choosing to become insensate rather than succumb to the Byrning legacy again.

That had been his father's solution. And it hadn't worked.

The man had had many rages afterwards, but mostly he'd been too drunk to harm anyone. In the end, he'd stumbled into the Thames and drowned, leaving his son in charge of the Dukedom.

'I have not had a rage since my adolescence,' he reminded his mother. 'My faculties are well in hand. I will find a bride of my own choosing.'

He said the words, but in his heart he knew his mother was right. All those qualities she listed were exactly the ones he needed. He must marry someone of even temperament and impeccable manners. She would help him remain calm and soothe over any missteps he might make along the way. And he would need to find her soon because he was an unwed duke who needed an heir.

And now, as he did every morning, he rededicated himself to staying rational, calm, and completely unaffected by emotion. And if he failed in that mission here was his mother, personally invested in keeping him in line.

'Do try to be logical,' his mother pressed. 'You need an heir while I am still young enough to ensure he is raised properly.' She leaned forward. 'So I can be sure the Byrning curse does not take root again.'

'It has not taken root in me!' he snapped.

She pursed her lips, then raised a single brow. That was all it took and once again he was a dirty boy with raised fists and a burning shame that his temper had once again made him go too far. Back then, he'd fight anyone who said a cross word to him. He'd found fights, he'd created fights, and he'd usually won them. Because he was heir to a dukedom and no one—even young boys—wanted to hurt him.

Time and constant admonishments from several people in his life had taught him to control his rage. He now buried his temper beneath logic and constant vigilance. He was not slipping now.

He took a long look at the mantel clock and arched a brow

back at his mother. 'Do you want me to meet Cedric's bride or not?'

She clucked her tongue in disgust. She was not subject to the Byrning legacy of rage, but she certainly had her moments of annoyance. Her pinched face, however, did not move him.

'Very well,' she said as she pushed to her feet. 'We will deal with Cedric first.'

As if she would do anything now that she'd set him to the task.

'Then I expect you to choose a bride immediately afterwards.'

'Good day, Mother.'

After a long-suffering sigh, she spun on her heels and departed. Which meant Declan had no excuse to remain seated in the dark as he nursed his sore head.

Damn his father for dying. This really ought to be his problem.

With a sigh, Declan rang for his valet and prepared to meet a 'miserably unsuitable' woman.

Chapter Two

Declan arrived at *The Integrity* within the hour. Given the quiet and relative dark of his carriage, his mood had steadily improved. Nothing cheered him so much as being left alone. That ended, of course, the moment he stepped out into the teeming noise of the dock. And it was made worse as he struggled to find the ship itself.

By the time he strode up the gangplank he wanted nothing more than to get this task over with as quickly as possible. Which made the absolute absence of anyone on board a frustrating annoyance.

'Hello?' he called as he looked about.

He heard nothing. Or rather he heard a million voices around him, the cry of the gulls, and the splash of things hitting or being hit by water. Sadly, he could not identify any as coming from within the confines of this boat. Bloody hell—how did anyone understand anything amid this cacophony?

'On deck!' came a bellowing voice from below.

Declan jolted as he turned to see the muscular, moustachioed man climbing up from below deck. He was dressed casually, but his weathered face and the easy way he moved suggested he was at home on this ship. The command in his tone implied he was the captain. Declan was about to speak when he realised the man was squinting up into the sails as he shook his head.

'Half monkey, half bird,' he muttered—apparently to himself, because he seemed startled when he turned and saw Declan standing there. 'What ho?'

'Hello,' Declan said, though his gaze was going up, up, up into the sails, where he could just make out a figure springing lightly through the mass of ropes. Half monkey, half bird was right. As he watched, the sailor took an impossible leap, caught a rope, then swung around before another long jump. It was breathtaking. And possibly life-taking if the man missed.

But he never did.

'Good God,' Declan muttered, envy in his tone.

Once upon a time he'd wanted to be a captain on the high seas, answerable to no one, free to challenge the elements however he wanted, and able to wander the world on his own whim. It had been a boy's fantasy, of course. No future duke could risk himself that way, and only a child thought life aboard ship was easy. And yet watching the sailor fly through the riggings, he felt his heart soar. Such freedom!

'Crazy,' the captain muttered as he followed the sailor's movements. 'Some are born to this life; some find it. That one found it and has the devil's own determination to make it fit.'

Declan had no idea what that meant, but he had no desire to dispel his private fantasy. In his mind, that sailor had no cares except to run the riggings for fun.

He pulled off his hat as he addressed the captain. 'Good morning, sir. I'm looking for my cousin Cedric, Lord Domac. I was told—'

'Yes, yes, he's due. Said he'd be here an hour ago, but I knew better than to expect him.'

Wise. Cedric had never managed time well. Or money. What he did manage well were people. Something about Cedric's sunny smile, bright hair, and the mischievous glint in his eyes had the most stiff-necked duchess softening. That put him in direct contrast to Declan, who had always been sober, restrained, and aloof. Thanks to the Byrning legacy, that was the only way for him to be without striking terror in his mother's heart.

'If you're his cousin, then I'm guessing you're the young Duke. Pleased to meet you, Your Grace. I'm Captain Banakos. Lord Domac asked me to show you around.'

'You were expecting me?'

The man grinned. 'I was, Your Grace, though I didn't know it would be today. Lord Domac said you'd be coming to inspect things. Said you'd be determined to understand everything about the gal's dowry.'

And now Declan began to understand. His cousin wasn't marrying an unsuitable girl. He was trying to get the lady's dowry.

'Please, show me everything,' he said.

And see it, he did. Every inch of the stripped-down, well-managed vessel. Everything was in place, everything was clean, and the hold was impressively full of cargo that had yet to be transported to a nearby warehouse.

Captain Banakos was a delightful guide, with several good stories to relay, and Declan forgot his sore head, forgot his irritating mother, and thoroughly enjoyed himself.

Indeed, he'd taken off his boots and was partway up the mainmast barefoot when his cousin finally made an appearance.

'Aren't you too old for that?'

Declan was looking up into the rigging, but paused when he recognised his cousin's voice. He noted as well the rough burr in it that indicated someone else likely had a sore head.

'Come on down, old man,' Cedric continued. 'It's too early to play monkey.'

Declan finally looked down. 'It's after noon, and you were expected several hours ago. Also, I'm only three years older than you.'

'That's old. Now, come down. I'd like to talk without craning my neck.'

Declan sighed. The air up here was clearer, and he'd discovered the unexpected thrill of challenging the sky by climbing. He hadn't got far, of course. Not yet. But he abruptly decided that he would someday. Unfortunately, now wasn't the moment. He needed to speak with Cedric, so he narrowed his eyes, planned his angle, and jumped.

He landed with a thud, the feel of the wood on his bare feet making him grin. He hadn't jumped like that since he was a boy. God, how he missed those days, when he hadn't been constantly aware of his violent legacy. When running and jumping had been fun and not an indication of generations of past misdeeds.

Meanwhile, Cedric was gazing up at the sailor still running about the rigging.

'Welcome back to England,' Declan said as he mentally closed the door on his boyhood dreams.

'Thanks. Isn't it your birthday today?' Cedric returned.

'Yesterday. And instead of birthday greetings the Duchess has ordered me to speak with you.'

'Has she?' Cedric drawled, his expression carefully blanked.

The poor man bore the moniker of 'The Inconsistent One', thanks to Declan's mother, so there was little love lost between the two. But rather than discuss that, he gestured around at the massive boat with a too-enthusiastic grin. 'Isn't she magnificent? Let me show you around.'

'I have been all over this boat already,' Declan said. 'And she's definitely seaworthy.'

It was the best compliment he could give to the efficient vessel. In truth, he liked it for being exactly what it needed to be, without luxuries, beautiful woodwork, or anything that would usually attract Cedric's attention.

'I know she's not much to look at, but she's exactly what she needs to be.'

Declan couldn't agree more, though he was surprised Cedric had echoed his thoughts. 'She's a fine ship,' he said in all honesty.

'And she's all mine.'

Had he married the girl already? Doubtful. His mother rarely got details like that wrong. What was more likely was that Cedric had yet to learn that wanting things and having things were entirely different. How like the young man to speak as if something were a fact when that was far from the truth.

'Truly?' he said.

Nothing more, but Cedric withered under Declan's stare.

'Um...well, it will be after the wedding.'

'Ah,' he said as Cedric ran his hand up and down the main-mast. 'About that...' he began.

But before he could go further, a voice interrupted from above.

'Beware below!'

Declan looked up, but Cedric was faster. He grabbed his cousin's arm and pulled him to the side rail. Then they watched in shock as the jumping sailor launched off the middle sail, flipped mid-air, then landed solidly on the deck. It was an impressive feat, and would have been a dangerous one if the ship had been full of people. Even relatively empty, the deck had coiled ropes and buckets all about. One slight miscalculation and the sailor would have a broken leg or worse.

Crazy! And yet Declan was impressed—especially as the leaper straightened up with an impish grin.

'I never get to do that when we're sailing,' said the boy.

At least Declan assumed it was a boy, given the grin, the diminutive stature, and the Asian slant to his features. Though Declan had met precious few Chinamen in his life—exactly two—he'd thought they all looked young, with features as refined as their porcelain. Smooth skin accentuated by dark slashes for brows and long, elegant fingers. This boy had the addition of a ready smile, a softly formed nose, and dark hair swept up into his sailor's cap.

'You're showing off!' Cedric said with a grin.

The boy laughed with a surprisingly musical treble, but Cedric hadn't finished.

'Did you have any problems getting here?'

'Took a hansom cab—as you suggested. But you're late.'

Cedric shrugged. 'You seem to have occupied yourself easily enough.'

'There's always something to do. I was checking the ropes. Rats are everywhere in London, and they'll eat the ropes if they're hungry.'

'There's too much good food in London,' Cedric scoffed. 'The rats will go for the better food and leave our boat alone.'

The sailor arched a brow but didn't speak. He didn't have to. Even Declan, who had spent little time on board a ship, knew that there were hungry rats everywhere, even in as wealthy a city as London. Especially in London.

'Very well,' Cedric continued. 'You can go back to it. We'll talk more in a bit, after I show my cousin around.'

The sailor grinned, then ducked away to climb the mizzen-mast. The two men watched for a moment, and Declan was impressed by the young man's thoroughness as he ran his fingers over every inch of rope while clinging like a monkey to the rigging.

But, as fascinating as the boy was, Declan had a purpose here and it was time he got to it. He turned to his cousin, watching as Cedric continued to stare at the boy with a cat-with-the-cream smile.

'Cedric...' he began, but his cousin interrupted.

'I'm not going to listen. I've found a course, and I like it.'

Damnation, this was not going to be easy.

'You've found many courses over your life, and you have loved every single one.'

Cedric grimaced. 'That's part of being young.' He turned to frown at Declan. 'Weren't you the one always climbing trees, exploring caves, talking about sailing away to fame and fortune?'

'I was a boy.'

'And now we're both men who can choose our own paths. I've found a taste for sailing.'

'What if this passion burns out like all the others?'

Cedric looked him in the eye, straightening his shoulders as he faced Declan. It was the most adult expression he'd seen on his younger cousin's face.

'I have listened and learned. I'm not sailing the ship myself. I'm hiring people to do that.'

'You're the financial backing,' Declan said.

And though it wasn't a question, Cedric answered it anyway.

'Yes. And it will be profitable. I swear it.'

'But not with your own money. With your wife's money.'

Cedric waved that way. 'After the wedding, it will be mine.'

That was true enough, but the words still grated. What a poor lot for the woman who was attached like a barnacle to the real asset of her dowry.

'There are other ways to get money than trapping a young woman.'

His cousin snorted. 'Will you loan me the money?'

'How much?'

'Ten thousand pounds.'

Now it was Declan's turn to snort. 'Absolutely not.'

At least not without a great deal more study.

'Then she is the only way. My father has burned through everything else.'

Declan grimaced. Whereas Declan's father had been a violent drunk, Cedric's father was a vicious gambler. It was just another manifestation of the Byrning legacy. And, as with all gamblers, he won for a time, and then he didn't. At last reckoning the Earl had lost everything that wasn't entailed. Which had left Cedric to find a way to finance his own life and his sisters' dowries.

It wasn't the worst idea to marry for money. Just a cruel one.

'Who is this woman?' Declan pressed. 'The Duchess said she's illegitimate.'

Cedric scrunched his face up in a mockery of Declan's expression. 'She's been claimed by her father. More important, she has a lovely dowry. Recall, please, that I'm an adult and can marry the woman of my choice.'

'Within reason.'

Cedric was a future earl. He might not have as many restrictions as a duke, but he couldn't marry willy-nilly either.

'Marrying a by-blow for her dowry isn't reasonable.'

'On the contrary. It's exactly what my father did when he married my mother. And my grandfather. And his father before that. It's our family legacy as much as the gambling, and you know it.'

He did know it. He also knew that Cedric had once sworn never to marry for any reason except love. The man was a romantic. He'd fallen head over heels in love at least three times before he was sixteen. And yet here he was, openly admitting to being a fortune-hunter.

'You're the grandson of a duke, the son of an earl,' Declan said. 'There are scores of wealthy women you could marry. It need not be this woman. Your mother will be all too happy to introduce you to—'

'Empty-headed misses who bore me?'

'Do you love her? Is that it? You know that love is a fleeting indulgence—'

'I'm not a child, longing for a woman's touch.' Cedric gripped the rail, his expression unreadable. 'I need ten thousand pounds to buy this ship and a cargo. If you will not loan me the money...' He slanted a look at Declan.

'Absolutely not.'

'Then I shall get it through her.'

Declan crossed his arms, doing his best to understand his cousin's bizarre actions. 'Are you sure of her dowry?'

'Yes. It is being proffered by her father, Lord Wenshire.'

Declan frowned. He'd never heard of Lord Wenshire.

'He's Lord Whitley's youngest brother.'

'The eccentric?'

'The explorer. He made his fortune through the East India Company.'

Now he remembered—but he'd never heard of a daughter. 'And this woman is his child?'

'Yes.'

Declan leaned back against the railing, his gaze naturally going to where the boy continued to inspect the ropes. It was merely a way to stall as he thought through the information.

'You're not infatuated with her? You are marrying her completely for her money?'

'I like her well enough.'

Society marriages had been built on less.

Declan started listing the facts, trying to sort through the issue. 'She is Lord Wenshire's daughter and dowered with ten thousand pounds.'

'She's dowered with this boat.'

Ah, now he understood. Still, he continued listing off her attributes. 'She was born illegitimate, but her father has acknowledged her and made her an heiress.'

'Yes.'

So why had the Duchess called the woman unsuitable?

'Our mothers think she's unacceptable. Is it really because she's a by-blow?'

Being born on the wrong side of the blanket was a black mark, but it wasn't an insurmountable one. Especially with a dowry worth ten thousand pounds.

'I cannot fathom their thought processes. I refuse to even try.'

Declan couldn't blame him for that. But what he couldn't understand was why his cousin had chosen a woman despised by his mother when there were so many others with good dowries?

'Out with it, Cedric. Why this girl? Surely there are dozens of well-dowered women your mother would celebrate. You can buy a boat then. Maybe not this one, but there are many others.'

His cousin arched a brow. 'You think so? Thanks to your mother, I have been dubbed "The Inconsistent One", and no wealthy woman wants that in a husband.' He crossed his arms. 'So, unless the family wants to loan me the money, I shall have to marry the girl I have chosen.'

'A by-blow foreigner?'

'Yes.'

'You are the son of an earl—'

'And the grandson of a duke. I know.'

'Why make things difficult? For her, if not for yourself. Do you know how hard it will be for any woman to go up against our mothers?'

His cousin tilted his head back as he looked up the mizzen-mast. 'I require ten thousand pounds, Declan. If you care so much for the family name, then find me another way of getting the funds I require.'

He heard the finality in his cousin's voice. Or perhaps it wasn't finality as much as something a great deal darker. Blackmail.

'You are using this woman as a threat.' It wasn't a question. 'You will marry an unsuitable girl unless we pay to stop you.'

Cedric arched his brows in challenge. 'What is the family name worth? Surely ten thousand pounds—'

'Is a ridiculous sum. You cannot think we have that kind of cash simply sitting around.'

'She does. Or rather her father.'

'Don't be a fool. I will not give in to blackmail, and you are a cad to use a woman so cavalierly.' He shook his head. 'Cedric, what has happened to you? You are not a man to use a woman this cruelly. In fact, you once swore you would marry only for love.'

His cousin rounded on him, the movement quick. It wasn't violent, though Declan tensed at it, but the words certainly carried a threat.

'And when was that, dear cousin? When did we last know each other?' Venom dripped from every word.

Declan frowned. 'At school—'

'Yes. Ten years ago. When my father still had my sisters' dowries. When the most difficult thing we had to do was spend our winnings at cards.'

Cedric had gambled at cards. Declan had been too afraid of the Byrning legacy to pick up the habit.

'Then you disappeared to play in Italy.' Cedric spat the words.

'It was my Grand Tour,' Declan shot back.

And it certainly hadn't been fun. Not at the end.

'I don't care! You disappeared. My family money disappeared. And there I was, all alone, trying to find an answer.' He gestured expansively at the boat. 'And here it is. My answer.'

Declan shook his head, wondering where he had gone wrong with his cousin. How had that romantic boy turned into this angry, bitter man?

'I will not give you ten thousand pounds.'

'Maybe not,' Cedric said, with a too-casual shrug. 'Or maybe you will change your tune after tea this afternoon.'

Declan narrowed his eyes. 'What are you planning?'

Cedric smiled in a way altogether too calculating to be charming. 'Obviously you have met the lady early, but I shall introduce her to the rest of the family this afternoon.'

'I have met no one,' Declan snapped.

'My apologies,' his cousin said. 'Pray let me introduce you properly—but don't mention anything about our nuptials, will you? I haven't proposed yet.'

Well, that was something. The lady need not know she was a ploy being used to blackmail Cedric's family.

'You can be sure she won't learn it from me.'

He was here to stop the wedding, not push the relationship.

Cedric nodded, then put his fingers to his lips and let out a loud whistle. The boy who was now up on the middle sails looked towards them.

'Come here!' Cedric bellowed as he gestured.

The boy understood. He immediately began scrambling down the rigging, pausing at much too high a height before doing another one of those acrobatic flips to the deck. It made Declan's heart leap to his throat—half in envy, half in fear—but the sailor landed with natural grace before rushing over.

'Yes?'

Cedric laughed. 'Take off your cap. Let me introduce you properly.'

Shock was already rolling through Declan's system. His mind kept saying, *No, it isn't possible*. And yet, with his cousin, of course this was possible. And, indeed, things proceeded with horrifying clarity.

He saw Cedric grin as the boy whipped off his cap and a short crop of straight black hair tumbled down, held back by a crude tie. The boy—who wasn't a boy at all—smiled at him. Declan noted straight white teeth and a healthy glow after the exertion. He saw laughing eyes that might well be mocking his shock.

And he saw a beautiful woman in boy's clothes with bare feet and trim ankles.

'Declan, please allow me to introduce Grace Richards, Lord Wenshire's daughter.'

Chapter Three

Grace had been enjoying the freedom up in the sails too much to pay attention to the men's conversation. She knew she'd be summoned eventually. Lord Domac was always planning something, and this morning would be no different. But she knew her father looked favourably on the man, so she did her best to treat him generously. Plus, the gentleman had given her cab money for this early-morning trip to the boat, where she could once again run free amid the sails and her sister could hide below deck with the accounts.

She hoped the girl had stayed hidden from the men. It wasn't appropriate for a lady to be seen doing accounts. It wasn't appropriate for Grace to be running around the sails, but she and her sister did what was needed when they felt too confined.

Stays and etiquette lessons had their place. This morning had been about breathing freely one last time before the Season began.

But when Lord Domac had called she'd done her best to make an entrance. Cedric loved it when she acted like an acrobat in the sails, so she'd performed a backflip to the deck before doing her dramatic reveal as a woman.

In truth, she relished the slack-jawed shock on the taller man's face. Men always underestimated her, and it was fun to see them surprised.

Though now that she was looking at the new gentleman's face, she had to admit that he hadn't reacted with as much shock as most men. Many grew furious at her reveal, so she tensed to run, but his movements were restrained. His brows rose, his mouth pressed tight. Rather than focus his anger on her, his glare skipped straight over her to land on Lord Domac.

Then it was gone. Two seconds later, he turned back to her with a warm smile and dipped his head in a formal greeting.

'A pleasure to meet you, Miss Richards. I am the Duke of Byrning, as my addled cousin neglected to say.'

'Stop being a prick,' Lord Domac groused. 'We're on board. We don't stand on ceremony here.'

The Duke arched his brows. 'Every woman deserves courtesy.'

That was a surprising attitude, and Grace pinkened in delight at his words, especially as he looked so steadily into her eyes. Normally men's gazes roved across her breasts or hips, looking for proof of her sex.

'My cousin is a stuffed popinjay,' Lord Domac said. 'He doesn't realise you prefer easy manners.'

Did she? She'd never met anyone who had used full manners with her. She'd seen from a distance as men bowed and demurred to other women, but never, ever had a man addressed her as if she deserved the full measure of his courtly manners. Not even Domac.

But this man did. He stood there in his gentleman's attire and gave her every courtesy. Even his bare feet didn't take away from the heavy impact of his regard. And so she gave him her best response.

'I am honoured to meet you, Your Grace.'

She curtsied as she'd been taught, though it probably looked ridiculous given that she wore a boy's clothing. Then she launched into the polite discourse her father had insisted she learn. First a comment on the weather, and then a question about the gentleman's interest.

'It's a sad wind today, I think. The boats are stuck without a breeze to lift their skirts. Have you an interest in sailing?'

Lord Domac grinned at her. 'You mean a breeze to lift their sails. Lifting skirts is something else entirely.'

Was he poking fun at her? He was the one who had taught her the phrase. 'Sails. My apology.'

Domac chuckled. 'Grace has learned most of her English from sailors and the like, but her father and I are teaching her how to go on.'

The Duke didn't even look at his cousin. Instead, he lifted his gaze to the slack sails. 'I know a little about boats and skirts, and the sails are definitely flat today. I am afraid my cousin has told me nothing about you. Were you born and raised in Canton?'

'I was.'

She could not be from anywhere else. Whites were only allowed in a small area of Canton. And half-whites, like herself, were lucky to be alive at all. Most were drowned at birth.

'Do you have much knowledge of China?'

Her father had told her that most would not know anything about her country. Indeed, they would not be able to find it on a map.

'More than most Englishmen,' he said, 'but nothing from someone who has lived there. I would love to learn more.'

She might have answered, but Lord Domac raised his hand to stop her. 'There is time enough to answer those questions at tea this afternoon. Grace has lived an extremely interesting life.'

The Duke's eyes narrowed, as if he was annoyed, but he didn't turn that rancour on Grace. Instead, he smiled at her. 'I look forward to learning all about it. Are you here for the Season, then? To find a husband?'

She was here because her only options in China were to become a nun or a prostitute. Lord Wenshire had offered her another option, and she'd grabbed it with both hands. But she couldn't say that now. Instead, she gestured towards London.

'My father wished me to see his homeland, and so I have indulged him.'

'You mean you have *obeyed* him,' Lord Domac corrected. 'As every good daughter does.'

She knew the difference between the two words and she had used the correct one. She had wanted to go to Africa, where she would be seen as foreign, but not a half-blood. In China, she was routinely cursed for her mixed blood. It would likely be the same here in England, since she was half English, half Chinese, but she had bowed to her father's wishes.

Rather than argue with Lord Domac, she continued to speak, working hard to act properly. 'My father came into my life only recently. He found me at a temple that is known to care for half-Chinese children. He claimed me as his own and offered to take me to England.'

'Extraordinary! And you went with him? Alone? Without even speaking English?'

'But she wasn't alone!' Lord Domac inserted. 'She has brought her sister along as well, and Lucy already knew English.'

Lucy had known *some* English, but it didn't matter. Neither of them had had a better option.

'Lucy isn't my sister through blood, but we were raised together. I couldn't imagine leaving China without her, so my father claimed us both.'

The Duke nodded slowly. 'Lord Wenshire is extremely generous.'

'Yes, he is,' she said, irritation making her voice hard.

Her father was indeed a generous man. The kind of person she couldn't believe truly existed, but months in his presence had shown her that he wanted the best for her and her sister. And it infuriated her whenever someone suggested otherwise.

He must have heard her tone because the Duke quickly dipped his head in apology. 'I meant no offence. Truly, I am simply impressed.'

She nodded, softening her own tone. 'I didn't believe it at first either,' she confessed. 'But he convinced me.'

The Duke's brows rose. 'I am desperate to hear more.'

'Which will happen at tea,' Lord Domac interrupted. He was always restless. 'Suffice it to say that Miss Richards is looking forward to an eventful Season.'

'Definitely,' she agreed.

Musicales, balls, and the theatre pulled at her curiosity. The way her father described them made her yearn to experience them. He made the Season sound like weeks spent in delight.

'Yes. Tea,' the Duke said, his voice dry as he shot a hard look at his cousin.

She had no idea what it meant, and no time to understand as he focused back on her.

'Do you attend with your father?'

'I don't know,' she said in full honesty. 'He does not often share his plans with me.'

Or his plans *for* her. He assumed that because she was new to English society, she had no idea how to manage herself. But she'd worked as a navigator on board a merchant ship for years. To think that she could not understand the niceties of appearing on time and dressing appropriately for this tea ceremony was an insult to her intelligence. But he was her parent, and she was here at his mercy. She would strive to hold back her temper.

'And does he know that you are here aboard ship this morning?' the Duke asked.

Although the man's tone was polite, Grace was accustomed to reading nuances in expression and tone. She read an implied criticism in the tightness of his face.

'Of course he does,' she said. 'I am on a morning outing with Lord Domac. My maid and my sister are below deck.' She straightened as his expression turned dark. 'I am completely safe here, and it is not your place to question my father's actions.'

Or her own.

It was a harsh response, but she'd learned young that men would take whatever authority over a woman they could. They might say they were protecting her, but it was merely a cover for their need to be in power. She had learned to strike back ruthlessly when a man sought to dictate to her, even in so small a thing as a dark look.

The Duke flushed, and his brows rose in an imperious expression equal to the haughtiest mandarin in China. 'I look to your *reputation*, Miss Richards. I do not blame *you*. I fear my cousin has been too lax with your safety.'

Her *reputation* was as a great navigator. If she weren't a

woman, she'd have her choice of ships. Instead, she'd been run off the docks the moment she'd developed a woman's body and could no longer hide. So she'd gone back to the temple where she'd been raised, and that was where her father had found her. But she supposed the Duke referred to her English reputation.

Meanwhile, Lord Domac had focused on a different aspect of the conversation. 'You have brought Lucy here?'

'Yes. She needed the outing as much as I did.'

Lord Domac made a sound that she could not decipher. Half grunt, half amused chuckle. Then he rocked back on his heels and grinned. 'I believe we're done here. Grace, please fetch your sister and your maid. I have a carriage nearby and will take you back to your father's house so you can get ready for tea.'

She frowned. 'Tea isn't until four.'

Just how much time did he think it took to change her clothing?

'But you have lessons, do you not? Dancing, deportment.' He looked at the Duke. 'She's even learning a smattering of French.'

He sounded as if he was showing off a prize dog. 'We should trade phrases, Lord Domac. I will match my French to your Chinese.'

'But why would I need to learn Chinese when you are here?' he asked.

She could think of a thousand reasons why knowing a language was better than having an interpreter, but she didn't argue. Instead, she looked back at the sails. This was the first time she'd been able to breathe free since coming to London three weeks ago. She didn't want to rush back to corsets and dance lessons.

'There are a few more things I'd like to check in the riggings,' she lied. 'Can we wait a bit longer?'

Lord Domac groaned. 'There's nothing of interest up there.'

'Perhaps I could be of assistance,' the other man said. 'I would be happy to wait here until you are ready to leave. It will be entirely proper if your maid stays alongside.' He smiled as he looked at her. 'And I should enjoy getting to know you better.'

She was tempted. There was gentleness in his smile, despite his criticisms, and he was quick to apologise when he overstepped. That was something even Lord Domac never did. But she knew too little of Englishmen to trust her judgement regarding them. She knew her father approved of Lord Domac, so why would she risk alienating him in favour of this other, more interesting man?

Because she was always drawn to the new, the different, and the generally intriguing. She'd survived by being bold, and she liked this handsome man.

She gestured to his bare feet. 'Have you ever climbed up to a crow's nest?'

'Never,' he said as he tilted his head all the way back.

'It's a long climb and a fall would be deadly,' she said. 'But the view is the loveliest in London.'

His brows rose. No doubt he heard the challenge in her voice. 'How can I resist an invitation like that?'

He couldn't. No man could.

'I'll have to tie a rope about your chest. I will not be the cause of your mother's tears.'

He agreed with a nod and a grin. 'I put myself in your hands.'

Another surprise. Most men dismissed the need for a rope, their pride getting in the way of common sense. Clearly, this man was not a fool, and she respected him all the more for it.

Not so Lord Domac, who hooted his disdain.

'She'll have you trussed up like a Christmas goose. I've seen her do it before.' Then he punched his cousin in the shoulder. 'There's no wind today. The rigging's safer than your mother's stairway.'

That wasn't at all true. Climbing ropes was still difficult if one wasn't used to it. And although this man looked fit, climbing was not a usual exercise for gentlemen.

Apparently he knew that, because he looked her in the eye. 'Do you tie me up as a joke? Or because it is necessary?'

'Necessary,' she answered honestly. Then she cast a look at Lord Domac. 'But I trussed *him* up like a fish in a net because it was fun.'

Lord Domac had joined their ship when they took port in India for the route back to England and had very quickly got bored. He had wanted to learn, and she had been happy to teach, but since her command of English had been weak, she had been forced to demonstrate rather than explain. That had involved wrapping ropes around him as they moved about the sails, especially at sea.

The Duke grinned as he shed his topcoat. 'Do as you see fit.'

'You won't get halfway,' his cousin taunted.

'How far did you get?'

'All the way up.'

Truth. But it had taken him several tries, and she'd had to wrap him until the ropes had practically carried him the whole way. She wasn't willing to do that again, just to salvage a man's pride. So while the Duke stepped over to the mainmast, she picked up a rope to steady him.

'This won't stop a fall on its own,' she warned. 'It's not a net. But it will slow your drop enough that you can catch hold yourself.'

He nodded as if he understood. She knew he didn't, but she liked the sparkle in his eyes. He was excited and, better yet, he was studying the ascent as he might a mathematical problem. She tied him in as best she could, and then secured the other end about her waist. If he fell badly, she would too, and then they would both die. But she'd done this several times before with other men. It was the only way to get new men up top. They couldn't let a woman get the best of them, so they went on when all reason told them to go down.

'Step where I step,' she said, 'and we'll both be fine.' Then she paused to raise her brows at Lord Domac. 'My sister is in the captain's quarters, looking at the accounts, if you'd like to speak with her. I'm sure she would enjoy seeing you.'

An understatement. For whatever reason, her sister had developed a keen interest in Lord Domac. If their father hadn't declared that Grace must marry first, Lucy—renamed from Lu-Jing—might very well be the one being shoved into stays and forced into tea ceremonies.

Lord Domac's eyes narrowed. 'She's below deck with the captain? *Alone?*'

'With our maid. We have made sure of the proprieties.'

He grunted—another one of those indecipherable sounds—

then headed immediately below deck. That left her alone with the Duke.

'Are you ready?'

'I am.'

'Then so am I.'

She began to climb the ratline, which was another word for the rope ladder. Without question, this was one of her biggest joys. The climb to new heights, the kiss of clean air, and the sheer physical exertion that kept her blood surging. She loved it, and apparently the Duke had no problems with it either. At least for the lowest sails.

His breath became laboured after that, and she pulled him to the platform at the top of the upper main to rest. He landed with an exhalation of breath and an eager look around.

'No need to stop,' he said. 'I can keep going.'

'That's not what the captain is saying.'

'What?'

She gestured down towards the deck, where the captain was now standing at the base of the mizzenmast.

'That be far enough!' he bellowed. 'Bring 'im down.'

The Duke tilted his head, clearly listening, but then he looked back up. 'I don't hear anything, and you promised me the best view in London. You're not backing out on a promise, are you?'

'Never,' she said with a grin. 'But look down again. It's a fair way—'

'I know. I saw.' He grabbed hold of the next ratline. 'Are you too tired to climb up?'

He meant it. He wanted to climb. So she shrugged and scrambled up the next set of ropes. He laboured behind her, his breath steady, so she knew he wasn't afraid. At least not yet. As long as she didn't hear the short, tight breath of panic, she would keep going.

There were seven sails on the mainmast, and he scrambled up six of them without hesitation. She'd gone slower than usual for her, making sure to wrap an arm around each rung in the ladder in case he missed his step and she had to support his weight. He never failed, and for that she was pleased. Clearly this was a man used to physical exercise.

By the top of the sixth sail—the main royal—she forced them both to stop on the platform. Even without a strong breeze, the wobble of the ship made it a dipping and swaying plank of wood. Many sailors had lost a meal from this height. Lord Domac had lost his dinner two sails below.

'How do you feel?' she asked. 'Do you get seasick?'

'No,' he said as he looked all around him. 'There's wind here. I can't imagine what it's like in a storm.'

'Terrifying,' she said with a grin. The height was dizzying, and the mainmast never felt as solid as it did on deck.

He looked at her with an assessing gaze. 'You've done it, haven't you? I can't imagine.'

He was speaking honestly, so she honoured him by giving him the truth in return. 'A ship in a storm is frightening wherever you are. Up there...' she pointed to the crow's nest '... I was able to do some good.'

He narrowed his eyes at the barrel that sat atop another thin platform, still a sail's height above them. 'Doing what?'

'Watching for land. We were off course and needed some place to shelter.' She shrugged. 'I have good eyes.'

'And nerves of steel,' he returned. Then he proved that he also had a full measure of nerve by looking down without blanching. 'Have you seen people fall?'

'Yes.'

He looked up at her clipped word. 'I'm sorry.'

She wouldn't have thought that two words would ease her memories. She still had nightmares. But his sympathy was genuine, and she took comfort from it.

'Thank you,' she whispered.

He gave her a firm nod, then looked back up to the crow's nest. 'Can it fit two of us?'

'It will be tight,' she answered. Then she touched his arm. 'You have come further than your cousin on his first trip. There is no shame—'

'I want to go up.'

And to prove it, he began to climb even before she did.

She watched him go, her hold on the ropes as firm as she could make it. It was actually more dangerous for him to be above her. The added height would make it that much harder for her to stay on the ratline if he fell.

He didn't.

He made it to the crow's nest while she admired the strength of his body and the pure grace in the way he moved. He wasn't a sailor, so he didn't have the flexibility of one. But he was strong, and sure, and never once did his breath shorten with panic. She couldn't even claim that for herself. The first time she'd climbed the ratlines her teeth had chattered from her terror.

He was even with the barrel-shaped crow's nest, and then climbed high enough to swing his feet into the barrel.

'Don't jump down hard,' she warned. 'The flooring isn't as strong as you think.'

He paused before jumping, looking down at her with wide eyes. 'I cannot tell if that's truth or jest.'

'Both,' she said with a wink. 'You're a big man who shouldn't be stomping around up there, but it will hold you.'

He didn't wait any longer before he jumped—lightly—into the nest. And she noted that, while he looked at the view with an awe-struck expression, he kept one hand on the rope and another on the mainmast.

She grinned as she scrambled up, but she'd underestimated his size. There was precious little room for her in the crow's nest, so she loitered above on the ropes.

'This is amazing,' he breathed as he looked all around. Then he glanced back at her. 'Do you know the sights of London?'

She shook her head, and he waved her in, moving back far enough that she could squeeze in beside him.

It was a delicate manoeuvre. She was not used to being touched by anyone, least of all a man she had just met, and yet there was a thrill in his heat and his hands. He let go of the rope and steadied her as she wriggled her way in. She felt his body as a large blanket of warmth, shrouding her from the wind, which was a good deal colder up top. But mostly she felt his breath in the expanse of his chest at her back, and the heat of it where it caressed her cheek. He must chew mint, she thought, for no man's breath smelled that sweet without it.

Then together they peered out over the masts of other boats

to the tableau of London before them. And although she'd said she'd show him the best view from up here, he was the one to show her.

'That way is Southwark,' he said. Then he moved her around, pointing to the city. He named Westminster Abbey and the Tower of London. She couldn't see them clearly, but she didn't need to. What she felt was his body pressed against hers, the certainty with which he stood, and the pride he so obviously felt in his city. He grew so confident that he released his grip on the mainmast, bracing his feet wide as he tucked her against him. And she relaxed as she strained to see what he saw.

'I suppose this means nothing to you without your going there,' he mused.

'Then I shall be sure to visit the places you have named.'

He grinned at her. 'I shall take you,' he said. 'And you shall tell me how it compares to Canton. Does your land have such grand edifices?'

'Different ones,' she said. 'But still grand.'

'I wish I could see,' he said, and she heard a longing in his voice that she did not understand.

'It only takes a ship and some time.'

'It takes a great deal more than that,' he countered. 'As a duke, I have many responsibilities that keep me tied to England. You cannot imagine the complaints I would get if I left for so much as a week, much less the time it would take to sail to China.'

'You are fortunate to have a family who values you.'

As a woman of mixed race, she had discovered most people wanted her dead. She was beyond lucky to have found her father. Indeed, without him she might right now have been forced into prostitution for her daily bowl of rice. Instead, she stood with a handsome English mandarin while watching a seagull swoop past.

'What happened to your mother?' he asked, his voice low.

She jolted, feeling his breath against her cheek and the compassion in his words. It was a heady mixture when she was so used to harsh tones.

'I don't know,' she confessed. 'I was left not yet a day old on the temple steps.'

'You don't know?' he asked. 'But surely Lord Wenshire has discovered what happened to your mother.'

She flinched, panic surging into her throat. Damn it, only one day with a new person and she was already slipping.

'He searched before coming to the temple. The woman he loved—my mother—' she almost choked on the lie '—was murdered by her husband. She was his fifth concubine and very lonely. But even so he had the right to kill her when she became pregnant with another man's child. I was lucky that a servant took me to the temple.'

He nodded slowly. 'Why didn't you say that at first?'

Because it was a lie.

'My father told me to keep the details secret. China can be a harsh country, and he did not want people to think less of me because of my past.'

It was a feeble excuse, but he seemed to accept it. Or at least did not argue it.

'Your life must have been very harsh.'

Yes and no. She knew many people who had had it worse. Many who had died.

'I found a way to survive as a navigator. At least for a time.' Until her true gender had been discovered. 'And then my father found me. I was very, very lucky.'

'And I am even more impressed,' he said.

They said nothing then. They watched the birds and the bobbing ships. She surprised herself by relaxing into the moment. Their bodies were touching, and she ought to be afraid. She had never allowed a man this close before. Certainly not since developing breasts. And yet, she was not afraid.

She accustomed herself to the press of this man's body, to his scent away from the dock smells, and the safety of looking at a view without being wary of any danger. They were docked in a safe harbour, and he was not a man to fear. He was a man who made her skin tingle and her thoughts spin in new directions. She had spent a decade on boats, learning her trade. She knew what men said and did. But never had her curiosity been sparked so strongly. And never had her thoughts turned so intimate, so fast.

And while she was thinking all that, he glanced down at her and smiled such that the skin wrinkled around his eyes. Odd that she found that handsome.

'You are so comfortable here. Have you lived most of your life on a boat?'

'I am one of the best navigators in China,' she said proudly.

'How...?' He shifted uncomfortably as he searched for the words.

'How was it possible for a woman?'

He nodded. 'Yes.'

'I saw that every person must have a way to make money. Without a family, my choices were limited.'

Since she was a half-white orphan, her choices had been to sell her body or find skills that were valuable despite her mixed race and sex.

'I learned how to navigate from an old man who had done the job before his eyes turned white. He introduced me to a captain who needed a smart navigator, even if she was a girl.'

'How old were you?'

'Eleven for my first sailing. But I worked hard and earned my place.'

His brows rose. 'I am impressed,' he said. 'To think of all the dangers you faced... Storms, pirates, brutal conditions...'

And her fellow sailors. Which was why she'd bound her breasts and kept to herself.

'I have fought for everything I've ever had,' she said. 'And I have had the protection of good men.'

If it hadn't been for the captain declaring her off-limits, she'd never have made it through her first voyage. Or any of the others.

She lifted her chin. 'I am lucky.'

'And a great deal more,' he said as his gaze travelled over her face. 'Cedric has excellent taste in women.'

She smiled, feeling the compliment warm her.

'But I do not think he has your best interests at heart.'

She arched a brow, already knowing this game. 'And you intend to save me?'

He mimicked her pose. 'Do you need someone to do so?'

She laughed and shook her head, knowing she lied. She had a vast array of skills, but she could not survive alone. Not without her father to support her or a ship's captain who would keep her safe while she worked. Or a husband to shelter her.

'I have come to England to be with my father and to see a new land.'

She kept her voice steady as she spoke, though inside she winced at the lie. She was here because it was the only safe way to escape China. It turned out that she would do a great deal to create a safe home for herself and her sister—including leaving everything she'd ever known and lying to a very kind Englishman.

Meanwhile, the Duke had twisted enough in the crow's nest to look at her face. 'I came here today to dissuade my cousin from marrying a woman, only to realise she is an intriguing prize.'

He touched her face then. A slow caress of his thumb across her jaw. Fire sizzled in its wake, and her breath caught and held. Certainly she had experienced flirtation before, but this man had seen her worth faster than anyone else. He looked at her with admiration mixed with desire, and she wanted to leap into his fire just to feel the burn.

Madness. And yet she wanted it. Even more so when he leaned forward as if to kiss her. But she couldn't allow that to happen. It would be leaping into something she could not control, and that was dangerous territory—especially for a woman.

So she leaped free. A quick jump and a grab and she was swinging herself away from him for all that they were still tied together.

'Miss Richards?' he said as she pulled herself up and away. 'Is everything well?'

'Yes,' she said, horrified to realise that her breath was short with panic. It took her a moment to slow it down, to steady her heart, and to dry the slickness from her palms. 'Yes,' she repeated more strongly. 'We must go back down.'

It was a lie. There was no need to go down for more than an hour except boredom. But he didn't question her. Instead, he took one last look at the world around them before reaching up and pulling himself from the crow's nest.

She watched his strong arms, noted the size of his hands, and admired the ease with which he managed his body. No wonder he was an English mandarin. He exuded power with every movement.

Then he smiled at her, gesturing for her to begin the descent. Normally she would warn him to be extra careful. The descent was harder than the climb, always. But she didn't have the breath. And for the first time in years she felt awed by a man.

Chapter Four

Descending the mast was much harder for Declan. Before, his attention had been on climbing, climbing, climbing...but now his thoughts were on *her*. They ought to be centred on not plummeting to his death, but his mind returned to thinking about how different she was from any other women in his life.

He slipped twice. His toes didn't catch properly, his legs were wobbly from the unaccustomed work. Thankfully his arms held him upright and he was able to refocus his attention. But, damnation, it was impossible *not* to think about her.

She was a female sailor. That alone was startling. She had the physical strength for the work and the bravery, too, if her account was true. He shouldn't be surprised that a bold woman could become a valuable member of a ship's crew.

What shocked him was her sudden modesty. He hadn't climbed up here to become intimate with her, but there was no denying that once they'd been in the crow's nest her body had held a great deal of appeal. He loved the dark silk of her hair and the smooth sweetness of her face. She was exotic, and that had a special lure. She'd also looked him directly in the eyes when she'd spoken, she had listened to what he said, and when the tight quarters had pressed their bodies together he'd been shocked by the force of lust that gripped him.

But he was not a man to be ruled by his lust, so he'd kept his tone polite, he'd given her what little space had been available, and then he'd begun to see if she were amenable to his attention. A touch here, a whispered word there. All subtle, all respectful, and all received as she'd sunk back against him. He'd felt her heat, he'd felt her curves, and he'd started to think of ways to further their association.

Then it had all changed.

One moment he was leaning in for a kiss, and the very next moment she was jumping onto the ropes as if he were a rabid dog. So abrupt had been her movement that he'd looked for some sort of vermin at their feet. No rats except himself. And she'd looked pale enough that he'd feared she'd faint and fall to her death.

She had recovered, thank God, but she'd wasted no time escaping him. If they hadn't been tied together, she'd probably have leaped to the deck minutes ago.

That was not the reaction of a seasoned courtesan or a rough sailor. What had happened there resembled the response of a frightened virgin, and he could not reconcile Grace's appearance in coarse sailor's clothing with her modest reaction.

The dichotomy had him replaying their entire acquaintance in his head to see if he'd missed clues. And the puzzle had him missing his footing.

'Easy now, guv,' said the captain from only a few feet below. 'That's a long, hard haul ye did there. I'm right impressed.'

Declan righted himself and dropped heavily to the deck. The shock of the impact reverberated through his heels up to his spine, and he was appalled by the weakness in his legs from the exertion. He was even more startled to discover that he couldn't see Miss Richards anywhere. Nor did he see his cousin, though that was less surprising.

'Lord Domac left about fifteen minutes ago,' the captain said. 'Said he wasn't going to loiter here waiting.'

Of course not.

'And Miss Richards?'

'Gone below to change into her fancy dress. She can't go back to her father's house looking like a sailor, now, can she?'

Somehow she'd been fast enough to make it to the deck, untie herself from him, and then dash away—all before he'd made it fully down.

'She's a quick one, isn't she?' he asked.

'Has to be as a woman on a ship. Quick with a knife, too, and a well-placed kick.'

'Really?' Declan leaned back against the mainmast as he pulled on his stockings and shoes. 'What do you know about her? How long has she been sailing?'

'I only know what her father told me. She's his daughter from the first time he went to China as a young man. Didn't know he'd fathered her until a year ago. Then he spent months finding her.'

'And she was aboard a ship?'

The captain grunted. 'That's not where he found her. She's a good navigator—best I've seen—but she got into some trouble. I don't know exactly what. She told me the captain who'd protected her had died and... Well, sailors can be an unruly lot. I've got a good crew, but she still had to kick some sense into a few. My guess is, once her protector died she was hard pressed by the crew, and not in a good way. She ran back to the temple where she was raised. That's where her father found her an' talked her into coming here with him.'

That was an extraordinary tale. So extraordinary that Declan wasn't sure he believed it. But then again, he didn't know any women who could climb a mainmast either.

'She can really navigate a ship?'

'Reads a map like you an' me sees colours. Just looks and knows. Sees the stars and does the mathematics in her head.'

'Did you let her navigate for you?'

'She's a curious creature, always poking her head into everything, wanting to know what and why. She started playing a game with my man, seeing who could chart a course faster or better. It was her. Always her. When he got a fever she took over, easy as you please.'

Declan doubted anything for this woman had been easy, but he liked the notion of someone who constantly wanted to learn more about the world. He often suffered from an excess of curiosity, needing to explore beyond what his mother said a duke ought to know. Sometimes he defied her. Other times he gave in for the peace. And even though he knew his mother would damn him for his interest in Miss Grace Richards, he refused to be cowed.

He wanted to know everything about her. Most important, he wanted to know details that he could verify because she sounded more like someone in a tall tale of exaggeration than the flesh-and-blood girl who'd just run away from him in the crow's nest.

He was interrupted by her reappearance.

He'd been watching for her to emerge from below deck and should not have been surprised by what he saw. She wore a modest gown, walking boots, and her hair was arranged in a short, but respectable style. All very proper.

But he hadn't been thinking of her as a proper girl. She was the acrobatic sailor who had turned out to be female. Except now he was staring at a woman dressed as any lady of the *ton*. She walked in small, demure steps, her gaze was downcast, and her face appeared flushed with health. If it hadn't been for the straight, dark hair and the exotic cast to her features, he would have thought her someone else entirely.

She said nothing as she approached, and he stood there staring, dumbstruck by the change in her appearance. She pressed her lips tightly together as she waited and waited…for something.

'Miss Richards?' he said, her name both a question and a statement.

'Yes,' she answered.

Then she glanced awkwardly to the side, where her maid stood in polite silence. He caught the woman's encouraging nod before she spoke.

'Lord Domac has left,' she said bluntly. 'I need a way back to my father's house—'

'But of course. I will escort you,' he said, mentally kicking himself for being so stupid.

Hadn't he already offered to do that before? But he couldn't stop staring at her. Such a change from sailor to debutante, and yet she was beautiful in both outfits.

'Um…are you ready, then?'

'Do you have room for my sister as well? If not, we can take a hansom cab. I believe I have enough coins.'

'No need. There is plenty of room in my carriage.'

'Thank you, Your Grace.'

Then she turned to the hatch, where a young woman was slowly climbing up to the main deck. Her head was cast down, her hair was in an elaborate coif, and…

He blinked in surprise.

She was perhaps the most gorgeous creature he had ever seen.

'May I introduce my sister, Lucy Richards? Lucy, this is Lord Domac's cousin, His Grace the Duke of Byrning.'

'An honour to meet you,' the girl said as she dropped into a deep curtsey.

It was done beautifully, with fluidity and a coy glance upward in the way a courtesan might. She was undeniably lovely, and yet he found the mystery of her older sister much more intriguing.

'A pleasure to meet you, Miss Richards,' he said as he bowed over her hand. 'Are you ready to go?'

'Whatever you wish,' she said, her voice husky.

He frowned at the seductive note to her words, but her expression was demure as she straightened. Had he imagined it? He looked to the much more intriguing sister and saw a frown marring her otherwise smooth face. She, too, was wondering what the younger girl was doing and looked disturbed by the thought.

Excellent. He hoped that there would be some good guidance from her in the future—assuming the younger girl would listen. Meanwhile, he offered his arms to both ladies to escort them off the gangplank.

The elder Miss Richards stayed long enough to give her thanks to the captain, who returned her smile in full measure, and then all three began the awkward process of returning to the docks and finding his carriage.

He watched the older sister closely during all this, trying to mentally connect the woman in the crow's nest to this uncertain society woman. He caught flashes. Moments like when she forgot to keep her steps small and leaped over a mud puddle rather than sidestep it. Other times he saw the maid surreptitiously correcting her and watched as she obeyed with alacrity—though twice he caught sight of her pursed lips as she no doubt silently cursed the restriction.

And then—finally—they were in his carriage and headed towards her father's home. Now he could ask some of the questions that had been burning on his tongue. While all three women sat with folded hands, and their gazes trained through the window to the London streets, he could begin to indulge his curiosity. He counted himself fortunate that the older sister sat across from him, so he could see the open play of emotions across her face. It was less fortunate that the younger sister sat beside him, pressed too close against him.

'Is it common to educate women in China?' he asked.

The elder Miss Richards shrugged. It was an indelicate movement, and it earned her a sharp look from her maid. She stilled as she answered.

'I cannot answer that except to say I had tutors at the temple. The monks taught me very young to be respectful in my questions and to listen to the answers. That it was the only way to survive.'

He noted that she said 'survive' not *learn*, but he could not think of a polite way to press into that. Meanwhile, she turned the questions on him.

'What did you learn as a boy? What can you do?'

How to answer that? It was akin to asking him how he breathed. 'I attended boarding school, where I learned reading and writing. Mathematics, of course, and science.'

She waited for him to continue, her attention fixed upon him. When he spoke no more, she tilted her head. 'Languages? Just English, or—?'

'Latin, Greek, French… A smattering of others.'

Her eyes brightened. 'Can you teach me?'

'What?'

'I have heard about those countries—Greece and France.' She paused. 'Who speaks Latin?'

'No one,' he said with a laugh.

He tried to explain about Rome and the history of that civilisation. It was a complicated thing to discuss, especially as he quickly found holes in her understanding of English. But she remained animated in her interest. She listened carefully and asked questions, and he found delight in explaining what he could.

'There has been a great deal of conquering in this part of the world,' she said. 'Rome has come and gone while we have remained China. Always.'

That was an interesting idea, and he wanted to learn more, but there was no time. They had arrived at the small London home rented by her father.

Declan stepped out, reluctant to lose the intimacy of the carriage, but happy to extend his hand to her and her sister. The older woman grasped it with a strength that shouldn't surprise him. He knew how physically capable she was. But her demure dress continued to confuse him. He kept expecting her to act as a normal society woman when he knew differently.

Being with her was like unwrapping surprise after surprise, and he was intrigued in a way that had not happened with a woman in such a long time.

He escorted them both up the steps, then enquired if Lord Wenshire were at home. Sadly, the man was out, so Declan had no excuse to further his investigation into the pair. Instead, he lingered on the front step while both sisters curtsied to him.

'I should like to call on you again, if I may,' he said.

The older sister wrinkled her nose as she glanced at the maid. 'Is that allowed?'

He answered himself, rather than wait for the maid's response. 'It is,' he said, 'but I shall obtain permission from your father as well. Perhaps I will see you at tea?'

She nodded. 'This afternoon? You'll be there?'

'Nothing could keep me away.'

But first he had to have a very serious discussion with his banker. He was not a man to give in to blackmail, but he was already determined to keep this woman out of his cousin's clutches.

First of all, she didn't deserve to be abused by his cousin in this way. She was far more intriguing a person than his mother had suggested. Capable, attractive, and so different from anyone he'd ever met. She definitely deserved a better match than Cedric.

Sadly, it was the second concern that tipped the scales. As intriguing as she was, she was not capable of handling the life of a countess. He cast no aspersions on her. It was the simple truth that Cedric's wife would need to manage the *haut ton*. That required a knowledge of the English aristocracy which obviously she did not have.

Some things could be learned. But, as a foreigner, she would never be accepted and would constantly have to fight for the smallest amount of respect. It would be a terrible life, and Cedric was not one to retire quietly into the countryside, where his foreign wife might find some peace.

All in all, Miss Richards was exactly what his mother claimed: unacceptable.

The knowledge depressed him. He longed for a world where 'different' was celebrated. Everywhere he turned he heard the same ideas, the same sentiments repeated over and over again. Where were the fresh ideas? Where were the new perspectives?

Nowhere in his circle. People like his own mother made sure of that.

So that was the way of things and he would be a fool to disregard it. But the question of how to separate her from Cedric remained.

What exactly would Declan do to prevent the marriage? Would he pay the ransom? That would be extraordinarily distasteful. Would he court the lady herself? Perhaps string her along long enough for her to realise Cedric's true nature? That, too, would be repugnant.

He would be no better than Cedric, pretending to court her without planning to wed her. Because he couldn't marry her either. If it was terrible to imagine her as a countess, how much worse would her life become if she were his duchess? She would be harassed and disparaged at every turn and, like Cedric, he could not leave London. He had responsibilities and political ambitions here.

Damn Cedric's irresponsible behaviour. And damn Declan's mother for dropping this disaster into his lap. There had to be a solution other than giving in to blackmail, and until he found it he would explore every option—even the most distasteful ones.

Chapter Five

Grace hopped into the carriage, her heart beating with excitement. Finally she was being allowed to mix with proper English company! She was to meet Lord Domac's parents—an earl and his countess—for tea. There would be other ladies and gentlemen there too, but with her father, Lord Domac, and the unsettling Duke of Byrning in attendance, she hoped that she would have enough friendly faces to do well.

And if that happened, then Father would allow her to attend her first ball!

She knew that plans were in place for her come-out. Her father's banker had a daughter ready for her come-out. Her name was Phoebe Gray, and she had wealth but no aristocratic heritage. It had been Mr Gray's suggestion that they come out together, and her father had thought it an excellent idea. They hoped to help one another launch into society that might or might not include the highest members of the *ton*.

But it all relied upon how well Grace performed this afternoon, and she was determined to make a good impression.

She only wished Lucy could come, too. The girl was almost painfully shy, and needed a lot of practice to make a good showing. But their father had insisted that, as the eldest, Grace was to enter society first. He had also pointed out—quietly, to

Grace only—that Lucy needed more time to grow up. For all that she was a genius at sorting ledgers, she still seemed like a duckling wandering lost in the world.

So Grace sat in the carriage and struggled to contain her excitement. It was the first day of a new life for her, or so her father kept saying. And, even though she doubted it was true, his enthusiasm had slipped into her and now she quivered with anticipation. Unfortunately her father kept focusing on something else.

'You are a proper lady now. You cannot let anyone know you spent your morning half-dressed around gentlemen.'

'Two of them were there, Father. They know.'

'Pray that they say nothing. Let us hope they are gentlemen.'

By which he meant that he hoped they were circumspect men who would not shame a woman? Privately she thought the odds very small that any man would hold his tongue if her actions were truly as scandalous as her father suggested. But the whole thing made no sense to her. She had brought her maid, she had been dressed properly on the way to the boat and on her return. And once on the boat she had dressed appropriately to the location. Wasn't that what a sane person did? Dress and act appropriately wherever she found herself?

But apparently English rules were different, so she held her tongue. She looked down at her clasped hands and held her breath. Arguing never changed anything. It only made unpleasantness linger and she was in a mood to be happy.

'You remember what to do during tea?' her father asked.

'I have practised,' she said.

And she had. *Often.* Did he really think her so stupid as to not remember the English tea ceremony? It wasn't even a ceremony, just a shared drink and sometimes a bit of food. And yet he put so much importance on it.

'I pour tea, I drink tea, and maybe I converse.'

'You won't be pouring the tea. It's the conversation that is important.'

She nodded. He'd already said that a dozen times in the last hour. 'I shall do my very best.'

And then he did the one thing that had convinced her to risk everything on this mad trip to England with him. He softened his voice, he smiled at her, and he looked at her with such paternal love that her heart swelled.

And then he apologised.

'I'm sorry. I am pestering you to death. It is only my pride in you that makes me want to show you off. But even if all is a disaster today, then it will make no difference. We will find a new place to live, another city to conquer.'

Guilt ate at her stomach and she glanced at her hands. She knew her father was ill. Though he hid it during the day, he coughed often at night—sometimes badly. She hoped it would get better, but one never knew. He'd often said how he wanted to spend his last years in England, and so she'd come with him here and would do her best to make him happy because he had made her and Lucy safe.

'I need not find a husband,' she said, as she had a hundred times before. 'We can live together wherever you want.'

He clasped her hands in his and pulled them to his lips to press a dry kiss there. 'You and Lucy have filled my heart when I thought myself nothing more than a dried-up old husk. I want to see you both settled before I die.'

'We can be settled without husbands.'

'A woman cannot inherit. She cannot manage her own affairs without a man to sign the papers. It is the same in China—'

'I know.'

'So I must find a good man to take care of you and your children.'

She tightened her hands in her lap. 'You think Lord Domac is that man?'

Her father nodded. 'He will inherit an earldom. That is no small thing. He is impatient, as so many young men are, but I think he will mature into a fine man. If you care for him, I think he will take care of you.'

'I think he cares for my dowry, not me.'

'Nevertheless, I have faith in his sense of honour. He will respect you as a husband ought.'

She nodded. In truth, that was a great deal more than she had ever thought to have. In China, her mixed blood made her an outcast. If her father thought this was the best way to secure her future, then she would consider marrying Lord Domac. After all, she put no faith in love. She only wanted safety. If he proved he could give her that, then she would be happy to marry him. But since she had not yet seen any proof of that, she made no promise to her father.

They arrived at the London residence of Lord Domac's mother. Apparently the woman lived with her sister, the Duke's mother. Her husband the Earl lived elsewhere, as the marriage was not a happy one. This did not surprise her. Many wealthy Chinese couples lived as strangers. Nevertheless, Lord Domac had assured her that his father would be there today to appreciate her beauty.

Or perhaps to ascertain the truth of her dowry.

Whatever the reason, she resolved to make her father proud. So when they arrived she grinned as he tucked her arm against his sleeve. Then they climbed the steps and knocked.

The butler was polite, the drawing room very lovely, and the Countess was dressed in a fine dress that was not silk and yet appeared beautiful nonetheless, thanks to some well-placed embroidery. Having once tried her hand at stitching, Grace knew how difficult the task was and appreciated the skill.

She and her father were introduced, and Grace made her curtsey. The Earl inspected her through his quizzing glass and the Countess looked at her as if she'd eaten something sour. Then, as one, they welcomed her father with polite phrases.

It was not an auspicious beginning, especially when the Earl rolled his eyes at his wife and headed for the door.

'I've seen enough and have an appointment. Good day.'

Then he grabbed his hat from the butler and departed.

Meanwhile, Grace looked about the room, seeing several plates of food in small cut bundles. But what stood out to her the most was Lord Domac as he lounged in a corner, a smirk on his handsome face.

'My lord,' she said. 'I did not see you there hidden behind the…the…' What was the name of the instrument? She couldn't remember. 'The music,' she said finally.

He grinned at her. 'It's the best seat in the house,' he said. 'I can watch everyone's expression from here.'

'Child,' the Countess said with a crisp tone. 'One cannot hide behind music. That instrument is a harpsichord. Harp. Si. Chord.'

Grace dipped her chin. 'Yes, my lady.'

'My daughter's name is Grace,' said her father, his voice cold. 'Or in this case Miss Richards.'

The Countess curled her lip. 'Of course. Miss Richards.'

Grace didn't know how to respond to that, so she kept her mouth shut and her head lowered. At any other time in her life she would have found a way to escape. Now she was glad Lucy wasn't here. The girl didn't need practice with this kind of disaster.

Internally, she sighed and accepted the inevitable. If Grace had one overriding strength, it was the ability to adjust when circumstances changed. She would do her best to mitigate the damage, but there was little more she could do.

Fortunately, the awkward moment ended as the knocker sounded again.

Lord Byrning? Her heart leaped at the thought, but the sound of female laughter filled the room. It was a very polite kind of laughter, quickly snuffed, and yet the sound lingered as three very lovely girls were introduced. They came with an older woman as chaperone, and every one of them was greeted with warmth by the Countess.

They were Miss Smythe, Miss Lockwood and Lady Jane, daughter of Lady Charton, who was their chaperone. Grace watched them carefully, so to emulate their mannerisms.

'Welcome, welcome!' the Countess enthused, then she shot a hard look at her son. 'Cedric, stop hiding in the corner. Come. Tell me you remember these lovely ladies?'

Lord Domac rose slowly to his feet. His smile was warm, and there was a languid kind of elegance to his bow. 'Of course I remember them. But pray, you cannot tell me that none of you caught husbands last season? I cannot credit it.'

'Why, sir,' said Miss Smythe, 'that is because you weren't there last Season.'

The other two girls giggled at that, and generally fidgeted where they stood. If Grace had been so wriggly at the temple, she would have been checked for fleas.

'Come in,' the Countess said as she gestured into the room. 'Let me introduce you to our other guest. Ladies, this is Miss Richards.'

'It is a pleasure to meet you,' she said, and she did a short-ened curtsey because they were of equal social status to her.

'Oh… Oh, dear,' Miss Lockwood said as she pressed a hand to her mouth. 'I'm afraid I can't fully understand her. What did she say?'

'Don't be a dolt,' Lady Jane cried. 'It was something polite, I'm sure. Wherever did you learn to speak English?' she asked.

'I learned from English sailors,' she said, doing her best to form the words clearly.

'*Sail*-ors,' said the Countess, correcting her pronunciation. Then she turned back to the women. 'How quaint.'

'Indeed,' echoed the girls as they wandered deeper into the room.

The three ladies and their chaperone immediately settled onto two settees while Grace remained standing. She hadn't been in-vited to sit and, frankly, the perfume the ladies used was mak-ing her nose itch. Her father smiled at her and gestured for her to sit in the chair where he'd been, but she knew better than to take an elder's seat, so she stood tall beside him.

There was a bouquet of flowers on a nearby table, and Miss Smythe complimented the arrangement. The Countess smiled, and then began a discussion of flowers that Grace had no ability to follow. She hadn't heard any of these words, much less as-sociated them with a bloom. And then Miss Smythe, who was apparently regarded as a flower expert, began to address Grace.

'You should wear daisies in your hair, Miss Richards. They would stand out so beautifully against all that darkness.'

'Don't be so rude,' chided Lady Jane. 'Her hair isn't long enough to support flowers.' She looked over with a confused expression. 'Is it customary to cut one's hair in China?'

Best to answer in a general way, thought Grace. 'Every na-tionality cuts hair, else we would all be caught on tree branches.'

Her father chuckled. At least she had pleased him.

Lady Jane was not so easily amused. 'In England, we are taught not to walk into trees.'

The women laughed at that, while Grace steeled herself to endure. As unpleasant tasks went, this didn't merit a mention, but she was disappointed nevertheless. Perhaps if she engaged Lord Domac in conversation the women would leave her alone. Her father had told her that English men were allowed to marry without parental approval. She'd even include a compliment to his mother.

'Lady Hillburn, the flower designs on your gown are most unusual.' Grace looked at Lord Domac. 'English flower designs might interest my countrymen if they were stitched well on silk. Perhaps you could sell them in China.'

They had, after all, talked a great deal about what he thought would sell in Canton. Unusual flower designs would do well, she thought, at least until every artisan began copying them. But it was the best thought she had at the moment.

'Of all the silly ideas,' said the Countess. 'Flowers do not last long enough to travel to China.'

'Not the flowers themselves—' she began.

'Of course not!' Lady Jane laughed. 'But the designs. Embroidered on fabric. I'm sure they have nothing so elegant over there.'

Actually, the Chinese had elaborate art depicting all kinds of flowers. 'Your blooms are different,' Grace explained. 'And isn't different always interesting?'

Lord Domac chuckled. 'It's always intriguing,' he said, with a warm smile to her.

She smiled back, relishing the kindness in his face. At least until he turned to his mother. 'Painted fans, Mama. Perhaps we could export parcels of those to Canton. Make it all the rage over there.'

'What a clever idea, Cedric,' his mother said. 'I'm sure they have seen nothing so lovely as an English rose on wood.'

It was possible, Grace thought. She had not seen many English fans.

She turned to the women. 'Yours are so lovely. Would it be possible for me to look at one?' she asked.

'Oh!' Lady Jane said as she pressed her closed fan to her chest. 'I... Well, I suppose so.' She passed hers over and the other women were quick to join in.

Grace looked at each carefully, evaluating them as she thought a merchant in China might. She inspected the paint, the quality of the wood, and even the craftmanship in the dangling ribbon. And while she looked the conversation flowed around her, all of it insulting.

'I'm sure you've never seen anything so beautiful,' Lady Jane laughed. 'But I promise you this is a poor example. Something I use every day for making calls. I save my nicer ones—'

'For the balls, of course,' interrupted Miss Smythe. 'The white one you had at the Weckstein rout was stunning.'

'Do you recall how funny Miss Bradley was, accidentally getting it caught in her hair?'

'My goodness, how we all laughed. Now, have a care, Miss Richards, we wouldn't want you to get my fan tangled, would we?'

'Don't be silly. Her hair's too short for that.'

Grace let the conversation wash away. They were just being spiteful, she knew. Women in China had disdained her as well. So long as they hadn't tried to beat her, she'd counted the words as nothing.

What she couldn't ignore was the way her father's face fell with each horrid interaction. He kept tapping his foot in annoyance and shooting her apologetic looks. He did not want her to endure humiliation at these women's hands.

What he didn't realise was that their barbs barely registered. She was more interested in the idea of selling fans to China. That was, after all, what interested Lord Domac, and he was her only friend in this room.

In time, she finished her inspection and passed the fans back to the girls with her thanks.

'Well?' Lady Jane pressed. 'What did you think of them?'

'They're very lovely, of course,' she returned.

'Then they'll be popular in China!' Lady Jane crowed. 'I

believe Lord Domac has landed upon a capital idea. Send fans to China!'

No, that wouldn't work at all—but Grace knew she couldn't say as much in front of these women. They would be insulted by her opinions. She maintained a wan smile as they began discussing which designs would work best, while Lord Domac listened with seeming fascination.

Though actually his attention wasn't on them, she noticed. It was on herself. And his face slowly lost its excitement as he read her expression.

'So not flowers,' he said finally, apparently ignoring everything the other women had said. 'Another design, perhaps? Something unique to England.'

'Perhaps—' Grace began, but before she could say more the door knocker sounded again.

Another visitor. Grace looked up with hope. She already knew where she stood with everyone here. Perhaps this newcomer would be more friendly and she could salvage something from this disastrous tea.

Like her, everyone turned to the door, waiting to see who entered. When a deep voice sounded in the hall, her heart soared and her entire body tightened. She had a simultaneous desire to run away from the man and to run towards him. In the end, she froze in indecision, her breath suspended as she stared at the doorway.

'The Duke of Byrning,' intoned the butler.

And there he was, looking as handsome in his gentlemanly attire as he had barefoot on the rigging, with the wind lifting his hair. He walked in with purpose, greeted his aunt with warmth, then nodded to his cousin. The women were all aflutter, each rising up to her feet to curtsey to the man. Thankfully, Grace was already on her feet, or she would have been left sitting there like an idiot. It took her father's not too subtle poke for her to remember to make her curtsey.

'Miss Richards,' he said. His voice seemed to wrap her in the same warmth as it had on the crow's nest. 'You look sensational.'

She felt her cheeks heat. Her father had said exactly the same thing, but every word from the Duke seemed to heat her to un-comfortable levels.

'I feel awkward in English clothing,' she admitted, 'but I am learning.'

'I would never guess.' Then he looked about. 'Has no one offered you a chair?' He turned and shot his aunt a hard glare. 'Pray, let me find one for you.'

'It is no matter,' she said, but it seemed he was determined.

Stepping out of the room, he directed the butler to bring a pair of chairs. A moment later two footmen appeared, each with a straight-backed chair. The Duke directed them easily, point-ing to the narrow spot where she'd been standing. Her father had to push his chair to the side, and then the new chairs were squeezed in such that they became a single bench. The Duke gestured for her to sit, which she did as gracefully as she could manage, and then he took the chair beside her.

It was a great deal of movement and activity, and in the end he was sitting pressed so tightly beside her that it felt more in-timate than it had in the crow's nest. She felt as if a deep breath would put her in his lap, and this time there was nowhere for her to run.

Even worse, she had absolutely no desire to move away.

Chapter Six

Declan liked his aunt as much as he liked all his older relatives. They were part of his life because they were family, and as the current duke he was responsible for their care. Certainly they had their own income and peccadillos, but once his father had passed he had become the head of the family. He would see to it that they did not disgrace their heritage, and indeed that they contributed to becoming the best England had to offer and not the worst.

So it was that he was quietly furious that no one had thought to offer Miss Richards a seat until he got there. It was unthinkable that she should be left to stand like a servant when all the others sat. Good manners required consideration for one's guests. Even if Napoleon himself had entered the room, he should be offered a chair while footmen went to gather the firing squad.

Unfortunately, he saw the embarrassment this had caused Miss Richards. Her cheeks had turned pink, her hands were clenched together, and her smile seemed frozen upon her face.

Thankfully, all was handled quickly enough and soon they were seated together so closely that he could measure the tempo of her breath by the pressure against his arm. And what a deliciously exciting feeling it was. What man *didn't* like being pressed up against a beautiful woman?

'Is everyone settled?' his aunt asked in hard tones. 'Shall I call for tea?'

Everyone murmured their delight at the idea, and his aunt rang a little bell in response. Declan didn't miss the envious looks the ladies shot Miss Richards, but he had no intention of indulging them. His focus was on making Grace more comfortable.

'I apologise for arriving so late and interrupting things. Tell me, what were you discussing?'

'Oh, my lord,' said Lady Jane, 'we were on the most fascinating topic. We were showing Miss Richards the extraordinary art in our fans.' She lifted hers up and snapped it open with a dramatic flick of her wrist.

'We're trying to think of a design that would be appealing to the Chinese. Then I'll export them and make a fortune,' Cedric said.

Declan glanced at Miss Richards' face, seeing the rigid way she smiled as she kept her eyes downcast. He might have mistaken it for a demure pose, but he felt the stiffness in her body growing tighter with every statement.

'What an interesting topic,' he said. 'Miss Richards, can you tell me what you find so different in our English fans?'

'They were talking about the meaning of the flowers,' she said. 'There is a whole language in them and I thought to learn it.'

'How very ambitious,' he said. 'I could never keep it straight.'

Miss Lockwood shifted towards him, her eyes alight with mischief. 'I was just about to teach her,' she said as she held out her fan and began pointing. 'This is a daffodil, and it means I am sending a message. This is an iris, suggesting preference. And here is a wild rose for passion.'

She tittered as she closed up her fan and pointed it directly at him with a flirtatious look.

Declan frowned, embarrassed for Miss Lockwood. She had named two of the flowers incorrectly, and he thought the meanings were wrong too. 'I believe I shall buy you a book, Miss Richards. One with the proper names of flowers and their meanings.' He leaned close. 'Don't try to memorise it now. Some things are best learned from a proper source.'

'What a very kind idea, my lord,' crowed Lady Jane. 'After all, it is important for all proper ladies to know the truth of these things.'

Then she raised her eyebrows and shot a glance at Miss Lockwood before rolling her eyes. It was her way of saying that she knew Miss Lockwood had her flowers all wrong, but she—a true lady—was better educated than to say so.

Honestly, it sickened him. The petty cruelty in this room had his blood heating to a dangerous degree. These women had a full world of conversational topics, but they could not resist poking at one another in the hopes of gaining favour with him. As if he'd care for any woman who would take pains to point out another's ignorance.

He turned away from her and allowed his attention to focus on Miss Richards. 'Surely the English are not the only ones to develop meanings from blossoms? What do the Chinese see in blooms?'

'The lotus flower is the most prized, of course. It rises from mud and blooms in perfection. It is called the seat of Buddha and it symbolises purity, long life, and honour.'

'How interesting—' he began, but his aunt tsked audibly.

'How very heathen to look at something that rises from the mud as a symbol of purity.'

Declan felt his teeth clench. His aunt had a difficult life, to be sure, but all she showed the world was bitterness—and he was tired of it.

'I find Miss Richards' knowledge extraordinary,' he said, with a pointed look at his aunt.

Unfortunately, her attention was focused on the butler as he appeared at the door with the tea tray.

'Here is the tea at last!' his aunt cried, effectively drowning him out. 'I declare that I am quite parched.'

Then she settled herself in front of the tray and began to pour for each person in turn. His aunt was a proper English lady, who had been taught the serving of tea in the schoolroom. She served him first, as he was the highest ranked person there, and correctly remembered his preference for milk. Then she continued about the room, her memory obviously serving her well as she poured for everyone save Miss Richards, who was addressed last.

The conversation continued and the ladies grew animated by the coming balls of the Season. Miss Richards did not participate, because obviously she didn't know any of the people discussed. Indeed, she was largely ignored by the company except for the occasional insult.

'Oh, Miss Richards, you wouldn't know this, but an earl is ranked higher than a viscount.'

'You must remember, Miss Richards, a waltz is a very exciting dance, but is not considered totally proper.'

He was moments away from the rude action of starting an entirely new conversation with her alone when Cedric beat him to the punch. Declan's cousin stood up under the pretence of selecting a sweetmeat in order to address her more closely.

'This must be terribly boring for you, Miss Richards. Perhaps let me divert your attention for a moment? I like the idea of exporting fans to China. Will you let me know if you think of a design that will appeal?' His gaze shot to Declan. 'That's what I need money for,' he said in an undertone. 'I want to sell goods to China and then bring back different things to sell in England. All our trade so far has been one-way, but the real profit is in going both directions.'

'A sound plan in theory—' Declan began, but Cedric was too caught up to listen.

'So...fans,' he said, facing Miss Richards. 'Could it be as simple as that? You'll be at lots of balls this Season, and you will see lots of different fans. Maybe a design will be intriguing to you.'

Miss Richards stiffened, and her face seemed to pale. 'I cannot speak to what the ladies of China would prefer, my lord. One would need to live inside the court to know.'

'But everyone likes novelty, yes? And English fans are different, yes?'

'Again, my lord, one would need access to the Imperial Court to know.'

Declan understood what she was saying, and knew it was the same here. Any man could bring his goods to England, but it wouldn't become popular unless a royal or an aristocrat declared it a delight. Without someone of influence in China praising English fans, Cedric would do as well tossing his fans into the ocean as he would in getting Chinese ladies to adopt them.

'What she means,' interrupted Cedric's mother, 'is that she's a nobody in China. She can't tell you what the ladies there want any more than my maid can.'

Miss Richards winced at that bold statement, as did her father, but she didn't contradict it either. And then his aunt passed her a cup of tea.

She hadn't asked for Miss Richards' preferences, and indeed, one glance at the cup told him that his aunt had purposely curdled the milk with lemon. It was a petty embarrassment, one that demonstrated a cruel streak, especially as she quickly made herself a cup and sat back with a smug smile.

'To your health, everyone,' she said.

Then she took a sip from her own cup while her eyes remained fixed on Miss Richards. Would she take a drink from the rancid tea? Would she make a noise of disgust? Or would she leave the cup on the edge of the table so everyone saw that it was curdled?

Declan's fury became a painful thing. The Byrning legacy was eating him from the inside out. He kept his expression placid by force of will, but determined that his aunt would feel his wrath eventually. This was not appropriate behaviour for a countess, and so he would tell her in no uncertain terms. There was little else he could do—she lived on his mother's charity—but he would make his displeasure known. Just not now. That would be exposing his family's dirty laundry in public.

Instead, he decided to correct her subtly and see if she was appropriately shamed.

'My apology,' Declan said with a loud voice. 'I'm afraid I accidentally picked up your teacup, Miss Richards. It appears I'm quite addled.'

Then he pressed his own teacup and saucer into her hands, before reaching forward to grab her curdled tea. Miss Richards didn't say a word, but watched him with a startled expression. She knew what he had done, and it had shocked her.

Meanwhile, he shifted his gaze to his aunt as he prepared to drink the disgusting brew. Would she stop him? Would she allow him to taste such a thing?

'Oh, don't, Your Grace!' she cried as she set down her teacup with an audible click. 'It's cold. I was slow in serving everyone, and yours was first.' She rang her little bell and when a footman appeared gestured to his tea. 'Take His Grace's cup away and bring more hot tea immediately.' Then she simpered. 'Really, it is so hard to get good servants these days. I'm mortified that I've served you cold tea.'

The other ladies rushed to reassure his aunt that they completely understood, thereby dropping them even further in his estimation. They shared tales of their displeasure with servants. They commiserated over how difficult it was to sack someone, but agreed that a lady understood how to do it with charm. And then, as if they had rehearsed it, they all turned to Miss Richards.

'Have you had that experience in China, Miss Richards?' asked Lady Jane. 'Servants who must be disciplined or who are simply too stupid to learn?'

They already knew the answer. Hadn't she just said that she had no entrée into the Imperial Court of China? As a bastard raised in a temple, Declan doubted she had experience with servants at all. But in this she surprised them all.

'Aboard ship there were always sailors who refused to take direction from a woman. I may have had the captain's trust as a navigator, but many men would not listen to my orders unless the captain relayed them. It was a constant problem.'

'I should imagine,' Declan said.

Meanwhile, Miss Smythe had abruptly leaned forward. 'You have worked as a navigator on board a ship?'

Miss Richards dipped her chin, her smile warming with pride. 'I have. I am very good at it.'

'But you're a *woman*!' In fairness to Miss Smythe, she didn't sound shocked so much as impressed. 'I cannot imagine any-one would listen to you. To any woman.'

'When I was younger, I hid my sex. Much easier to be a young boy than a vulnerable girl. But as I grew older there were constant problems. I was fortunate to have the protection of a good captain, who made sure I was obeyed. And he had a solution for when I was not.'

Declan could not get over how difficult her life must have been. 'What was it?' he asked.

'What is always done. It was the captain's idea. I was too young to know what to do, but he taught me.'

Everyone looked around, confused.

Finally, it was her father who explained. 'If a sailor disobeys, he is flogged. It is the same on English ships.'

Lady Jane's lip curled in shock. 'You had men whipped? That sounds barbaric.'

'It sounds like necessary discipline to me,' Cedric said, nodding to Miss Richards as a way of showing his support. 'Ships can be lawless places.'

But Miss Richards shook her head. 'No, you misunderstand. The captain had men flogged many times, but I was still treated with disrespect.'

'What did you do?' Declan asked.

She looked into his eyes, her expression calm. 'I wielded the whip myself.'

Declan believed it. He had seen the proof of her muscles, felt the strength in her, and he had been in her company enough to know that she had hidden talents. He would not have guessed that she could flog a man, but that made more sense than that she would be anxious to learn flower language.

But the others did not have that advantage or perception. His aunt, in particular, pushed to her feet.

'Miss Richards,' she said in strident tones. 'In England, la-dies do not lie. To think we would believe such a preposterous statement merely betrays your ignorance. I suggest you apolo-gise immediately for your egregious actions.'

And here Grace must have finally reached her limit. She stood and, though she was not nearly as large a woman as his aunt, her composure radiated a confidence that he'd only seen in royalty.

'Should you like me to teach you how to do it?' Miss Richards asked. 'You think to belittle me, but you only damage yourselves.' She looked to the other ladies in the room. 'How can you accept being so small? Even your attacks are tiny, when you are capable of so much more than bad tea and ugly fans.'

The ladies gasped, his aunt louder than the rest, but did they understand what she was saying? Declan wondered. That she not only saw their slights, but counted them as less than nothing compared to what she had done with her life. She wasn't yet thirty and she had lived well beyond the bounds of anything these women considered possible.

In truth, he barely credited it. But far from being outraged, he was filled with admiration. Her sheer audacity impressed him, and her accomplishments were far beyond that.

'Would you care to ride with me in Hyde Park?' he asked abruptly. 'I should love to hear more.'

She blinked at him, and he watched as her expression turned uncertain. She didn't know the value of such an invitation, and had to look to her father for guidance. His aunt, however, didn't give her time for an answer as she voiced her outrage in the loudest voice.

'Your Grace! You cannot mean to foist such mendacity upon society!'

Mr Richards had found his feet, and he extended his arm to his daughter. 'Grace has not lied,' he said sternly. 'And I think we've had enough of your *polite society.*'

These last words were sneered, and well they should be. And now Declan was forced to apologise for his bitter aunt.

'Lord Wenshire, pray allow me to apologise for this terrible display. My aunt has been unwell, and I believe it has affected her temperament. I assure you, she and I will have words later.'

He shot his aunt a look that did nothing to assuage the fury in his blood.

His aunt's mouth fell open in shock. The other ladies gasped in horror, but he turned his back on them. They were no longer women to whom he wished to extend any courtesy. Meanwhile, he continued his apology.

'Pray, allow me to show your daughter that English society is not always so crass.'

'Declan!' his aunt snapped, her voice imperious. 'You are overcome with emotion.'

He froze, her words slipping like ice into his veins. Those were the exact words his mother had used whenever he'd grown the least bit upset about anything as a boy. A broken toy, a lame horse—all had been dismissed as Declan being overly emotional. And, given the legacy of his blood, it was the one thing that terrified him.

Was he overreacting to his aunt's horrendous display of bad manners? Damn her for making him second-guess himself. He took a moment to re-evaluate and decided—again—that she was in the wrong.

'Drink your tea, Aunt. I am finished speaking with you.'

She gasped in shock, her hand pressed to her breast. She had a weak heart, he knew. She often grew breathless when distressed. He wondered anew if he had gone too far, especially when she collapsed back down into her seat. Of course he knew that she might be faking that, but he also knew her condition was real. How awful if his display of temper ended up killing his aunt.

But it was too late to change that now. He turned back to Miss Richards, though a part of him remained aware of his aunt's shortened breath. If she really did faint, he would call for a doctor.

She didn't.

'Miss Richards, I should also like you to join me at the theatre. With your father's permission, of course.'

No fool, the man dipped his chin in agreement. 'A wonderful idea. Grace has been hoping to see our theatre.'

'Then it is settled. A walk in Hyde Park tomorrow and the theatre the next day.'

Surprisingly, Grace shook her head. 'My come-out ball isn't until next week. I cannot go to the theatre beforehand.'

He nodded. 'Quite right. But we can walk tomorrow. Theatre as soon as you are out. And I shall expect an invitation to your ball.'

She dipped her chin. 'You honour me.'

He could do no less, given how abominably she'd been treated this afternoon.

'Perhaps your father would join us in Hyde Park tomorrow—but may I have the pleasure of escorting you home now?'

He lifted his arm for her, while her gaze hopped between him and her father. It was as if she couldn't understand a man extending such a courtesy to her. But in this her father helped.

He took her hand and placed it on Declan's arm. 'It's too far to walk home, but since it's a fine day you should enjoy a meander, yes? There's been so little time for me to show you the best of London. I'll have the carriage waiting nearby when you're finished.'

Now that she had her father's permission, Miss Richards nodded to him with the poise of a queen. 'I should enjoy a walk, Your Grace. If that is what you wish.'

And so began the most extraordinary discussion of his life as they walked out, without giving anyone else in the room so much as a backward glance.

Chapter Seven

Grace couldn't wait to get outside. London did not have the cleanest air, but it was better than the stuffiness inside. Not to mention the spiteful, small women right now exclaiming their outrage. She lifted her chin and ignored the catty whispers. After all, people had whispered, pointed or outright thrown things at her for her entire life. She had come too far to bend now.

She took her wrap from the haughty butler, but was forced to wait as the Duke looked around.

'Where is your maid?' he asked.

She frowned at him. 'We didn't bring her.'

It had been just her and her father in the carriage. Why would she need a servant's escort?

The Duke shook his head. 'Your father is too casual with your reputation.'

'I am not to walk abroad with my father?'

'No, Miss Richards. You are not to walk alone with me.'

Then he snapped his fingers at the butler, who bowed.

'Right away, Your Grace,' he intoned, before stepping over to whisper to a footman.

Grace watched the exchange with confusion, before turning her attention back to the Duke.

'I am not helpless,' she said.

She could fight, and she could run fast when the situation called for it. She was likely the most capable woman in this house, but she didn't say so—especially when the Duke shook his head.

'I protect your reputation, Miss Richards. Your person is safe with me.'

A moment later, a maid rushed up from below stairs, pulling on a cloak likely too heavy for the spring weather. She looked flushed, and her hands were raw, but her demeanour was cheerful enough.

'This is Millie, Your Grace,' said the butler. 'She is quiet and respectful.'

Those last words were aimed at the girl, as if she needed reminding how to act. The Duke nodded and turned to go, but Grace was not willing to dismiss anyone so quickly.

'We must have pulled you from a task. Do you need to return quickly?'

Millie's eyes widened in shock. 'Er…yes, miss. I were kneading the dough for tonight, but—'

Her words were cut off at the butler's imperious sniff. Then the man turned to the Duke. 'Millie is at your disposal for as long as you require,' he said loudly.

'Is someone else covering your tasks, then?' Grace pressed.

The girl dropped her gaze to the floor. 'You need not concern yourself with that, miss.'

Which meant, no. This walk was an added burden. But one look at the men's faces told Grace that her enquiry had infuriated the butler and confused the Duke. Additional discussion would not be looked upon favourably. The best she could do to mitigate the situation was to give the girl a gentle smile.

'We will not keep you away from your duties for long,' she said.

'Yes, miss. I will enjoy the respite. It is a fine—'

Her words were cut off again, this time by the snap of the butler's fingers.

Grace flashed an apologetic smile to the girl, then turned towards the door. She was momentarily confused when the Duke held out his arm, but she adapted quickly enough. She set her fingers on his forearm, as she had been taught, and they stepped out into the fine afternoon.

She didn't dare look behind her to see if Millie followed, but she could hear the girl's footsteps.

A few moments later, she spoke softly to the Duke. 'You are right. We should have brought my maid.'

He slanted her a glance. 'You are also right, but I don't think we agree on the reasons. You shouldn't worry about the girl's duties. That is Nagel's responsibility.'

'Nagel is the butler?'

'Yes. Generally, the butler manages the servants, along with the housekeeper.'

She nodded. She'd been taught as much. 'And does Nagel seem a forgiving kind of man? Does he understand what it takes to make bread, or that she will not have time to finish her other tasks?'

He was silent for a long moment. 'I have no idea what kind of man he is below stairs, though my aunt has praised his efficiency.'

She didn't respond. She knew what that meant in a Chinese household. A ruthless master often meant that the higher servants were equally ruthless, if not more so. She would have liked to believe that it was different in England. Her father treated his manservant well, and the maid who had been hired for herself and Lucy seemed kind enough. Indeed, Grace had learned nearly as much from her talkative maid as she had her tutors. But she could not speak to what happened in other households.

The Duke turned them to the right, his expression distracted. 'I will say something to Nagel to be sure that she is not illtreated for this outing.'

He said the words, but she could tell from his tone that he thought it a needless action. And indeed, she agreed. If the butler were a tyrant, then a word from the Duke would make things worse rather than better. The only way to know would be to ask Millie what she would prefer.

She turned around to address the maid. 'Would that be helpful?' she asked. 'If the Duke were to say something to Mr Nagel? Or would it make things harder?'

The girl's mouth dropped open in shock. Indeed, so startled was she at being addressed that she couldn't seem to form any words, especially when the Duke himself turned to look at her.

'Well?' he enquired.

Thankfully, his tone wasn't abrupt, but she could tell the girl was nearly shaking in terror at being so addressed.

'Never mind,' Grace said, as she turned back. 'I think it best if we let things be.'

At least she hoped so. Millie didn't sport any obvious bruises, and she walked with a happy lift to her heels. If she were being mistreated, then it was well hidden.

They walked a few more steps before the Duke spoke again, his tone thoughtful. 'Is that common in China? Are servants usually...?' His voice trailed off as if he couldn't find the right words.

'Beaten? Raped? Terrified into submission?'

'Good God!' he gasped, clearly horrified. 'Is that how your underclass is treated?'

She turned to watch his reaction to her next words. 'Do you suppose that never happens in England? If women are so safe, why do we need maids to go with us everywhere?'

He frowned, clearing his throat. 'Well, of course there are some instances. Horrible, terrible things. We most certainly don't condone it!'

'Neither is it condoned in China,' she said softly. 'But it happens nonetheless.'

He gaped at her. 'Were you—?' He swallowed. 'I mean—um...'

'No. I am whole.'

By which she meant she was still a virgin. However, she knew that for a discarded child such as her, she was the exception rather than the rule.

'The monks taught us how to fight. Even the girls.' Her lips twisted. 'Especially the girls.'

He nodded, though he still appeared flustered. 'I should not have asked. That was wrong of me.'

'Then you would have wondered—or assumed.'

He didn't respond to that, though she could tell he wanted to. Her father had wanted to ask as well, and it had taken many months of getting to know him aboard ship for them to become easy enough together to speak of it. Indeed, it had been Lord Domac who'd broached the question, thereby forcing the discussion between herself and her father.

'My parentage rests upon my face. Anyone who looks at me knows I am not of a blessed union. As such, I deserve less respect in China than even the lowest beggar of clear race.'

'That's despicable,' he said, his voice hard.

She glanced at him, startled at the vehemence in his tone.

It took him a moment to register her expression, and then his voice turned rueful. 'You seem shocked, Miss Richards. Do you think English men would treat you so shabbily?'

'Your aunt and her guests believe I am less than they.'

He snorted. 'My aunt and her guests believe *everyone* is less than they. It has nothing to do with your race.'

She arched her brows at him, and he flushed.

'Very well, you are right. It has a great deal to do with your race, and I am sorry for that. I had not thought that they could be so mean.'

She snorted, and then abruptly covered her mouth. She should not have expressed her doubt so openly. When he looked at her, his mouth agape, she tried to apologise. 'I meant no harm,' she said quickly. 'I do not know your customs. I should not venture an opinion.'

He sighed. 'I welcome your opinion, even when it is expressed inadvertently.'

Was that a kind way of referring to her snort?

'But believe me,' he pressed, 'some of the most despicable people I know are full-blooded Englishmen of high rank. And some of the kindest come from the lowest rungs of society. I do not think title or bloodline are accurate measures of one's humanity.'

That surprised her. How did a wealthy mandarin meet anyone—kind or not—from the lowest caste?

He shook his head. 'You are shocked?'

'I do not understand England well enough to be shocked. In China, the rich children are kept well away from the poor.'

He nodded. 'Many are here, but I was a wanderer.'

She was not surprised. She remembered the way he had ached to go up the mast, and the hunger in his eyes as he'd looked around in the crow's nest. Many in this world were content in their very tiny corner, but she had spent years on boats or by docks. She knew the yearning in some to explore. She wondered if his responsibilities as a duke prevented him from indulging his desires.

'Where did you go?' she asked.

He smiled. 'Everywhere I could. Our nannies were always busy.' He glanced at her. 'I have a younger brother and three younger sisters. And two who did not live long.' His tone dipped at that, but he did not seem to dwell on it. 'Whenever they were busy with the younger children, I escaped to my own amusements.'

'I cannot believe your servants were so careless.'

'I was lucky in that,' he said with a grin. 'And I was lucky to befriend our gamekeeper. He had a boy a little older than I, whom I worshipped.'

She smiled trying to envisage this large man as a young boy. 'Did you try to do everything he could?'

'I did. And I assumed that because I was the ducal heir I should do everything better than everyone else.' He shrugged. 'I couldn't, of course. And I learned to stuff away my pride when dealing with Jacky or any of his older siblings.' He looked off into the distance. 'It wasn't easy. I had no control over my rage.' His lips quirked. 'Fortunately, I wasn't large enough to cause any damage. They were well protected from me.'

'Were they unkind to you?'

'No. Not unkind, exactly, but it gave me the experience of being the youngest.'

'Did they have a mother?'

'God, yes.' His tone and his expression softened. 'She told the most amazing stories. Tales of poor beggars who needed a helping hand, old men whom nobody listened to but who knew great secrets.' His gaze was soft in memory. 'I never heard those stories from anyone else. Honestly, I think she made them up, but she could tell them so well we believed them. And when she was too tired to speak she got her husband to tell them. And her father as well, who came to live with them.' He shook his head. 'That whole family was a never-ending source of stories, and always with a moral pointed at someone.'

'At you?' she asked.

'Often. Usually the ones about pride and wilful ignorance.' He chuckled. 'But I was not the only one who needed a lesson or three.'

She could hear the humour in his voice, and knew he had enjoyed a happy childhood—at least when in the gamekeeper's cottage.

'The monks had many such tales as well,' she said.

'I should like to hear them.'

'Lucy remembers them more than I do. I always wanted to learn how to slay the demons myself. I didn't believe that someone mystical would do the slaying for me.'

'A practical mind, then?'

She nodded. 'And too restless to sit still.'

She looked at him, wishing he had joined them on the boat four months ago instead of Lord Domac. She would have preferred learning English from him. She would have enjoyed long nights staring at the stars with him. But it had been his cousin who'd stepped onto the boat in India, and his cousin who had befriended her father. And it was his cousin her father had formed a friendship with.

She kept her thoughts to herself. Her father had told her to be discerning with the gentlemen she met. He wanted her to evaluate them honestly. So she tried to separate her feelings—which were definitely confused—from the facts.

The Duke seemed to be a man of influence and intelligence without the rashness she feared in Lord Domac. But he also seemed to dislike her restless nature. Hadn't he chastised her for travelling without a maid? And he was constantly worried about her reputation. The man was excruciatingly aware of all the tiny rules of society that she could never remember. She had no idea if he was right or wrong in his assessment, and she disliked not understanding the rules.

Fortunately, he didn't seem to be angry when correcting her. What irritation did colour his voice seemed to be directed at other people. Nevertheless, she was wary. He lived under a myriad of rules that seemed to apply to every detail of his life. Why wasn't he screaming in frustration at their constant weight?

She turned away, wishing she were naturally quiet, like Lucy. Would she never find a place where she could be herself safely? Of all the people she had met, this man interested her the most. But he clearly did not approve of her, so she would have to think more about Lord Domac.

That made her heart twist in a way that startled her. She liked the Duke, but she had liked many different men in her life. Turning away from them had never made her chest tighten with regret. What made him so different that her body seemed to want to linger near him?

Meanwhile, the Duke had guided them around a corner to reveal a wide open space of green set in the middle of the city. And not just green. She heard the happy babble of water nearby, not to mention the laughter of children and the murmur of voices from nannies talking as they watched their charges.

'This is St James's Park,' he said. 'It's one of the lovelier places in London.'

'It is huge,' she said as she stepped forward. Because it was spring, the flowers were a gorgeous riot of colour. 'This is available to everyone?' she asked as she looked around.

There were no gates that she could see. Only people enjoying the beautiful day.

'Do you not have public parks in China?'

'Yes, but most gardens are enclosed. Private places enjoyed by the wealthy families who tend them.'

'Then I am pleased to bring you here.'

She lifted her face to the sky, wishing to pull off her hat to feel the wind in her hair. She supposed it was enough to feel the sun on her face, if only for a few moments.

He let her bask for a bit, before directing her along a path. 'There is something I want to show you,' he said. 'Down this way.'

She followed, her steps lighter. 'So much space...' she murmured.

'I suppose things can feel crowded aboard ship.'

'Very much so,' she responded. 'And even in the temple there were people everywhere.'

Someone had always been watching, and many would take any excuse to discipline the half-children.

'Do you miss it?'

'What?'

'The temple. The boat. This must feel very different to you.'

'Everything is different, and yet so much feels the same. The clothes and language are different, but one city feels the same as the next to me. So many people, all thinking about their own lives, all crowded together.' She looked around. 'But I am learning your customs.'

'Indeed, you are. I do not think I could be half so easy in another place as you are here.'

He overestimated how 'easy' she was, but she smiled to pretend he was correct. 'Have you travelled much?' she asked.

'I have. I took my Grand Tour of the continent several years ago. My tutor insisted I go, despite Napoleon's antics.' He shook his head. 'Looking back, it was not as safe a choice as we thought, but obviously I survived. I think I was lucky, rather than wise, and I do have very fond memories of Italy.'

She faced him, intrigued by his far-off look. 'What was it like?'

'I was a young man of title and wealth. It was all parties and new foods. Parties and lovely weather. Parties and unbearable heat and beautiful women.'

'I thought you went with a tutor.'

He chuckled. 'I did. But he was a tutor who enjoyed—'

'Parties?'

'Yes.' He focused again on her. 'But I have never been so far as China. Or even Africa. You must have seen so much.'

'I saw views from the boat, and I tasted strange foods, but I was rarely allowed to explore.'

'That must have chafed.'

'No,' she said. 'I preferred the safety of a place I knew, with people who would protect me. I loved hearing tales when the sailors returned, but I had no desire to risk myself by exploring.'

'Truly? I would guess that anyone who jumps the riggings like you do would want to test herself.'

'On land? As a lone girl? No.'

She had seen enough in China by the time she was ten to know that she would not be safe in a city she did not know. Not without the protection of wealthy men and strong servants. Better to stay on the ship and listen to tales from a place of safety. Life aboard ship had been dangerous enough. She had not needed to seek out more dangers just for their novelty.

'I envy your freedom to wander as you chose.'

He shrugged. 'As I said, it was not so prudent a choice. I was young and stupid, and we paid the price.'

His tone was bitter, but not closed, so she dared ask the question. 'What price?'

'My tutor was murdered. I was nearly so.'

She winced. 'I am sorry. Was it the French?'

She had learned from her father about the war with Napoleon.

'That would have been more honourable. No, it was footpads. I lost my purse, not my life. My tutor was cut. Not so bad a wound, or so we thought, but then infection set in. He died eight days later, and I had to manage my return to England when I hadn't the least idea how it was done. If we hadn't squandered so much on wine and women I would have done better. I learned very quickly that my title did not protect me from much of anything.'

She watched him closely as he spoke, seeing shadows in his eyes. He knew, then, what it was to live in danger.

'How long did it take you to return home?'

'Several months.' His lips twisted in a rueful expression. 'Not so long in the grand scheme of things, but I have never forgotten what it was like to be hungry or afraid.'

A difficult lesson, then, but she could see he was a better man for it.

Then, before she could say more, he looked up and gestured ahead. 'Ah, here we are. What do you think?'

Chapter Eight

Declan watched her face as they stepped out through a set of trees to see the Chinese Bridge in all its glory. Though the yellow and blue paint had faded over the last year, it was still a lovely sight. Not as pretty were the burned remains of the pagoda, but from this angle it didn't look so bad.

It took her a moment to take in the view, and though she didn't immediately gasp about the sight before her, she did smile. 'That's quite lovely,' she said politely.

'It was constructed for the Grand Jubilee last year. There was a seven-storey pagoda right there, but it caught fire during the fireworks display. It was a sad end to the celebration, but impressive at the time.'

'You were here?' she asked.

'My whole family came to celebrate with the royal house. There were so many people here it looked like a sea of bodies. They were even in the trees—which made it all the more frightening when the pagoda caught fire.'

'Were many people hurt?'

'Several.' They started walking, heading towards the bridge. 'But only two deaths, thankfully. The Queen was most distressed.'

'What were you celebrating?'

'A hundred years since the Hanovers ascended to the English throne.'

'A hundred years?'

Her eyes widened before she quickly looked away, and he knew she was hiding her thoughts.

'Are you surprised by that?' he asked. 'That England has had the same ruling family that long?'

She shook her head, biting her lip as she stared at the water.

It took a moment before he realised *why* she had been surprised.

'How long has your emperor's family ruled?'

She smiled. 'The Qing dynasty began nearly two hundred years ago. The Ming dynasty lasted nearly three hundred years before that.' She glanced around, as if she could see the King and Queen in the shrubbery. 'China has stood for thousands of years. Twenty dynasties in all. I had not realised how young your country is.'

His brows arched. 'The Hanovers aren't our first ruling family, you know. But I suppose...' He counted on his fingers. 'We are only six dynasties compared to your twenty, so you have us there.'

She shrugged. 'China is very old and very large, but I am looking forward to seeing all the best spots in London. You did promise to show me.'

'I did indeed.'

'Perhaps we could go at a time when my sister could join us. She has been cooped up inside for so long. She longs to get out.'

'It would be my honour,' he said slowly, 'but I don't believe she is out yet, is she?' She looked disappointed at this reminder, and he flashed her a quick smile. 'I know our customs are strange, but they are for your own protection.'

'I understand. The wealthy Chinese hide girls away, too.' Then her next words surprised him.

'They think it keeps them safe.'

She didn't sneer as she spoke, but he heard the implied criticism.

'Women should be cherished and protected,' he said.

She faced him, her expression rueful. 'I have never thought ignorance was useful. Indeed, it can be dangerous.'

'But you stayed hidden on the boat rather than explore new cities. You chose protection.'

She nodded. 'Some risks are not worth the reward. I had found safety aboard ship.'

'So you think I am wrong,' he said, 'to worry about your sister's reputation and your own?'

How startling that he found himself smiling at that. No one had dared disagree with him in so long.

'I have no experience of your customs. How can I judge if you are right or wrong?'

'But I can tell by your expression—'

'Do not ask me questions when you will not like my answer.'

Her voice was curt, and he could see how she had tensed as if to run.

Damnation, he was making a muddle of this. After his family had treated her so abominably, he'd wanted to show her that not everyone in England was rude. More than that, he longed to return to their easy camaraderie from the boat.

But how to reassure her without going too far? He was not accustomed to navigating these seas.

'Miss Richards...' he began, daring to touch her arm.

Not hard, and not in a way that would restrain her, but to keep their connection for a little longer. He brushed his hand across her upper arm, and that seemed to be enough to keep her nearby even as he let his hand drop away.

'You recall me telling you about the gamekeeper's wife? The one who told me story after story?'

'Yes.'

He winced at the stupidity of his own question. Of course she remembered their conversation. It had occurred five minutes ago.

'Well,' he continued, 'some things she did not put in fables. Some things she said, and then she enforced. Do you know what one of her favourite dictums was?'

'I do not know what a dictum is,' she responded.

'It is a rule to live by. She said it was my responsibility to listen to everyone's thoughts, no matter how ridiculous. To listen carefully and decide. Not listening, according to her, was the gravest sin of any man, but it was worse for powerful ones. It would be their downfall.'

She arched her brows, challenging him without even saying a word.

He chuckled in response. The woman would not give him an inch that he did not work for. Odd how he found that attractive.

'What that means is that I don't want you to hold back your thoughts from me. Others might not be so open, but I demand it from everyone in my circle.'

'Everyone?' she pressed. 'Even your mother?'

He snorted. 'She gives her opinion whether I ask for it or not.'

He lifted his arm, offering to escort her onto the bridge. Given that she had run ratlines in a storm, the gesture was ridiculous. She had no need for any man to guide her, and yet she smiled at his offer. It was as if no one had ever thought to be polite towards her and, given his aunt's treatment of her, perhaps that was true.

'So you wish to hear my unbound thoughts.' She said it as a statement, not a question.

'I am eager for it.'

She shot him an arch look. 'Then you cannot get angry when I do as you ask.'

'Of course not.' Then he challenged her. 'Will you extend me the same courtesy?'

'Of not getting angry?' She pursed her lips, clearly thinking. 'I cannot remember a time when I wasn't angry,' she murmured, as if startled by her own thoughts. 'But I am not angry with you.'

'I am pleased to hear it.'

That was an understatement. Inside, he was whooping for joy. He guessed that she did not say such things to many people.

'Very well,' she said as she made an expansive gesture towards the park. 'I think this is my favourite place in London.'

It was not the topic they had been on, but he allowed her the pretence.

'I think you have seen little of the city. London has many other beautiful spots.'

And he wanted to show them all to her.

They were walking now under the remains of the pagoda. It had been rebuilt a little, and repainted, but they could see the remains of the fire in the ragged edges of some of the wood. Paint could not cover everything.

She stopped beneath it and looked up. 'It must have been a sight.'

He glanced at her. 'Are you being polite? Surely real pagodas are much more impressive.'

She nodded. 'They are, but they are structures used for worship. They need to be large. This must have been lovely as a decoration.'

She smiled at him, and he had the feeling that she was meeting him halfway.

'It is very pleasant now, even without the extra storeys.'

He grinned back at her. 'Do you know, I haven't the least idea what to ask you. I want to know everything, but what does one ask first when one wants to know everything?'

He must have surprised her, because she burst out in a delighted laugh. She immediately covered her mouth with her hand, clearly embarrassed, but he gently pulled it down.

'Do not hide something as wonderful as a laugh,' he said. 'I told you, I want to know everything about you.'

She faced him squarely then, her eyes dancing as she studied him. 'I believe I feel the same. Please, start at the beginning. What did you do as a child, before you went to your gamekeeper's cottage?'

'Ran around terrorising my nanny. I ran, I played, I was king of my castle. Or a little prince.'

She frowned. 'Do you have a castle?'

'I do, but it is old and crumbling away. No one lives there any more but mice and—'

'The gamekeeper?'

He shook his head. 'Goodness, no. My father pensioned him off years ago. He has a handsome cottage nearby, where he plays with his grandchildren and teaches them how to hunt and fish.'

He leaned back against the railing, looking at her. He was fascinated by the mixture of races in her face. Square English jaw topped by golden skin that probably never burned like his did. She had a strong nose, from her father, and a fascinating shape to her exotic eyes. He could stare at her all day, but that would mean he missed all her other fascinating attributes.

He'd never met anyone who challenged his thoughts about the most common things. Who else among his set would bother worrying about a servant's tasks? Not to mention live her extraordinary life.

'What did you do as a child?' he asked. 'And do not mince your words. I truly want to know.'

She looked away, her shoulders hunching slightly as she spoke. 'I spent my days stealing food, hiding wherever I could, and getting viciously angry when anyone caught me.'

'How often did they catch you?'

She shrugged. 'Very often. I was not very fast as a child, or very smart.' She looked up to the top of the pagoda, her gaze distant. 'But I was very, very lucky.'

He was surprised by that. 'I cannot imagine that you thought yourself lucky. Did you ever have a home?'

'The temple was my home.'

'Didn't they feed you there? Why would you steal food?'

She grinned. 'Because I was angry. I wanted a family. I wanted nice clothes. I wanted everything I did not have, so I tried to steal it.'

He shuddered at the idea. His parents had been difficult, but at least he'd had everything he'd ever wanted materially. 'You were caught.'

It wasn't a question. She'd already said as much.

'Often. But not everyone in the world is vicious. I was taken back again and again to the temple, where children like me were managed.'

'Like you?'

She pointed to her face. 'Those of mixed race.'

'I think it makes you look stunningly beautiful.'

It was no more than the truth, but she seemed shocked to hear it. Enough that it took her another moment before she continued her story.

'There was one monk who made it his mission to raise us. No one wanted us, you see, and for a girl that meant the temple or prostitution.'

He nodded. 'I am glad you chose wisely.'

'I didn't choose,' she scoffed. 'I was hauled back there, locked in, and treated harshly until I learned to listen.'

He jolted at that, his mind reeling from the way she had been treated for no other reason than the fact that her parents had been from different lands. She'd had no choice in her birth, but even so she'd been reviled.

What kind of resilience would it take to survive something like that? And to come through it as this beautiful, composed woman?

His esteem for her rose.

'How are you not a bitter, angry shrew of a woman? I mean no disrespect, but my aunt has suffered nothing so severe, and yet she spews venom everywhere.'

Her expression shifted to a kind of resigned acceptance. 'I am angry. I am bitter. And yet if I remain in those feelings how will I appreciate this beautiful day? This beautiful park? Or the truth that I am dressed in fine clothing and have eaten good food.'

'Remarkable.'

'The monks taught me well.' She chuckled. 'Probably much like the wife of your gamekeeper and her lessons. I fought like a demon, but they were stronger and smarter than I.'

Amazing. He had not thought they had anything in common, and yet he could see her point. Someone had raised each of them, and that someone had not been a parent.

'What else did the monks teach you?'

'To fight. I liked those lessons. And to speak respectfully. But mostly I learned to listen.'

'To religious lessons?'

'I didn't listen very well to those.' Her voice was rueful. 'The one monk in particular who took care of me taught me how to listen to what people wanted from me. He said once I knew how to do that, then I could choose my path. I could choose whether I wanted to give it to them or not.'

Such a valuable skill.

'And are you good at it? At knowing what others want from you?'

She shrugged. 'Good enough to survive.' Then she looked around at the park surrounding them. 'Perhaps I can even thrive. That's what I want,' she said, her voice growing softer. 'Somewhere I can be safe to choose any path I want. To do whatever I want.'

'And what is that?' he pressed, fascinated as much by the shifting planes of her face as the emotions they revealed.

'I don't really know. There are so many things I want to try. My father wants me to paint. He says I have talent. And I've been reading books in English. It's slow, but I am learning. Lucy wants to manage the buying and selling of cargo. She learned a great deal from the captain.' She stretched out her arms. 'I just want to try everything.' Her arms dropped to her sides. 'But instead of doing that, I'm learning how to serve tea and dance.'

'You don't like those things?'

She seemed to pull herself inward, pressing her hands to her belly. 'I am doing what I need to.'

To survive. She didn't say the words, but he heard them nonetheless.

'Your father wants you to marry,' he said. It wasn't a question.

'He says Lord Domac would make a good husband.'

How gratifying to hear the deadness in her voice at that. He did not wish his cousin ill, but he couldn't stomach the idea that this extraordinary woman would be married merely for her dowry. She was worth so much more than a boat or a cargo. And his cousin was a fool not to see that.

She would be wasted on Cedric. She deserved so much better.

'Do you know what my cousin wants?'

She nodded. 'He wants to impress people. He told me once that he already has a title, and most people bow to that. But those who don't will bow to money.' She turned to him. 'So he wants a great deal of money.'

He nodded slowly as he straightened up from the railing. Then he offered her his arm and they began to stroll again. He didn't want to completely disparage his cousin. Cedric had some very good qualities, but he was immature. He'd always been impatient, looking for a quick reward. He and his father shared that vice, whereas Declan's problem was in a dark, explosive temper. It had destroyed his father's life and had come perilously close to ending his several times.

Thanks to the Byrning legacy, rage was his constant companion. He kept it under control now, but there had been times in his childhood when that hadn't been the case. Now, as always when he met someone interesting, he resolved anew never, ever to show Grace his temper. It had already lost him good friends and one possible wife. She'd seen him nearly come to blows with a political rival who had drummed up heinous lies about himself and his family. That was the experience that had taught him that lies and insults were commonplace. Their only purpose was to goad him into a violent reaction that would show him in a dreadful light.

He would not let his temper get the better of him again.

Which meant he had mastered his legacy.

Cedric needed more time to master his problem.

'Do you know what Cedric will do to gain that money?' he asked.

'He will marry me for my dowry. But Father says he will honour me as his wife.'

She did understand. He didn't know if that made things better or worse.

'Are you in love with him? Do you want to marry him?'

She shook her head, as if that was the silliest question. 'I want safety. If he is my safest path, then I will choose him.'

'And if he is not?'

She twisted to study his face. 'Can a woman be forced to wed in this country?'

He flinched at her words, hating it that she had to think about these things. It was not something he cared to think about ever—but that was his failing, not hers.

'Yes. Women can be forced. But I will not allow that to happen to you.'

She searched his eyes, her head tilted as if she studied the stars for direction. 'How will you do that?'

How will you keep me safe?

She hadn't spoken those words, but he heard the question nevertheless. Inside, he felt every part of him respond to the call. As if she were indeed a woman looking for a saviour, and he a knight of old, searching for a quest.

It was a silly thought, but he would swear he'd heard the trumpet sound.

'I am a duke, and the head of my family. My cousin is…' He shook his head. 'If you do not wish to marry Lord Domac, send word to me. I will see that you are not forced.'

'Do you think my father would force me?'

His eyes abruptly widened. 'I…um… I don't know your father well. Do you think he would?'

'I don't think so. He is not a violent man,' she said. 'But he has strong beliefs in how I should behave—including whom I marry.' Her lips curved. 'That I *should* marry.'

Declan nodded. 'A woman is safer in this world with a good husband.'

'That's what my father says.'

'You disagree?'

It seemed as if they were throwing leaves at one another, questions that had no true weight. After all, the world had its rules, whether or not they agreed with them. And yet he found he enjoyed this discussion. She seemed to like it as well. And together they both seemed well pleased.

'I want to choose my path,' she said. 'And I want very much to make a good choice not just for myself, but also for Lucy.'

He could hear her devotion to her sister in her tone, but also the longing of a woman who had never had control of her life. And yet for someone without resources, she had done amazing things with her life.

'You are the best navigator in China,' he said, his tone teasing. 'Surely you can successfully navigate the *haut ton*.'

She snorted, the sound very unladylike and yet so charming.

'When your aunt is guided by the position of the stars, then I shall have faith in my ability to steer clear of her.'

'A fair point,' he admitted.

'You know,' she said, her words teasing, 'I am not the only

female sailor in China. I had the example of a woman far more powerful than I could ever be.'

'A female sailor?'

'More than a sailor Ching Shih captains a fleet of boats.'

He shook his head. 'I cannot imagine it.'

This story was likely a fairy tale, when he preferred the comfort of facts. But he could not deny the animation in her when she spoke the name. And what did he know? China was a very different place from England.

'I can see you at the forefront of a fleet of ships. You have the strength of will to do it.'

'Then you have more imagination than most. No one thought I could be a good navigator, but I am one of the very best.' She arched a brow at him. 'Will you listen to the tale of China's famous pirate captain Ching Shih?'

'I cannot think of anything I want to hear more.'

Chapter Nine

'Why would you tell him that story?' Lucy gaped at her sister, clearly confused by Grace's contradictory behaviour.

They sat in Lucy's bedroom as it was the closest to their father's. It allowed them to hear his cough without hovering beside his bed. They both wanted to know if the tonic they'd given him this afternoon had helped ease his dry hack. So far it hadn't, but perhaps the medicine took a while to work.

Either way, they were passing the time by discussing in detail everything that had happened that afternoon—much of which made no sense to Lucy.

'You told me that men do not like powerful women. You told me to be meek. So why would you tell the Duke about China's pirate queen?'

'He was interested,' Grace said with an apologetic shrug.

How did she explain that once she'd started talking with the Duke, it had been so hard for her to stop? He seemed to value her thoughts and her opinions. And he never did anything that made her feel threatened. Even better, he clearly wanted to protect her. That was a potent lure for her, and she had been unable to control her words. As for her thoughts—well, they had gone rampant with ideas she did not want to express.

He excited her body and her mind. And that was as danger-ous as it was wonderful.

'What did he think?' Lucy pressed. 'Did he believe a woman can lead a fleet?'

'As it happens, the Irish claim a pirate queen named Granu-aile, so it wasn't a great shock to him.'

Lucy shook her head, clearly not understanding the spell the Duke seemed to have thrown over Grace. 'You told him you *ad-mire* Ching Shih. You cannot admire a powerful woman with-out him thinking you want to be one.'

It was true. Grace understood the risk. No man, be he Eng-lish or Chinese, wanted a woman who would dominate him. But she didn't want to rule over the Duke. She just wanted to spend more time with him.

'He kept asking questions. I promised I would answer hon-estly.'

Her sister leaned back against the wall. They were whisper-ing together, just as they'd always done in the temple. But in this moment Lucy could not control her tone.

'I don't understand,' she said with clear irritation. 'Did you tell him that Ching Shih is bloodthirsty?'

'I did. Or at least that the sailors believe it.'

'And that you admire her?'

'I admire her strength. She didn't collapse and die when her husband did. She has forged her own path.' Her brows narrowed at Lucy. 'You know how much I have clung to those tales.'

Of course she did. Lucy knew everything about Grace. The two of them had been paired together since their earliest mem-ories in the temple. Grace had never been able to sit still un-less she held Lucy. And Lucy had rarely stopped crying except when near Grace. Or so the monks had told them.

As they'd aged, they helped one another survive. Grace was always faster, stealing food for them both when the temple didn't have enough for everyone. Lucy was the quiet one, the shy one—the one who watched and understood much more than anyone guessed. She was also the one who could apply logic in private but completely crumpled when interacting in person. Thank heaven numbers didn't change when she grew flustered. If she hadn't been a half-person, she would have made a merchant a great wife. As it was, she'd been doomed to live as a nun in the temple, counting sacks of rice and rationing it out to hungry children.

It had been the tales of Ching Shih that had shown them both that women could be strong enough to make a new kind of life for themselves. The two of them had hung on the stories of the pirate queen's life. They'd inspired Grace to seek out a man to teach her how to be useful on a boat. And they'd encouraged Lucy to want more than life as a silent temple nun.

It had taken years, and the special providence of luck, but now she and Grace were here with a father, who cared for them both. None of this would be possible were it not for those tales of Ching Shih.

Lucy gripped Grace's fingers, squeezing them tightly. 'Men want docile women. You have told me that a thousand times!'

Grace twisted her fingers out of Lucy's grip. 'He loved my tales. He begged me to tell him more.'

'Men will beg at the feet of their mistresses, but they will not marry them. How many girls have we known who believed the promises of men?'

Grace sighed as she flopped backwards onto the bed. 'He is different from the others. He listened to me. He wanted to hear what I thought. No other man has shown me such respect. Even Father tells me what I want instead of hearing my words.'

Lucy crossed her arms. 'What have you told me about men who make you feel good?'

'That they are lying,' Grace answered. 'That only you know what you want.'

'Yes!'

'But he's not like that!' Grace abruptly rolled over, to look at her sister. 'He's a good man. He's not violent. He enjoys new things.' She dropped her chin on her palm. 'He wanted the experience of climbing the rigging, so he did it. He wants to learn about me because I am so different. That's why I had to tell him about Ching Shih. It's a tale that he has never heard before, about a woman he never imagined existed.'

'How does that help you?' Lucy pressed.

Grace looked away. 'Perhaps it makes me seem less strange.'

Lucy shook her head and dropped down beside Grace on the bed. 'All men enjoy new toys,' she said, echoing the monks, who had taught something similar. 'That path leads to suffering.'

Grace flopped onto her back again and stared at the ceiling, her words coming as if she were talking to herself. 'He seemed impressed by what I can do on the sails. And he believes that I am a good navigator.'

'Anyone who knows boats knows you're a great navigator.'

'Yes, but Lord Domac needed to be convinced. The Duke just believed me.'

'Or he didn't see any reason to argue about what isn't important to him.'

Grace sat up, her face flushed. 'He believes me. He doesn't treat me as a child when I say things. He listens!'

Didn't Lucy know how rare that was?

Lucy softened her expression. 'Do you love him?'

The words cut straight to Grace's heart. It was possible, she supposed. If she allowed herself, she might fall in love with him. But to risk everything on a feeling was madness.

'Oh, *mei mei...*' Grace moaned, calling Lucy 'little sister' in the most tender way. 'Half-people like us don't find love. You know that. We must look for safety. For us and any children that may come.'

Lucy shook her head. 'I still want love. And I know that's naïve.' She spread her arms and spoke her words to the ceiling. 'I want a man to fall madly in love with me. I want his thoughts on me at all hours of the day and night. I want him to sing songs to me, give me sweet food and kiss me all night long.'

Grace couldn't quite stifle her sigh. 'You're dreaming of Lord Domac.'

It was half statement, half accusation. After all, she could see the truth in her sister's dreamy eyes.

'What happened between the two of you that you would build such a fantasy around him?'

'Nothing,' Lucy answered—but in a way that Grace knew she lied. Something had sparked this dream.

'I cannot help you if you lie to me.'

Her sister flushed a dark red. 'There *was* something that happened between us. Not like you think. It was this morning when you were in the sails with the Duke.'

Fear clutched her heart. Had Lord Domac attacked her sister? She quickly scanned her from head to toe. There was no injury that she could see. And she wasn't acting like a woman hurt.

Grace swallowed down her fear and spoke calmly. 'What happened?'

'We were talking. He was asking about our life together in the temple.'

'Everyone seems very interested in that,' Grace drawled.

She supposed it was because there were no Buddhists in England, or so her father had said.

'He wanted to know about our parents. About how your father found us.'

Ice slid down her veins. This was something she and Lucy had sworn never to discuss, even between themselves. And yet she could already see that her sister had talked. 'You told him the truth?' she said.

'I didn't mean to. It just… He was asking questions and—'

'You wanted to please him. So you told him.' She groaned. 'How could you?'

'I didn't mean to!'

'What did you say? Exactly?'

Her sister bit her lip, but then she told the tale. 'He wanted to know how your father found you. How he knew you were his daughter.'

Even knowing the tale that was coming, Grace flinched. Back then, she hadn't spoken English. She hadn't known the monks had lied to Lord Wenshire. She hadn't known they'd played him for a fool.

'Lord Domac has worked out that we three are not related by blood. He guessed and I confirmed. He said you don't look like him. And I don't look like either of you.'

Guilt twisted in her insides. 'We don't know the truth,' she said, trying to convince herself. 'I'm the right age to be his child. And we have never pretended you are Lord Wenshire's child. But to me you're my sister. I would not leave China without you.'

Lucy smiled and squeezed Grace's hand. 'I know. I wanted to go with you. I wanted a new life.'

They both had. They'd both known their future in China was bleak. But that didn't solve the immediate problem.

'So now Lord Domac knows what even Lord Wenshire does not. That I am not truly his daughter.'

By the time she had understood enough English to realise what had happened, it had been too late. She hadn't been able to tell Lord Wenshire that she wasn't his true daughter. They had already sailed away, and he had shown her such love that she hadn't been able to hurt him with the truth.

'Lord Domac won't tell. He has no reason to. He knows that revealing it would destroy you. It would destroy us both, and he doesn't want that.'

She hoped so. She did not want to hurt her adopted father. He was a kind man, desperate for a family, and she and Lucy were all too happy to have what had never been theirs. Together, they made a loving unit, and she did not want that to change.

'You cannot tell anyone else,' Grace stressed.

'I know!' Lucy sighed. 'I didn't mean to tell him, but I'm glad I did. We'll soon find out if he wants you or the boat.'

Grace threw up her hands. Hadn't they been over this? 'He wants the boat!'

'Then he is not the husband for you!'

Lucy abruptly sat up, folding her legs in front of her so she sat like a monk teaching his class.

'If you believe the Duke is safe, then he is your man. Which means you are giving up on Lord Domac.'

Grace could hear the hope in her sister's voice.

'You are too enamoured of Lord Domac. He does not love you.'

At least she prayed he didn't. He had made it clear that he intended to marry Grace. What a disaster that would be if there were real feelings between him and her sister.

Meanwhile, Lucy twisted her fingers in the blanket. 'He might...'

'We were with him for four months aboard ship. If he loved

you, he would have approached you. He would have done something.' She narrowed her eyes at her sister. 'Did he?'

'No!'

Was that too vehement a denial? She couldn't tell.

'In any event,' Grace continued. 'Father thinks I should marry him. And we all believe he is safe.'

'Because we know what he wants.'

'Yes. The boat. And he will let me navigate the boat and I can live safely on it.'

'For how long?' pressed Lucy. 'How will you climb the ratlines when you are pregnant with his child?'

'Ching Shih did.'

'And will he kill to protect you? You have said that a boat is too small a place, that it is too difficult to hide when everyone knows you are a woman.'

She leaned forward, and Grace could see the sheen of tears in her sister's eyes.

'Remember your last voyage before you came back to the temple? You said the sailors had blamed you for the storms. They'd tried to kill you—their only navigator—because you were a woman. You said you could not risk that again.'

'And we sailed to England.'

'You don't want to sail any more. Admit it.'

Grace's eyes dropped, because they both knew it was true. A short voyage with a trustworthy crew would be all right. But a long voyage such as Lord Domac planned would be too dangerous for a woman to risk. Even his wife.

Now that her point had been made, Lucy turned the conversation back to the Duke. 'What do you think Lord Byrning wants?'

Grace pursed her lips. 'I told you. Novelty. He seems to delight in learning about new things.'

And she admired that. So few men ever wanted to learn new things simply for the joy of learning. But that character trait came with a flaw. The moment she ceased being new or different, he would look somewhere else.

She gripped her sister's fingers. 'He will not be interested in me once I have told him all my tales.'

'Maybe… Or maybe not. Father said the Duke has to take a wife because he must have children. It's an English rule. Perhaps you can measure out your tales? Keep him interested long enough to marry you.' She leaned forward, her words light. 'The Duke is very handsome, isn't he?'

Grace's lips curved in an embarrassed smile. 'There was a moment on the bridge when he stepped into the sun. *Mei mei*, he was surrounded by light as if heaven blessed him. I felt such heat inside me. Just being near him burned the air from my lungs. And every time he smiles I see that again. I *feel* that again.'

She would not confess that to any other person, but she and Lucy had been sharing secrets since their youngest days. These feelings the Duke created in her were so large she had to tell someone. She had to understand why she ached every time she thought of him.

'You are in love,' Lucy said.

Grace dropped back onto the bed, her disdain obvious. 'Love or not, I do not make decisions based on *feelings*.' She all but sneered the word.

Lucy was silent for a while, and then she spoke, her words gentle. 'I think you should marry the Duke. He is rich and powerful and he will keep you safe.'

Grace stared at the ceiling for a long time, trying to sort through all the emotions churning within her. But in the end one question lifted to the top. One question that must be answered first before anything else could be decided.

'Do you really think it is possible?' she asked. 'That we could marry so well? Us?'

They were both of mixed blood. Half-people. That made them undesirable in China. Could the English be so very different?

'I don't know,' Lucy answered. 'Maybe if they fall madly in love with us they will not think that we are half-people.'

'I do not think the Duke is a man to fall madly in love,' Grace said.

He was too even-tempered for that. Even angry—and he had certainly been furious with his aunt—he had kept his tone even and his mannerisms controlled. No, the Duke was not a man to be ruled by any emotions, even one as pretty as love.

Lucy settled down beside her sister. 'I think I should spend some time with the Duke. If it is only novelty he wants then he will look to me, because I'll be new and different. But...' She grinned as she met her sister eye to eye. 'If he still looks at you, then you will know he wants you.'

Or else she would know that his eye would always turn to the next new thing. She didn't want to guess what she would feel if the Duke began looking at Lucy instead of her. The very idea cut her deep inside.

Lucy would not let the subject drop. 'Do you think we can convince Father to let me join you in Hyde Park?' she asked. 'That will be proper.'

'Everyone will be looking at us. Two half-Chinese girls in Hyde Park.'

Lucy flinched. She never liked being the centre of attention. 'That will be awful.'

'Maybe. But you cannot hide away for ever.' Grace touched her arm. 'You need the practice in public, and I will be there to keep you safe.'

'Very well...' Lucy pretended to give in, even though she had been the one to suggest the outing in the first place. 'But I'm only going because you need someone to keep you from spouting nonsense about pirate queens.'

Grace snorted. 'He loved those tales!'

'Remember not to overwhelm him with strange stories. We want him to think that we are normal women. Women who can be good wives.'

'I will try,' Grace said, her voice low.

All her faults rolled through her head, the things the monks had said over and over until she heard the words in her sleep.

'But we both know that I am too restless to be a good wife. I am too much like a man. I am too loud—'

'Stop it!' Her sister hit her with her fist, but there was no power behind it. 'You will stop repeating those lies.'

'But—'

'We are half-people, *da jie*,' she said, using the loving term for big sister. 'We must be double in order to be whole. So you cannot be too much of anything. It is not logical.'

Grace slanted her sister a fond look. 'Well, if it is not logical, then it must be a lie.'

'Exactly.'

'Because the world—and most especially men—always act logically.'

'Just because men are flawed, it does not mean we must be.' Lucy lifted her chin. 'Stop worrying. We will learn more tomorrow, when we go to the park. And if the Duke doesn't immediately fall at your feet then I will be on hand to make sure he tumbles deeply in love.'

Grace groaned. 'Even you cannot be so foolish.'

'Try to believe, *da jie*. It is possible for both of us.'

Grace didn't say anything. She didn't want to crush her sister's childish dreams. But in her head she repeated what she knew was the wisest course. She would make no decisions based on emotion. In that, she and the Duke were the same.

Which meant neither of them would ever tumble into love with the other.

Chapter Ten

Declan arrived on Miss Richards' doorstep in a surprisingly unsettled mood. He was known in public as an even-tempered man. His reputation in the family, of course, was as a violent, ungoverned child prone to temper tantrums. That had been true when he was a boy, but thanks to the care of the gamekeeper's wife, not to mention the constant reprimands from his mother, he believed he'd outgrown such things.

It still required constant vigilance.

God knew, he had no desire to horrify Miss Richards with an intemperate display. So this disquiet as he approached her home bore some examination lest it lead to becoming overly emotional.

He had decided on a clear, logical list of facts.

Item One—this morning he had awoken in clear disarray. One minute he'd eagerly anticipated this visit, and then the next he'd dreaded it akin to attending a funeral. Such mood swings hadn't happened to him since adolescence. This fact was labelled *troublesome*.

Item Two—since leaving Grace yesterday he had ruminated on the story of a Chinese pirate queen. He had hung on her words even as he'd doubted them, and now he eagerly anticipated their next moments together and equally wanted to discard the whole discussion as poppycock.

The Irish tale of Granuaile was just as fanciful, but he knew of several who believed it. Perhaps many cultures created tales of pirate queens exactly because they were so much fun to imagine. Of course, an abandoned girl child would seize upon tales of a powerful woman as a means of giving herself hope. Therefore he would not discredit her belief until he found proof that it was false.

This fact he labelled *acceptable*. She believed the tale, and whether it was true or not made no difference. She admired the pirate's strength and independence. These were qualities he also admired. Therefore, the matter was settled in his mind.

Item Three—last night he had thought about the shape of Grace's body as she moved, the way her breasts shaped the modest gown she'd worn, and how he'd looked at her mouth and visualised things he'd never wanted to do with other society ladies. Lust had slammed through him, desire mixed with a need so strong that he had given in to the fantasy while in his own bed. He'd shamelessly pleasured himself while dreaming of her. And when was the last time he'd done that? Not since he was a randy boy, discovering women for the first time.

He wanted Miss Grace Richards—that much was clear. And damned if that want wasn't coursing through his blood now, even as he mounted the steps towards her door.

This item he labelled as *distressing* because his mother was right. The girl was unsuitable for marriage to his cousin or to himself.

It wasn't simple snobbishness. His duchess would have to understand polite society and would need to help him politically. She must make good connections and soothe ruffled feathers. And she absolutely must be able to face down the spiteful, vicious women in society, of which his mother and aunt were only moderate examples.

Miss Richards might be able to swing from the ratlines in a storm, but she had no understanding of the cruelty that could be inflicted upon a woman in society. He had seen strong women destroyed by daily attacks. At its worst, it drove some women mad. At best, it drove the unschooled away. They often found their own society, while hidden somewhere in the countryside.

But *his* wife could not run away. His political life was in London, where he enjoyed a robust discussion of the direction of this country. He meant to lead it in this new century, not wait on the sidelines as men too old or too stupid tried to keep everything *the same*. As if change was a dirty word.

Therefore he refused to marry a woman only to have her disappear to the country. He wanted children, and he wanted to know them. That wouldn't happen if whomever he married lived elsewhere.

Which meant that, even though Miss Richards stirred his loins, she was not the wife for him. And yet he longed to be with her, to hear the tales of her life, to understand more of the world beyond England's shores. How much further could one go than China?

She fascinated him, and yet he could not have her. Which, naturally, left him in a far darker place than he liked. Logic and reason had left him with one measly 'acceptable' against very powerful 'troublesome' and 'distressing'. He did not like that. Not at all.

Which meant that by the time he'd climbed the steps to her house he was holding on to his placid expression of polite interest by the tiniest thread. And yet he would not miss this outing for the world.

He was greeted at the door by Lord Wenshire himself. 'Your Grace, please do come in. I'm afraid we haven't been in London long enough to get a proper butler.'

Declan's brows went up. Hadn't they been in London for weeks now? 'Do you need assistance with that? I'm sure my housekeeper could help you find someone appropriate.'

The man sighed. 'I would be very grateful. Our last three have not…' He shook his head. 'The candidates have not lasted long.'

Declan frowned. Good servants were hard to find, but surely there was someone who could meet their needs. 'I shall have my housekeeper contact you immediately.'

'If she could be with Grace, that would be most helpful. I have been trying to teach her how to manage a household, including hiring the servants, but it seems I haven't the knowledge either. Not much call for a butler when travelling the way I have been.'

'No, I suppose not.'

By all accounts Lord Wenshire had wandered the world with little more than a knife and his wallet. Though Declan supposed that was an exaggeration. The man had worked for the East India Company and made his fortune there. Surely that company had given him more than a knife?

'I should love to hear about your adventures,' he said.

'I should enjoy speaking about them with you, though they are not as exciting as you might imagine.'

He might have said more, but at that moment the two ladies appeared, and Declan lost all track of anything but their appearance. Or, more specifically, Grace's.

Who the hell had put her in that awful pastel gown?

In his mind, Grace burned the way she had appeared on the boat, when she'd guided him up to the crow's nest. Her skin had caught the light differently from any way he'd ever seen before, shown smooth with a golden tan. Her cheeks had been flushed from exertion, and she'd listened to his words about London as if memorising every word. And then she'd turned to him, her eyes alight and her mouth so sweet. Her hair had been tangled and she'd worn a sailor's garb, but she'd been beautiful.

He saw the same slope to her cheeks now, and the same curve to her delectable mouth, but this time her casually short hair had been pulled back into a ruthless bun. There were tendrils of hair about her face that were meant to curl and bounce by her cheeks. That was the style that all the girls wore, but on Grace it looked appalling. Her hair dragged like tattered strings, out of place and clearly annoying her, given how she kept trying to tuck the strands behind her ears.

And that was nothing compared to the pale, washed-out puce of her gown. She was ten times more vibrant than that awful colour, and yet it seemed the dress was wearing her rather than the other way around. Especially with the horrendously large bow at the front, which appeared larger than her breasts.

'Good afternoon, Miss Richards,' he said as he bowed over her hand. 'I'm so pleased to see you again,' he said honestly.

Then he turned to her sister and did the same.

At least the younger sister had a decent gown. Less fashionable, less decorated, it fell in simple lines without décor, and that made it less of an atrocity.

He would have to tell his housekeeper to help with the girls' wardrobe too, if possible.

Meanwhile, Lord Wenshire spoke up. 'I thought to invite Lucy to join us. It's a fine day and she has been cooped up inside for so long.'

'Of course—' he began, but was cut off at a firm bang of the knocker.

'Goodness, who could that be?' Lord Wenshire asked.

The moment the door opened to show Cedric standing there Declan knew he should have expected it. Of course his cousin wouldn't allow Declan to escort Grace alone. He would force himself in if only to establish his ownership of the girl. Or rather her dowry.

It was Declan's fault for making the invitation at that thrice-blasted tea.

'Lord Domac! What a surprise!' exclaimed Lord Wenshire. 'Have we forgotten an appointment?'

'Not at all, but I couldn't allow His Grace to have all the fun.' He stepped past Lord Wenshire to bow over the ladies' hands. 'Miss Richards,' he said to the younger daughter, as he clearly caressed the girl's hand. 'Grace,' he murmured as he bowed again. 'You look ravishing.'

Had there been extra warmth in his greeting to the younger girl? Declan couldn't be sure, but the question was in his mind. Meanwhile, Grace was blushing prettily at Cedric's compliment.

'Lord Domac, welcome to our home,' she said, clearly a little flustered.

'He forgets his manners,' Declan interrupted. 'He is to address you as Miss Richards. A gentleman does not use a lady's first name unless the pair are engaged. Which you are not.'

His voice was cold, his attitude worse.

What the devil was wrong with him? He knew a thousand better ways to correct his cousin than calling the man out in public. But seeing his cousin fawning over Miss Richards had set his teeth on edge. The man was playing her false, and that heated Declan's blood to a dangerous degree.

He needed to control himself, but Cedric had always known how to irritate his 'older and more boring' cousin. As children, it had caused the man untold delight to needle Declan, until he lost control and punched back physically. Then Declan would be punished, and Cedric given special treats. It had been infuriating, but it had been the byplay of children—boys in particular—and Declan refused to give in to it now.

And yet despite his determination Declan felt his temper rise. And, damn it, Cedric knew, because his face shifted into a mischievous grin.

'Oh, goodness, I'm forgetting myself,' Cedric drawled.

Damn, the man could be charming.

'It was Miss Richards' beauty that overtook my wits.'

It was the size of her dowry that had overcome him, and the joy he had at tweaking Declan—but, again, that could not be spoken of out loud.

'Well, we must be off,' Declan declared. 'So sorry, cousin, but my carriage will only take four. I'm afraid you'll have to make your own way to Hyde Park.'

'Don't be ridiculous. You and I have squeezed in together in carriages before. We can handle it for the short ride to Hyde Park.'

Of course they could. But if he knew anything about his cousin, the man would 'squeeze in' next to Grace—probably between both ladies.

'Don't be silly,' Lord Wenshire said, his voice calm. 'I can follow on foot. It's not that far, and I've been aching for a little exercise. The city is so confining, and I'm used to a more active life.'

Good God, did the man know nothing about randy young men?

'Please, Lord Wenshire,' he said quickly, 'you take my carriage with your beautiful daughters. My cousin and I will meet you there.'

And on the way he would have some choice words with the man.

His hard tone left no room for argument, and the logistics were quickly managed. And then, as soon as the carriage had rumbled away, he rounded on Cedric with a tone that was a good deal frostier than he'd ever used before in his life.

'What the devil are you about, Cedric?'

'At last,' his cousin drawled. 'I have your attention.'

'Of course you have my attention. What bloody good does that do you? I'm furious, and you're gloating about God only knows what.'

Cedric snorted. 'I'm gloating? Good God, you are in your dotage. Let me make this clear.'

'About time!'

His cousin continued as if he hadn't been interrupted. 'Miss Richards is to be my wife, and you are trying to take her away merely because you can.'

Of all the idiot complaints!

'Cedric,' he said, with as much patience as he could muster. 'I'm doing nothing of the sort. Damn it, we aren't children. She isn't a toy to fight over. Haven't you outgrown this by now?'

Cedric threw up his hands in disgust. 'I'm not playing. I am warning you, cousin, do not stand in my way.'

Declan gaped at his cousin, seeing a hardness he'd never witnessed before. Far from being the irritating little boy Declan remembered, Cedric had matured into a man with dark intent.

'Cedric, what has happened? We used to be friends.'

When the boy hadn't been torturing him.

'Friends? We rubbed along well enough when we were at school. You with your stuffy old chums and I with the fun ones.'

Declan tried not to roll his eyes at that. *Stuffy. Irresponsible.* These were insults they'd thrown at each other as they'd passed in the school halls. Hadn't they grown past these things?

'But then you disappeared,' Cedric all but spat.

'I was on my Grand Tour.'

And what a long disaster that had been, though he realised now he'd never told his cousin the fullness of what had happened to him during that awful time.

'And what about afterwards?'

Declan frowned. 'What *about* afterwards?'

'When my father gambled away our money? When he lost my sisters' dowries on some bizarre investment. Where were you then, when I needed help stopping him?'

He had no idea.

'How was I supposed to stop your father? I couldn't control my own.'

'I came to you. I begged you for help.'

'You came to the House of Lords during a vote! I couldn't drop everything to see you.'

'You sent me away. You wouldn't hear a thing.'

'We met later. We had dinner and some very fine brandy.'

'You laughed at my ideas.'

Oh, good God, they were back to this! 'You hadn't done any research. You had no idea if the investments would work.'

'I did research it!'

'Not enough. Damn it—'

'My sisters have no dowries!'

Declan folded his arms across his chest. It was one of the ways he made sure he appeared stern when inside he was holding back a scream. Or a punch.

'You should be discussing this with your father.'

'He's back in the duns again and you know it.'

He did. The Dukedom had long since cut off any support to his uncle. The man was nothing but an endless pit of gambling losses.

Cedric lifted his chin. 'I need to get my sisters something for their dowries.'

'Then bring them to me. We'll all sit down and discuss plans. The Dukedom will provide for their dowries. It will not cover your blackmail.'

Cedric shook his head. 'Miss Richards is my plan.'

'Miss Richards is your blackmail. It's cruel, Cedric, and it's beneath you. You and I both know she's not up to the task of being your countess. The *haut ton* would crucify her.'

Cedric tilted his head and stared at him. There was a darkness in the man's eyes that made Declan step back. Something he had never seen in the younger man's eyes and hoped never to see again. And yet as they stood there the blackness only worsened.

'Cedric,' Declan said softly. 'We will find a way to get you a boat. You need not marry—'

'Will it come with a navigator like her? Will it come with her father's money? Do you know how much Lord Wenshire made in the East India Company?'

No. Declan had made discreet enquiries, of course, but even those who had worked with the man knew nothing about his income.

'I do not,' he said softly. 'And neither do you.'

Cedric lifted his chin. 'I know enough. He is wealthy and he loves his daughters.'

'You are taking advantage—'

'I am marrying a woman whom I will treat well. I will let her be a navigator on a boat she loves. I will let her travel back to her home, and she will make me a dragon's hoard of wealth. Then you will come to *me* for money, you will beg my forgiveness, and you will take your supercilious nose and stick it—'

'You are not engaged to her yet!' Rage filled Declan's tone. He felt it burn as hot and dark as Cedric's hatred. And it dripped from his words like acid. 'You don't love her, and don't want to marry her. You are using her to blackmail the family.'

'Is it working?'

'Of course not!'

Cedric laughed, and the sound was not pleasant. 'I think it is.'

And then he had the infuriating gall to start walking towards the park with a jaunty step and a merry whistle.

Declan stared at his cousin, lava in his veins as his rage burned darker and colder, settling into lines he scarce knew were forming. This was something he had never felt before, something that overwhelmed him, darkened him, and then hardened into feelings that were deep and ugly.

His cousin would not have Grace. He would not abuse a girl too naïve about English customs to know what she was doing. And if Cedric tried anything that ended up damaging Grace, he would know such pain as only a duke could inflict.

Chapter Eleven

'I knew this dress was wrong,' Grace said once the carriage started moving.

'Why ever would you say that?' her father asked, without even looking at the hideous bow of her gown. 'The modiste said it was the peak of fashion. And both His Grace and Lord Domac said you look lovely.'

Grace looked at her sister. 'He said he was pleased to see me. Lord Domac said I looked beautiful.'

By which she meant that the Duke was not a man to lie, whereas Lord Domac clearly was.

She watched as Lucy's eyes widened, and she nodded as if she understood. But her father was oblivious.

'There you go,' he said as he smiled warmly at her. 'You are in the height of fashion.'

She did not argue. What was the point? He would see what he wanted to see, and thankfully he saw them both through the eyes of love.

'Father,' she said as she took his hands, 'thank you for that, but you know you do not have a head for fashion.'

'Fashion is ridiculous all the world over, and there is no putting logic to it. I am merely pleased that you have garnered the attention of not one, but two exalted gentlemen. Just imagine what it will be like tomorrow night at your first ball.'

Her smile grew strained. If her gown today was as wrong as she believed it might be, then her ball gown would be a disaster. The modiste had been too busy to give them much attention and had pulled the gown from somewhere in the back of her shop. She'd said it was all the rage, and Grace had no ability to disagree. Now she wondered if the woman had palmed off a terrible gown upon a person who didn't know better.

There was no help for it, of course. She was wearing it now.

Meanwhile, her sister poked her in the side. 'The Duke looked very handsome, didn't he?'

Grace felt her face flush. The Duke always looked handsome, but he'd seemed tense to her. His movements had been tight, his jaw clenched. There was a fight brewing between him and his cousin, and she wondered what words were being spoken.

Lucy gave her a mischievous smile. 'Maybe you think Lord Domac outshone him.'

'I think Lord Domac has a flatterer's tongue. I never know what to believe when he speaks.'

'Don't be silly. All you have to do is look at his mouth. When his smile is tight, with a lot of teeth, he has not spoken the full truth. He never lies outright. But when his lips are parted and relaxed he is open and honest.'

Grace frowned, trying to remember Lord Domac's mouth. 'How was he when he talked about my dress?'

Lucy shrugged. 'I couldn't see.'

Which was no help at all. And it didn't matter anyway because their carriage came to a stop.

Their father stepped out first, and then turned to help them. It was only as she cleared the carriage that she got her first look at the madness that was Hyde Park at the fashionable hour.

Circling the park were a slow promenade of dozens of carriages. A row of palanquins would have moved faster than those plodding horses, with men and women preening from their seats. The colours were dizzying to see, not to mention the abundance of ribbons and feathers. Even some of the men wore fabrics in bright patterns that made it so she could only see the colours and not their faces. It was as if she stared at a parade of attire.

Perhaps her bow was not as much out of style as she'd thought.

But a more narrow-eyed look around told her that no woman wore a bow as large as hers. And, worse, none of the elaborate knots were at the front, preceding the body like the bow of a ship. Good Lord, she looked ridiculous.

'Oh, dear,' she said as she turned to her sister. 'I think the modiste was playing a joke on us.'

'Nonsense!' Her father laughed. 'Do you not see the feathers on that woman's head? Or whatever pattern that is on the gentleman there? Fashion is nonsense. You fit right in.'

She didn't think so. And the moment she saw a pair of girls eye her and burst out laughing she knew she had the right of it. She grabbed her sister's hand. 'Quick. Pull this wretched thing off me. Rip it if you have to.'

Her sister's eyes widened, but she quickly agreed—though the movement was awkward, given that they were still in view of everyone. Grace tried to shield herself in the carriage, but it could hardly be done in secret. Worse, there was a telltale ripping sound as the stitches were pulled.

Fortunately, the ribbon had been attached to the top of the gown, not as part of the seam. So long as she was careful, her gown would stay in place. She hoped...

'There,' her sister said as the knotted fabric fell away.

'Oh, dear!' came a masculine voice from the opposite side from the park. 'Did you rip your gown?'

It was Lord Domac, striding forward with a sunny smile on his face. Since Lucy was busy tossing the bow behind her into the carriage, Grace was left to face the man alone.

'Yes, I'm afraid I was clumsy and stepped on it,' she lied. Then she frowned, looking over Lord Domac's shoulder. 'Whatever happened to the Duke?'

'Oh, he'll be along in a minute. He's older, you know. One has to allow for his advanced age.'

Advanced age? That was a lie if ever there was one. She knew the Duke had climbed the rigging more easily than Lord Domac. And now that she looked closely at the future earl, she saw sweat darkening his shirt collar. More likely Lord Domac had run ahead while the Duke had maintained a sedate pace.

'Did you race one another here?' she asked.

'And I won!' he quipped happily.

Then she spied the Duke, sauntering up the street. His steps were long, his movement steady, but there was a tightness in his gait that she'd never seen before. She glanced to her sister, wondering if Lucy saw the same thing, but her sister was gazing up at Lord Domac with a worshipful air.

Damn! The girl's infatuation hadn't dimmed.

Grace stepped forward, coming between her sister and Lord Domac. 'There is the Duke,' she said, too loudly. 'Look at the way the sun shines on his hair. I've never seen such a thing before.'

Well, not since walking on the bridge in St James's Park with him.

Lord Domac snorted. 'Blond locks are commonplace here. It's really nothing special.'

Possibly not, but she liked it that the man kept his hair clean. It was one of the things that she appreciated on land—the fact that one could bathe more often than only whenever there was a storm.

'Never mind that,' Lord Domac said. 'Shall we begin our promenade? Unless,' he said after a pause, 'you wish to put that bow back on? I believe we could make it stay close to where it is meant to be.'

Or it might fall off at the most awful time.

Fortunately, another voice interrupted before she could form a response.

'I believe that the gown is much improved,' said the Duke as he joined them.

His voice was a low rumble that didn't startle her so much as shiver down her spine all the way to her toes. And why were they curling as if they had been touched?

She meant to say something. She even opened her mouth. But her mind was blank. He stood right beside her, his body large, his expression congenial, and his eyes...

Oh, dear.

There was something in his eyes. Something dark and heated. Something that made her tense even as it thrilled her. She was not a woman who ran towards danger. Indeed, she was the exact opposite. She was looking for a safe harbour from the world. And right now she really ought to be running away.

'Your Grace?' she said, her voice a bare whisper.

'Come,' he said as he held out his arm. 'I believe I promised you my escort.'

She knew she was supposed to set her fingers on his forearm. But he held his arm out to her as if it were a club. Was she to grab it and bludgeon someone?

She hesitated, uncertain of him in this mood. And in the middle of her hesitation, Lord Domac chortled.

'Sweet heaven, Declan. Stop being such an imperious prig. You're frightening the girl.'

Then he smiled his most charming smile and held out his arm for her. She knew it was his most charming look because they had practised exactly this kind of promenade on the boat from China. She hadn't had full command of English then, so she had memorised all his different expressions instead.

And now she was wondering if that meant his mouth was tight with teeth or parted and relaxed. She had no idea. And yet she couldn't quite bring herself to cling to the Duke. He was obviously in a strange mood.

So she did what she'd always done in China when she was unsure. She stayed on her own until she knew exactly who was offering what.

'If I can run the ratlines aboard ship, then I can surely walk without aid in a park. Yes?'

'Grace!' her father said, his tone exasperated. 'You are not to mention that.'

'My apology, Father,' she said quickly. Then she looked at her sister, who had not said one word since the men had arrived. 'Lucy, let us walk arm and arm, yes? I see several ladies doing that.'

'Oh, yes!' her sister said.

And so they began their walk, with herself and Lucy leading while the three men trailed behind. Grace and her sister whispered between each other, commenting on the clothing they saw as they smiled at everyone who looked their way. And indeed there were several people who looked directly at them. So many that Grace began to memorise the pattern of their every glance.

First their eyes widened in surprise, then there was a slow pinch to their lips as their gazes hopped to the men, and then they leaned close to a companion, be it male or female. All too soon sneering laughter would erupt, and all the while Grace felt her belly tighten with dread. She knew mocking laughter when she heard it. And she knew disgust in every glance. After all, such was the reaction in China when anyone saw her half-white face.

'I do not think this was a wise idea,' she said in Chinese.

'Not if we were alone,' came her sister's response in the same language. 'But we are with powerful men. We must use it.'

'How?'

Her sister tensed, then whispered urgently. 'Pick your man now. Either the Duke or Lord Domac.'

'You cannot simply demand—'

'The Duke. I agree.'

Then she abruptly shoved Grace sideways, hard enough that Grace stumbled...straight into the Duke's arms.

Chapter Twelve

Declan was still struggling with his rage when Grace stumbled. He saw the way her body jerked, but had no time to do anything more than lift his hands before she careened into him. He kept himself upright, his hands gripping her waist, even as her head bumped hard against his chest.

She found her footing quickly once she'd gripped his arm. Indeed, he felt her muscles adjust as she straightened her slender frame.

'I am so sorry,' she breathed, her face inches from his own.

He stared at her, moved by her beauty despite the ugliness raging inside him. His hands spasmed, unwilling to release her, and then, to his shock, his index finger slipped through the thin seam of her gown. He had been holding her tightly, but a well-made gown would not have given way so easily. He touched warm flesh, his finger sinking into the space between two ribs. He shifted his finger just to be sure, and felt the seam give even more.

Then he saw her eyes widen as she too realised that her dress had ripped.

'Good God, Declan,' his cousin drawled. 'Cease man-handling the girl.' Then he took hold of Miss Richards' arm, his dark, thick hand wrapping like a stain around her skin.

'Don't touch her,' Declan said, his voice hard and menacing.

The sound of his own voice shocked him, but there was nothing he could do to stop the deadly threat in it.

His idiot cousin didn't hear it, of course. The man had always been oblivious to his own stupidity.

'Come away, Miss Richards,' his cousin continued. 'The Duke is a clumsy oaf. I should not like him to hurt your gown with his bumbling.'

'I am fine,' the woman said, her voice soft as she turned her eyes towards Cedric.

Of course she was fine—not that his cousin had asked about her welfare. No, he had addressed her gown, which Declan had, in fact, already damaged.

'Step away, Cedric,' Declan said.

His cousin had not released Grace's arm, and Declan's fury was pulsing on its leash. It was an irrational fury, burning through him as it sought a target.

'Let her go,' Declan repeated, doing everything in his tone and body to warn his cousin.

Cedric's expression darkened. 'You arrogant—'

Declan struck. A single fist straight to Cedric's jaw. His cousin's head snapped round but his neck did not break, thank God. It did nothing to ease the black lava in Declan's blood.

Cedric stumbled backwards, but didn't fall. All too soon his shoulders squared, and his fists were quickly raised.

'Stop this!' Lord Wenshire bellowed. 'This is London! You're English!'

The other Miss Richards cried out as well. She reached a hand out to Cedric, but thankfully was clever enough to keep out of the way.

Declan noted these things in the way of a man hearing a distant noise. His attention was focused on the red mark on Miss Richards' arm. Cedric had hurt her, and for that there would be retribution.

Some part of him recognised his rage. Some tiny piece of his mind registered that for all his smug assurance that he had the Byrning legacy under control, it was here now—in full control of him. And it had decided to strike down any soul who dared defy him. In this case, his own cousin. It would not just strike Cedric down, but destroy him in the most primal way.

He stepped into Cedric's reach, already knowing his cousin would take the bait. Cedric did, putting power into his blow, but no real skill.

Declan had spent years since Italy learning how to defend himself from footpads and worse. He blocked it easily, and then he struck again. Blow after blow while his cousin struggled. He didn't care, and he didn't hear. All he did was feel the impact of his fist on Cedric's flesh.

Rage. Hatred. How it burned.

Until someone else's elbow hit his face, jerking him around.

As he wheeled back his arm was pulled hard with his momentum, and brought abruptly up and behind his back. It was a shocking change, since he was sure there had been no other attacker at hand. Not someone who could hit that hard nor manoeuvre him so easily.

Then white-hot pain cut through his focus.

He tried to jerk away, but the grip on his arm didn't tighten. No, it shifted, raising his arm more painfully until he was stooped over from the agony. He tried any number of manoeuvres, but he already knew it was useless. He was caught fast. Whoever held him kept the pressure strong, while around him was…noise.

So much noise.

Voices. Gasps.

He blinked as he looked around. Hyde Park at the fashionable hour was filled with all the *haut ton*. And every lord, lady, and miss was staring at him in shock.

'Are you calm?' came a voice behind him.

Miss Grace Richards.

He took a heaving breath. Had he been panting? Blood still coursed hot in his body, but his mind began to clear. He looked down to see Cedric on the ground, his face a bloody mess as he sent Declan a seething glare.

'Cedric?'

The man didn't acknowledge the question. Instead, he straightened to his feet to stand tall before Declan.

'I told you to let go of her,' Declan growled.

'I didn't hurt her,' Cedric snarled. He was always one to bluster when faced with a difficult situation. 'You, on the other hand—'

'Miss Richards?' Declan interrupted, alarm shooting through him. Had he hurt her? Where was she?

'I am well,' came a quiet voice behind him. Not just behind him, but right at his shoulder.

'You are the one restraining me,' he said.

It wasn't a question. He could plainly see the other Miss Richards, and her father too, both watching him with guarded expressions.

'Are you calm enough to be released?' she asked.

Was he? In truth he wasn't exactly sure. Rage still seethed inside him, but he thought it was under control. He took another full breath, using it to slow the heavy thud of his heart. His shoulders were still tight, his jaw still clenched, and all the people staring at him did not help. Nevertheless, he nodded.

'I will not hit him again, provided he keeps his hands off you.'

He felt the angle of his arm ease and breathed a sigh of relief despite the throbbing pain.

Miss Richards stepped around to face him. 'Why did you attack your cousin?' she asked, her expression almost bland.

'He hurt you,' he said.

'I did not!' Cedric snapped. 'You did.'

Declan's gaze dropped to Miss Richard's forearm. He remembered Cedric's hand there, he remembered a red mark, but there wasn't one there now. Her skin was flushed, but unmarked. And the more he stared, the more her skin remained smooth and clear.

'He hurt you,' Declan repeated, but there was fear in his tone. Had he imagined it?

He looked at Miss Richards' face. She was watching him with a steady, clear gaze.

'I have run the sails in a storm,' she said softly. 'I am stronger than I look.'

Of that, he had no doubt. He touched his throbbing jaw. She'd effectively stopped him, and even his own father had been unable to do that.

'Look at her dress, you idiot!' Cedric snarled. 'You did that.'

Declan quickly scanned her body. She stood straight, with no marks, no injuries. It was only her dress which... He flinched. Bloody hell, her dress had a gaping hole in the side where the seam had ripped.

He frowned as memory crystallised in his mind.

He'd put his fingers through her dress. Oh, God. What had he done to her reputation?

With quick movements, he stripped off his coat and extended it to her.

She frowned at it. 'I am not cold.'

'You are in dishabille,' he whispered.

How had this happened? Panic was beginning to thrum in his veins. He knew that shame would come in an overwhelming cascade soon. His only defence, and the only way to keep the legacy in check, was to regain his full faculties.

But, oh, the pain in realising that he had not only failed to control himself, but he had also lost his temper so viciously in front of her. In front of everyone. She was the one he'd most wanted to show the best of himself. Instead, she'd seen the worst.

God, he was a disaster.

And it wasn't over.

He had to recall himself to the present, so he strove for rationality.

He started by pulling in his memories. He recalled that she'd stumbled sideways. But she was more sure-footed than a cat, which meant she hadn't tripped. Her action had been deliberate. She'd meant to fall into his arms...she'd meant to have him catch her and rip her dress.

His eyes narrowed as he remembered. 'You did this on purpose,' he said. 'Why?'

The answer was obvious, wasn't it? He was a duke. She was an unwed miss. Many had done worse to trap him into marriage. But he couldn't believe it. And yet he couldn't make sense of the situation any other way.

'What?' she cried.

And yet he couldn't stop seeing it in his mind's eye. She'd jerked sideways, right into his arms. He'd grabbed her and her dress had torn—in front of everyone in the *haut ton*.

Meanwhile, her father cursed and shrugged out of his own coat. Knocking aside Declan's offering, he gently set his own coat around Grace's shoulders. Then he put her hand on her dress and spoke softly to her. 'You need to hold the seam together.'

She nodded, her gaze downcast as she gripped the side of her dress. Then she turned to her sister. 'Come along, Lucy,' she said, defeat in her tone. 'We should go home.'

'No,' Declan said as he straightened up to his full height. 'No, you and your father will ride with me in my carriage.' Then he glanced about at the assembled gawkers, spying the sister of one of his oldest friends. 'Lady Bowles, would you mind escorting Miss Lucy Richards back to her home?' He cast a dismissive look at his cousin. 'I believe my cousin is indisposed.'

His cousin was bloody, one eye already swelling. His nose didn't look broken, but it was hard to tell as the man pressed a handkerchief to his eye.

Meanwhile, the lady stepped forward, her expression equally guarded as she turned to the younger Miss Richards.

'Hello, dear,' she said kindly. 'Let's step away from all this. Men can be such children sometimes.'

The disgust was heavy in her tone and Declan felt his blood heat again. She was right. He'd thought he'd outgrown his legacy years ago. Hadn't he said as much to his mother that morning after his birthday when this whole thing had begun? And now he was once again a ten-year-old boy, with aching knuckles and a growing, crushing shame.

He fought it the way his father always had—by putting on a ducal air that was a hideous lie. 'Commentary is not necessary, my lady. I merely require your assistance.'

'Oh,' the lady retorted as she gently guided Miss Lucy Richards out of the park, 'commentary will most certainly be made and not only by me.'

She was right, of course. He could already see the scandal

whipping through the *ton*. Every tongue here was wagging, even as the onlookers waited to see if there would be more spectacle.

'Cedric,' Lady Bowles called. 'Do come and escort us, will you?'

His cousin had been fingering his split lip, but after another dark look at Declan he stomped away. Which left Declan with Lord Wenshire and Grace.

Lord Wenshire arched a brow. 'I believe,' he said darkly, 'your carriage is this way.'

Yes, it was. As was his doom.

How the hell had this happened? How had he allowed Cedric to goad him again? How had he not changed from when he was twelve and they'd brawled over toy soldiers. But Grace was not a toy. She was a debutante. And he had torn her dress in full view of the *haut ton*.

Was he now honour-bound to offer marriage?

He shook his head, clenching and unclenching his fists as he trailed behind Miss Richards and her father. Good God, he couldn't think straight. He shouldn't have come here this day. He should have realised that he was in no mood to control his temper. He should have realised the moment Cedric appeared that he could not stay vigilant against his legacy. It was always there, ready to destroy him when he let down his guard.

Had he ruined Grace? Had he destroyed his cousin's face? Why had he allowed Cedric to get to him? Hadn't he learned by now? God, he should not have come this morning. Hadn't he said that he faced something both *troublesome* and *distressing*?

He was such an idiot!

And now he was honour-bound to marry Grace.

And why did that idea not bother him, when he had just this morning decided she was unsuitable?

Chapter Thirteen

Grace climbed into the carriage feeling acutely uncomfortable. She knew she ought to feel afraid, or even horrified by the Duke's outburst. Instead, she felt unaccountably attracted to him.

She understood violence. Indeed, aboard ship she'd seen a great deal of things that had rightly terrified her. Now she had seen the Duke's fighting skill, and his rage, and she knew how dangerous that was. She never, ever wanted to see such things again.

But for the first time in her life such rage had been focused in her *defence*. Moreover, the Duke had given warnings to his cousin. He had told him what to do in no uncertain terms. It was Lord Domac's idiocy that he had not recognised the signs and heeded them. In truth, some demon inside Cedric had goaded the Duke into the attack. Who was so stupid as to taunt an enraged beast?

That was Lord Domac's error. Hers was to look at the Duke and see a man, not an animal. She knew from experience that a man who sank into rages was a beast in a man's clothing. He was unpredictable and dangerous. Her best bet was to stay as far away from him as possible.

But he had *protected* her.

It didn't matter that she hadn't felt any danger. That she was perfectly capable of defending herself from Lord Domac. The Duke had seen the way she'd been manhandled by his cousin and had issued his warning. Twice.

That was the act of a man, not a beast. It was only the rage that had overcome him that had brought him low.

And the Duke did look low. She was already seated beside her father in his carriage when he shouldered his way into the vehicle. His jaw was tight, his shoulders hunched, and when he lifted his gaze to look at her she saw guilt, pain, and anger, all warring for pre-eminence. One of them would dominate, and that would tell her if she faced a man or beast. Unreasonable anger would end their association, no matter how handsome he appeared.

Pain at that thought cut sharp and deep, but she had long since hardened herself against pain.

Guilt, however, could not be pushed away. That was something she understood. She had only to look at her father's kind face to feel her own twist of guilt. What was so special about her and Lucy that he had claimed them and not the others? A dozen other mixed-race children lived at the temple, but he had taken her and Lucy.

But she couldn't think about that now. Instead, she studied the Duke as he settled into his seat and looked down at his clenched fists.

A moment later, the carriage started moving. It was not a long drive to her home, so they had little time. Unfortunately she had no understanding of what the English required in a situation like this. That was until her father started speaking.

'What you have done has shamed us all,' her father said, his tone hard.

The Duke's head snapped up, his eyes blazing with fury. 'What *I* have done? It began when she purposely threw herself at me!'

Her father stiffened, nearly rising out of his seat. 'How dare you say such a thing? My daughter is honest!'

Grace winced. It had been deliberate, just not by her hand.

She touched her father's arm and looked the Duke in the eye. 'The Duke is correct. The fall was on purpose.'

Her father twisted to stare at her. 'You would not do such a thing,' he stated flatly. 'You have little interest in catching a man, even a duke. Why would you—'

'Your sister did it, didn't she?'

The Duke's tone was defeated. She could see that he'd replayed the action in his mind and deduced the truth.

Grace nodded. 'Yes.'

'She knew your dress would rip. Why is it made so badly?'

She arched a brow at him, wondering if he would deduce that answer as well. A moment later, she saw him grimace.

'Your modiste is terrible.'

'What did you think of that bow, Your Grace?' she asked.

'It was hideous. You realised that and tore it off.' He took a deep breath. 'And there was no time to restitch it.' He shook his head. 'I shall have Lady Bowles take you to her modiste.'

Her father snorted. 'That is all to the good, but what will we do now? You have ruined her reputation.'

'I… I am not fit to marry,' he said. 'Not until I can control this.' The Duke leaned back against the squabs, his expression completely defeated. 'I am aware that this is not your daughter's fault, but it is the truth nevertheless. I will not propose.'

Her heart sank, even as she completely agreed with him. 'I cannot marry a man with no control,' she said. She looked to her father, who was already shaking his head. 'You know this to be true. I will not tie myself to a man who endangers me.'

She watched as her father pressed his lips together, clearly unhappy with the way this conversation was going.

Meanwhile, she looked to the Duke. 'Can you explain yourself?' she asked. She held up her arm. 'You can see that I was not hurt.'

The Duke's gaze rested hard on her skin. 'He was gripping you tightly. I saw it. He could have hurt you.'

'Yes,' she agreed. 'But I do not bruise easily, and I have endured much worse.'

His tortured gaze went to hers. 'I shudder to imagine what you have been through. It is not how a woman should be treated.'

She admired him for that statement. She knew he meant it. And so many men wouldn't say it, much less mean it.

'Why do you feel this so deeply?'

One thing about living among people who spoke a different language was that she'd become adept at reading their bodies and faces, despite their words. She watched as the Duke fought his own nature to hide from her question. She saw him try to gather his haughty air around him like a cloak, but then toss it aside with a clench of his jaw. He wanted to answer her as much as he wanted to hide from it. But in the end honesty won out and he faced her squarely.

'You are too new to England to have heard of my family's legacy. It's what we receive with the Byrning title.'

Beside her, she felt her father stiffen.

'Oh, dear...' the man murmured.

'You remember, then?' the Duke asked.

'As a boy at school.' He shook his head. 'Your father had a temper, but so did many other boys.'

'So did my grandfather and his father. All the way back for hundreds of years.' He looked directly at her. 'We are not known as men who control our anger.'

'Did your ancestors burn things?'

'Whole villages of our enemies. It's a bloody past, in a time when kings rewarded such viciousness.'

She watched him as he spoke. There was no pride in his tone.

'Were your rages rewarded?' she asked. 'As a boy, were they encouraged?'

He shook his head. 'Indulged is the better word. When I was a boy. But Mrs Wood—the gamekeeper's wife—would not let me get away with them. She taught me that a man controls himself. A duke even more so.'

There was more to the tale. She could see it in the tense set of his shoulders and the way his gaze slid away whenever he tried to meet hers.

'You became enraged when you thought I was in danger,' she said.

'Yes.'

'Were you hurt by your father as a boy?'

He shook his head slowly. 'Even at his worst, my father knew I was his heir. He did not touch me.'

'Then someone else.' It was not a question.

'Many someone elses.'

This time his gaze went to the window, though she knew his thoughts were not on the view.

'I had a sister...' He swallowed. 'She tried to defend her nanny from one of my father's rages. She ran into his blow. He threw her against the wall. Her neck was broken.' He took a shuddering breath. 'It was quick, at least. My father became a drunkard that night. He never raised his fist again—at least not with any power.' He snorted. 'He grew angry. He stormed and bellowed. But mostly he drank himself insensate. I think he was relieved when death finally came for him.'

He had told her some of this before, but now she understood it so much better. His family legacy was one of rage, but he was trying to fight it. And it was Lord Domac's perversion to ignore it or perhaps to encourage the disaster.

'You are the Duke now,' her father intoned.

'Yes.'

'And you just beat your cousin in Hyde Park at the fashionable hour.'

He paled, but didn't disagree.

She didn't say that he had done it in her defence, or that his obvious misery touched her deeply.

'How long has it been since you were gripped by such a rage?' she asked.

He slumped backwards against the squabs. 'Since I was in Italy, when I was attacked by footpads. That wasn't rage so much as terror. The spells were common when I was a teen. My sister was dead, my father a drunkard, and everything had changed.' He shook his head. 'But I learned to control them. I swear—' He cut off his words. 'I thought I'd learned.' He looked to her arm. 'I thought he was hurting you.'

What did she say to that? To a man who had carefully controlled his worst nature until the moment he'd seen someone hurting her? Mistaken or not, he had believed her in danger and had allowed his inner beast to fight on her behalf.

How could she not be grateful for that? How could she damn him?

She knew that a man who rages might turn his violence towards her at any moment. She had seen sailors who used any excuse to explode. But he was not that kind of man. He hated this fury inside him. The only question was how well did he control it? And could she risk being in his presence long enough to find out?

The answer, of course, was no. Logic and self-preservation told her that violent men were not to be tolerated. They always turned. This was not a kind world, and at some point a situation would turn against him. Something would happen, someone would defeat him, and he would react with violence. Such was the nature of violent men.

But she could not discard a man who had defended her. So few ever had. And none without conditions. Her father defended her because such was the duty of a man to his child. He didn't know it was a lie. The ships' captains had kept her safe because she had been their only navigator. All had got something from her in exchange for their help.

The Duke, on the other hand, had defended her because he'd thought her wronged.

After a lifetime of standing—afraid—on her own, the idea of having such a defender was a powerful temptation. And one that she was loath to give up.

'We should not marry,' she said, and the words were for herself, not him. She needed the ability to escape if necessary, and she could not do that if they were wed.

Her father disagreed. 'But what about your reputation? You are to be launched tomorrow night!'

She had no answer. This was his country, his customs.

'I shall court her,' the Duke said.

'What?' her father gasped. 'You have just said you will not marry her.'

'I shall let it be known that she has refused me. That she was shocked by my outburst.'

That was true, but she had not been shocked by his violence. Only by his defence of her and her attraction to him.

'Will that serve?' her father pressed.

'It will. I shall make my interest known. I will take the blame for my outburst solely upon myself.'

'As well you should,' said her father.

'And that should make her attractive to everyone else.'

She frowned. 'How?'

'Because I am an unwed duke. I will not attend any outing that does not have you included in it. And every society matron will want me there.'

He was so confident in his attractiveness. Usually, she would doubt such arrogance. Men often overestimated their influence over women. But she couldn't deny his appeal, so she nodded.

'I will allow you to court me,' she said, marvelling at her own arrogance.

If he wanted to pursue her, then she could do nothing to stop him. Except this wasn't a true pursuit, was it? He would only pretend to court her because it was the best he could do without marrying her.

He nodded, clearly satisfied.

Her father, of course, wasn't nearly as content, but he gave in with a grumble. 'Very well,' he said. 'Then you should take her out for her first dance tomorrow.'

'And then the first waltz,' the Duke agreed.

'There must be at least one other outing.'

'I have already offered to take her to the theatre.'

'Yes. And perhaps Vauxhall?'

Her father was pushing. He clearly wanted these things for her.

'It would be my pleasure,' the Duke responded.

The two men shook hands, as if she had no part in the discussion. She stared at them both, seeing satisfaction in their faces. Then, to her shock, the Duke turned to her. Leaning forward, he grasped her fingers and pressed a kiss to the back of her hand.

'Truly, Miss Richards, I apologise for the disaster of today's meeting. It is my hope that you can forgive me today's lapse and that we can begin anew. I swear to show myself a better man if you will allow it.'

He waited for her answer, her hand still clasped in his.

Heaven, what could she say to that? Her heart was beating triple time, her muscles were tensed as if to run, but where would she go? Out through the door or into his arms? He made her feel such contradictory things.

And still he waited for her answer.

The carriage stopped and the footman opened the door, but he did not move. He held her hand, he looked into her eyes, and he waited for her response.

'I will allow it,' she finally said, but what exactly had she just agreed to do? To dance with him? To attend the theatre with him as well as a pleasure garden? Or to let him tease her emotions in ways that had never tempted her before? Until she bit by bit opened herself to him?

That sounded like the height of folly.

And yet she had already agreed.

Chapter Fourteen

Declan didn't have much time. After his disastrous brawl in Hyde Park, he had to face the political consequences. No one in Parliament wanted a member of the Whigs making public displays of any kind, and they were understandably horrified by his actions.

He spent the rest of the evening and the next day soothing feathers and debating ways to make life better for the whole country. It was exhausting, but necessary. And if he'd thought he would get a moment's reprieve once he returned home, he soon discovered his error. He was met there by his solicitor, who had a ridiculously long list of legal matters to address regarding the ducal estates. And again he found himself reassuring the man that he wasn't impetuous or brash, despite the fact that he had recently been seen decking his cousin in Hyde Park.

The Byrning legacy was not taking over his personality. Everyone could remain calm. That was what he kept saying while privately he prayed it was true.

Damn it, he needed a wife. Someone who could help him calm his political allies, reassure his solicitor that he hadn't lost his mind, and generally share the burden of all his tasks. A foreign woman—be she Chinese, French, or from the moon—

could not move through his world with ease. Not without extensive training, and maybe even not then.

It was a simple practicality: he needed help. And it was traditional: he was of an age to marry. It was the reality of life as a duke.

Meanwhile, the clock in his library ticked along like a reminder of the world rushing ahead whether he was prepared for it or not. He finished up as quickly as possible with his solicitor, cognizant that he still had a pile of urgent correspondence on his desk.

The man had just left when Declan was interrupted again.

'Just like your father!' a voice exclaimed as the door to his library burst open.

Declan tensed, but he didn't look up from the letter from his steward. He had yet to find a way to manage his mother's tendency to burst in on him whenever she felt the urge. To date, his best strategy had been to ignore her until she paid some homage to the niceties of his title.

'And now you're drinking just like him, too!' she exclaimed as she pointed to the glass of brandy on his desk.

Behind her, his butler came rushing in, face red with apology. 'Your Grace, I stepped away for a moment. She has a key, and I was not—'

Declan held up his hand. 'Mother,' he drawled, 'you do not live here. Please surrender the key.'

'Oh, good God, you're being ridiculous. I am a duchess and you are my son. I will not—'

'Mother, you will surrender the key or I will ban you from my presence.'

'Now you're being dramatic,' she huffed.

At that, he turned to face his mother directly and slowly pushed to his feet to face her. 'Mother, I recently beat Cedric bloody in Hyde Park. This is not the time to test me.'

'Don't I know it!' she cried. 'Everyone is agog—'

'Key! Now!'

The two words exploded out of him, bellowed and cold. He saw his mother shrink back, her eyes widening with fear, and he cursed himself for being a damned beast. Her gaze dropped to his glass of brandy. He hadn't taken a single sip, but she stared at it as if it were the devil's own piss.

'Do not become him,' she whispered.

'I'm not.'

'The cuts on your knuckles say different. Not to mention every Christmas when you were young and beat up poor Cedric. I thought you had gained some measure of control, but now I see—'

With a grunt of disgust, he grabbed the brandy and threw it into the fire. The glass and the alcohol exploded with a satisfying cacophony, but it did nothing to ease the turmoil inside him. His mother was right. How many times had she told him that his temper would destroy him? How many times had she punished him for the least outburst?

Countless. And all of it for naught because he was thirty-one years old and still beating up his young cousin. What the hell was wrong with him? Was he doomed to be controlled by a legacy he couldn't escape? The agony of that thought nearly broke him.

Meanwhile, his mother would not relent, though she took a different tack.

'Declan, my dear, I am concerned about you,' she said, her voice taking on a soothing quality that he couldn't help but warm to. There had been times in his childhood when she had been a doting parent. He had learned in adulthood that it was simply a character she adopted when she needed it. His mother did not have it in her to be truly motherly.

'Do not say another word until you set the key on my desk.'

'But—'

'I will not tell you again.'

He waited in indifference for her response. She would either comply or not. If she complied, he would win. If she did not, he would throw her out and be done with her for this minute. Either way, it was a welcome distraction from the shame of his actions in Hyde Park.

He heard the key drop onto his desk.

'There,' she said haughtily.

He straightened and turned back to face her.

But before he could speak, she waved vaguely at the ornate key. 'I have several more, you know. This is a game your father and I played ad nauseum.' She donned the exact arrogant expression she'd worn for her portrait. 'I am the Duchess of Byrning, and I have a right to be here as much as I choose to be.'

'You are the Dowager Duchess—'

'Until such time as you marry I have a right to be here.' She waved her finger at him. 'Everyone expects it. You might as well get used to it. Even the servants cannot stop me.'

That was the best reason to marry that he had ever heard. But in the meantime he would have all the locks changed.

'Mother, you must learn the limits of your influence. Barging in on me at your whim shrinks my respect for your intelligence.'

'Well!' she said as she sat down. 'I believe the one who's intelligence is lacking is you. How could you hit your cousin in front of everybody? It boggles the mind.'

'He was hurting her.'

'Who? That Chinese girl? Well, that's between them, isn't it? If they're engaged and all that.'

'They're not engaged!'

'Thank heaven for that. Was this afternoon's display your attempt to dissuade him? Was that what you were doing? If so, then I applaud your reason, but I don't think it was effective. According to his mother, Cedric is as determined as ever to marry the chit.'

'He doesn't want to marry her. He wants her dowry.'

She snorted. 'Obviously! How does brawling in Hyde Park change anything?'

It didn't.

'I'm going to court her.'

'Who?'

Declan ground his teeth together but managed to answer civilly enough. 'Miss Richards.'

'How will that help anything?'

'For one, it will save her reputation. She was shocked by my temper—'

'As is everyone, though I suppose few are surprised.'

'She refused my offer of marriage.'

No fool, his mother stared at him long and hard. Then she shook her head slowly. 'You did not offer for her.'

It was a statement, not a question. And he was unable to lie directly to his mother's face.

'I... I did not. But that doesn't matter. This saves her reputation.'

'And makes her quite popular, I assume?'

'Yes.'

'Giving her someone else to fall in love with besides Cedric.'

He looked down into the fire, wishing now for the brandy that had just exploded. 'She does not seem especially enamoured of him. Or me.'

'That is her mistake and our good fortune. I assume you are to dance with her tonight?'

Of course his mother knew about her come-out ball.

'Yes,' he answered.

'Very well. Do the bare minimum and then send every possible gentleman over to her. Someone will turn her head quickly enough.'

Declan grimaced. 'I doubt she can be easily swayed. She seems...' *Capable, intelligent, remarkably composed...* 'A discerning sort of woman.'

His mother looked to him and shook her head. 'All young girls can be swayed. It merely takes the right application of pressure. Never mind,' she said as she pushed to her feet. 'I'll take care of it. Just play your part and no more.'

Part of him wanted to let his mother leave. Why poke the bear when she was already on her way out? But he knew from experience that he had to set down rules clearly or she would trample them.

'Mother,' he said coolly.

She stopped with one foot out the door. 'What is it now?'

'You are to do nothing to discredit Miss Richards or her family. Consider the lady untouchable.'

'Don't be ridiculous. She's the epitome of touchable. Her father's barely in society and she's a by-blow of mixed race. No one wants her here, and no one respectable will marry her. The sooner she gets that message, the better for everyone.'

Declan folded his arms. It kept him from choking her.

'She has done nothing wrong. You will not smear her.'

His mother threw up her hands in disgust. 'I begin to regret bringing you in on this business. She is *inappropriate*.' Her words were stated with diction as hard as glass.

'I am making her appropriate.'

'Not unless you marry her.'

He arched his brows. 'Do you doubt me?'

'Never,' his mother said. 'You've always been a man of your word. Unless you get angry or start drinking, that is.'

And there it was, the reason he let her run roughshod over him and the truth of why he never put her in her place or truly banished her for her tart tongue.

She was right.

Until he got his temper under control he was a lying fool, swearing to something one moment, then breaking his word the next time something upset him. That was how his father had been until his death. And that was how Declan had been in his teens and early twenties. It wasn't until after his Grand Tour that he had reconsidered his life.

And now that he'd pummelled his cousin, in full view of the *ton*, she had reason to doubt him again. If he tossed her aside now, when she was speaking the truth, then he would be no better than his father who'd been destroyed by the Byrning legacy. He needed to keep his mother's sharp tongue nearby, but he also needed her to be clear about the boundaries.

God, he needed a wife soon. One who knew how to manage his mother while keeping Declan calm. Naturally Miss Richards floated through his mind, but she was neither appropriate nor soothing. Indeed, when in her presence he felt hot and alive in all the best ways. But that made his temper short, and that led to...

Beating up Cedric in Hyde Park.

No, as much as he might wish it, Miss Richards would not make him an appropriate wife. God, how that thought hurt. But at least he could help her in other ways. He would make her acceptable and maybe she would find a man far removed from Cedric's greed or Declan's rage.

'You will leave Miss Richards alone,' he said flatly.

'Or what?' His mother threw up her hands in disgust. 'Honestly, it's almost endearing how you keep laying down the rules. Leave the key. Don't bother the girl. I am the Duchess of Byrning. I shall do exactly as I wish. And you will have to accept it because that is what a son does for his mother.'

He folded his arms. 'I do control your purse, Mother.'

Her expression darkened into her cold face, the one that had terrified him as a child. 'And you swore to me that as long as I kept my expenses reasonable you would never restrict my purse. Are my expenses over limit?'

'No.'

'Indeed, I think I'm well below my allotment this season.'

She was probably right. She kept better track of her finances than he did.

'Do you intend to go back on your word?'

'No,' he said again.

He couldn't in good conscience take her money away. It had been a stupid move to try to threaten her purse. But failing that he had no way to control her.

'Then I believe the matter is settled.'

'No, Mother, it is not. You will push and push until I must do something drastic that neither of us want.'

She waved a negligent hand at him, supremely confident in her ability to manipulate others to her will. 'Just do as you have promised. Pretend to court the girl while I throw handsome young men in her direction. Between the two of us she will be happily married to some nobody within a few weeks. Then she can retire to the country and have all the mixed-race brats she wants.'

She smiled at him.

'See? I can compromise. I shall do nothing to harm her.' She abruptly frowned as the grandfather clock in the hall clanged the time. 'Goodness, now we're both going to be late. I'll see myself out. And you must go and get dressed. Something restrained, to reassure everyone that you've not gone mad.'

She shook her head, speaking to herself as she pulled on her gloves.

'Why ever did I marry a Byrning? Violent beasts, every one of them. And they never change.'

Declan felt his throat close at her words. It was all he could do to remain upright and placid as she spun on her heel and left. But the moment the front door closed behind her, he collapsed into his chair.

Was it true? He looked at the space on the wall that had once held a portrait of his father. He'd ordered it removed the minute he'd ascended the ducal throne. But that didn't free him of the image of his father, of his grandfather, of all the Byrnings before him, who had been driven by their own vicious tempers.

Was he fated to be just like them, no matter what he told himself? If he married the wrong woman would he accidentally kill his own child in a temper? No, no, no! He didn't believe he was capable of that. But the scrapes on his knuckles said he was doomed.

Damn it, why did he have to have strong feelings for Miss Grace Richards? She interested him as none other, but obviously that made the rage burn hotter. She did not quiet him. She challenged him, aroused him, and made everything feel more alive.

He couldn't marry her. He shouldn't even be near her. But circumstances had forced his hand. And now he had to bathe before doing the pretty with her.

Odd how that thought brought a smile to his face. Looking at him now, no one would ever imagine the horror that lay just beneath his skin.

Well, no one but Cedric and his mother. Not to mention Miss Richards and her father. Plus anyone else who had seen him in Hyde Park.

Chapter Fifteen

Grace couldn't stop feeling the fabric of her dress. She had never worn anything so fine. It was *silk*. Certainly, she had seen great ladies in China in such attire, but never had she thought she'd be one of them. And here she was, far away from home, attired in silk that whispered delightfully across her skin.

'You look stunning,' her father said.

Her sister had said the same, as had their maid. But none of their breathless words could match the giddy unreality of the situation.

She was wearing silk. She was going to a ball. She was going to dance while gentlemen courted her. *Her!* A half-person worth nothing in China, a crazy navigator who had pretended to be a boy, and the mixed-race child of a kind old man who looked at her as if she had the moon and the stars in her hair.

'I cannot believe this is me,' she whispered as she continued to finger the fabric of her dress.

It was simple yellow silk with flowers embroidered upon the bodice. This gown was well made and came from Lady Bowle's own modiste.

'I cannot believe I am walking my daughter into a *haut ton* ball,' her father murmured. 'It is funny how a man doesn't think of these things until it's nearly too late.'

She reached out and squeezed his hand, feeling the icy cold of his fingers. Her father wasn't healthy, though he hid it well. Out of respect, she kept quiet as she watched his face for signs of illness as she would watch the night sky for the path forward. She saw nothing but his usual kind expression and his sallow skin. If only his cough would ease, then he would sleep at night and be healthy again. But, failing that, she would do her best to make him proud tonight.

It wouldn't work. She would not be well received tonight. Half-breed children never were. But in this moment, in the dark carriage with her father, she was well content.

'You have given me more than I ever dreamed possible,' she said.

'You have given me more than I ever thought I could have,' he said back.

And then they were there, arriving early to her come-out ball.

It wasn't her night alone. She was to share the event with Miss Phoebe Gray. The girl was young, sweet, but had no claim to an aristocratic heritage. Her father was rich, but her only hope of a successful match into the highest level of society was if someone like Grace, whose father was of the aristocracy, joined her come-out. The hope was that together they'd draw enough of the *haut ton* for them both to catch someone's attention.

Grace wasn't supposed to know this, of course. Her father wanted her to be giddy about her come-out, so he pretended that everyone would accept them as wholeheartedly as he had. But living in fantasy had never worked for her or her sister, and so they had both questioned the servants until they'd understood what was happening.

Still, they allowed him the pretence, and… Well, she would wear silk and attend a ball.

Grace was smiling as the door to the rented ballroom was thrown open and Miss Phoebe Gray waved her in. 'I'm so glad it is warmer now,' the girl said by way of greeting. 'We can open the French doors at the back. People can walk on the lawn. Isn't it perfect? Everything is going to be so perfect!'

Grace smiled. It was impossible not to in the face of such sweet exuberance.

'And you look gorgeous in yellow!' Phoebe continued. 'I could never do yellow. It makes me look like a badly made candle with a head for a wick.'

Phoebe slapped her hands to her sides and opened her eyes wide. If that made her look like a candle, Grace didn't see it, but it didn't matter. The girl was off onto another topic almost immediately.

'I've checked everything three times. The flowers are lovely. Have you seen them?'

'Only the roses in your hair,' Grace answered. 'They match your dress perfectly.'

Pink roses, pink gown and pink cheeks on a sweet face. Add in her blue eyes and golden hair, and the girl was English perfection made into a woman.

'You look perfect,' she said, wishing she knew better English words to describe the girl.

Phoebe giggled. 'I'm so nervous I'm afraid I'm going to burst into pieces!'

'Settle down, dear,' came a man's fond voice. It was Phoebe's father. The banker wore a genial expression as he bowed over Grace's hand. 'Allow them to take off their coats.'

'Of course. So sorry,' Phoebe said. The moment that was done, she grabbed Grace's hands and tugged her inside. 'There are yellow roses for you, too. Come and see! My maid is a whiz at adding flowers to gowns and hair and everything!'

Grace smiled and allowed herself to be pulled along, while behind her the gentlemen greeted one another. Phoebe continued to talk, her excitement infectious, and Grace let herself be swept up in the wonder of it all. Tonight she was the daughter of a wealthy aristocrat, no matter what the truth might be. And tonight she would enjoy herself no matter what.

She dutifully praised the food, the decorations and the musicians. She allowed Phoebe's maid to put a yellow rose in her hair. And then she and Phoebe stood in their places in the receiving line to greet their guests.

And there were a great many guests.

Unfortunately, there weren't many *titled* guests.

It would appear that the aristocrats had no interest in lowering themselves to attend the come-out ball of the daughter of a banker and a foreign girl with a titled father. It hardly mattered to Grace, but she could see that her father was disappointed in the turn-out, as was Phoebe. Despite the many people who came through the door, the girl's eyes seemed to dim with every Mr So-and-So or Mrs Whoever who greeted her.

Every so often Phoebe would whisper to her.

'I thought Lord Someone-or-Other would come. He was ever so nice to me in Hyde Park.'

Or, 'Maybe Lady This-or-That isn't feeling well tonight. I thought she'd come, but I haven't seen her.'

Grace had no answer to such things. She didn't understand who was more important than someone else. But she recognised disappointment when the girl's smile faltered and her shoulders drooped.

As the arriving guests dwindled, Grace squeezed Phoebe's hand. 'We are two beautiful girls having a party in our honour. So many people are alone and hungry. If we cannot be happy tonight, then we are the miserable ones who will never know joy.'

She wasn't sure she'd said her words clearly. She was trying to paraphrase a sentiment taught at the temple. But her meaning must have been clear because Phoebe slowly nodded.

'You are right, of course,' Phoebe said as she lifted her chin. 'This is our night, and no one can take my happiness from me.' Then she grabbed Grace's hand and tugged her away. 'Let's get some lemonade before the dancing begins. I'm parched.'

Grace was gulping down lemonade when *he* walked in. She'd known he was coming, of course, but she hadn't expected him to make the kind of entrance he did. Late, and yet supremely confident as he was announced. Handsome, of course, but in the English way. Tall, and dressed in austere black with a cravat of perfect white, a large, brilliant blue sapphire set in the centre.

She was not one to be enamoured of English attire. At least not what the women wore. But the English gentlemen emphasised a lean elegance that she appreciated. And the Duke took her breath away. He stood a hand's breadth taller than the other men, he carried himself with unhurried power, and he took the time to greet his hosts with respect, including an apology for his tardiness.

'Oh, my God!' Phoebe gasped. 'You said he was coming but I didn't *believe* you! Are you finished drinking? Hurry! We must greet him! But we can't run. Don't run!'

Grace wasn't running. Indeed, Phoebe appeared to be talking to herself as she rushed forward, then abruptly moderated her pace. Ten seconds later she was in her spot in the receiving line and going into a very deep curtsey. The Duke hadn't even turned her way yet, but she dropped down as if her legs couldn't hold her up.

'My goodness,' the Duke said, amusement crinkling the corners of his eyes. 'What loveliness has appeared before me? Please, Miss Gray, let me see your gorgeous face.'

Phoebe rose, her cheeks pink and her eyes sparkling. 'A pleasure to greet you, Your Grace. I'm so, so happy you could attend.'

'The pleasure is all mine,' he returned as he kissed her hand.

And then, at last, he turned to greet Grace.

She didn't know what she expected when he saw her. Hopefully as warm a greeting as the one he had given Phoebe. Her focus was on quieting her own racing heart. But the moment he turned to her all other thought fled. She watched his expression change as his gaze softened and his brows rose. Where there had been amusement, she now saw heat. His eyes flickered, taking in the whole of her, but that lasted less than a moment. For the most part he stood there, apparently transfixed, while she watched him and wondered if she measured up.

She hadn't been nervous before, but as he stared, her heart trembled. What had she done wrong?

'Miss Richards,' he finally managed, clearing his throat as he spoke.

'Your Grace.' She dropped into a curtsey, as she had been taught, but he quickly tugged her upright.

'I did not think you could be any lovelier,' he said. 'I thought I was prepared to see you dressed...' He shook his head. 'I have never seen a more beautiful woman. And I have seen many.'

His words were mere flattery, of course. She knew better

than to be taken in by overblown words. But they did not seem overblown. Everything in his face and body seemed earnest. And she could not help the flush of heat that filled her body. Did he really think her the most beautiful woman he'd ever seen?

'Your Grace,' she whispered again, not knowing what else she could say.

Thankfully her father saved her.

'You have arrived just in time,' he said loudly. 'I'm afraid my old bones aren't up to dancing any more. Would you mind taking my place for the opening dance?'

This had been planned in the carriage yesterday afternoon, but hearing it played out like this, Grace knew it sounded as if it were a surprise happenstance. And it felt as if it were the most startling thing as the Duke raised her hand to his lips.

'It would be my very great honour,' he said, before he pressed his mouth to the back of her hand.

Damn, damn, damn, why must she wear these stupid gloves? She wanted to feel his mouth on her skin. She wanted to know the calluses on his fingertips without the blunting fabric between them. She wanted to touch the man—and that thought was as shocking to her as it was thrilling.

Never in her life had she wanted to touch a man as she did right then. Indeed, it was as if all her body ached for a caress.

She heard the musicians readying.

She heard Phoebe's father chuckle as he came to Phoebe's side.

And she heard her own heartbeat loud in her ears.

Great heaven, what was happening to her? She tried to pull herself together. She forced some semblance of a smile as the Duke took her hand in his. And she managed, somehow, to walk to the centre of the ballroom.

Her father spoke first, of course. He uttered words of greeting, echoed by Phoebe's father. And then, with great fanfare, Grace and the Duke began to dance. Phoebe and her father were also part of the set. All this had been decided beforehand. And Grace knew the steps. She'd practised them! But she'd never done them with the Duke before. She'd never held his hand as he drew her close, nor stepped around him as if flirting without touching. She'd never done anything like this with him, and…and…

And it was *wonderful*!

Her heart trembled, her breath stuttered, and nothing mattered except for the way he looked at her. He held her hand and her feet moved exactly as they ought. He smiled at her and her heart sang. And then their steps drew them close, and he whispered the most glorious words to her.

'This is just the beginning.'

Chapter Sixteen

Declan smiled, hoping to ease the anxiety on Grace's face. Clearly she knew that her debut was already a failure. Except for him, none of the *ton* were here. They wouldn't deign to attend the come-out of an illegitimate woman of mixed heritage and the daughter of a banker. He doubted that Grace truly cared, but he could see her worry for Miss Gray.

That was why he'd whispered to her that this was just the beginning. He'd known girls who had contemplated suicide after a bad launch. Every debutante needed to understand that the come-out ball was just the beginning of a long and hopefully glorious life. Surely Grace knew that elite society was only a small fraction of the wide world?

Thankfully, she seemed to understand. The dazed look in her eyes had cleared, her smile had strengthened, and she moved with increasing poise on the dance floor. She was athletic, so the movements of the dance were not difficult for her. She'd obviously had lessons and knew where to go when. But the more he looked at her, the more she seemed to come into her own.

He was no poet, able to express how beautiful she was while she blossomed in his arms. But one moment she was placing her feet where they belonged with obvious intent. Then the next moment she was *dancing*. The girl who'd begun the set had become a woman, who moved for the sheer delight of the music and the night.

He could not credit himself with her change, much though he wanted to. But he could thank God that he was here to witness her delight.

She was even daring to cast him a flirtatious look now and again. Obviously, she was not a practised courtesan. Her coy regard was not that assured. But she showed flashes of daring when her eyes, her hips or some slight lift of her shoulder tempted him to touch her.

And with each glance he dared to draw her closer. How he wanted to take her to places best reserved for fantasies that could not be indulged in the middle of the ballroom. But, oh, he thought about them. Imagined them in graphic detail. And he delighted in the shocking lust he felt for her.

When was the last time he'd felt such a pull to a woman? *Never.* And the realisation of what he felt was as wonderful a sensation as it was frustrating. Because of course she was off-limits, except in the very proscribed manner of the dance.

In. out. A bow. A spin. And through it all a desire to kiss her until he was senseless with hunger. Worse, he could see the desire in her. Every time their gazes connected, their hands touched or her lips curved as if just for him he knew she felt it, too. She wanted him. Despite what she'd seen him do in Hyde Park and how horribly his family had treated her. Despite everything, she desired him, and he was both humbled and deeply aroused by that thought.

'Excuse me, old chum, I wonder if I might impose for an introduction?'

A male voice interrupted his thoughts. And it wasn't until the broad shoulders of an old schoolmate jostled him aside that Declan realised the dance had stopped.

'What?' he said, forcing his thoughts to beat back his lust.

'Never mind him,' the voice continued. 'Declan and I are old schoolfriends. No doubt he's addled by your beauty. Propriety demands that he do the honours, but since he's been struck dumb I shall introduce myself. Lord Cubitt, at your service. Might I have the pleasure of the next dance? Or the next one you have free?'

Grace smiled, her expression uncertain. Apparently, Lord Cubitt was prepared for such a reaction, and quickly charmed his way around it.

'Pray, don't be afraid. You may tell me that your dance card is full. I shall be crushed, of course, but will survive somehow.'

He'd survive on the food offered during supper, because his title was completely impoverished. Still, he was a charming fellow, with a respectable title, and so Declan forced himself to do the pretty.

'Lord Cubitt will not step on your toes, Miss Richards. Indeed, he is accounted quite a good *dance* partner.'

Had he emphasised the word *dance*? Did she understand that he was not a marriage prospect? He could only hope.

Meanwhile, Grace nodded, flashing a sweet smile at the bounder. 'I believe you have no need to sulk, my lord. I do indeed have space on my dance card. As does Phoebe, I think.'

'She will be my next request,' the man said as he grinned and scrawled his name.

As Lord Cubitt did his work, Declan chanced to glance up. Good God, where had all these men come from? A steady stream of bucks, bounders and jack-a-napes were sauntering through the doors. Enough that Grace's father and Phoebe's parents were scrambling to greet them all.

Why ever were this lot here? Had the gaming hells and brothels closed for the night?

'There, that's done,' said Lord Cubitt. 'But lest I think I can keep you all to myself, I have a few more friends who are desperate for an introduction.'

What? Declan's eyes widened as he saw a queue of gentlemen lining up, all vying for an introduction and a slot on Grace's dance card. Good God, it was as if all the reprobates in London had decided to come and court her.

Then, to his shock, he realised that was *exactly* the case. Every fortune-hunter in London was here, paying homage to Grace. And she, damn it, had no idea who she was allowing to touch her arm, to write their names on her dance card, to demand every single one of her waltzes.

Hell! He was supposed to have the first waltz. Her father had already agreed to it. But he had been too overcome with desire to think of writing down his name, and now... Her card was full while he stood there like an idiot.

Where was her father? Where were Phoebe's parents? They were supposed to protect the girls from reprobates. But of course her father didn't know who was who in London, and Phoebe's mother was at the door, keeping the worst ruffians from coming in. After all, none of these men had a proper invitation. Indeed, he now saw that both fathers were at the French doors at the back, preventing God only knew who from entering.

Damn it! Someone needed to help at the front entrance or Mrs Gray would be overwhelmed.

Bloody hell. He'd have to go.

He glanced back at Grace. The worst she might suffer was if a man took liberties with her on the dance floor. Mrs Gray, on the other hand, might very well be hurt as a few of the bigger men tried to muscle their way in.

'I'll be back,' he said into Grace's ear. 'Don't go outside with any of them!'

Then he ducked away before he could hear her response, crossing in quick strides to the ballroom door.

'Mrs Gray,' he said in his darkest tones, 'may I be of assistance?'

'Your Grace,' the lady said, clearly relieved. 'Thank you. These *gentlemen*...' her tone cast doubt upon the term '...do not have an invitation, and yet they seem to think they can simply descend—'

'Aw, milady, we mean no disrespect,' countered an infamous card sharp who existed on the fringe of polite society. 'We were asked to give Miss Richards a boost, so to speak. Just a dance—'

Declan interrupted, his tone hard. 'Miss Richards does not need "a boost" in a dance or otherwise. Pray be gone.' He reached out to slam the door shut, but was stopped by none other than his own cousin.

'They don't have an invitation,' Cedric said, 'but I do. My deepest apologies, Mrs Gray, for my tardiness.'

He stepped forward, neatly shoving the others back, while Declan winced at the dark purple bruises on the man's face. There was paste covering the worst of them, but the injuries were there for all to see.

'Cedric—' Declan began, though God knew how he was going to apologise for what he'd done.

It didn't matter. His cousin was addressing the other men crowding forward.

'Go on, now,' he said. 'I hear there's a new girl at The Rose Garden. Pray give her my regards and she might bestow a kiss upon you for the association.'

Only his cousin would barter a tart's kisses as a way to quiet an altercation. Though, to be fair, it was effective. Crass, for sure, but effective. The unwanted gentlemen left with a tip of their hats and a grin.

Meanwhile, Mrs Gray had greeted his cousin with a relieved smile. 'Thank you for your assistance, my lord.' Then she looked behind her at the dance set now forming. 'Though I'm afraid the bulk of the fortune-hunters got through the door before I could stop them.'

'Yes...' Cedric drawled. 'I can see that.'

Declan shot him a hard look. 'Was this your doing?'

'Mine? Good God, no! Do you think I want more competition for her hand? You're bad enough. Thank God you're old and boring, otherwise I'd never stand a chance.'

'I'm barely three years your senior,' Declan growled, his gaze on the men now surrounding Grace.

'And yet you act a dozen years older or more.'

'You cannot fault me just because you want to remain in your adolescence.'

'Oh, yes, I can, cousin. I absolutely can.'

Declan ground his teeth together, annoyed with himself. This was unseemly of them, sniping at each other in front of Mrs Gray. So, rather than respond, Declan bowed to the lady.

'If you would excuse us, Mrs Gray? I would like a word with my cousin.'

'Of course,' the woman answered, her worried gaze still scanning the newcomers. 'I should find Phoebe...'

'Yes,' Declan agreed. 'I think that would be wise.'

He waited while the lady hurried away before he turned to his cousin. But before he could speak Cedric forestalled him, holding up a hand as if to block a punch.

'I have no interest in anything you say,' said Cedric, and then pointedly ignored his cousin as he looked for Grace. 'I believe I shall go and claim my dance.'

'Her card's full already. I'm out, too.'

Declan didn't touch his cousin. He knew better. The man was just as likely to punch him as to treat him with restraint. And could Declan really blame him?

Cedric stopped moving, clearly frustrated. 'What the hell is all this? Every fortune-hunter in England...'

His voice trailed away as he came to the same conclusion Declan had. They looked at one another and spoke the word at the same time.

'Mother.'

Meaning both their mothers together. And hadn't the Dowager Duchess declared this very thing not two hours ago? Her speed and thoroughness were daunting.

Cedric sighed, turning his bruised face towards Declan. 'You should just give me the ten thousand pounds, and then we can both be done with this charade.'

'Never.'

'You owe me.'

Declan winced. He did, but not ten thousand pounds' worth. 'I'm sorry, Cedric. I shouldn't have gone off like that, and I am genuinely remorseful. But you're not going to use my failing to destroy my family's coffers.'

'I'm part of your family.'

'Nevertheless.'

He could hear Cedric grinding his teeth together and, given the swelling along his jaw, knew that must hurt.

'A loan, then,' his cousin finally said.

Declan gave his cousin a long look. Damnation, he was actually considering it. Ten thousand pounds and this whole mess would be done. He could stop pretending to pursue Grace, his cousin would go away, and...

'No. What you are doing to Miss Richards is criminal.'

His cousin scoffed. 'Criminal? I intend to marry her. You, on the other hand, are simply toying with her.'

'You want her dowry, nothing more.'

Cedric didn't need to respond except with a raised brow. It was considered normal for a man to marry for a dowry. It was downright commonplace. Though one would think a future earl might have more self-respect.

'Leave her alone, Cedric,' Declan growled.

'No.'

'There are dozens of other fortunes around. Try Miss Gray.'

Though from the crowd of men around her, Phoebe's dance card was likely full as well.

'No.'

And there it was. Far from being a lost lamb, ignored by the *ton*, Miss Richards was now the most sought-after woman in London. And, far from dissuading his cousin, he had made Cedric dig his heels in even further.

It was exactly as Declan had planned, and yet, his body physically rebelled at the idea of Cedric or anyone else having Miss Richards. He was nauseous—and furious. It was all he could do to stand there, watching her dance with those blighters, without decking every single one.

If the sight of Cedric touching Grace had brought him to violence in Hyde Park, how would he handle seeing her wed someone else?

Chapter Seventeen

Grace had never been the focus of so much flattery. At first it had given her a sweet flush of joy. She had never been called beautiful so many times. But before long the compliments had begun to get repetitive. Then they had become ridiculous. And then, when even the most overblown compliment had served only to tighten her lips in annoyance, gentlemen had begun calling her the Ice Queen, who destroyed their confidence with a single frown.

She should have been disgusted, but they were so ridiculous that she hadn't been able to help laughing. And the moment she'd begun to laugh, they'd had her.

Everyone had gone to new heights of silliness for her smile. Gentlemen had pretended to fall prostrate at her feet with every giggle. And when even the most serious had declared they lived or died on her barest glance, she'd felt the attention go to her head.

How easily she fell as the flattery filled her to bursting. And why did it give her an extra measure of glee when every one of her laughs elicited a dark glower from the Duke? What cause had he to glare at her as men vied for her attention? Why did he cross his arms as if chastising a recalcitrant child when she was nothing of the sort?

She had survived on the streets of Canton and in the some-times more frightening bowels of a merchant ship on the China Sea. This was fun. And he could go to Diyu if he would steal this evening's entertainment from her.

So she danced and she laughed. And when even Lord Domac—despite his bruised face—found a way to be charm-ing during the supper buffet, she felt herself lighten for the first time in years. She was safe, warm, and well fed. She had men bowing over her hand and making themselves pleasing to her. And if only her father would smile everything would be perfect in her world, no matter what the Duke thought.

But her father was not well. The supper buffet was closing when she saw him stumble. Several gentlemen helped him to a seat. Her father had been celebrated almost as much as she, but she saw his pallor and knew that he was too tired to remain at the ball past midnight.

Within moments, she had made it to his side. 'Father, I think it is late enough,' she said as she clasped his frail hand. 'We should go home now.'

'What? And miss your triumph? We couldn't possibly.'

Did he truly think it was a triumph to have men vying for the chance to spend her dowry? Or did he think her too stupid to know why these grasping men were suddenly at her feet?

'This is no triumph if you are ill.'

'I am merely tired, my dear.'

He was more than tired, but she would not shame him by pointing that out.

Instead, Lord Domac offered a suggestion.

'Pray seek your bed, my lord. I shall see your daughter safely home.'

'You will do no such thing,' said a cold voice. It was the Duke, of course. 'She is not safe—'

'Have a care, cousin,' Lord Domac interrupted, his voice threatening.

The Duke looked as if he would argue, but then he swal-lowed. 'Her reputation will not be safe without her father. Per-haps it would be best if they both went home.'

Grace agreed, but her father would not budge. 'I will not cut short your fun,' he said as he squeezed her hand. 'The next set will begin soon. I shall simply wait—'

'No, Father,' Grace said. 'I shall spend the night with Phoebe. She will want to discuss every aspect of the evening. My reputation will be safe and my...my fun will be extended with my dear friend.'

This was the only compromise her stubborn father might accept, and indeed he finally agreed, once Phoebe's father was apprised of the situation.

With that matter handled, she watched as the Duke called for her father's carriage and saw the elderly man safely away.

But all that took time, and while she trusted her father with the Duke, she did not trust Phoebe with all the attention being showered upon her. If Grace felt herself caught up in the flattery, how much harder would it be for a sheltered girl? Especially since Phoebe was considered an eligible heiress despite her lack of aristocratic heritage.

Where was the girl?

The musicians had begun tuning their instruments for the final set, and Phoebe was nowhere to be found.

'Oh, no,' she murmured. 'Has anyone seen where Phoebe has gone?'

'Likely the ladies' retiring room,' one gentleman said.

'Goodness, no,' said another. 'She is probably taking some air outside. Shall we go and look?'

Go outside with them after the Duke had specifically warned her not to? Absolutely not.

'Where is her mother?'

'Never mind that,' intoned another gentleman. 'The set will form soon, and I have been waiting an eternity to have you in my arms.'

'And you will be waiting a great deal longer if we do not find Phoebe.'

Thankfully Lord Domac understood her concerns. 'I'll go outside,' he said quietly. 'You look in the ladies' retiring room.'

She nodded and headed to the ladies' room. As it was late in the evening, the retiring room looked like a disaster. There were torn bits of fabric discarded in the corner, several tired maids stitching gowns or redoing hair, and a bevy of ladies talking in excited whispers. They all looked up when she came in, their expressions ranging from disdain to sweetness, depending on the woman.

Grace barely had time to acknowledge them all. Indeed, she'd only met them for ten seconds each in the receiving line.

'Hello,' she said calmly. 'Has anyone seen Phoebe?'

None had an answer.

And then one girl's head jerked up. 'That's the musicians! The last set is forming!'

With a gasp, everyone jumped from their places throughout the room and gave quick pats to their attire before scrambling out through the door. Grace had to leap sideways to avoid being trampled.

Once all the guests had departed, Grace took one last look around before turning to leave, but she was stopped by an older maid with a pinched expression.

'Miss,' the woman said in a low voice. 'Miss...' Then she pointed to a screen that shielded the room from the chamber pot.

Oh. But why would Phoebe need the chamber pot for so long? Unless... Oh, dear.

Grace carefully peered behind the screen. There stood Phoebe with a torn dress, a maid quietly stitching up her skirt and her face streaked with tears. Of all the things Grace had been imagining, this was the worst.

'Phoebe,' Grace whispered. 'Are you all right?'

The girl's head snapped up, her gaze sharpening from distracted to terrified. 'Don't let anyone see me,' she rasped.

'I am alone,' Grace responded as she stepped fully behind the curtain. 'What has happened?'

'I didn't want to go outside,' Phoebe said. 'I know better. I didn't want to.'

Grace felt her blood go cold. She had experience with this. Not personal experience, but she had sat with other girls, not all of them biracial like her. She knew the best thing to do was to hold the girl's hand and wait for the full story. Or enough of it that she would know what to do next.

Except Phoebe wasn't speaking.

She gripped Grace's hand and stared fixedly at the floor.

'How badly are you hurt?' Grace finally asked.

'It's nothing.'

'It's never nothing.'

Phoebe held up her arms. Her gloves were off, and her arms appeared scrubbed raw. Clearly she had tried to wash off the bruises that were dark on her pale skin.

'I kicked him and ran. But he...' She shook her head. 'He'd already torn my dress, and now there are dirt stains on the back.'

She pointed to where a dark, wet spot showed. Grace didn't see any dirt, but it didn't matter. The girl's absence from the ball and her torn dress would tell a tale to anyone who cared to look.

'You are not hurt in...in any other way?'

Phoebe shook her head. 'I don't think he expected me to fight.'

'I'm very glad you did. You should be proud of yourself.'

'It doesn't matter. My reputation is ruined,' she said on a choked-off sob. 'He said that I was ruined and that I would have to marry him now.'

'Is your father that cruel? Does he have no care for your feelings?'

It was an honest question. Many girls had suffered more at the hands of their fathers than from any suitor.

'What? No! My father will—'

'Will be very pleased that you fought.' Grace squeezed Pheobe's hands. 'Tell me who this man was.'

'What? No! I—' She dropped her face into her hands. 'It's over. I just want to forget it ever happened.'

How many times had Grace heard those exact words? All sorts of people had come to the temple for help, for safety, for counsel. If they were injured, the half-Chinese girls were often sent in to tend them. And in that capacity Grace had heard many awful tales. Women who were hurt simply wanted it to be over, but that could never be.

'You will never forget, Phoebe, as long as you live. Best face it now.' She lifted the girl's chin, being as delicate as possible but keeping her resolve clear. 'What is the man's name?'

'I didn't want to go outside with him. He was so much stronger than me, and I didn't want to make a scene. Not at our come-out ball.'

'Of course you didn't. But I need to know—'

'Lord Jasper, miss,' said the maid. She was another older woman, with a worn face and tired eyes, but her chin lifted as she spoke in a clear voice. 'I've already whispered it about to them that will listen. Stay away from him.'

'Thank you,' Grace said to the maid. 'You will take care of her?'

'Yes, miss. Ain't the first time I've had to mend a gown at a ball for all the wrong reasons.'

Well, that was truly horrible. Fortunately, in this case, there was something Grace could do. Something that had burned in her soul from the very first moment she'd come upon a girl crying while hiding. Never before had she the strength to do anything about it. Never before had she been able to strike back at men who thought they were untouchable. But she was not a weak, sheltered girl like Phoebe. Neither was she a shunned biracial child in a temple. She was an adult woman now, and she had learned a few tricks of her own.

She pressed a kiss to Phoebe's cheek. 'It doesn't feel like it now, but you'll be all right. You'll see. Your father loves you and would never see you hurt. You know it as well as I.'

There was fear in Phoebe's eyes. Probably worry that she had disappointed her father. Hopefully, the man would be the parent Phoebe needed. If not... Well, then that too was something girls often had to live with.

But Lord Jasper was an entirely different matter.

Grace stepped out from behind the curtain, then boldly left the retiring room. A few steps took her back inside the ballroom, where the ball was continuing as if nothing had happened. And along the walls, loitering in clumps, were the men who had come without invitation to the party.

She scanned the room quickly, looking for the Duke or Lord Domac, but neither was in view. Very well, then. It was up to her. And by the fury growing in her blood this was something she longed to do.

She crossed to the musicians. 'Stop playing. Now.'

It took a moment for them to comply. The music faltered and then stopped. And then the dancers stumbled to a halt, all looking to where she stood before the players.

She stepped forward, pleased when the guests separated before her.

'Where is Lord Jasper?' she called.

No one answered. No one, that was, except Phoebe's mother, who rushed forward with a harsh whisper. 'Grace, this is unseemly. You must stop this—'

'Go to the retiring room. See to your daughter.'

The lady's mouth dropped open, her eyes widening with shock. Without another word, she rushed away.

Meanwhile, Grace turned back to the room at large. 'Come, come, Lord Jasper. I am the reason for this event. Myself and Phoebe. Surely you can present yourself to me, even though you had no invitation to attend.'

'I was invited by another lady,' drawled a man as he gestured vaguely to a bevy of girls in the corner. 'And was most welcomed once I arrived.'

'That is no true invitation, sir.'

'Nevertheless, I am here.' He grinned as he bowed before her. 'Lord Jasper at your service.'

She looked him up and down, seeing in him a genial face, a body neither exceptionally strong nor overly fat. Truthfully, to her eye, he looked harmless, almost kind. But there was a cruel joy in his eyes that spoke of arrogance and privilege. And her blood boiled even hotter.

'You have heard, have you not, that I meted out discipline on the ship where I served as navigator?'

'I know nothing of your heathen ways, Miss Richards, but I can already see how unnatural you are as a woman.'

He called her unnatural? When he had forced a naïve girl outside at her own ball?

'Aboard ship, if there was a crime against a woman I was the one to administer justice. Do you claim that an English ballroom has less justice than a Chinese ship?'

He arched a brow. 'Again, *miss*.' He sneered that last word as if her very sex were suspect. 'I know nothing of your heathen ways.'

'Then let me enlighten you.'

She slammed a hand against his throat, cutting off his breath. And while he reeled from that she kicked him as hard as she could straight between his thighs. He could not scream. She had cut off his breath. But he could crumple to the ground, his eyes bulging and his body twitching in agony.

Good.

'I thought Englishmen were different,' she hissed. 'I thought that with your fancy clothes and your smooth manners I could expect more from you. How disgusted I was to learn that you are worse than a common sailor.'

She reared back and kicked him again, straight in the groin. She did not examine the fury that built inside her. She didn't restrain it. Instead, she let all the hatred flow from her as she kicked and kicked, until she prayed that organ he cherished so much was crushed to oblivion.

She had not meant to lose control. She had not meant to become ruled by her fury. But once she had begun hitting the man, she had not been able to stop. She saw Pheobe and so many other girls in her mind's eye. She saw their tears, felt their agony, and she knew the terror that had dogged her from her earliest memory. Women were often vicious to one another, but men were casual brutes. Men took their strength and their power, and they hurt women. This man—and so many others—deserved to die.

So she kicked him again, until strong arms wrapped around her. A powerful body lifted her up, dragged her away, and held her aloft as if she was a child.

She screamed her fury. She bellowed like an animal. But she was not released.

'Enough. Grace... Enough!'

It was the Duke's voice and the Duke's arms. It was his body that she railed against, and his arms that held her away. No, she belatedly realised. He held her safe. Safe from the man on the floor. And safe from descending into the mindless disaster of her fury.

It took her some time. Still she kicked the air and heard the Duke's grunt when her feet found him.

'Grace!' came another voice. Phoebe's. 'Grace, I'm all right. He only bruised me.'

That did not make it right, but it was enough to quiet her. Enough to make reason push to the fore. Enough for her to realise that she flailed like a wildcat in the Duke's arms.

'Are you all right?' the Duke asked her, his voice strong in her ear. 'Are you calm now?'

'He hurt her!' she rasped.

'And you have delivered justice.'

She doubted it. She suspected that Lord Jasper had abused many more innocents than Phoebe. But the message was delivered. She needed to gain control of herself.

And while she was quieting her pounding heart, the Duke turned to the people surrounding them. 'Isn't that right?' the Duke asked everyone, his voice raised to carry throughout the ballroom. 'Miss Richards did exactly what was needed, and Lord Jasper got exactly what he deserved.'

Silence greeted his words. Silence and an uncomfortable shifting of feet.

'If I hear one word different,' the Duke continued. 'If any whisper against these ladies reaches my ears, I will destroy the speaker. Do you understand me? Lord Jasper...' He paused to glower at the wheezing man. 'Got exactly what he deserved.'

Again there was no answer, just the gaping, dumbfounded looks of stunned people. No one spoke against the Duke. But then again, no one spoke to agree with him.

'Do I make myself clear?' he all but shouted.

As a group, every soul nodded his or her head. Every soul looked not at Lord Jasper but at the Duke. And every soul began to murmur.

'Yes, of course, Your Grace.'

'Completely agree, Your Grace.'

'Quite right.'

And there Grace saw true power. The Duke had not raised

a fist. He had not beaten anyone bloody and he'd barely raised his voice. But the entire assemblage bowed to his wishes.

'You may put me down now,' she whispered, ashamed of her outburst but not regretting it. 'I am calm.'

'Are you hurt?' he asked her.

'Only because I could not save Phoebe beforehand.'

'Tonight or another night, it would have happened eventually. Her dowry is too large to prevent such things.'

Meanwhile, Phoebe's father stepped forward. 'I believe that is the end of this evening's entertainment.' He pointed to Lord Jasper's nearest compatriots. 'Take that rubbish away. And be sure that your names will be remembered. Bankers are in close community with barristers,' he drawled. 'Your families will find credit hard to come by. Not to mention legal assistance.'

Grace had no understanding of what that meant, but she could see satisfaction cross the Duke's face. Also a flinch as he looked at Phoebe and her mother.

'You should take her home,' the Duke said to Mrs Gray. 'I will see that the ballroom is managed.'

The lady agreed and started ushering Phoebe to the door. But then she stopped, turning back to face him. 'Grace is supposed to stay with us tonight.'

'I will see her safely home,' the Duke said.

Lord Domac stepped to her opposite side. 'That will not help her reputation any more than this has.'

'A maid,' Grace said, looking at the woman who had helped Phoebe. The woman stood at the edge of the ballroom with a satisfied smile on her lips. 'Do you mind?'

'Not at all, miss.'

And so it was decided. While Phoebe's parents took her home, the servants and the Duke supervised the clearing of the ballroom. Grace didn't see what became of Lord Jasper. Honestly, some part of her hoped he'd die from his injuries, though she feared that would bring further harm to her. The death of a nobleman, whether English or Chinese, always drew a penalty.

But she had no time to worry about that now. All her attention was occupied with learning how to end a ball. And once that was accomplished she settled beside the maid into a dark, intimate carriage with the Duke. She stretched out her feet and sighed. How lovely to finally sit.

But all too soon the darkness closed in, and she was deeply aware of the Duke seated across from her. Especially when he spoke gently into the darkness.

'Are you all right?' he asked. 'Are you hurt?'

'I was not hurt at all.'

'Was Miss Gray badly injured?'

Meaning was she raped?

'No. She was frightened, and it was a great disappointment for her come-out ball. She was so excited when the night began.'

'Large dowries always bring out the worst. Truly, I am ashamed of my fellow men.'

'I expect she will be better prepared in the future.'

He was silent for a long moment, and then he spoke again, his voice rough. 'I have never seen anyone fight as you did.'

She all but rolled her eyes. 'Your women need to learn how to defend themselves.'

'We have women who fight. Bare-knuckle punching, even, and people bet on the outcome.' He shook his head. 'What you did was different. That style of fighting...' There was awe in his voice. 'I have never seen the like before.'

That was not surprising. It was a style taught only by the monks to other monks. Except at her temple, where the children were allowed to learn it as a means of self-defence.

'The monk who taught me is the same one who believes a mixed-race child deserves a full life as much as anyone else. He said I was not worthless, but that I would need to defend my worth often.'

'That is a wise man.'

Did he sound surprised? 'Do you believe the Chinese are all savages?' Her face twisted into a grimace. 'I would not blame you. They believe you whites are all apes.'

'I believe that men do terrible things. We allow our worst impulses to rule. Lord Jasper is one terrible example, and Cedric gambles with people, using blackmail to meet his needs. And I have such feelings,' he said, his tone achingly hollow. 'It seems that every moment in my life is aimed at controlling my temper. Every choice, every breath, is governed by that need.'

She frowned. 'But I was the one who lost control tonight. You stopped me.'

He nodded. 'Righteous fury is understandable. And he deserved everything he got.'

Grace took a moment to think, seeing something she had not understood before. The Duke obviously damned himself for every display of temper, but he forgave her.

'How is what I did different from your fight with Cedric?' she asked. 'You thought he was hurting me.'

The Duke turned away, his gaze focused somewhere outside the carriage. 'I could have killed Cedric.'

'I could have killed Lord Jasper. We both needed each other to stop.'

He looked back at her, and when he spoke his voice was barely audible. 'You are astounding,' he said. 'How can you forgive me? I was a beast against Cedric.'

'How can you forgive *me*?'

He had no answer, and neither did she. It would seem they both had the same fault in an explosive temper. That might be disastrous. Or else they could be good checks, one upon the other, keeping each other in line.

'I think,' she said finally, 'that we are just people. Arrogant and small, powerful and weak, all thrown together in a very large world where we manage to hurt one another.'

'That is a very dark statement.'

'But,' she continued, 'we can choose to help each other. Stop the worst, encourage the best.'

'Some of us do. Some of us try very hard to be better.'

He was referring to himself, and she respected him for it.

'Have you taught your women to fight?' she asked.

He snorted. 'My mother doesn't need any more weapons. She's dangerous enough. And the others have never asked.'

She let that hang in the silence, uncertain how to respond until the maid sitting beside her spoke up.

'I should like to learn, miss. Unless I'm too old.'

Grace turned to her. 'All ages can learn.'

'I saw what you did to him. We all did. And I have a daughter, miss. A right pretty one. She needs to learn.'

'Yes,' Grace agreed. 'She does.'

But before she could say more, they had arrived at her father's home. The carriage stopped and the Duke's servant quickly opened the door, leaving no time to plan.

'I give you leave to contact me,' she said to the maid. 'My sister can teach you as well. If your daughter is pretty, then there is no time to waste.' She squeezed the woman's hand. 'And even if she is not.'

Then she allowed the Duke to help her out of the carriage. He walked her to the door, his steps slow.

'That is kind of you,' he said quietly. 'But it will not endear you to the *ton*.'

'Do you think that was ever a possibility? Even before tonight's events?'

He sighed. 'Probably not. But you are notorious now.'

She wondered what that meant, but there was no time to ask.

He squeezed her hand. 'Which room is yours?'

'What?'

'What bedroom is yours? Light a candle in it so that I know you are safely within.'

'Do you fear I will be attacked in my own home?'

'No, but I wish to be sure.'

It made no sense. She was safe in her father's home. And yet she appreciated the sweetness of his worry.

'My room is at the back. You will not see it from the street. But I will light a candle in the parlour there, before I see my father.' She pointed to the parlour window.

He nodded, then lifted her hand to his lips. It was a courtly gesture, one that was foreign to her eyes, and yet it thrilled her nonetheless. That glow was in his eyes, luminescent in the moonlight as he bent over her hand. He did not look down even as he kissed her glove.

She gazed at him, feeling a tightness in her belly. Was that yearning? Desire? She didn't have a word for this feeling. In a life dominated by fear, this was something altogether different and she relished it.

He straightened from his bow, but he did not break the connection of their gazes. And so they looked at one another, saying nothing, and yet she felt so much. A tingle in her breasts. A dryness on her lips. An ache between her thighs.

This was desire, and it felt wonderful. Sharp, hungry, and so exciting. She understood now why people sought it so fiercely. And when he straightened up she abruptly twisted her hand, gripping his wrist.

He froze, his eyes dark in the shadow, but the air was filled with need. Hers? His? She didn't know. But her heart was fluttering, and her body ached for him.

'Grace,' he whispered.

'Yes.'

She didn't say it as a question. It was an answer to the question he hadn't asked and the desire she couldn't voice.

He leaned closer, without touching her, his body large and the shadows dark. He was shielding her from view while his breath grew short.

'A kiss?' he asked.

She could barely hear him over the beating of her heart.

'Yes, please.'

How bold she was. She had run all her life from sex, knowing it was dangerous. And yet here she was, begging him for it. She was begging him. And he was not going to refuse.

He didn't take the kiss. Instead, he touched her cheek, his glove warm and soft as he caressed her. A finger slipped below her jaw, and she lifted her face to his. Already her lips were parted. Already they tingled with awareness.

His thumb brushed across her lower lip and she felt heat in its wake. Was it always like this? Did his body tingle as hers did? Did he feel as if he would die if their mouths didn't touch?

He leaned forward, the air between them narrowing until their breath mingled. His was sweet. Hers was hot.

Then it happened. He touched his lips to hers.

They were clever as they moved across hers. That was what she thought. What a clever mouth he had, teasing hers as she stretched for him, nipping against her flesh before soothing it with his tongue. How clever of him to delight so easily. Just his mouth and his tongue, and she was desperate for more.

She stepped forward, pushed up against his chest and angled her head. She wanted more. She needed to feel more. He matched her, wrapping an arm around her back as he tugged her high against him. She arched her back and he thrust his tongue inside.

The dance they shared now was overwhelming. Tongues parrying as they stroked across and around each other. And all the while he thrust in and out of her mouth while she clutched at his coat. She wanted to climb higher on his body, she wanted to surrender completely to his kiss, but she knew that it was too dangerous to continue.

Too much! Too fast! And altogether too exciting for her to stop.

Thank Heaven that he did. Thank the Divine that he ended it with a slow withdrawal. She had not the strength. Indeed, as he set her back onto her feet she wondered if her knees would support her.

'This is dangerous,' he whispered.

'I know.'

'I do not regret it,' he confessed.

'Neither do I.'

They stood there, slowly disentangling their bodies. They were on her front step. It might be in shadow, but it was not safe.

She stepped back, banging into the front door. He stepped back too, a proper gentleman once again. And then they heard footsteps.

By the time the door was opened they stood in proper distance from one another.

'Miss Grace!' the footman said. Then his eyes widened. 'Your Grace!' he said as he fumbled with a bow.

'Good evening, Samuel,' she said as she turned away from the Duke. 'How is my father?'

'Resting comfortably, miss.'

'Thank you.'

She didn't look back, though her whole body tingled with awareness of where the Duke stood. She entered the house, taking the candle from the footman's hand. And then, finally, she turned around.

'Goodnight, Your Grace.' She kept her tone level, or she tried to, but there was a hesitancy in her voice. Or perhaps it was a yearning that seemed to echo in his gaze. 'Thank you for escorting me home.'

'It was my pleasure,' he said as he bowed.

How could words be felt physically? As if he were caressing her with his voice? Madness... And yet she relished every sensation even as she dipped into a shallow curtsey and firmly shut the door.

Meanwhile, Samuel stifled a yawn. 'The house is abed, miss. Your father said you wouldn't come back tonight.'

'There was an incident at the ball,' she said as she crossed into the parlour. 'I had to come home.'

She set a candle in the window, pausing as she watched the Duke return to his carriage. Such a large man. Normally, she disliked men of such imposing size. She was often frightened of someone so physically powerful. But not of him. Instead of fear, she felt longing. She wanted to be surrounded by him, protected by him, and...and more.

She waited there at the parlour window until the Duke's carriage pulled away. It was as though her body strained to be with him, lingered over the thought of him, wanted...

Well, what she wanted was obvious. She understood carnal desire. There had been a time when she had been fascinated by it, talking to older girls about what they did and why. She'd even spent time with the prostitutes who had come to the temple. She'd wanted to understand, and they had wanted to explain.

But it hadn't been long before she'd decided to forego that nonsense, to learn navigation from the old sailor with milky white eyes. She'd thought the whole business of copulation something too fraught with danger for her to pursue. Even when she'd developed breasts and begun to feel attraction, she'd ruthlessly suppressed the urge.

Too dangerous. Too tricky. She would not risk her survival on something as unmanageable as passion.

Until now, when her place in her father's affection was secure, and when an English mandarin—of all people—spoke to her with respect while hunger burned in his eyes. Now she thought about it. Now she *yearned* for it.

Could she risk it? What folly! And yet as she headed for her bed he remained in her thoughts and in the tingles that still teased her body.

Chapter Eighteen

Declan had ample time to think as he returned the maid to her home. Naturally he had known that women were often abused in one way or another, but he'd always made sure those in his household were protected. And certainly he disliked those men who abused their physical and societal power to exploit ladies who should be under their protection.

It had never occurred to him to teach the women around him how to fight. That wasn't ladylike. And yet Grace had fought, and she had never seemed more powerful or more attractive to him.

That she had so obviously lost control of herself only increased her allure. Here was a woman who understood his struggle to maintain his composure. That turned her into a Valkyrie in his mind. She was a warrior woman, to be respected if not revered.

He said nothing to the maid. He was not in the habit of conversing with other people's servants. But before they stopped, he did venture a comment.

'If you or your daughter feel unsafe in your current employment, you may apply to my housekeeper. I am sure she can find a place for you both.'

The woman's eyes widened with shock. 'Your Grace?'

'What name should I give Mrs Williams? In case you choose to communicate with her?'

'I am quite happy, Your Grace, but my daughter...her name is Molly Smithee.'

'Molly Smithee,' he repeated, committing it to memory.

'She wants to be a lady's maid, Your Grace, but will be happy in whatever capacity is available.'

'I'll let Mrs Williams know, though I cannot promise advancement. I am a bachelor without need of a lady's maid.'

'I will trust to your good judgement, Your Grace. And that of Mrs Williams.'

And with that she curtsied as best she could in the carriage and stepped out. Once he had seen her into her home, the Duke stared into the space where Grace had sat. He stared at it and thought about the evening. He thought of her and he lusted. He thought of her and he...

'Home, Your Grace?'

'What?'

'Should we head for—?'

'No.' He quickly thought about the London streets. The Richards lived not so far from a few of the better-quality gaming hells. He grinned. 'Drop me off at the Lady's Delight,' he said.

'Your Grace?'

His coachman was shocked, and well he might be. It had been years since he'd stepped into that infamous gaming hell, but he was not averse to pretending.

'The Lady's Delight,' he repeated forcefully.

And then he sat back and allowed his mind to wander. It went to her, of course, and he let it. He had no exact plan as to what he would do, and he didn't want to examine his thoughts too closely. So he let his mind wander to the lascivious and the carnal. And when he stepped down from his carriage his gait was a bit stiff.

'Go home,' he said to his coachman. 'I shall take a hackney back.'

'Aye, Your Grace.'

The man eyed him for a long moment. He was twice Declan's age and had known him since he was boy. He no doubt had guessed what might happen, but he didn't say anything before he left.

Soon Declan was whistling as he walked not into the gaming hell but down the street, towards where Grace lived.

He wanted to see her again, he thought, without prying eyes or shocked gossipmongers. He wanted to speak to her as a man might to a fellow soul who had piqued his interest.

His thoughts were a lot less clear when he walked by the dark house and then wandered, oh-so-casually, behind it. There was a small alley, no light except for the waxing moon, and not even a tree to ease the sight of dirty bricks and rubbish. Then he looked up at her window and wondered what he was doing.

She was likely abed, her face freshly washed and her legs stretched naked beneath the sheets. She wore a nightrail, he imagined, made of soft cotton or sensuous silk. But beneath that simple gown would be her plump breasts and her narrow waist. He imagined he could feel the muscles in the strength of her arms and the grip of her legs. He thought of her kisses and her sighs. And he wished—

'What are you doing here?' she hissed.

He was jolted out of his fantasy only to see her for real, wrapped in colourful silk as she peeked out from behind the back door.

'Grace?'

'Why are you standing there, Your Grace?'

'Call me Declan.' He wanted to hear his name on her lips.

'That's not proper.'

'I won't tell.'

She stared at him, and then she jumped as a dog barked in the distance.

'This isn't proper,' she repeated, but then she waved him in.

He grinned as he moved inside. They were in the dark kitchen, quiet and still, without even a cat to hunt for mice.

'How did you know I was out there?' he asked. 'Why aren't you in bed?'

She sighed and lifted her hands in a gesture of futility. 'I have a temper, too,' she whispered. 'And it doesn't let me sleep.'

He understood. 'I applaud what you did to Lord Jasper.'

'Will he survive?' she asked.

'Probably. Either way, I've made it clear that it was what he deserved.'

Grace folded her arms across her chest. It was a gesture of anger or fear, he wasn't sure which.

'What will your mother say when she hears?' she pressed. 'Will she blame Lord Jasper? Or will she say that the heathen has shown her true colours?'

There was a wealth of disgust and self-recrimination in her tone. He touched her shoulder and pulled her gently to face him.

'Do not blame yourself. He deserved—'

'I don't,' she interrupted. 'But I know that the lower caste always shoulders the blame.'

'That's not true.' He lifted her chin until she was looking at him. There was very little light here, but he could see her eyes widen in her pale face. 'That's not *always* true,' he hedged.

And then he did what had been burning in his thoughts all night long, even before they had reached her front door.

He kissed her.

He cupped her cheeks, tilted her mouth to his, and kissed her more thoroughly than he had managed before.

He went slowly. He could tell that she was not experienced. Her mouth was soft, her lips only slightly parted. She was willing, but unschooled, and the roar in his blood nearly overcame him.

He brushed his lips across hers, then gently teased his tongue against her lips. She stretched up towards him and he felt the brush of silk against his legs as her dressing gown fell open.

He slipped his tongue inside her mouth, tangling with hers and then withdrawing before plunging in again. He felt her breath catch as her body moved towards him. Or maybe he had simply pulled her tightly, such that he could feel the swell of her breasts and the length of her thighs. So hot. So sweet. So very much *his*.

He felt her hands press flat against his chest. Did she mean to push him away? He felt her palms skim across his chest, restless and uncertain.

He drew back, looking into her dark eyes. 'Have you never been kissed before tonight?'

'Yes. By sailors and others.'

'Kissed like that?'

Kissed in a way that had made her breath stop and her heart thunder?

As he spoke, he brushed his thumb across her swollen lips while he slipped his other hand beneath her dressing gown.

She wore simple cotton beneath, the fabric soft and without restriction. He outlined the curve of her waist, the strength of her ribs and the swell of her breast. He had not meant to be so free with her, but he could not stop himself.

'Have you ever felt pleasure, Grace?'

He was speaking obliquely, but she understood.

'Not as you mean.' She curved her fingers around his waistcoat. 'I have never wanted it before. The risk was too great.'

His hand trembled beneath her breast. How he wanted to go further. It was taking all his willpower to hold himself back.

'Do you want me to touch you?'

She nodded, the movement of her chin jerky. 'Yes,' she whispered. 'Just…a little.'

Could he do it? Could he pleasure her 'just a little'?

He curved his hand up until he palmed her breast. He felt the sharp point of her nipple and the full weight of her. She was small compared to many women he had known, but her shape was exquisite. And even better was the way her breath caught as he held her.

Her eyes widened and her mouth parted on a pant. Then he rubbed his thumb back and forth across her peak and she trembled as she swayed towards him.

'Has anyone ever touched you like this?' he asked.

'Just you.'

He dropped his head to her neck, nuzzling beneath her ear and rubbing his teeth along the curve of her jaw. Her dark hair fell from its coil, spreading out across her shoulder. It was still short, but the feel of it made his knees weaken. Dark hair, golden skin, and the scent of sandalwood and honey.

He untied the ribbon of her nightrail. He used his mouth to brush apart the flap of cotton that shielded her breast.

'Declan...?' she whispered.

Her hands were tight on his waistcoat, and he idly wondered if she would tear the fabric. He didn't care if she ripped it apart.

'I want to show you pleasure,' he said. 'I want to teach you.'

So saying, he tried to tongue her nipple, but the cotton shift did not open far enough. So he adjusted. He lifted her breast with his hand and set his mouth above the fabric. It was thin enough that he could use his teeth to bite her nipple, then suck it far into his mouth.

She cried out at that. A soft mew of delight. He caught her hips then, steadying her as she arched beneath him. Tightening his grip, he lifted her up and set her onto the table in the centre of the kitchen. It was sturdy wood and the right height. He could touch her this way, but not take her. The table was too high.

'I want to show you,' he murmured against her skin. 'I want to feel your first time.'

He set his hands to her knees, gently spreading them. The length of her nightrail prevented him opening her as he wished, but it was enough. He felt the heat between her thighs and smelled her musky scent.

But before he could touch her she gripped his arm. 'Even I know this is wrong.'

'I won't take you. I swear.'

'This is allowed?'

No, not exactly.

'This is something women teach each other,' he said. At least he had been told so. 'Where to touch. How it feels.' He shifted, pulling his hand away while setting hers on her own body. 'I won't do more,' he swore. 'But I will tell you what to do.'

And he would watch.

She bit her lip, clearly tempted.

'Can you be silent?' he asked.

She nodded, her eyes lighting with hunger.

'Is everyone asleep?'

'Yes,' she whispered.

'Then let me tell you what to do.'

He backed to the other side of the room until he was well out of reach.

'Has no one ever spoken of this to you before?'

'I have heard about when it can be good, but...'

'You didn't believe?'

'I didn't want to be tempted. I had other things to learn. How to navigate. How to fight.'

He nodded, awed again by her intelligence. But now she was tempted. *He* tempted her. And the thought surged heat through his body.

'I will tell you, and then you can learn on your own.' He gripped the back of a chair rather than reach for her. 'Widen your legs and lean back.'

She did as he bade. Slowly, carefully, and with a shyness that had the lust pounding through him. What a sight! Her muscular legs spread until her gown strained. She didn't mean to be seductive, but nothing was more enthralling to him than her inexpert motions as she pulled her nightrail up and up.

She stopped just short of giving him the full view. All he saw was shadow, though her scent tantalised.

'Set your fingers between your nether lips.'

'What?'

'There are folds between your legs.'

Her fingers began to explore.

'Move around until—'

She gasped, and he knew she had found it.

'Feel how wet you are?'

She nodded.

'Dip inside. Take that sweetness and stroke it up and down. Up and down. You'll find what you want.'

What an exquisite pleasure to watch her explore. Her one candle barely lighted her, but he could see her face, hear the sounds she made and see the changes in her body.

'Adjust how you touch, move your fingers in different ways. Discover yourself.' His voice rasped and his body pulsed with need, but he didn't move.

She looked at him, doubt in her eyes.

He did not know what the Chinese believed, but he knew what the priests here said about women pleasuring themselves.

'This isn't wrong,' he said, to himself as much as her. 'This is what you should learn about your own body.'

He said nothing more. Let her choose what she wanted. And he gloried in seeing her intimate explorations. He felt her every gasp like a gong in his body. He knew when her speed increased how wonderful she would be feeling. And he watched with his breath held because she was beautiful in her bliss.

Soon she was moving faster.

Soon her breath became soft gasps.

And then…

A single cry.

Her body shuddered. Her head dropped back.

'Yes,' he whispered. 'Oh, yes.'

He was ready to catch her if she fell. He was ready to kiss her into silence if need be. He was ready for any excuse to touch her, but she kept herself apart from him. Her body, even in the midst of bliss, was wholly her own. And he couldn't have been more impressed.

When she was spent, she sagged back against the table. She let her hand slip away and her legs fall together.

He dared come close then. He gently resettled her nightrail around her knees. Then he took the hand that she had used to pleasure herself and kissed it. Indeed, he drew the scent into his lungs and the taste into his mouth. He kissed her hand as he'd wanted to kiss her most intimate places. And she returned the favour by touching his face, his hair, and the long stretch of his jaw.

'All Englishwomen know this?' she asked.

'No. But they should.'

'Then how do you?'

'There are women who teach men like me. Women who introduce us to pleasure.'

She nodded. 'Prostitutes.' There was no condemnation in her tone.

'Usually.'

'They offered to teach me.'

He winced that she had been in such close quarters with such women. The dangers they faced were myriad and often lethal.

'I chose to become China's greatest navigator instead.'

'A wise choice.' He pressed another kiss into her palm. 'And now you know their secrets.'

She shook her head, her gaze still languid. 'I bet there are many more to learn.'

He grinned. 'There are.'

'And you want to teach me.'

'Oh, yes.'

'No.'

The bluntness of her word jolted him. After what he had just witnessed, he had not expected such a final response. And into his confusion she smiled. It was a sweet expression, but it did not hide the determination beneath her words.

'I wanted to learn this,' she said, her voice a low whisper. 'I wanted you to teach me.'

His body jerked with hunger at that, but he knew better than to act on it.

'But this was improper.' It wasn't a question. 'And you said—'

'That women teach each other.'

'Because it's improper for a man to do it outside of marriage. Yes?'

He swallowed. 'Yes.'

She straightened and pulled the silk dressing gown about her shoulders. 'I wanted to learn this,' she said. 'I do not say you are at fault.'

Now he understood. 'But you will not risk more with me?'

'With anyone.'

That was something at least.

'It is time for you to leave,' she said.

Long past time. But he couldn't depart without asking one more thing. Why it was so important to him, he had no idea, but it had brought him to her door in the middle of the night just to see if she would answer.

'Will you tell me…?' His voice faded away. What an awkward question to ask.

'Yes?'

'What is your name in Chinese?'

She blinked, startled. 'Nayao. It means a person with grace or beauty. Enough that it is a unique quality that stands out.'

His brows rose. 'That is an excellent name for you.'

'What does your name mean?'

He frowned. 'Declan means that I am the Tenth Duke of Byrning.'

Her eyes widened. 'Your name is the same as your title?'

He shrugged. 'I suppose you could look at it that way.'

'Then you have no identity apart from that?'

'I—'

He clapped his mouth shut. He'd been about to claim that of course he was more than the title he'd been destined to inherit. Of course his identity was vastly more than his title. And yet from his earliest days he had been reared to be the Duke of Byrning and all that entailed. Even his middle names were attributed to one ancestor or another, not to mention a saint thrown in there for good measure.

'I suppose my name is my heritage.'

'And I have no heritage except my name.'

Did that mean they were opposites? That there was a gulf between them that made them unsuitable?

Obviously not, given what they had just done. He couldn't think of a more suitable woman right now. And yet, despite what they had shared, she felt so far away from him. And exponentially more intriguing.

He opened his mouth to say something—he wasn't even sure what. Perhaps he just wanted to say her name again, to make it more familiar. But before he could form the syllables a thump sounded above them, then a series of weak coughs.

'Father,' she whispered.

Oh, dear. Lord Wenshire did not sound good.

'You must go!' she said, gesturing him out the door.

'Do I call a doctor?'

She shook his head. 'No. No, this is common.'

That was even worse. But as another thump sounded above stairs he knew his time was up. He had to leave without even a goodnight kiss. If he touched her even once now, he would not be able to tear himself away.

He gave her a last look. One that was filled with the desire for *more*. More conversation, more interaction, more touching. Instead, he gave her a quick bow and hurried away.

Chapter Nineteen

Declan barely slept that night. His thoughts kept returning to the sight of Grace—Nayao—bringing herself pleasure under his direction. What a sight! And he pleasured himself while remembering it.

But now it was morning, and he had a task to accomplish. He'd decided on this course several days ago, perhaps from the moment he'd first met Nayao. But last night's display required him to be more aggressive in his campaign. Which meant the mid-morning sun found him banging on his mother's door.

Once the haughty butler opened the door, he was tempted to barge straight upstairs into his mother's bedroom. After all, she'd done the same to him. But that was petty, so he opted for the manners appropriate to his title.

'Tell my mother that I await her in the library.'

His words and tone were abrupt. He preferred to be polite with his servants, but he knew that in this case Nagel approved of only the rudest manners from his superiors. It made no sense to him, but then the whims of polite society—even among their servants—rarely made rational sense.

Appropriately, Nagel bowed deeply to him and intoned, 'Yes, Your Grace. I have already sent for tea and a morning biscuit, if you'd like.'

'Yes, thank you.'

Damn it, he should have remembered not to thank him. He could hear the man's disapproving sigh as he headed for the library. His mother certainly did hire servants who reflected her attitudes.

He found his way to the library and seated himself at the desk there. It was his mother's desk, the drawers filled with her correspondence. As was normal for her, the top was pristine, the desk locked. He sat here merely for effect. This was his mother's seat of power, but he was the Duke. And he had every right to everything she owned.

She took her time coming downstairs. Long enough for him to enjoy several morning biscuits and a proper cup of tea, not to mention a good portion of the morning paper which Nagel had brought with breakfast.

'Have you lost all your money, Declan? Have you come to move in on my peace?'

'Good morning to you too, Mother.' His tone was rather cheerful, he thought. Must be the biscuits. They had put him in a good frame of mind.

'You're being overbearing. You're invading my library just because I woke you up on your birthday.'

He couldn't tell if she approved or if that was chastisement. Either way, she wasn't wrong. He leaned back in her chair and smiled at her.

'It was the day after my birthday, and you didn't remember it.'

'You're not a child who needs sweets.' She dropped down into the chair opposite the desk. 'What is it? Your aunt will be down at any moment and she'll want to know what Cedric is doing.'

'You already know what he's doing. He's trying to blackmail me into giving him ten thousand pounds.'

'It would be a loan.'

'It would not, and you know it, because he won't pay it back. And since when did you start defending Cedric?'

'When the alternative was him marrying that awful woman.'

Declan sighed. He really disliked going over the same ground with his mother. 'Miss Richards is not awful. Indeed, I find her rather compelling.'

The Duchess rolled her eyes at him. 'Every man enjoys watching a brawl, but that does not mean it belongs at a come-out ball.'

Ah. So she had heard about last night.

'Lord Jasper deserved punishment.'

'Then *you* should have given it to him outside of the ball-room. Ladies of the *ton* do not mete out justice like common ruffians.'

He didn't respond because he knew it was true. Gentlemen were supposed to keep each other in check, but the opposite was often true. They egged each other on into wilder acts all in the name of fun, and be damned to whoever got hurt in the process.

'Neither she nor I would have had to do anything had you not sent the worst of society to that ball. So I lay what happened at your feet, Mother.'

Far from being chastised, she smiled. 'I merely created a situation whereby everyone could see her true colours.' His mother lifted her chin to peer down her nose at him. 'Miss Richards will never be accepted in polite society now.'

'Really?'

'Really. Lord Jasper may never be able to have children. Did you know that?'

'I don't care.' Indeed, part of him hoped it was true.

'Well, his mother cares. And see how I was able to accomplish what I directed you to do without even being present?'

'And what do you think you have accomplished?'

'She's banned from society. Cedric can't marry her now.'

And there was his mother's greatest flaw. She seemed to think that the world was made up of the *haut ton* alone. All other people existed to serve. Ergo, if Miss Richards was not in society, Cedric could not marry her.

'You're wrong, Mother. Cedric will marry her for her dowry. He's never cared for society or its games. All you have done is play directly into his hands.'

'Don't be ridiculous. He has a great deal of pride. He will never marry someone so outré.'

He shook his head. 'You underestimate him, Mother. The

only way to keep Cedric from marrying her is to get her married to someone else.'

'Just give him the money!' snapped a voice from the hallway. It was his aunt.

As was appropriate, Declan rose from his seat and bowed to the Countess. But when he straightened, his expression and his voice were hard.

'No.'

'Why ever not?' His aunt dropped her hands to her hips. 'You don't spend it. Everyone else is buying houses and boats and whatnot. Cedric should get the same as everyone else.'

Declan sighed, looking at the drawn face of his aunt. He usually avoided the woman because she was so shrewish, but also because he knew he would be equally awful if he had to live her life. Her husband was an inveterate gambler who had charmed her when she was too young to know better. Now she lived on his mother's generosity and was pitied throughout the *ton*. Her only hope for salvation was in Cedric, whom she coddled as if he were a babe in the woods.

Except now he saw how his forbearance had damaged the entire family. Cedric thought he could blackmail the duchy, Cedric's father was off gambling money he did not have, and now his mother stood here speaking to him as if he were her maid.

This could not continue, and so he set his own hands on his hips.

'Cedric gets what his parents give him.' Which, as everyone in this room knew, was nothing but debt. 'You get food, clothing, and a home because of my mother. And if you are very careful I will find a way to help your daughters, whom you seem to have abandoned.'

'Do not speak to me of my children!'

'Very well,' he said. 'I will not dower them.'

It was a lie. He already sent regular funds to his female cousins, and he definitely planned to help with their dowries when the time came.

'We are your family!' the woman cried.

'And I am the head of that family, so mind your tongue.'

His aunt tried to object. She puffed herself up to her largest height to glare down her nose at him, which was hard, given that he was taller than her. But such a position had no effect on him. Indeed, he was ready to throw her back to her country estate, where she could work the fields as his cousins sometimes did. Though, to be fair, his cousin Cora claimed she enjoyed farming.

In any event, he did not move except to slowly raise one eyebrow at her. That was enough for her to collapse sideways into a chair, where she began to weep with great drama.

'You see,' his mother said as she patted his aunt on the shoulder. 'We cannot accept that woman into our family. It would destroy everything.'

'No, Mother, it would not. And you are a fool to suggest such a thing.'

The Duchess's eyes widened in shock at his statement, and he honestly couldn't understand why. Then it came to him. He had not spoken in anger, and neither had he swallowed down his thoughts out of fear that he was overreacting. His words had been calm, rational, and implacable. And apparently she could not believe that he could be so controlled.

'Are you well, Declan? You are speaking like a mad man.' When his aunt set off on another wail, she squeezed the woman's shoulder. 'Leave us, Agatha. You're upsetting the Duke.'

Agatha gaped at the Duchess for a moment, but she quickly realised she was not helping her own cause. Burying her face in her handkerchief, she headed out of the room, though her sobs continued.

Meanwhile, his mother focused on him and continued her campaign.

'It's my fault,' she said as she claimed his aunt's chair. 'I was so terrified of your father's moods that I kept him away from you. He couldn't teach you the proper way to be a duke. If he were here now, he would tell you that a Chinese girl cannot marry Cedric. It's simply not proper.'

'Mother—'

'Think, Declan. Do you know anyone with a foreign wife?'

'Yes, I do.'

'Not *Chinese* foreign! Good God, even a Spanish wife is frowned upon. You know it is true.'

He did know. But it was true because women like his mother and aunt were leaders in society. They decided who was allowed and who was not. So what she was truly saying was that *she* would not accept a foreign girl, and she would make sure everyone else reviled her, too.

Thank God he was the head of the family. He now realised he had been too lax, choosing to ignore society, avoid his mother and aunt, and generally bury his head in his ledgers while he set the ducal estates to rights. But now he saw how arrogant his relatives had become, thinking they could dictate not only his actions, but society's as well.

This had to end now.

'Mother, I will not bandy words with you. You will repair the damage to Miss Richards' reputation.' He spoke calmly, but he could see that his mother wasn't receptive.

'No one could do that!' she exclaimed. 'The moment Miss Richards punched Lord Jasper, she put herself beyond the pale. No hostess will accept her now.'

'Nevertheless, you will do it. You will do as I ask because I am the Duke. You will do it because Cedric will marry her if she doesn't have another option.' Those words choked him, but he continued. 'And you will do it because I will no longer tolerate your ridiculous games. If you must meddle in people's lives, sponsor a charity. What you are doing here—setting yourself against a woman merely because she is Chinese—is beneath you. It is beneath the title you hold, and I will not allow it.'

'You will not allow it?' she cried, gaping at him.

'That is correct.' He tapped his chin, as if he hadn't already decided on what would happen now. 'I believe vouchers to Almack's will be a good start.'

'Almack's! Never!'

'And you must tell all your friends to invite her to their social events.'

'You have gone mad!'

'It is either find her a new husband or accept that Cedric will marry her.'

The words burned in his gut, but he kept his expression bored, as if he cared not one whit what she chose. It was a lie, of course. He was here championing Nayao's cause because he very much cared that Cedric did *not* marry her. Nor anyone else for that matter.

Somehow, during the night, he had decided that she would be his. He didn't know how he'd manage it. Indeed, he feared that she set off so many feelings inside him that it would be a terrible disaster. But he had now realised how much more of a disaster it would be if she went to anyone else.

He might very well go insane if that were the case.

Oblivious to his decision, his mother made a gesture of frustration. 'You cannot think she is remotely attractive. Perhaps as a mistress, but a wife?' She shook her head. 'No, even Cedric is not so reckless.'

'Mother, Miss Richards is strong, clever, and so much more than any woman I have ever met. Different, powerful, and capable of things I have never seen before.'

His admiration for her rang loudly in the suddenly quiet room. He could see that his mother was genuinely confused. She wasn't arguing his decree, necessarily, but trying to talk around his logic.

'Every man enjoys novelty, Declan. A cow is novel, too, but one doesn't marry it.'

A cow was one of the least novel things in England, and damn his mother for comparing Nayao to cattle! He sighed, trying to work out a path here. Yesterday had opened his eyes on so many levels. Ever since he'd met Nayao she'd quietly challenged his blind assumptions. His mind felt open for the first time in his life, open and willing to look at the world through new eyes. And not just the world, but his own family and their limitations.

'Miss Richards is like a wild rose, growing against all odds.'

'On a dung heap? Even you must admit the stench.'

No, he did not. To his mother, everything but a very tiny corner of England was a dung heap. To him, there was a very large world out there, and Nayao tempted him as no one else.

'I think she is fascinating,' he said. 'And I am not the only one. So if you don't want her marrying Cedric, I suggest you make her appealing to respectable men.'

'Respectable! But then I would have to see her at parties. She would become part of the *ton,* if not the *haut ton.*'

He shrugged. 'Would you prefer her at the family Christmas dinner?'

His mother shuddered at the thought, but Declan smiled at the image. He would enjoy seeing Nayao lighting the yule log. And he would definitely enjoy kissing her under the mistletoe.

'Get her a voucher, Mother,' he instructed as he headed for the door. 'Immediately.'

'Or what?'

A very good question.

'Or I shall pay for Cedric's special licence myself.'

He walked out on her gasp of outrage and headed to his club. Or that was what he'd intended. Instead, he directed his coachman to take him home. He wanted a bath before he showed up on Miss Richards' doorstep and asked to take her riding in Hyde Park.

And bathe he did. He even allowed his valet to tie his cravat in a complicated affair that took twenty minutes to settle right. His boots were polished to a mirror shine, and his signet ring had a quick clean.

Which was why it was rather upsetting that when he finally presented himself at Miss Richards' home he found he was not the first to command her attention. Indeed, the parlour was filled with blackguards and fortune-hunters. And that included his cousin.

Chapter Twenty

Grace knew the moment the Duke entered the room. Of course she did. He was dressed to perfection, he carried himself as if he were the Emperor himself, and yet in his eyes she saw a clear hunger. She felt it across the room, she knew it every time their eyes met, and she burned with it whenever she heard his voice.

He burned for her. And she for him.

She could not forget his touch, his kiss, or the low rasp of his voice as he had instructed her. He had not touched her most intimate places, and yet last night she had felt as if every stroke had been made by him. She'd tried to recreate the experience alone, but it was not nearly as satisfying without him.

They exchanged the usual pleasantries. He was one of a throng of men who apparently wished to further their acquaintance with her. She knew it was because of her dowry, but that didn't stop her from appreciating the flattery. Never before had she been the subject of such approval—even if it was false. Even Lucy seemed to glow from the attention. She had been allowed to join the salon, and her normally composed demeanour was flushed pink.

This was heady stuff for two girls who had lived in constant danger of being killed just because they were neither white nor Chinese.

When the Duke's face tightened with anger whenever she smiled at someone other than him, she felt a surge of satisfaction. It was petty of her, but he had consumed her thoughts for so long there was a measure of satisfaction in seeing him think he was only one among many. It wasn't true, of course. She saw only him. She felt only him. But she pretended to be fascinated by all the others, including his cousin.

Her walk to Hyde Park later was uneventful, probably because the Duke did not join the crowd that went to promenade. And the ball she attended that night was equally boring.

The Duke arrived late, so she had no dances left for him. He arrived on time the next night and managed to write his name down twice on her card. But when he swept her into his arms for the waltz they said not one word to one another.

They didn't need to.

When his hands touched her body she was right back in the kitchen. She was touching herself as he told her what to do, what to feel. It all rushed back into her mind and body, such that their waltz left her breathless with need.

When the dance was done, he slowly released her body. His gaze roved over her, burning everything it touched, and then he spoke.

'I cannot stop thinking about you.'

'I am the same.'

Her words didn't make logical sense. But when he looked at her like that she became too lost to think clearly in another language.

And then the chance was over as her next partner claimed her.

He left soon after that.

The next night was an excursion to the theatre. At the Duke's invitation, both her father and Lucy were allowed to attend too. Grace had never seen a theatre before, and the experience enchanted her. Best of all was the way he walked with her during the interval. They went from box to box, with her on his arm. She was introduced to important people who greeted her kindly merely because he stood beside her. She exchanged pleasantries with powerful Englishmen and their haughty wives. Another time, she might have trembled at their reluctant acceptance.

She knew how quickly that would change if ever she was away from the Duke.

But she was not apart from him, and so she stood tall and spoke clearly.

When the interval was over, the Duke patted her hand and smiled at her.

'You did very well,' he murmured as they headed back to his box. 'I'm impressed.'

'That was nothing to do with me,' she said. 'That was about your power here in England. They sought not to offend you.'

'And they found no fault with you.'

She doubted that. There would be whispers, but with him beside her she didn't care.

She cared even less when he abruptly ducked them into a side corridor. It was dark, and secluded, and she should have been terrified to be caught like that.

She wasn't.

She was thrilled as he pressed her against the wall.

'Grace... Nayao.' He spoke her name reverently as he caressed her cheek, framing her face with his hands. 'I dream of you every night.'

She nodded. He hadn't even asked her if she did the same, but she answered nonetheless. 'You are in my thoughts always.'

Then their lust overcame their senses as he slowly, inexorably, pressed his full body against hers.

She gasped at the feel of him on top of her. She could not run, she could not escape, and all she wanted to do was raise her knee along his flank as he kissed her.

He lowered his mouth to her ear, the heat of his breath stirring the hair along her face and neck. He said nothing, though she was tensed for words. Instead, he stroked his tongue along her flesh, her jaw, her neck.

She felt his thickness against her groin. She knew when it pulsed with need. She didn't even realise she had pressed upwards against him until she heard his hiss.

'What am I to do?' he murmured.

As if she knew.

'I cannot stay away from you.'

He kissed her then, deep and hard, while his hands roved over her breasts. She arched into his touch. She ached to give him everything. And when they broke apart to breathe he continued to touch her everywhere, even as he whispered into her ear.

'You cannot marry any of those men. They want only your fortune.'

She knew that. 'No one wants me for myself.'

He pulled back. He looked her in the eyes. 'I do,' he said. 'I think this is love.'

He spoke the words as if they terrified him. As if loving her were a terrible thing.

'Why do you say it like that?' she asked. 'Why is love so awful?'

His head drooped then, setting gently against her forehead. 'Is love enough?' he asked, and the words sounded more for himself than for her. But then he raised his head up to look her in the eye. 'Do you want to be part of this world? Do you know how people will treat you when I am not by your side?'

She did. After all, she'd been to balls, teas, and musical evenings. He hadn't been at all of them, and he certainly hadn't been at her side the whole time. Most people were polite to her. A few said mean things. Several wanted to further their acquaintance with her. But she didn't know if it was for herself or because they wanted the connection to him.

In his world, she had only him as a bulwark against hate. And yet that was still more than she'd ever had in her life. There'd been people who had supported her, else she never would have survived. But he was different. He loved her. She could feel it in his touch. She knew it in his desperation to be with her. And she felt in her thrumming heart.

She loved him.

The knowledge rolled through her with the force of a tidal wave, and she embraced the feeling as new and exciting.

But one look at him destroyed all her budding happiness.

He saw it as a disaster. For him, the truth was obvious.

'Love is not enough for you,' she said. It might be for her, but clearly it wasn't for him. 'You don't want a wife who detracts.'

'You don't *detract* from anything!'

And yet in his eyes she saw doubt and fear.

'I feel so much when I am with you,' he said. 'It's not you I fear,' he said. 'It's myself.'

She couldn't help him, then.

He had to resolve this in his own mind before they could have a future.

But still she couldn't resist touching his face, stroking his lips and whispering her own words into his mouth. As if she could make him say the words to her.

'I love you,' she said, but she didn't think he heard it.

He was too busy kissing her throat, stroking her breasts, making her insane with need. And then he plundered her mouth, twisting his tongue around hers, teasing the roof of her mouth and thrusting in and out as if they could make love right there in the theatre.

Her knees weakened and she gripped his shoulders to hold herself upright. He curled an arm around her back. He supported her as he thrust against her—above and below—over and over. Was it possible to attain bliss from just this? A kiss and a thrust through thick layers of fabric?

She thought it was.

Her heart was thundering, her body willing. He could have done it. He could have lifted her skirts right then and she would not have stopped him.

How he found the strength to resist, she didn't know.

But, with a growl that reverberated from his body into hers, he drew back. Then he slammed his palm down hard on the wall beside her body. He hung his head as his breath heaved in and out.

'I cannot,' he growled.

He could have. She would have allowed it. And what madness was that?

She didn't argue with him. What good would that do? But she could ask him what he meant by this. By kissing her in a dark corridor and then stopping.

'What do you want?' she whispered.

He lifted his head. His gaze roved over her face. His body trembled, still close enough to her that she knew he ached.

'What I cannot have.'

'Why not? Aren't you a great mandarin among your people? A leader? A duke? Every soul here bows to your presence.'

'Only to my face.' He snorted. 'I cannot explain the intricacies of English politics to you.'

'I could learn.'

His head tilted as he looked to her. 'I suppose you could... But why ever would you want to descend into that madness?'

For him.

'You say you are afraid of yourself with me. That makes no sense. What do I do to you?'

'You make me feel!' he all but shouted. Then he sighed. 'And when I feel, I am afraid of what I will do.'

He meant his rages. He meant beating up his cousin in Hyde Park. He meant his legacy of destruction.

'But I am not afraid of you,' she said. 'Even at your worst I was never afraid.'

It was the truth, and she saw her words hit him full force. His body jolted, his eyes widened, and hunger burned hot in his eyes. But she still saw doubt in his face, and knew he held himself back from her, as he held himself away from everything.

He was a man so controlled that he denied himself everything, she realised. Even love.

And then they were out of time. She heard a noise from down the corridor. People. Whispers. A couple no doubt doing exactly as they were. It was enough to make the Duke jerk back from her.

'Do you know where my box is?' he asked.

'What?'

'Do you know how to return to my box?'

She nodded. They were barely ten steps from it.

'Apologise to your father for me. I shall leave my carriage for your use.'

'What? Why?'

He stroked his thumb across her lower lip. And as he did so he wet his own. She lifted her hand to his face, but it never arrived there. He grasped it quickly, then slowly, inexorably, lowered it down his body. While her breath caught, he pressed her hand to his organ.

She felt heat and thickness. The thrum of a heartbeat, or perhaps it was the rumble of her own. Either way, he thrust into her palm. His eyes fluttered closed and he dropped his head back.

She began to grip him. How could she not?

But he pulled her hand away.

'I cannot be seen like this. And I cannot stay near you without it.'

'But—'

He kissed her again. His tongue nearly undid her. But then he pulled away.

He scanned her quickly, then twisted to open a side door.

'It's empty,' he whispered. 'Go quickly.'

'But—'

He gave her no time to speak. He pushed her firmly through the door, then closed it behind her. What could she do but exactly as he wanted?

She went back to his box, she made apologies for him, and then she sat down next to her sister while her entire body throbbed with need.

That was bad enough.

But then it happened again in a secluded alcove at the next night's ball. And again in the instrument room during a musical evening. It was crazy. They would get caught eventually. But she could not seem to stop herself. Or him.

Which was why, when the summons came, she went immediately to see his mother. If anyone understood the Duke's intentions, then it would be the Dowager Duchess. Didn't English men revere their mothers? If she could get through the lady's arrogant disdain, she might finally understand what he wanted.

Chapter Twenty-One

Grace tried not to be impressed by the London abode of the Dowager Duchess of Byrning. She'd been there before, for that first disastrous tea, but she hadn't understood things as well as she did now. Now she knew that this place was owned by the Duchess alone and housed herself and her sister. The large staff supported only two souls, and that made it a grand palace.

Certainly there were such edifices in China, but she'd been a half-white orphan who could only look at them from afar. Today she was walking into one by invitation. And, though she'd attended balls in other private residences, she had been one of many attending a party. Today she entered alone except for her maid, who was immediately swept away below stairs.

That left her feeling small behind a sour-looking butler as he escorted her past footmen to a different parlour from the one she had been in before. This one was called 'intimate', and it was larger than some boats.

The butler left her one step inside the door. It took her a moment to survey the room and see—fully at the opposite end— the Duchess of Byrning and the Countess of Hillburn, sitting on ornate chairs as if they were thrones. They were, of course, the mothers of Declan and Cedric, and they did not look friendly, for all that they smiled and gestured for her to sit.

She could already tell this was not going to be easy, but she also knew that they wouldn't beat her or whip her.

'I'm so glad you could join us, Miss Richards,' intoned the Duchess. 'I assume you know who we are?'

She did, and she curtseyed to each in turn, with her head bowed and her legs steady. 'Your Grace, my lady,' she said. 'I am pleased to renew our acquaintance.'

They will not beat me. They will not beat me.

She repeated that over and over, to give herself perspective. No matter how intimidating the circumstances, these women would not physically harm her. It wasn't done in England—at least not between women who shared tea with one another—so she was safe. And, even more important, if her physical body was not in danger, what harm could a few words do? Worst case, she would be insulted, and that had been so common in her life that it felt no more substantial than air.

She sat down in a chair placed opposite them. The tea tray arrived without use of a bell or any kind of signal. There was also a display of sandwiches and tarts, which no one touched.

'How do you take your tea, Miss Richards?' the Duchess asked.

'Strong,' she answered, 'and without addition.'

It wasn't meant to be a challenge. It was merely the truth. To her, sugar and milk were luxuries, and she was not used to such things.

'Ah,' the Duchess said as she set the pot down. 'Then we shall allow it to sit a while longer.'

'Pray do not wait on my account,' she said with a smile. 'There is no reason to deny yourself your preference.' She meant it as a courtesy, but the Countess sniffed in an expression of disapproval.

'That is not the way it is done,' the lady intoned. 'If the guest waits, then we all wait.'

What was she to say to that? If the women wanted to drink tea they disliked, she was in no position to stop them. She dipped her chin and waited. After a dozen breaths, she finally spoke.

'I'm sure the tea is fine now. I should be very grateful for a cup.'

The Duchess poured. She served Grace first, then the Countess, before pouring her own. And when the beverage was adjusted to their liking, they both lifted their cups in a single co-ordinated movement. With their gazes fixed on Grace, they sipped their tea.

She scrambled to drink as well. She didn't know the exact timing. Was she to delay drinking while they sipped? Were they all to drink at once? Surely she should know this by now? And wasn't that a measure of how rattled she was, that she couldn't remember even so simple a thing as the English tea ceremony?

The tea wasn't bracing enough. But then, no tea could be strong enough to combat the sheer intimidation of these two women. The contrast to her first cup of tea in this house was marked. Where the Countess had been mean and petty, the Duchess was reserved, careful with the niceties, and appeared every inch an empress.

They will not beat me.

They would, however, make her sit in uncomfortable silence as they drank and stared at her. Until now, she had not realised how a long stare would be so much more effective when given in exquisite timing with another. These two women had perfected it to the point that she was beginning to sweat.

'I suppose you are wondering why you have been asked to tea,' the Duchess intoned.

'I do not ask such questions, Your Grace,' she said, in full honesty.

'Wise of you,' the woman said. 'Nevertheless, we shall alleviate your curiosity.'

Grace set her teacup down into its saucer. She waited. And she waited even longer. Oddly enough, this game of pauses was having a calming effect on her. Only women with nothing else to do could spend so much time in pauses. She had been trained at the temple in meditative silences. So she sat, she breathed, and she waited. Eventually they would come to their point.

Besides, this was the worst they could do to her. There was nothing to fear.

Eventually Cedric's mother spoke, her voice stiff and her expression one of extreme distaste. 'It has come to our attention that our sons have behaved with an extraordinary lack of kindness.'

What?

The Duchess set down her teacup. 'To you, Miss Richards. They have been unkind towards you.'

What was she supposed to say to that? 'I don't know—'

'Don't interrupt,' the Countess chided. 'They are men, and therefore unaware that their games can have a profound effect upon the fairer sex.'

'We taught them better,' said the Duchess.

'Most assuredly so,' said the Countess.

'But men play games and never think twice about us.'

The Countess nodded, and they both looked to her as if it were her turn to speak.

'About us?' Grace asked.

'Yes. Us women,' the Countess stressed. 'They don't think about us.'

'About *you*, Miss Richards,' inserted the Duchess. 'They don't think about how their game might affect you, and for that we have brought you here to explain.'

'Explain?' Grace asked.

'Yes, Miss Richards. Pay attention,' the Countess huffed. 'My son Cedric—Lord Domac to you—needs ten thousand pounds to buy a boat and cargo. Some business about selling things to the Chinese?'

Grace nodded. She already knew this. He'd been very open about how he would spend her dowry.

'It is difficult,' said the Duchess, 'to admit that one's nephew is a fortune-hunter, but there it is. He was courting you for your dowry.'

'That's not true,' said the Countess, and she turned away from Grace to address the Duchess directly. 'He had no plan to actually marry her. He was just using her to get the family to invest with him.' She turned back to Grace. 'You're unsuitable, you see. You must know that. He's to be an earl one day, and he must marry a woman of appropriate breeding. It was just one of his games. A way to get money from the family because they'd rather that than see him marry someone unsuitable.' She paused for a long moment, then curled her lip. 'You.'

Grace held her tongue. She already knew this, and yet they were speaking as if it was the deepest secret.

'It's all very distasteful,' the Duchess fumed. 'Lord Domac threatened to marry you if the family did not give him ten thousand pounds.' She shook her head. 'I knew I had to intervene, and I went straight to Declan.' She pointed her fan at Grace. 'The Duke of Byrning to you.'

Yes, she knew who Declan was.

'You did the sensible thing, my dear,' the Countess said with a fond smile. Then she turned back to Grace. 'She asked her son to intervene and put an end to Cedric's nonsense.'

'I meant him to speak to Cedric,' the Duchess huffed. 'Instead, he thought he would have some fun—'

'Fun!' the Countess sniffed.

'Fun—the idiot boy.' The Duchess shook her head. 'He set about gathering the funds, of course, but he had to delay your growing infatuation with Lord Domac. I did not think he'd make such a spectacle of himself by courting you.'

'To be fair,' the Countess said, '*she* is the spectacle, not him. Nevertheless, Miss Richards, it was cruel of him to engage your affections.'

'Most cruel...' said the Duchess.

'And so you have been brought to tea so that we can explain the way of things.'

'So you will understand.' The Duchess leaned forward. 'You do understand, do you not?'

She did, she supposed. These ladies were explaining the shallowest aspects of what was happening between herself and their sons as if she could not understand them on her own.

'It is a boy's game,' the Duchess emphasised.

'It isn't real. None of it,' the Countess continued.

'And you are telling me this because it's cruel?' She didn't elaborate on who was being cruel—these ladies or their sons.

The Countess pursed her lips. 'We are telling you this so you will not put any thought to marriage with either of our sons.'

The Duchess tapped her fan into her palm several times before she spoke again. 'Pray, let me be blunt. You are a foreigner, not versed in our ways. We fear that you do not understand that there are expectations of a duke's wife—'

'And an earl's!'

'—that a foreigner is simply not able to fulfil.'

Now they were getting to the point. But she needed them to put it more plainly. 'What kind of expectations?'

'Duties. Tasks. They're quite significant,' said the Duchess.

'Exhausting and unending,' echoed the Countess.

That wasn't specific enough.

'I am a hard worker, my ladies,' Grace said. 'And a quick study. Both your sons have expressed awe at my accomplishments.'

The Duchess waved her fan in the air. 'But they would, you see. That was all part of their game.'

The Countess released a heavy sigh. 'She doesn't understand. Look at her. She hasn't the wits to comprehend.'

If anyone was lacking in wits, it was them, for underestimating her so thoroughly. She'd known from the beginning that it wasn't likely that the English would accept her any more than the Chinese had. Both countries saw her as half of a whole rather than a full person. But her father had told her his status would change things. No one had protected her in China, he'd argued, but he would protect her in England. His name would keep her from being discarded.

And she now saw it was true. After all, she'd known from the first moment that his status would prevent her from being beaten by these women. She would not be whipped for daring to speak to their sons. She would not be poisoned or stabbed or in any way physically damaged for her audacity.

What she hadn't realised until this very moment was that lies could hurt so much more than a beating. She knew that every moment she had spent with Declan had been more than a game. She felt it in her heart. But her head questioned it.

Could a man reared by such women truly feel love for her? Or had she simply believed what her heart wanted her to? Was it likely that most English gentlemen were like her very unusual and generous father? Or was it more likely that her father was unique and that the men of his country were like the men everywhere else in the world? They play with lives—with *her* life—as a game with each other?

And while she struggled with her doubts she heard the door behind her burst open. The next sound was loud, the heavy tread of boot heels echoing in the large chamber. She knew who it was before she heard his voice. But even so, she braced herself from the sheer impact of his tones. They were heavy with fury, for all that his words sounded polite.

'Mother! Aunt!' said the Duke. 'What tales are you spreading today?'

Chapter Twenty-Two

Information came to Declan in a variety of ways. Rarely, however, did it come from his valet in the middle of the afternoon, and in his library, no less. Turner had walked right in, held up a cravat, and offered to help him put it on before tea at his mother's.

Declan hadn't intended to go anywhere near his mother, but at his valet's significant look he'd agreed.

Which was when he had learned that Turner had heard that a maid had overheard the footman saying to someone else… He couldn't follow it all. But the main point was that Grace was set to have tea with his mother and his aunt, and that could not be good.

He'd headed straight for his mother's house, to discover that everything Turner had said was correct. There sat his mother and aunt, as if in judgement over Grace, who was looking pale but seemingly composed.

Not a good sign. Grace became animated when happy, and right now a statue would show more signs of life.

'Mother! Aunt! What tales are you spreading today?' he asked.

When all three women looked at him with shocked expressions, he turned his question into a joke. 'I hope you're not telling that silly tale of me running out of the house naked when I was four.'

'You were five,' his mother said as she lifted her face for a kiss, 'and you were protesting the need for a bath.'

'Good thing Nanny caught me before I became lost.' He turned and greeted his aunt, then finally was able to bow over Miss Richards' hand. 'You must share what stories they have been telling. Allow me to defend my honour.'

He kept his tone light, but the words were meant with his whole heart. He knew his mother and aunt could be intimidating, especially to a woman only recently thrust into the social whirl. Which was why he had rushed over here. He did not like the idea of them anywhere around her, much less alone with her and in such a setting.

'They told me the tale of my dowry,' Grace said, her voice flat. 'And that neither you nor Cedric will ever marry me. Indeed, they said it was all a game from Cedric to extort ten thousand pounds.' She waved her hand vaguely in the air. 'I don't quite understand the details. Only that you and Lord Domac have been courting me in a game and I was the...' She winced as the word left her mouth. 'Toy.'

He shot an angry glare at his relations, but he didn't bother with them. Instead, he touched her hand. 'You know that's not true.'

She arched a brow at him. 'I know it *is* true. At least in part. I have known Cedric's purpose from the beginning.'

'But not mine.'

She met his gaze, her feelings completely unreadable.

'No,' she agreed, 'not yours.'

He swallowed. This was not something he wished to discuss with his mother and aunt watching. So he squeezed her fingers. 'Let us go for a walk. We can discuss this in private.'

He watched her eyes flicker, and he read so many conflicting emotions in them. But none had a chance to settle because his mother refused to be ignored.

'Step away from her, Declan. You've been cruel,' she said, her voice as cold as the arctic. 'It is heinous to raise a woman's hopes when you have no intention—when you *never* had any intention—of fulfilling them.'

'What hopes?'

'Marriage, you idiot boy!' his mother snapped. 'You let her believe you'd wed her!'

He straightened up to his full height, the familiar tide of fury burning dark in his vision. In that one moment he remembered all the times his father had raged at his mother. All the reasons why his cold, calculating mother deserved the hatred that burned in him.

'She thinks she is protecting you,' Grace said, her voice low.

When he looked down at her, he watched her gaze turn troubled.

'Is she?' she asked.

'What?'

'Protecting you from your feelings for me? Protecting you from a disastrous choice in marriage?'

'That is not her concern!' he snapped.

Grace had the audacity to roll her eyes. 'She is your mother. You are her son and heir. Your choices affect her profoundly. Of course she is concerned.'

He gaped at her, but not for the reason she likely suspected. He was shocked that the rage in his blood had cooled. A few simple words from Grace, and the black tide receded.

That had never happened before.

Meanwhile, Grace slowly stood to her full height, matching him in dignity. 'Is she right?'

He blinked, trying to shift his thoughts from his rationality to what he was being asked. It was true, his mother was indeed worried about exactly the same things he was. Marriage to a mixed-race woman would damage his power in politics, his influence in social circles, and it would definitely carry down to his children.

He now saw how ridiculous that thought was. Indeed, he'd spent the entire night thinking about just what she meant to him, and how little he cared about everything else. Political and social influence ruled his mother's mind, but meant little to him.

Whatever sway they'd once had over him was now dwarfed by what Grace gave to him.

Around her, he felt alive. She calmed his rages and brought new thoughts into his world.

That was worth everything to him!

Meanwhile, his mother snorted in satisfaction. She thought that his silence was an admission.

'I believe we have made our point, Miss Richards.' She held up a large engraved envelope. And while she waited for Grace's attention, she spread her fingers to show that there were actually three envelopes. 'I have in my hand a voucher to Almack's. Not just one, but three—one for you, one for your sister, and one for that chit Miss Phoebe Gray. I have invitations for them all—'

'Mother,' he interrupted. 'You cannot buy her off—'

His mother continued as if he hadn't spoken. 'You aren't aware of it, but admission there—especially at my invitation—will establish all three of you with the *haut ton*. You will become respectable, and every man in attendance will also be respectable. No more of those fortune-hunters and card sharps.'

'You forget that Cedric is one of those fortune-hunters,' he growled.

His aunt sent him a caustic look before she stepped in. 'We shall give you our support. We shall make each of you a viable flower on the Marriage Mart—'

'Provided,' continued his mother, 'that you do not look to our sons.'

Declan folded his arms. 'You will give her the vouchers and support them either way, or I shall make life very unpleasant for you both.'

Grace sighed. 'Do not threaten them. It only makes them more afraid.'

He turned to her. 'But what does it mean for you?' He gestured to his relations. 'They are not unique. They will never accept you, no matter what you do. Not as I do, Nayao.'

He used her Chinese name deliberately, so she knew he referred to all of her. But in his mind she was always Grace—not as a name, but as an attribute. For all that she had suffered in life, she was the epitome of poise and refinement.

He watched her eyes grow sharp. They hopped between him and the ladies.

'And what of your children?' she asked. 'Would they accept them?'

He flinched. He already knew the answer. His mother would decry the blood in her grandchildren. Their every fault would be laid at Grace's door. Their every gain declared due to his blue blood.

The light in Grace's eyes died out. 'I know what it is to be without family. It is a terrible thing.' Tears welled in her eyes, but she blinked them back. 'I will not do that to your children.'

They had never talked about children before this moment, but at her words he saw them in his mind's eye. Bright, inquisitive, exploring the world in ways he'd never managed.

'Our children will be raised in a way we never were,' he said. He touched her hand. 'You will be an incredible mother. And I will do everything to guide our children.'

He would make sure that the legacy of rage ended with him.

'But you said it yesterday,' she pressed. 'You said that love was not enough.'

'You said that,' he corrected. 'And I think you are wrong.'

She looked at him, then back at his mother and aunt.

'Don't look at them. They don't matter. Talk to me,' he said as he gently drew her face back to his.

'Yesterday you said you cannot have me. Now you are here telling me to ignore them and their fears. What has changed?'

How did he explain the extraordinary changes she had wrought in him? How did he tell her that the things he'd once valued seemed unimportant now? That there were emotions beyond rage and intellectual curiosity, feelings that he wanted to experience with her?

These were not easy things to say, and certainly not in front of his mother, but he'd try his best.

'I heard you,' he whispered. 'I heard you say you love me.'

He saw her wince, as if her love was painful for her. And apparently it was, because she stepped away from him.

'Love does not solve everything,' she said. Then she looked to his mother and aunt. 'I had love growing up. The monk who raised me, the navigator who taught me and the captain who protected me—they were each like a parent to me. They showed me love and taught me things that fill me even now.' Her voice broke as she looked back to Declan. 'You have never known that kind of love. One that is generous and supportive. So when you finally experience it, you grab it with both hands.'

She looked down at her own hands as she spoke and slowly curled them into fists.

'But it is not enough,' she said loudly. 'Love, no matter how strong, cannot fill your emptiness when an entire society reviles you. Better never to have children than to watch them suffer when their own grandmother despises them.' She lifted her chin to look directly at Declan. 'And I hope I may not be here when you realise my love is not enough for you.'

'Nayao, of course it is—' he began, but he never got the chance to say more.

Her gaze had swept back to his mother. 'I accept your vouchers and their conditions. I shall enjoy meeting the best of English society. And then I shall happily turn my back on all of you. My father and I will live in Italy without any of you.'

She turned to leave, but he caught her arm. 'Please, Grace. You were never my toy. And this has never been a game to me.'

'I know,' she said, her voice barely audible. 'But it is for them. And I can never be a winner in it. Which means you will always be the loser, and your children even more so. Eventually you will realise that, and whatever is between us will end.'

He shook his head. 'That's not true. That doesn't even make sense!'

'Maybe not to you, but your children will know. And I will know. It is a terrible life.'

And with that, she swept forward. His mother was ready, holding the vouchers out. Grace took them and departed.

He didn't stop her. He knew now was not the time to confront her. But what pain seared through him, watching her leave!

More than he'd expected, more than he thought rational. More, indeed, than he had ever experienced before.

What was this agony? Why did rage burst through him as the door shut behind her? Rage directed at his mother and his aunt. Rage at the pain Grace had suffered. Rage at anyone and anything that would set a wedge between himself and her.

He knew the answer even as he stood frozen in shock at the realisation.

He was in love with Nayao.

He loved everything about her.

Her strength, her beauty, even her determination to protect their children. Especially that!

Never had he thought anything could feel as strong as his rage, but he felt it now.

Love.

Such love that it tamed his fury. The anger wasn't gone, but it was tempered. It didn't rule him. And that was yet another shock.

He had been such a fool! He'd been afraid of his legacy of rage, afraid to risk hurting anyone, so he had hidden away from society and allowed his relatives to run roughshod over him. He'd never had an inkling of how powerful love could be. He'd never guessed that there was any woman who could tame his rage and show him how love changed everything!

He now knew he would up-end his entire life for her. She was everything he needed, everything he wanted, and everything he loved. But before he could claim her he had to make his world as safe as possible for her and for their children.

While the thud of the door behind Grace still echoed in the chamber, Declan turned to his mother and aunt. He spoke calmly. He would not have them blame this on the Byrning legacy. He didn't want to frighten them with his anger. He meant to impress his decision upon them.

'I did not realise until this very moment how poisonous you both are,' he said. 'I thought my anger was a curse, but I think the real curses are your narrow minds, your bitter manipulations and how very small your world is.'

His mother snorted. 'Do not cut up at me. We have solved the problem. We said nothing but the truth, and now her reputation is assured. Just as you ordered.'

Perhaps that was true. She had obeyed the letter of his command, but not the meaning. And he saw now that he could not force her to change. Therefore, he must look to protecting those who would be harmed by them.

'Hear me well, both of you. You shall have no knowledge of my children. You are wrong. Your judgement is flawed because your minds are closed. You cannot imagine that anyone could have value but yourselves.' He shook his head as he finally saw how small they were. 'I will not allow your poison to damage the next generation.'

And with that he departed. He had a great deal to do before tomorrow night's dance at Almack's. Much to do before he apologised to Grace in the only way possible.

Chapter Twenty-Three

Grace dressed slowly for Almack's. She knew what a triumph it was for her to get not one but three vouchers. Indeed, Phoebe and Lucy were chattering like old friends, giggling about one thing or another. But she couldn't share their excitement. Perhaps they would find their future husbands tonight. Perhaps they would find love. But she knew her future was set. There would be no grand experience tonight. There would be nothing but the certainty of a life spent alone.

Because she had already found her love. She had already fallen for Declan. No other man saw her so clearly. He called her by her Chinese name, he defended her reputation, and even fought his own mother on her behalf. She tried to find an exact moment when she'd tumbled into love, but it had been a gradual thing. The way he had looked at her in the crow's nest. The way he had appeared beneath the burned pagoda. She relived his kiss. She felt his need. And she ached whenever she saw him.

But that wasn't love. She knew that. That was lust and desire. What had made her realise that it was love was the devastation she'd felt at the idea that her foreign blood would taint him and his children. He was the epitome of English perfection, and she would only poison his power and his position.

She would not do that to him. And that willingness to sacrifice her feelings for him told her as clearly as a full sail where the wind blew. She loved him. She loved his children, who didn't even exist yet. She loved his seeking mind and his open heart.

And so she would leave for Italy, or Africa, or wherever the wind took her, rather than poison Declan with her tainted heritage.

Her sister took her hand, jolting her out of her dark thoughts. 'You can always sail again,' she said softly.

Grace nodded, knowing it was true. But it wouldn't be the answer she wanted. She'd sailed as a way to find a safety that hadn't existed in China. She'd become an excellent navigator as a way to create value for herself. And when she had no longer been protected aboard ship, and no longer allowed at the temple because of her age, she'd found safety with Lord Wenshire as he sailed for England.

Everything she had ever done had been to find a safe space where she could live and thrive. She'd never expected to find it with an English mandarin. But Declan had proved himself strong, respectful, and generous. And she loved him.

'I am tired of sailing,' she said honestly. 'Perhaps Father and I will find a place in Italy.'

'No!' Phoebe exclaimed as she came to Grace's side. 'You will find true love tonight. We all will!'

Grace exchanged a knowing look with her sister. Phoebe had a generous heart, but also a naïve one. She still believed in fairy tales and Grace found that charming.

'Maybe I will,' she finally said. 'Who knows where the wind will blow?'

'Exactly!' Phoebe declared.

And then she all but dragged the two girls downstairs, where Lord Wenshire was waiting with Phoebe's parents.

'My goodness. I cannot credit such loveliness,' he said. 'You three astound me.'

'You are the best of fathers,' Grace said, feeling every word.

And Lucy echoed it a thousandfold.

In the end, the three girls climbed into a single carriage with Lord Wenshire. Phoebe's parents weren't allowed in Almack's without vouchers, whereas Grace's father had a title and would not be turned aside. Grace counted it a mistake that she hadn't thought to demand vouchers for Phoebe's parents, but everyone assured her they were well pleased with the situation.

After all, Pheobe would not have got a voucher at all without her.

They entered Almack's amid the usual crowds of debutantes. There were whispers, of course, and pointed stares, but Grace was used to them. Lucy seemed unnerved, but Phoebe shone brighter than them both. She heard the sneers. None of them could avoid it. But the girl simply grinned brightly and talked with excitement about how wonderful it was that the Duchess had sponsored them all.

It wouldn't have worked if the Duchess and Countess hadn't played their part. But they were there, right by the front entrance, when Grace presented their vouchers. The ladies exclaimed at their beauty, applauded their curtsies, and immediately introduced all three of them to an entire line of gentlemen.

Clearly they were working very hard to make all three of them acceptable to any man who wasn't one of their sons. And the girls did their best to charm, enchant, and otherwise dazzle the men who bowed before them.

But Grace's heart wasn't in it.

That was until Declan strode in.

He looked every inch the Duke he was. He wore black, with a red ruby in his white cravat. His boots gleamed, but not as brightly as his eyes as he scanned the crowd until his gaze landed on her. Then he smiled, and her heart tripped in her chest.

How she loved that man. Just looking at him made her feel safe. She knew, despite everything to the contrary, that he would make sure nothing harmed her in his presence. Not even his mother, who was just then coming to his side with a furious expression.

'Declan,' the woman said. 'What are you doing here?' Her voice wasn't loud enough for people to hear clearly, but the question was there on her face for all to see.

'I am here,' he said, 'to make my choice.'

And with those words he disentangled his mother's hand

from his forearm and walked straight into the pattern of the dance.

It was incredibly disruptive. Dancers scattered before him, and the music faltered until everything was in disarray. But of course the dance had already been disrupted, because Grace hadn't been able to move from the moment he'd entered the hall.

It had been one thing to see him, to talk to him, to do such secret things with him when she hadn't been aware of her feelings. It was desire, it was distraction, it was excitement. But now she knew it was love. She was in love with him. And he was stepping through the crowd of people like a warrior of old, coming to stand directly before her.

'Your Grace,' she murmured as she dipped into a curtsey.

'Miss Richards,' he said as he pulled her up.

And he kept drawing her hand up, higher and higher, as he pressed his mouth to the back of her glove.

Somewhere in the distant part of her mind she was aware of people staring at them. She heard outraged murmurs, and the Duchess saying something sharp to someone. She didn't care. All that mattered was that he was looking into her eyes as if she were the wind in his sails after a long stillness.

'Marry me.'

She read the words from his lips because she could not hear over the roaring in her ears.

'What?'

His lips curved and he stepped forward. 'I'm such an idiot. You kept saying that love was not enough. It's not enough if it's yours alone. That's what you meant. You love me, but that's not enough.'

She swallowed, tears destroying her vision. 'Your Grace—' she began, but her words were choked off as he dropped down to one knee before her.

'I love you. That's what I forgot to say. I love you. I want to marry you.'

She stared at him, not knowing what to do.

'I am the best that England has to offer. I am clever, educated, and titled. I lay all that at your feet, Miss Grace Nayao

Richards. And I want more than the best of England at my side. I want the best of China.'

She blinked. 'But I am not the best of China or of anywhere.'

'You are beautiful and clever. You question things and learn. And you have taught me so much that I never even thought to wonder about.' He pressed his lips to her hands. 'There is a whole wide world beyond England, and I want to share every bit of it with you.'

'Have you lost your mind?'

A male voice cut through the crowd. She didn't even know who it was until Cedric grabbed Declan's arm.

'You can't marry her any more than I could!'

Declan didn't rise from where he still knelt on one knee. Instead, he rolled his eyes. 'Cousin, you are a boor.'

'And she's a thief and a liar.'

Her head jerked round. She heard the condemnation in Cedric's voice but did not understand it. Both men knew she had stolen to survive and lied to escape danger. But she had only done such out of necessity. Why would Cedric condemn her for that now?

'She's not really Lord Wenshire's daughter,' Cedric continued, his voice echoing loudly in the silent room. 'She lied about it in China and she's still lying to him. She is not his child.'

Grace's mouth dropped open. How could he know this? Then she remembered. Lucy had told him and had sworn him to secrecy. And now he had betrayed them both.

A slap rang out, loud and sharp. Grace had not seen her sister step forward, but the sound was clear as it echoed through the room. Not to mention the sight of Lucy's bright red handprint on Lord Domac's cheek.

'I did not think you could stoop any lower,' Lucy cried. 'And to think I once thought you clever. Safe, clever, and kind.' She shook her head. 'You have fooled me just as your father fooled your mother. You are a villain worse than Lord Jasper.'

Cedric reared up, his expression changing to one of horror as he looked at Lucy. Then he looked around at the crowd, and he flushed a dark red. 'Lucy, I didn't mean—'

'Step away, Cedric. Or I swear to God I will put you into the ground.'

That was Declan, his voice cold and hard as he stood to face his cousin.

'Not a penny, Cedric. Not a penny to you or your sisters. You know that is how they survive now. It is upon my charity. But I will end it.'

'You can't—' Cedric began.

But it all was forestalled by Grace's father. He began swinging his cane as he cleared a path forward.

'Stop it!' he bellowed as he whipped the cane up and down between the men. 'Good God, I am ashamed to be English. Stop it!'

Both men had no choice but to back away, and in that space Grace looked to her father. She had tried so many times to tell him the truth, but it had always seemed too dangerous. And now she was exposed.

'I'm so sorry,' she said. 'I didn't speak English. I didn't know why you had chosen me. I didn't realise what you believed.'

She truly hadn't known he thought her his daughter. All she'd been told by the monks was that he was taking her away from China. And that was exactly where she'd wanted to be— away and safe.

'Hush...hush, child,' her father said as he set his cane on the floor. 'I knew the truth from the beginning. The woman I loved and our child died years before. I knew that long before I went to the temple.'

Grace gasped in surprise.

Lucy did as well, her hands clasped tight in front of her.

'You knew?' Lucy whispered.

'I did.' He touched Lucy's cheek, and then he smiled at Grace. 'I could not save my child, but I could save you. I could bring you here and give you a life such as I would have given my own flesh and blood.' He looked disdainfully about them. 'But I can see that was foolish. My own people are as ignorant and cruel as yours.' He lifted his chin. 'If you wish, we can leave at once for Italy, or Morocco, or any other land. We can try again to live without such idiocy.'

This was too much. Grace could not understand it. She stood there, looking at her sister, looking too at her father, who offered her a safe place far away from here.

What was she to do?

'Forget them,' Declan said. 'Forget them all. Look at me.'

She turned to him and felt her face heat with embarrassment. He was back on one knee before her.

'You should not be on the floor,' she whispered.

'It is our custom. I will stay here until you answer.'

'But you cannot want me,' she whispered. 'I am...'

'What?' he pressed. 'What are you? A by-blow of mixed blood? I don't care. A woman who has survived on her wit and her skills? Absolutely. A woman who can choose her future. A future with her father, who loves her, or...' He gathered her hands and tugged her closer to him. 'Or a future with me. You are the woman I love, Nayao. Stay with me.'

He loved her? Not possible.

And yet she saw it in his eyes. She felt it in his hands where he held her. And she knew it in her heart. He did love her.

'But your mother...' she whispered.

'Do you know why I have proposed this way? Here in front of the *haut ton*? Because it will be a huge scandal. It will be spoken of from this day on, long after we are dead and buried. I want everyone to know that you are exquisite and that I love you. That I will defend you and honour you until the end of my days. And any who speak against you will have to answer to me.'

How his words filled her. Everything she wanted, everything she hadn't dared dream of, was right here before her.

On one knee before her.

'And our children?'

'I adore them already.' He drew her forward. 'Don't be afraid. Remember the people who loved and protected you. Our children will have us. They will know more than this tiny corner of England. They will thrive, no matter what others say, because we will love them.'

Would that be enough? She didn't know.

'I never want them to be alone.'

'Neither do I,' he said. 'I will never abandon them, and I will never abandon you. I love you.'

She didn't have an answer. Not one that came from her lips. And yet she heard herself gasp. She felt her knees buckle as he steadied her coming down to the floor. Soon they were face to face, both on their knees, and he braced her even as he touched her face.

'Could you love me?' he whispered.

She nodded, unable to force the words out. But then other words came. 'How can you love me?'

'How can I not? You are everything I want.'

Then he kissed her. Right in front of his mother, his aunt, and all the *haut ton*. He pressed his lips to her mouth and wrapped an arm around her shoulders until she was deep in his embrace. And from that position she opened to him. She gripped him tight as he supported her. And when they separated to draw breath, he whispered into her ear.

'Will you marry me?'

What could she say? He was her safety. He was her love.

'Yes.'

'I have a special licence. We can be wed tonight.'

'What?'

'I will not let you change your mind.'

Or perhaps he would not let his mother or those around him force his hand.

Her gaze flickered to the people who surrounded them, all with their mouths agape.

'No,' he whispered. 'Don't doubt me. I will wait until you are ready or I will marry you this very night. Nothing will change my mind.'

'What of our children? What of your political power?'

'Both stronger for my being with you.' He touched her cheek. 'Do you not feel it? How we teach each other? How we make each other better?'

She did. She knew it because with him she felt free enough to do anything.

'Now,' she said. 'Tonight.'

'An excellent choice, Your Grace!' he cried as he pushed to his feet.

She didn't realise he was carrying her until she began to rise with him. Somehow he'd slipped his arm under her, and now he settled her against his solid chest.

'Your Grace!' she cried, alarmed.

'Declan,' he corrected. 'Call me by my given name.'

She smiled. 'I love you, Declan.'

'I love you.'

Chapter Twenty-Four

They were married by special licence that evening. Her father gave her away. Her sister and Phoebe stood radiantly by her side. They were her support.

The Duchess and her sister also attended, as did Lord Domac, using every possible moment to dissuade Declan.

Grace said nothing, waiting to see if he would allow their constant interference.

He did not.

After his mother's first interruption—just as the priest entered the church—he told them all to be silent or to be gone. And by gone, he continued, he meant that they would be gone from his life and his support.

Such was the power of his statement that they all stood silent. Then he turned to her.

'I love you,' he said. 'But if they are too much for you—'

'Will you always defend me? Against them? Against others?'

'I vow it before them and before God.'

She smiled. 'I vow it as well. I will stand by you, aid you, and love you until my last breath. As I will our children.'

His smile was radiant. His kiss was passionate. And for her, that was the promise that sealed their marriage bond well before the priest spoke his words or either of them said, 'I do.'

Twenty minutes later it was done. They were married.

And that night, as he brought her to his home, she knew all would be well.

Except for one small, but enormous detail.

The marriage bed.

The English and the Chinese alike prized virgins. And though she had never had relations with a man, she could not prove her virginity. She understood better than most what men looked for to prove virginity. They wanted blood on their marriage sheets. They wanted pain during the coupling. She didn't know if such a thing was possible for her. So many men had told her that she was unnatural. What if she could not prove what she knew to be true?

She did not say anything about her concerns as they travelled to his home. She did not say anything as he introduced the staff. Nor did she say anything when her new maid was presented to her. It was Molly Smithee, the daughter of the servant at her come-out ball, come to be her abigail.

The girl was indeed pretty, but she was also smart and capable, ready with soothing words as she helped Grace into the bath already prepared for her. There hadn't been time since her come-out for Grace to teach the girl how to defend herself, but there would be plenty now, she supposed.

'I've set a salve for your use by the bedside,' Molly said, her voice low as she pointed. 'Mama says it will help with the ache.'

Grace nodded. She had heard of such things as well. Molly said other things, but Grace couldn't think. So much had happened this night. She could not believe she was married.

It wasn't until she was dried, and dressed in a gown of sheer silk, that she thought to grab the girl's hand.

'What will he do?' she asked. 'What will he do if he thinks I am not a virgin?'

The girl's eyes widened with shock, then she shook her head. 'He can have the marriage annulled.'

'Annulled?' She did not know this word.

'Ended as if it had never happened.'

No. *No!* He would not take it away now, would he? Not after their vows, not after all he had said.

'I cannot prove it,' she whispered. 'I have climbed ratlines, fought with sails in storms. I have whipped men and done things no woman has done before.' She swallowed. 'I have been told many times that because of that there will be no blood when I am married. That I will not be able to prove whether this is my first time or not.'

Molly nodded, but had no answer.

Every girl heard such things growing up. *Do not do these things. It will take away your virginity, whether or not you have been with a man.*

'In China,' Grace whispered, 'a woman can be killed for this.'

'Would the Duke do that?' Molly asked.

Grace bit her lip, trying to think rationally. She could not believe a man who had just vowed to love her for ever would do such a thing. But men were not always rational when it came to the marriage bed. And by his own admission his Byrning blood was prone to rages.

'He won't kill me,' she said, her voice strengthening. 'He will believe me.' She wrapped her arms tight around her belly. 'He will believe me,' she repeated.

And then there was no more time. There was a knock at the door that joined their rooms and Declan entered. He, too, had bathed, and his hair was still damp. His eyes gleamed in the firelight, and he walked with a predatory kind of grace. Not as a man who lived on a sailing ship, but as a creature who was wholly sure of himself in his domain.

Grace adored the sight of him.

But he paused when he saw her, and his steps slowed. 'You are afraid,' he said.

She didn't answer.

'That's natural. In the span of a few hours, everything has changed for you. For me as well.'

'I am not a natural woman,' she said, meaning that she was an orphan of mixed blood who had navigated ships and only just come to England. Nothing about that was normal or natural.

He touched her cheek, stroking it gently with his fingers. 'You seem completely natural to me.' He caressed the edge of her jaw before trailing his hand down the length of her neck. 'Exquisitely beautiful.' He grinned. 'And now you are mine.'

She had no time to search his face for subtle meanings. For all that he seemed a gentle man, she did not like his words of ownership. And yet, perversely, she thrilled to the mastery in his kiss. She enjoyed surrendering to him.

She opened her mouth to his. She felt his fingers slide across the ribbon of her gown and she trembled when she felt him pull it free. The silk gaped open across her chest, and his mouth followed the trail set by his fingers. Her body heated, her knees weakened, and her breath caught with each scrape of his teeth across her flesh. She gripped his shoulders to stay upright, but he clearly had no desire to stay standing.

He scooped her up in his arms and laid her gently on the bed. She pushed herself up, supporting herself on her elbows—not because she wanted to stand, but because she wanted a better view of her husband as he stripped out of his dressing gown.

She had never seen him naked before. She knew the shapes of men's bodies, knew how to evaluate them for strength against the sails or nimbleness in the rigging. He was neither bulky nor wiry. He was tall and powerful, his muscles reddish gold in the firelight. And his power seemed to ripple across his whole body as he came forward.

'What do you see,' he whispered, 'when you look at me like that?'

'A fortress,' she said as she skimmed her hand across his shoulder. 'And a sail,' she went on as she stroked the breadth of his chest.

He arched a brow at her. 'Those don't usually go together.'

'No, they don't…'

But she saw it in him. Strong shoulders to protect her, and the power to take her wherever they might need to go, even if it was nowhere but right here.

She shook her head. 'My head is muddled.'

He grinned. 'Good.'

Then he kissed her again, gently pressing her back into the bed. He thrust his tongue inside her mouth, he duelled with hers and he used his hands to push away her gown. First off her shoulders, then down to her waist. Her arms were pinned then, caught by the fabric. She knew she could rip her hands free if she wanted to. She knew she could fight if she needed to. But she didn't want to.

Instead, she let herself arch into the stroke of his hands on her breasts. Her head pressed back as his mouth trailed across her body. Such attention he gave to her breasts. His hands shaped her, his fingers pinched her nipples, and then his mouth suckled until she was writhing beneath him.

Then she felt the weight on the bed shift. While she lay panting, he stroked his hands across her feet and up her calves. His fingers were strong as they kneaded her flesh, and he moved steadily upward, bringing her gown with him until it lay tangled across her hips while he knelt between her knees.

She was open before him, and it was nothing like what had happened in the kitchen. This time it was his hands on her legs, his thumbs stroking her wetness. He spread her open, and when she thought to tense he leaned forward and blew air across her wet nipple.

The experience was so shocking—the cold on the wet—that she gasped. And then he captured her nipple between his lips while his fingers did wonderful things between her thighs.

She cried out as pleasure shot between her breast and her groin. And then her breath caught again as he rolled over the spot between her thighs. That wonderful place he had taught her. Over and over he stroked her, while her legs trembled.

Then he bit her nipple. Not hard, but sharp. Enough to shock her. And as she arched from the sensation he entered her. One hard thrust.

She felt the intrusion like a bolt of lightning. One that stretched her wide and filled her to bursting. It was too much, and it was wonderful.

She lifted her knees, not even knowing what she wanted.

But he did.

He began to move and she revelled in it. Harder, faster.

She gripped him with her knees. She clung to his shoulders. She arched down against each thrust.

She heard his breath, harsh against her ear. Or was that hers?

Again and again he drove into her.

Climbing.

Building.

Bursting!

She flew on waves of bliss.

She had no idea how long she floated, but when she returned to herself she realised he had collapsed beside her, and she was snuggled into his side. She heard his breath steady. Hers, too. And she smiled for a while.

Until she remembered.

'It didn't hurt,' she whispered.

Her body stiffened when she realised she'd said that aloud. Afraid, she opened her eyes. Then she panicked when she saw him watching her.

'Grace?'

She swallowed, then adjusted herself on the bed. If there wasn't blood, she'd cut herself to make sure there was. But how would she do it without him seeing? Oh, heaven, she was flustered.

'Grace, what's wrong?'

'I...um... I need...'

She needed to fool him. He couldn't know. But—

He grabbed her arm, stilling her with the strength in his grip. It wasn't bruising, but it was firm.

'What do you need?'

His voice was calm, no sign of his fury, but there was a tightness in his face. If she'd thought ahead she could have had a convenient lie ready. But she'd never expected... She'd never thought...

'It didn't hurt,' she said.

'That's good.'

'I know I'm not a natural woman,' she said, her voice low. 'I know—'

'You are natural to me.'

'I have never been with a man before. Never before you. I swear. But—'

His expression abruptly softened. 'It doesn't always hurt for a virgin.' He flashed her a quick grin. 'Not if it's done right.'

'Oh.' No one had ever told her that. 'But there should be blood, yes?'

She moved to lift the coverlet, but he held her still.

'I don't need to see any blood. I know you were a virgin.'

'But—'

'I know.'

She blinked. 'How?'

He chuckled. 'Because you know nothing of sex. Because you haven't the wiles of a courtesan. No woman could lie so effectively.' He pressed a kiss to her lips. 'And besides, I don't care. So long as there is no one else after me, I am well content.'

'After you?' She didn't understand what he meant. 'I will not service your friends!'

He nodded, pulling her in tight. 'Damn right, you won't.'

He used his weight to gently settle her down against him. She curled tighter into his body. She smelled his scent, and immediately felt her body begin to relax. It took a while, but in time she felt her tension slide away.

'Is that why you were afraid?' he asked. 'Because you thought I was worried about your virginity?'

She shrugged. 'Yes and no. I think I was afraid about many things. This is very new.'

He was silent as he held her more securely against him. 'Were you afraid I would rage at you?'

She thought of his legacy and shook her head. 'I can defend myself. You are large, but I am quick.'

She felt him grin. 'Good.'

Then he pressed a kiss to her temple. He was silent for a long time. Long enough for her to think he had fallen asleep. She was nearly there herself.

And then he spoke again, his words barely above a whisper.

'Do you know why I love you?'

She was wide awake now. 'Why?'

'Because you make my world new. Before I met you, I had endless days and nights of the same damn thing. Certainly there were happy times, and there were bad times, but all in all the same thing. And every day I grew duller, emptier and colder.'

'So I am...' She searched for the right word. 'I am a novelty?'

'No!' He pressed a kiss to her temple. 'You have shown me that there is more to life than England. There is a whole world out there. And I want to share it with you.' He smiled as he looked at her. 'I told you this at Almack's. Did you not believe me?'

She had. She did. But hearing it now, like this, naked and enfolded in his arms, it came to her why she loved him back.

'You are a novelty to me,' she said. 'You have offered me a world that I never knew was possible. A life where I can be safe and new.' She pressed a kiss to his lips. 'I would not change that for anything. I love you.'

'And I love you.'

This time when they made love it was slow and sweet. And since she knew what was coming she could enjoy it more. And he could teach her more.

When it was done, she stretched out beside him. She was fully sated, fully delighted. And together they slept.

Chapter Twenty-Five

Reality didn't intrude until the next morning. They'd awoken late, eaten lazily, and spoken of things they could do another day. Tomorrow or the next. They were still at the breakfast table when the butler arrived with the mail. On one of the letters Grace read the name of her father's solicitor.

'What is that?' she asked as Declan slit open the letter.

'Your dowry.'

'The boat? Now it is yours.'

'Yes.'

He was quiet, his expression relaxed, and she wasn't sure what that meant.

'What are you going to do with it?'

He smiled at her, the letter in his hand. And then he set it on the table near her. 'What do you want to do with it?'

'Me?'

'Yes, you. Whatever you want, I'll see it done.'

She thought long and hard about that. She toyed with her teacup and she traced the letters on the linen paper.

'Your cousin did everything so that he could have the boat,' she said.

'Yes.'

'So let him have it.'

Her husband reared back. 'What? Reward him for every-thing—?'

'We would not be married were it not for him.'

Declan frowned, clearly thinking. 'I do not like giving Cedric what he wants. He needs to earn his keep.'

She agreed. 'He will.' She grinned at him. 'I may have sailed the ship, but it was my sister who advised on the cargo, who balanced the accounts, and handled the money. We had many ports of call along the way. She barely spoke English at first, but she knew what to sell and what to buy.'

He frowned at her. 'How could she know such a thing?'

'While I spent my days learning how to navigate, she spent her days with the merchants. She learned a very great deal.' She leaned forward. 'She is more clever than I am.'

He snorted. 'I doubt that.'

'I don't.'

'So, do you think she should have the management of *The Integrity*?'

Her husband was quick. He understood exactly. 'I think she should. And let Cedric work on it.'

'As a sailor? He'd never agree.'

She shrugged. 'Then he cannot have it. But it is what he wants more than anything. He told me so himself.'

'He would work as a sailor, completely under her control?'

'Not exactly. There are a few improvements to the boat that Captain Banakos wants, and selecting a cargo can take months. We shall give Lucy control during that time and see how it goes.'

'Then we shall give it to Cedric?'

She shrugged. 'Then we will ask Lucy what she recommends.'

He pursed his lips, considering. 'Cedric, supervised by your sister? Will Lucy agree?'

'Lucy will be thrilled.'

Epilogue

One month later, Grace was sharing tea with her sister. Lucy had found some Chinese tea at an apothecary, and they both relished the taste. But what Grace relished more was the moment when her new husband sauntered in. He'd been closeted in his library with his steward for hours, but now he strode into the parlour with an excited grin on his face.

'What has you so happy?' she asked as he came for a kiss.

'I have finished with my solicitor, my banker, and my steward, not to mention my valet and your maid.'

She blinked. 'Why ever would you be talking to my maid?'

'Because we must go. Now.'

He tugged her upright. She went willingly, but stopped when she was fully upright. 'Let me say goodbye to my sister—'

'No, no. She is coming with us.' He turned to Lucy. 'If you will join us, please?'

Lucy frowned, but nodded. In truth, her eyes were dancing. She enjoyed surprises much more than Grace ever had.

Soon enough they were all in a carriage, headed towards… the docks? Grace could smell the air and knew that terrible, wonderful scent from far away.

'What have you up your sleeve?' she asked her husband.

'Only what we have already discussed.'

She couldn't think of it. This last month of their marriage had been a delight. Nights of passion coupled with long hours of learning about one another. They had discussed boats and crops, Parliament and royalty, and every other topic under the sun. Too much to give her a hint as to what was coming and why it involved Lucy.

Until they arrived at *The Integrity*.

Captain Banakos was there, a broad grin on his weathered face, as was…

'Why is Lord Domac here?' Lucy whispered. 'I will not—'

'Oh, I remember now!' Grace exclaimed. And then she squeezed her sister's arm. 'Don't worry. You shall love this.'

Meanwhile, Declan rushed ahead, leaping with joy onto the deck of the large merchant ship. He greeted the captain with a warm embrace, and then arched a brow at his cousin, who was looking daggers at all of them.

'I'll make this quick, shall I?' Declan said as everyone made it on board. 'Miss Lucy Richards, your father and I have discussed things and come to an arrangement. The repairs on *The Integrity* are underway. It will take another month at least, but then she will be ready to set sail with a new cargo.' He leaned forward. 'Would you like to choose it?'

The girl's eyes widened as her hands flew to her mouth. It appeared she could not speak.

'Damn it!' Cedric snapped.

But he did not have a chance to continue as Declan turned to address him.

'I'm willing to give you a portion of that cargo, cousin. I'll let you supervise it, sail with it, and sell it in China as you initially planned. Any profit will be allotted to you and your sisters' dowries evenly.'

'What?' The man gaped at him.

'One condition, though.' He grinned as he turned to Lucy. 'She will be the one deciding on the cargo. She will be the one to set the price. And you will work under her and Captain Banakos. Prove your mettle and we can discuss the next sailing.'

'I'm to be her lackey?' Cedric asked, bristling.

'Yes,' Declan said cheerfully. 'For the next two months. If

you want the boat.' He looked to Captain Banakos. 'I trust you will treat him as he deserves?'

The captain chuckled as he set his thumbs inside his waistband. 'That I will, Yer Grace. That I will.'

'Excellent,' Declan said as he grabbed Grace's hand. 'And now for your surprise.'

'What?' she said.

She'd been vastly entertained, watching her sister's reaction. Finally the girl was going to be able to put her skills to use. Few understood exactly how precious that was. Indeed, she'd been on the verge of asking if she could work on the crew as well. They'd need a navigator...

But she had no desire to leave Declan.

'Come along, my love,' he said as he tugged her down the gangplank.

They didn't go far, simply crossed to the bottom of the next gangplank. She frowned at the boat, seeing a sleek pleasure craft, large enough to weather turbulent seas, but not strong enough to carry a profitable cargo.

'What is this?' she asked.

'It's *The Duchess*,' he said as he gestured expansively at it. 'Or *The Duchess's Gift*. Or *The Duke's Pleasure*. I don't know. It's a yacht, and it's yours, my love.'

He scooped her up and began carrying her up the gangplank.

She squealed in surprise, but her eyes were on the sails, the lines, and everything else she could study.

'It's mine?' she whispered.

'It is,' he answered as he set her feet down. 'Will you teach me to sail, my love? Will you help me with the sails and the wheel and the...? I don't know what else?'

'But where are we going?'

He grinned as he spun her around. 'Wherever you want, so long as we are back within a month. Do you think I have been killing myself in my study these last weeks for no reason? It was to set everything in place so that we can sail to the Continent, or to Spain, or to wherever you choose, so long as we do it together. I want to see the world, and I want to do it with you.'

'The whole world?'

He shrugged. 'Or as much of it as we can see in a month. Possibly two the next time. But for now—'

'You must come back for Parliament.'

She had spent a great deal of time lately, learning the workings of his government.

He nodded, showing he was pleased, then shrugged. 'I must also be sure the crops are handled well.'

Farming. That was another thing she would need to study. Perhaps while they were sailing this beautiful boat.

'So we can play for a time now? We can sail—'

'Wherever you like for as long as it takes you to teach me everything.'

She laughed, knowing that would take a lifetime. 'I should like that very much,' she said.

'Good because we sail with the evening tide.'

She opened her mouth to argue, but he pressed a hand to her lips.

'I have a small crew who will help. Your bags are already on board, though I believe Molly was shocked by the clothes I have had made for you. And...' He waggled his eyebrows. 'We even have a crow's nest large enough for two. That took the longest time to arrange, but it's done now.'

He pointed up, so that she could see the double-sized barrel up top.

He had thought of everything, and she couldn't believe how happy she was. They would sail together! And even more than her own joy at the idea was seeing how absolutely thrilled he was. What a pleasure to see him so happy!

Then she looked at his clothes. 'Do you have equally scandalous attire?'

'I do.'

'Good. Then I believe we should both change, and I shall race you to the top.'

'Agreed.'

Then he dropped a kiss on her lips before dashing below decks. She was startled by how fast he moved. She had to jump to follow him.

It took longer than it should have for them to change. They

were, after all, in the same stateroom together, and the bed was quite comfortable. But soon enough they were climbing the ratlines while she pointed out things that he needed to know. It wasn't until they were both settled one against the other in the crow's nest that she realised how incredibly happy she was.

'I never thought to be this lucky,' she whispered as she leaned back against him.

'Nor I,' he said. Then he pressed a kiss to her head. 'I love you, Nayao. I cannot imagine my life without you.'

'I love you,' she answered.

Then she twisted to kiss him. But just before her lips found his, he burst out laughing.

She pulled back, shocked and a little insulted, and then she looked to where he pointed.

There, still on the deck of *The Integrity*, stood Lucy and Cedric. They were nose to nose, both gesturing with hard, angry slashes.

'Oh, dear,' Grace said, fear skating up her spine. 'Maybe this wasn't a great idea.'

Cedric was much larger than her sister. He could hurt—

No, he couldn't.

While they watched, Captain Banakos grabbed Cedric in a casual headlock. Grace knew the position, knew as well how humiliating it was. And there he stood, holding Lord Domac in place, while Lucy leaned down and continued speaking. They couldn't hear the words, of course, but Grace knew her sister well.

Lucy was telling him exactly what cargo they would carry, and exactly what his responsibilities would be. Likely scrubbing the deck until his hands bled.

'She won't be too hard on him, will she?' Declan asked. 'He is a titled peer, or rather he will be eventually. I want him to learn what is needed on a boat, not—'

'She'll be fair with him…eventually. I trust Captain Banakos will keep them both in line.'

'Well, that will be an adventure for them, won't it?' Declan asked.

'That's their story,' she said as she twisted again to face her husband. 'I'm more interested in ours.'

'Me, too,' he said.

Then he pulled her into a kiss, one that they both knew would be repeated a hundred or more times up here. Because they had the time, now, and the freedom to be themselves. And the love to keep them afloat for the rest of their lives.

* * * * *

HISTORICAL

Your romantic escape to the past.

Available Next Month

Only An Heiress Will Do Virginia Heath
The Duchess Charade Emily E K Murdoch

....

The Unexpected Duke Julia Justiss
Winning His Manhattan Heiress Lauri Robinson

Keep reading for an excerpt of a new title
from the Historical series,
MISS ANNA AND THE EARL by Catherine Tinley

Prologue

Elgin, Scotland,
1797

'Mama, tell us the story about ZanZan and Milady!' Anna gazed at her mother adoringly.

Mama laughed. 'Again? I declare it is your favourite story. Very well, but you must promise to go to sleep immediately afterwards. Now, move over a little, and I shall sit on your bed.'

The triplets—Anna, Izzy and Rose—shuffled over in their large, comfortable bed and Mama stretched out beside them, smoothing her simple dun gown. There was an ink stain on her hand from her long hours clerking that day.

'Once upon a time,' she began, 'There were three little princesses. They lived in a beautiful castle—'

'Not like our cottage!' declared Izzy, briefly taking her thumb from her mouth.

'No, indeed. Our little cottage is beautiful in its own way, though, and we are very grateful for it. Now, the princesses lived in a beautiful castle with their dear friends—'

'Milady!' Rose jumped in with the name.

'And ZanZan!' added Anna. ZanZan was her favourite.

'Yes, the princesses and their mother lived with ZanZan and

his mama in the beautiful castle. It had nearly a hundred rooms, and the children played and laughed all day long.'

'There was a big, big staircase,' said Rose, lifting her little arms and spreading her hands to show how large the staircase had been.

'And a piano!' said Izzy.

'And secret places. Tell us the part about the secret places, Mama!' Anna could see some of them in her mind's eye: the bookcase in the library that was really a door; the hidden drawer in Mama's desk that would pop open when she pressed the third carved flower from the left; the loft in the stables that no one would know was there. She remembered *everything*.

'And another time,' Mama said, and there was a different tone to her voice, 'The mother of the princesses stayed in an inn for three whole weeks!'

'Why, Mama? Why did she stay there?'

'It was when the princesses' mother was getting ready to be married to their father. Her husband-to-be stayed in a different place, as was proper, and each Sunday the minister read out their names in the church to see if anyone might try to stop the wedding.'

Anna was fascinated. 'Why would someone do that?'

'His family did not wish him to marry. But they did not find them.' Mama shook her head. 'It was a happy time for them both.'

'Like now, Mama?' asked Rose.

Mama smiled. 'Yes, like now.' There were more stories then, until finally Mama said, 'Now, let us sing *The Lady Blue* together, and then we shall say our prayers. But remember, you are never to speak of your father. Now, promise me!'

'I promise, Mama.'

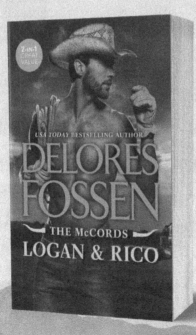

Subscribe and fall in love with a Mills & Boon series today!

You'll be among the first to read stories delivered to your door monthly and enjoy great savings.

WE SIMPLY LOVE ROMANCE